The Revenger
Book 8 in the Dan Stone series

A Novel

By
David Nees

Copyright © 2023 David E. Nees

All rights reserved

To keep up with my new releases, please visit my website at www.davidnees.com. You can join my Reader Group by signing up using the prompt window. I never overload my readers, but offer insights to my writing, thoughts on the creative process, and advance notice of new releases and promotions. When you sign up, I'll send you a free copy of *Training Camp*, my novella that fills in the time between *Payback* and *The Shaman*.

You can also visit my Amazon author page. Click the "Follow" button under my picture on the Amazon book page to get notices about any new releases.

Manufactured in the United States
ISBN 9798867036621

For Carla
You always inspire me to be my best.

Many thanks to my alpha readers, especially Judy and Ed. You not only encourage, but give critical feedback that makes a rough text shine. Your generous gift of time and attention is very much appreciated.

Further thanks go to my beta readers. These are people who have enjoyed my stories over time and unselfishly contributed to this book's success with their critical reads. You have made this novel a better one.

The Revenger

"When justice is done, it brings joy to the righteous but terror to evildoers."—Proverbs 21:15

"If you prick us, do we not bleed? If you tickle us, do we not laugh? If you poison us do, we not die? And if you wrong us, shall we not revenge?"—William Shakespeare

Chapter 1

I t was an early spring day in Washington, D.C., one of those days that offered a prelude to the full delights of spring. The cherry blossoms were nearing the end of their blooming, drawing a large influx of people to view their glorious array. Now, the pathways around the tidal basin were strewn with an ever-deepening pink carpet. Late arrivers still walked the grounds around the reflecting pool and along the borders of the monuments to wonder at the dense collection of trees that produced such a delight. The air was sweet and fresh, even in the city. The sun shone brightly, and the world looked somehow more pure and more innocent. People smiled at one another, and you felt a sense of optimism in the air. Spring was here. The weather was beautiful. The world was good.

Baruch Mier was a member of Israel's team of negotiators involved in the Abraham Peace Accords, so named because the Abraham of the Bible is considered a common ancestor of both Jews and Muslims and revered as a prophet by both religions. He was working with a senior State Department diplomat named Jonathan Bishop. The two were planning their next steps to bring the Saudis on board. They had shown increased interest in recent months as Iran progressed further in its attempts to dominate the region. The war in Yemen, a lightly disguised proxy war between the two countries, was at a stalemate. Weeks ago, arms heading to the Houthi rebels from Iran were intercepted, but the intelligence indicated many had gotten through. The re-arming would bring about renewed fighting. Increasingly, many Middle East countries were looking at the accords as a way to hedge in Iran, whose sworn enemies were Israel and the U.S.

Bishop led the efforts to capitalize on this development and finally bring the Saudis to the table. With them on board, the agreement would be more substantial, and the other wavering Mideast states would re-examine their reluctance.

On that day, full of the promise of spring, Mier and Bishop met for lunch at Blackfinn, a restaurant on I Street near 16th. It was not far from Farragut Square. The restaurant had a high-end pub feel and offered a wide selection of entrees that would please a variety of tastes. It featured outdoor seating, perfect for this early but warm spring day.

The two men took advantage of the mild day and were seated outside near the curb. They had just ordered and were relaxing with glasses of white wine. The sidewalk was filled with pedestrians as it was lunch hour, and the weather was inviting.

"We are going to change the world, Jonathan," Baruch said as he raised his glass in a toast.

"Maybe. The time is certainly ripe for the next step." Jonathan saluted his counterpart with his glass. "You think the Saudis are finally giving up their antagonism towards Israel?"

Baruch shook his head. "I only wish. They are the keepers of the faith, remember. They walk a tightrope—"

"The royal family."

"Yes. They must protect the center of Islam while pushing back against the Iranians. It is this Shia-Sunni split that we exploit at the moment. If they can still be seen as the protectors of Islam while befriending Israel, we will prevail. We must set the path, so that the economic benefits can start to flow. The Saudis are a practical people, after all. The oil won't last forever and alternate energy sources are forcing them to think beyond their oil dominance."

"They put Iran more into a corner while moving their economy forward."

Baruch nodded. "But the clerics have to be placated. The royals must allow them to enforce their strict rules on the populace, while not going so far as to cause a rebellion."

"They walk a tightrope, as you say."

Jonathan thought for a moment.

"To stretch that analogy further, we must help stabilize the rope, so they don't slip and fall."

Baruch smiled. "You're reaching the limits of the analogy, but I don't disagree."

"Do you think a rebellion is possible?"

Baruch shook his head. "Probably not in my lifetime. Still, you never know what the future will bring. There is so much imported labor in the country. They can't do without it. These people have no rights and could be a volatile segment if they ever got fed up."

"Or organized."

At that moment, a van drove up to the curb. The two men glanced at it since it stopped in front of a fire hydrant. Expensive cars often drove up to dislodge passengers to the restaurant, but not a plain, commercial-type van. Those went around back to an alley to unload supplies for businesses. The driver got out and quickly walked across the street.

"He's going to get a ticket," Baruch remarked.

They watched the man enter a car that had pulled up and then drive off.

"Something's up," Jonathan said, rising from his chair.

Baruch gave him a questioning look. A question he never got to ask. The explosion ripped the van apart. All the eardrums of the patrons sitting at the sidewalk tables burst just as the shrapnel tore through their bodies, shredding them into body parts. The blast continued through the front windows into the restaurant, killing more. Staff in the kitchen were spared death but were injured by flying debris. Fire broke out and began to spread inside. The adjacent buildings suffered damage, with broken windows and metal shards tearing through the ground floors. Across the street, the façade of the glass-fronted building shattered. The crowded sidewalk instantly turned into a debris and body-laden battleground. Anyone in the way was either injured or killed. It was the luck of the draw as to where the metal ripped through them.

The beauty and hope of the fresh spring day were blown apart that noon. The tourists strolling along the Mall heard the blast as a muffled whoomp accompanied by a slight pressure wave. Shortly, the wail of many sirens pierced the air. They understood. Despite the beauty of the day, D.C. was a dangerous city, and like all such cities, bad things happened; people got robbed, beaten, or worse.

Within minutes, the rising notes of the sirens multiplied as the fire trucks raced to the scene. Once there, they unloaded their hoses and ran through the human debris to quench the growing fire inside the building. The injured were helped to safety and to the numerous ambulances arriving. Once the fire was under control, the true horror of what had taken place showed its face. The police arrived and tried to set up a perimeter. The firefighters were intent on ensuring the fire was out, but their activities seemed to be contaminating the crime scene with all its bodies and body parts strewn about the sidewalk.

Finally, the fire department retreated and turned the scene over to the police, with a fire investigator assigned to work with them. An hour later, the FBI showed up, and the three agencies began coordinating their work to pick over the ruins and piece together what had happened. By the end of the day, they understood that a van had driven up, parked, and exploded. They could find no body parts in the van, so they assumed the driver had fled the scene. There were no witnesses to testify; everyone who had been close to the truck was dead.

Chapter 2

He was walking down Connecticut Avenue from Dupont Circle, heading towards Lafayette Park on his way to the National Gallery on the Mall. As he strolled along on this glorious spring day, his mind was disturbed; images kept emerging out of the dark. Images of a disaster, possibly an explosion, only to recede again before he could grab them and see them more clearly.

His name was Geoffrey; he was a Watcher, a loosely connected group of people worldwide with special sight—supernatural vision, some might say. They worked on the side of the good against the forces of darkness that tirelessly attacked the order in the world to create chaos and death. He was one of the few in the District, a place of power, intrigue, and darkness. He stopped and stood aside from the other pedestrians. Geoffrey concentrated, using his powers of extended sight. He would force the images to show themselves, even if they tried to hide from him.

Then he saw it. The shock of the vision caused him to gasp. He paused for a moment. Watchers did not involve themselves directly; they only provided guidance. His hesitation lasted for only a moment. He could not, would not, ignore the immediacy of the threat and the possibility that he could save lives.

Geoffrey started sprinting down Connecticut Avenue. He reached the intersection of Connecticut and I Street and looked to his left. A car with two men turned from I Street onto 17th, almost striking him and bringing him to an abrupt halt. Its driver looked over at him before he accelerated up the road. The Watcher imprinted the man's face in his mind.

The next moment, a blast threw him to the ground. His mind reeled from the force of the shock wave. He rolled over, groaning, and slowly got to his feet, trying to clear the confusion from his head. With his ears ringing, he stood up and looked down the street. Tables were flung against the walls of the building. Chairs scattered. Blood was everywhere. People and parts of people were strewn all around the patio. The restaurant's front windows were blown out. The Watcher could see the flicker of a fire starting to burn inside. The windows were blown out across and up and down the street, and people were lying on the pavement, either dead or wounded.

He started forward. People along the street were screaming in pain. Curiously, no sounds came from the destroyed patio. There was no one there alive to scream. Some survivors stumbled out of the restaurant and wobbled away from the horror they saw. They were bloody and injured but alive.

The sirens came next. Within minutes, the scene became chaotic as fire trucks roared up, and men jumped out to connect hoses and attack the fire. The police arrived and began to cordon off the area to keep back the growing assembly of spectators.

Geoffrey waited. He could not help. He felt a deep anguish in the pit of his stomach. Sometimes, the darkness won. He understood the magnitude of the struggle and that it would ebb and flow, with each side getting the upper hand at times. This was a day for the darkness. He leaned against the wall of a building. It was hard to do good but so easy to destroy, to cause chaos, to be a tool of the darkness.

Many people were useful dupes who could be used for dark purposes, working from a misguided ideology. This attack, however, was the action of those directly working on the dark side, those who knew evil and were serving it, working to undermine the stability of the West in general and the U.S. in particular.

The police now had some officers working their way through the crowd to find anyone who had witnessed the bombing and could give them some information. One of them reached Geoffery.

"Did you see anything?" The officer asked.

Geoffrey nodded.

"Tell me what you saw."

"I had just gotten to the corner. A blue car, a BMW I think, turned from I onto 17th. Right in front of me. It ran the light and almost hit me. That's why I noticed."

"Did you get the license number?"

Geoffrey nodded. "Partly."

He recited the plate number as far as he knew it. The officer nodded as he wrote it down.

"Anything else?"

"There were two men in the car. The driver looked at me. We locked eyes for a second. He was dark with dark hair. He looked Hispanic or Middle-Eastern."

The officer wrote everything down, along with Geoffrey's phone number and address.

"Thank you."

He gave him his card.

"If you think of anything else, call me. However, an investigator will follow up with you in a few days to get a more detailed statement.

Geoffrey nodded, and the officer moved on. He stood staring at the carnage. The yellow tape had gone up, and the injured were being loaded into ambulances. Triage work was being done on those waiting to be transported to a hospital. There would be many casualties.

Geoffrey turned to go, his visit to the gallery forgotten. He started walking back to his apartment located between O and P Streets. On the way, he reviewed the sequence of events in his mind. He'd known of something coming for a couple of weeks. It was hidden and only had gradually begun to emerge. All the Watchers knew of this with their ability to share information. However, someone had precipitously accelerated the action date, catching him and the others off guard. He only "saw" it at the last moment, and that had been too late.

Geoffrey had not told the whole truth to the officer. He knew exactly what the driver looked like with a less complete picture of the passenger; the one Geoffrey assumed drove the van. He would find the warriors, the ones fighting on the front lines, and give them the complete picture. They would know what to do with the information. If he gave it to the FBI or D.C. Police, it would only serve to alert the perpetrators and make them more careful.

He arrived at his apartment. There was much to communicate with the others. The warriors would be called into action. He would do his part in identifying the bombers. Others would respond to this assault, and he would play his small role.

Chapter 3

A day before the D.C. explosion, the driver embarked in a delivery van loaded with boxes of dry goods to stock a grocery store or supply a restaurant. His cargo included bins of aromatic spices, such as borage, cumin, cardamom, and Bahārāt, which gave the inside of the van a complex array of scents. The C4 was carefully triple-wrapped and sealed, then put inside some of the spice bins. The hope was that the spices would throw off any dogs that might be employed at the checkpoint. If they indicated any whiff of explosives, the guards would search the van and the material found. His destination was Jerusalem, which would take just under two hours.

He drove slowly down the highway from Nablus, crossing into Israel proper from the West Bank at Qalqiliya. He wore the uniform of a food distribution company. It was a recognizable name, one that was known to most people and therefore generated little suspicion. The driver would deliver the van to a small, nondescript warehouse outside the city. There, the C4 would be assembled and packaged along with a large quantity of diesel fuel, purchased in small amounts over some months. Tanks of acetylene used for welding were also added to the assemblage being built into the delivery van. The diesel and acetylene were innocent products, but together with the C4, capable of creating an enhanced explosion.

The plan had been to spend a week assembling the components and waiting for the right moment to detonate. They had two targets in mind: Ariel Weiss and Natan Yitzhaki. Both men worked at the Ministry of Foreign Affairs. They were members of the negotiating team involved with the Abraham Accords. Ariel was the special envoy and had great sway on the team. Natan was considered his protégé.

His *nom de guerre* was Muntaqim, Arabic for "Avenger" or "Revenger." He was in charge of both attacks. When Muntaqim decided to advance the schedule for the Washington, D.C. attack, the plan for the attack in Jerusalem had to be moved up as well. Both bombs were to go off on the same day. His seemingly random changes of plans and pacing frustrated many of his men. They didn't understand his thinking, and he never offered an explanation, but no one was willing to criticize him. They just grumbled quietly to themselves and doubled down on their efforts to meet Muntaqim's ever-shifting schedule. Now, they had less than 24 hours to complete their task.

When the van pulled into the warehouse, a team of men descended on it. The pace was intense. The work had to be done by the following afternoon.

Before the van had arrived, Muntaqim sent a letter via delivery service to Weiss's office. He hoped the letter would assure the two targeted men would be where he wanted. The letter was on official Saudi diplomatic stationery. It asked Ariel and Natan to meet with a Saudi diplomat concerning new issues in the ongoing discussions. The communication clearly stated that it was urgent and secret and specified precisely where and when the Saudi would meet them. The designated location was the Imma

Restaurant at the corner of Harav Shmuel Baragh Street and Itzhak Ben-Zvi Boulevard. Five o'clock in the afternoon was set for the meeting, just before the dinner hours would begin. Both streets were busy with much traffic, but most importantly, the restaurant had sidewalk seating. The letter clearly stated that they should sit outside, making it harder for anyone to listen to their conversation.

The letter raised much discussion at the Ministry. Some worried that it might be a set-up for an assassination attempt. Ariel was adamant that they should go since the stationary was legitimate and hard to forge.

"Everything in life is a risk," he said. "It would be foolish to disregard this invitation. It looks suspicious only because the Saudis want it to be covert. We all know they have to move carefully on these matters. They take a risk. We take a risk."

"I don't like it," the Chief of Operations for Mossad said.

Ariel patted the man on his shoulder. "It is okay, Doron. We go back a long way. You know I don't act foolishly but I see this as a risk we should take."

Doron demanded that Mossad plant its agents in the area, including one seated near them, to defend against any threat that might materialize. With nothing in the daily briefings to indicate increased terror activity and the agreed-to flooding of the area with agents, he finally gave his approval. Ariel was sure that uncovering any snag confidentially boded well for the interest of the Saudis in making progress. He looked forward to the pending meeting.

The next day, the two men were dropped off at the restaurant twenty minutes before the scheduled time. The security team had been in place for over an hour with one rotation. Ariel and Natan sat down and ordered two glasses of a popular Cabernet Sauvignon, Yarden, from the Golan Heights Winery.

"Here's to a real break-through," Natan said, lifting his glass.

"It's a step," Ariel replied as he sipped the wine, "but don't be disappointed if not much comes of the meeting. The Saudis must tip-toe forward, take tiny steps. It will seem frustrating, but remember, they're moving in the right direction."

They were almost finished with their first glass when a van pulled up at the appointed meeting time. The agent sitting near the diplomats noticed it and spoke into his hidden mic. One of the other agents approached the vehicle. When it stopped, some cars stuck behind the van honked their horns since it was in an active traffic lane. The agent near the two diplomats got up and walked quickly over to them.

"You must get up. There is a problem."

"What's wrong?" Ariel asked. Natan began to get out of his seat.

"I'll explain later. Now get up."

Ariel reluctantly stood. The other agent reached the van. As the two diplomats stood, the man talking to Ariel and Natan looked towards the van to see what was happening.

The blast obliterated the agent standing next to the van. It picked up the three men at the table along with the other patrons. Before they hit the ground, shrapnel, both implanted in the device and from the torn van, flayed their bodies. The blast wave shattered the windows, not only in the restaurant but up and down the street. Pedestrians for fifty yards on each side of the van were thrown to the ground, killed, or injured. The blast severely damaged any cars near the explosion, with their occupants torn apart.

In a split second, the corner had become a scene of devastation. The sound of sirens rose in the air as the police and ambulances were dispatched to the scene. There were injuries all along the block and across the street from the blast and window fragments.

Chapter 4

I t was the day after the D.C. and Jerusalem explosions, which had happened nearly simultaneously. Four people were crammed into Jane's basement office at CIA Headquarters. It wasn't tiny, but it certainly wasn't spacious, and with four agitated people inside, it felt cramped. Dan Stone stalking back and forth like a caged predator didn't help. He had been to the site of the explosion and took a long time looking at the ruin it had caused—both in lives and property.

"Dan, can you please sit down?" Jane asked. "Your pacing around is making everyone nervous."

Jane Tanner was the head of a small, deep-black operation. It didn't have a clever code name; it was just Jane and her team of two tech assistants, Fred Burke and Warren Thomas. The other member of the group was Dan Stone, her assassin. She had discovered Dan as he was pursuing a successful vendetta against the Brooklyn mob for their killing of his wife and unborn child. When she had intervened, Dan was in a precarious position. The mob was after him, along with the FBI and NYPD. After realizing his options were limited, he had decided to work for her newly formed team.

Fred and Warren had worked for Jane since she had formed the team under the direction of Henry Mason, her boss, a long-time cold warrior and CIA veteran. They had been together for years, yet the two assistants had never fully gotten used to being around Dan. He always made them nervous. Now, he looked like an angry tiger as he paced around the room. His body bristled with tension, ready to unleash on some unfortunate victim. His eyes flashed with anger as they swept across the room.

Dan ignored Jane's request and continued his pacing.

"The DHS has issued a National Terrorism Advisory System bulletin," Fred said. "It's at 'Imminent' level."

"Nothing imminent about it. It already happened," Dan said. His voice was barely audible but hard as a rock.

"That will screw up the whole transportation system," Fred continued. "No one's going to get where they're headed on time."

"They'll tighten security checks at the airports," Jane said. "Also train and bus stations."

"Useless." Dan spoke up again. "The scum who did this are long gone."

"We don't know that," Jane said. "They could be holed up somewhere in the area, waiting for things to cool down."

Dan shook his head. He was now standing in a corner with his eyes darting around the room.

"For God's sake, will you sit down?" Jane's eyes now flashed with anger.

"What the hell are we doing here?" Dan asked. "I can't operate domestically. You know that created a crisis for us all the last time." He paused momentarily, then added, "I need to go hunting."

"Henry was told it was all hands on deck. Even the black ops. This explosion is going to have serious consequences." Jane turned to look directly at Dan. "And you don't go, hunting, as you say, around Europe and the Mideast, creating havoc and more problems."

"It's what I do. I need to be back out in the field, chasing down the usual suspects...hunting and killing them." He looked at Jane. "The same type of attack occurred in Jerusalem, at almost the same time. What do we know about that?"

"I'm working on it," Jane replied.

"They're linked," Dan said.

Jane nodded. "I agree. I've reached out to Eitan."

Eitan Malkah was the head of METSADA, the operational arm of Mossad. Eitan and Jane had run joint covert ops together some years ago, and more recently, he had recruited someone, off the record, to help Dan track down the Scorpion.

"For right now, word has come down that, along with DHS, FBI, we're to get all our assets in place to hunt down these perpetrators. Even our dark ops."

"So, we're to break the law?" Dan asked.

"No, but we've got eyes and ears overseas that might help uncover the perps. Will you sit down?"

Dan shook his head. "I can't. They've won this round. It will embolden them to try more. They figured out simple works. Simple is hard to defend against...and they're right. I need to go hunt them down, not spend time doing the FBI's work here."

"You'll get your chance."

Just then, Jane's cell phone rang. She looked but didn't recognize the number.

"You should answer it," Dan said. "It could be something useful."

She picked it up. "Hello?"

She listened for a moment, started to speak, and then caught herself. After a moment, she said, "I'll meet you at my apartment in Arlington. Since you know my number, I assume you also know where I live."

"Who was that?" Dan asked when she put down her phone.

"That was a Watcher." She had a concerned look on her face. "It seems like they're also in D.C. And they know where I live."

"Not surprising, really. Remember they're on our side. Or maybe we're on their side. They seem to have recognized this battle long before we got into it. What does this Watcher want?"

"He wants to meet with us, you, and me. He won't come here—"

"I don't blame him."

"He wants to meet at my apartment...now."

Dan pushed away from the wall. "He must have some useful information. Time sensitive as well."

Jane turned to her two assistants. "You two get your eyes and ears out. Look for anything that could lead us to the perpetrators. You know what to do."

"I'll contact my NSA buddy," Warren said. "I'm sure they're hard at work re-sifting communications to see if they missed something."

"Have him send you anything, however tenuous. And drill into all communications with the usual overseas characters. Only expand it to quasi government agencies."

"I'll start searching for any data on missing explosives," Fred said. "Do we know what was used?"

"Not yet. FBI forensics is working the site right now, but it may take some time."

"They going to share?" Dan asked.

"No holding back." Jane got up and pointed to Dan, "You and I are going to my place and see what this guy has for us." She turned to Fred and Warren, who were getting out of their seats. "I'll check back with you two tomorrow morning. You need to have something for me."

The room emptied.

Chapter 5

Six months earlier

Muntaqim made his way through the crowds in the streets of Al Qamishli in northern Syria. It was a dusty, ancient city. He walked with his head down on a circuitous path that eventually took him to a bridge connecting to an island in the middle of the Jaghjagh River. Here, the city was older, more rundown, with empty buildings, some without roofs. It was just the place he needed.

Before going over the bridge, he went down an alleyway and entered a nondescript door. It opened to the house of a supporter, a Sunni Arab living among the predominantly Shia population. Muntaqim knew he could safely wait here for nightfall. One could not be too careful. Danger came not only from Shia militants who would kill him for his activities but also from the sky—from Western powers that seemed to have eyes everywhere.

After dark enveloped the city, he crossed the bridge and continued to an empty warehouse. It was located on the island amid other abandoned buildings, some of them showing the effects of the brutal civil war that had been going on in the country. There, he met with his fellow fighters in the Sunni cause.

"Salam alaikum," peace be upon you, he said to the man who met him at the door.

"Wa-alaikum as-salam," the man said in response.

"Where is he?" Muntaqim asked.

"Inside."

The two men entered an inner room. There were no windows, and it was lit by a lantern hung from the ceiling. Seated in a chair pulled up to a table was a man, a local, looking nervous. His hands were tied behind his back.

"Kalil, do you know why you are here?" Muntaqim asked.

"No *zaeim.* I have done nothing wrong." He used a respectful title for leader.

"So, you say. But our attack on the police barracks was foiled. Someone knew about it and they were ready for us."

"It was not me. I told no one."

"Yet my investigation has revealed that you had a visit from the Shia militia." Muntaqim opened his cell phone, pulled up a picture, and put it in front of Kalil. It showed him talking with another man in an alley near his house.

"Is this not you?"

Kalil hung his head.

"And is this not a member of the militia?"

He began to shake. "He threatened my family. If I didn't help them, he would kidnap my family and take them far away. I'd never see them again."

"So, you betrayed us."

Kalil looked up, his eyes pleading. "I only wanted to deliver information that would not damage us yet keep them away from my family."

"You didn't think to come to me? To tell me what was going on?"

The man continued to look at Muntaqim. "How could I? I was afraid of what you would do."

"You tried to find a path between loyalty and betrayal for your safety."

The man looked down at the floor. "I am sorry, forgive me."

"That path you sought. It does not exist. You are either in this fight or you are not. And when you join, there is no getting out. You would let the apostates, the ones who corrupt Islam, who preach a heresy, to continue? And to force you to help?"

The man only shook his head as if to say "no."

"Unlike them, I will spare your family. But you have broken your vow to us. You cannot continue."

"Please, my family will be desperate. How will they survive?" His voice was now almost a whisper.

"That is the problem you created for them when you chose this path."

Muntaqim stepped around behind Kalil. He took out his knife. With his left hand, he grabbed Kalil's hair and pulled his head back. He swiped the blade across the man's throat. Blood flowed onto the man's chest and drowned out the scream that tried to erupt. Muntaqim let Kalil's head fall. After a few moments of gasping, he expired.

"Take him to his neighborhood and drop him in an alley. His family will find him. They can mourn and bury him. Some will know he collaborated and understand the price. Others will not know and blame it on the Shias. So much the better." He walked to the door. "I must leave. Remember, there are many fronts on which we battle. Continue your path of sabotage and ambush. I must go see others who battle the apostates."

"As you command, *zaeim*."

Muntaqim drove east from Al Qamishli towards the Syrian-Iraqi border, heading for Mosul. The road crossed over at the border towns of Tall Kushik and Rabiah. He constantly varied his routine. It didn't matter. Muntaqim suspected there were other forces at play. Something seemed to disrupt some of the best-laid plans. Being unpredictable might help protect against such disruption. Much to the consternation of those he commanded, he had begun to employ the tactic. It was not conducive to efficiency but seemed to help protect his actions against discovery.

His grandmother sometimes had spoken of people blessed with extraordinary gifts, "special sight," she called it. Muntaqim had been close to his grandmother. His father had been a stern and distant figure, killed by the police while he was a boy. His mother was distracted with trying to survive with four children. He found solace and comfort in his grandmother and her stories. They seemed to be from another age, steeped in practices and beliefs that hadn't changed for hundreds of years.

She often spoke of these people. She knew one in her village that many people looked to for advice and guidance. But sometimes they were persecuted and shunned, which is what she spoke of happening in her village after a particularly bad harvest. These memories had come back to him. Could something like that now be arrayed against him? Muntaqim didn't know, but he took steps to shield himself as well as he could.

Mosul, the ancient city of Nineveh of the Bible, was home to a majority of Sunnis. It had a rich tradition of multiculturalism that had been largely destroyed by ISIS's rule. Before their ascension to power, the city had contained Muslims, Christians, Jews, and Yazidis. The latter followed a mixture of Islam and Zoroastrianism, often misunderstood to be devil worship.

Oil discovered in the 1920s helped the city prosper. Saddam Hussein enjoyed the city, and it thrived during his rule. The current leader of Iraq, a Shiite, had not directed aid and support to the city, leaving it to struggle on its own to recover from the ruin of ISIS rule. UNESCO had gone in to work on the many archeological sites, providing some employment for the local population. Muntaqim had much support there and used the city as a *de facto* base of operations in his war against the Shia.

His phone rang as he drove down the empty highway.

"Who is this?" he asked as he answered the call. He did not recognize the number.

"I speak for a potential benefactor," came the reply. "One who would like to meet with you."

"I do not meet with strangers."

"That would be unfortunate. My *zaeim* is a very wealthy Sunni. He has observed your activities and wants to offer you a role in a larger struggle."

"How did you get my number? How do you know about me?"

"We have followed you for a while. My *zaeim* has many resources."

"Who is this rich Sunni?"

"That can be only revealed by him. This is an opportunity to act on a much larger stage. He's inviting you to become part of a larger jihad. We can arrange a safe meeting place. One of your choosing."

"I will think on this and call you back."

"Don't delay. This phone will only be operational for the next six hours."

The man ended the call. Muntaqim drove on towards Mosul. Who was this wealthy Sunni? A Saudi? He had heard talk of a billionaire Saudi who quietly financed attacks on the West. Could this be the one?

Chapter 6

Jane and Dan made their way to the parking garage. It was not far from her basement office, an unexpected perk of being stuck out of the way, out of sight. They brought a sketch artist with them. The Watcher had insisted on it. He said he could give them a good description of one of the bombers. No one said much. The mood throughout the headquarters of the CIA was that of crisis management with overlays of anxiety, CYA activity, and genuine effort to bring some resources to bear on the tragedy that had occurred.

They parked in the garage of Jane's apartment building and entered. Instead of going up to Jane's floor, they went to the lobby and met the man who placed the phone call. Dan recognized him at once as the man he had spoken to in Georgetown over a year ago. He noted to himself that he had never gotten the man's name.

The Watcher nodded to Dan and introduced himself to Jane.

"My name is Geoffrey. I see you brought the artist like I asked." He looked around. "Shall we go up to your apartment?"

"You know which one it is?" Jane asked.

Geoffrey smiled. "No, that is not an important piece of information for me to acquire."

"But you could if you wanted to?"

Geoffrey didn't lose his smile. "Please, I want to help."

"Let's go," Dan said.

Jane turned to the elevators. Once in her apartment, she offered the Watcher something to drink. He accepted tea. Dan poured himself a small glass of bourbon and sat to one side.

Jane cradled a cup of tea and sat down while the artist set up her computer. She and Geoffrey began to work together.

A quiet back-and-forth discussion ensued between them, with the Watcher pointing out parts of an emerging portrait, the artist making the corrections. A half-hour later, a surprisingly clear picture of the driver, along with a less detailed view of the passenger, emerged on the artist's screen. The driver's image was more complete and realistic than most police sketches.

"Wow," Jane said, "this will definitely work with our facial recognition system." She turned to the Watcher. "How did you get this so realistic?"

Geoffrey smiled. "It's the power of observation." He gave her a knowing wink. Jane seemed to understand that he didn't want to say more in front of the artist. Only Jane and Dan knew the significance of a Watcher's powers of observation.

Jane turned to the artist. "Send this to my computer." She gave her the encrypted email address. The artist sent the picture and then stood up.

"Can you wait for me in the lobby? I need to talk with this person in private. It will help me to better assess the image you just produced."

She nodded and packed up her computer.

"You're not to share this outside of our group. I'll distribute the picture as is best for the investigation."

The artist didn't say anything but gave Jane a questioning look.

"It's important to not let the perpetrators, wherever they might be, know we have such a good image of one of them," Jane said.

The artist nodded and stepped out of the apartment.

When they were alone, Jane spoke. "Can you share that image with other Watchers? Now that you've created it?"

Geoffrey nodded. "It will be shared. One of us may have some insight into the faces...a person and where he might be."

"That will help," Jane replied. "We may not have these two in our government data files. We'll look, but we might have to depend on your network."

"We may be able to give you a starting point, a place to begin your hunt."

"That's what I need," Dan said.

"I know. We all know. You are the tip of the spear." He straightened in his chair, and his face took on a serious look as he turned to encompass Jane and Dan in his intense gaze. "There is something odd going on. We had intimations of an impending attack. It was well-shrouded, so we could not establish the details. It also did not appear imminent. Then, the day of the attack, I was walking only blocks away and got a flash of what was going to happen."

He paused to find the right words.

"It was like someone took the cover off, or pulled back the curtain, just before the action began. As if they didn't care about being discovered, because it was too late to intervene."

He looked down.

"It was as if they understood they were being watched. That is not comforting. That could present a problem in this battle going forward."

Geoffrey had a pained look on his face.

"Yet you got there, not in time to prevent the attack, but in time to identify one of the perpetrators. That's something," Jane said.

Geoffrey nodded. "Let us hope so."

Chapter 7

Four months earlier

Their meeting was set for the afternoon in a small but secure office in Jeddah. It was an anonymous space, which Rashid liked. He could not bring a front-line fighter like Muntaqim to his more lavish offices in Riyadh.

Rashid watched the man closely when he entered. His men had already checked him for weapons. Rashid was interested in how he carried himself. The body gave away much that words tried to hide. This knowledge served him well in business as in war.

"*Salam alaikum*," peace be upon you, he said as Muntaqim entered the office.

"*Wa-alaikum as-salam*," came the response.

The man's eyes scanned the room. It looked as though he was evaluating his surroundings, noting where Rashid's men stood, how many there were, and where they wore their weapons. His manner evidenced instincts honed in battle. A man not to let his guard down, thought Rashid.

"Please sit," Rashid pointed to the couch opposite him. On the table between them there was an array of food and drink. "We can eat and talk in safety and peace here. My men are also outside, watching the streets. Nothing can get through to us."

Muntaqim gave Rashid a faint smile. "So you say."

"You don't trust my security?"

"I am ever cautious, especially of becoming too comfortable, assuming people don't make mistakes."

"Yes, mistakes can happen. Redundancy is important. Also, hiring the best one can."

"Then never assume they can't."

Rashid smiled and took a sip of his tea. "One must relax sometimes."

"Maybe for you. I stay alive because I relax very little."

Rashid leaned slightly forward as if to begin a more serious conversation.

"You have been very successful against the apostates."

Muntaqim nodded.

"But you fight the wrong battle."

"How is that?"

"Our battle ultimately is with the west, specifically the U.S."

Muntaqim looked thoughtful. "They will fall of their own accord. They are turning on themselves and seem to have lost the will to prevail. Self-doubt is growing along with a loss of belief in their basic principles."

"You read them correctly, but I am not so sure this trend will continue. Their society seems to have the ability to keep swinging back to the center from its extremes."

He took a sip of his tea.

"I prefer to see their destabilization accelerated."

"And you will help it along?"

Rashid nodded.

"And you are interested in me for that end?"

Rashid nodded again. He appreciated that this fighter could come to the point quickly.

"I understand that the man that was called Scorpion is now missing and presumed dead. He was your man, was he not?"

Rashid did not answer but nodded a third time. He preferred to let the other party move the conversation forward, interested in where they would take it.

"Someone...or something has been foiling your plans for a number of years. I hear reports of Mexico, Frankfort, Marseille, Africa, and now an elaborate scheme in the U.S."

Muntaqim paused to pour himself a cup of coffee.

"These were all your enterprises, were they not?"

Rashid smiled but kept silent. The man had done some careful research.

After a moment, Muntaqim continued. "Don't you find it odd? Don't you wonder how so many of your best fighters have been killed?"

"There are no leaks in my organization. I have already examined that possibility and dismissed it."

"And yet, someone tracked your most secret and deadly agent, Scorpion, to his home territory, Yemen, and is now gone, probably food for the carrion birds in the desert. And," Muntaqim now leaned forward, "you have no idea of where he died and who killed him."

"As I told you, I have investigated this issue. My small organization has no leaks."

"But you keep getting foiled and your best warriors killed."

"You shy away from the larger battle? You are afraid of taking on the greater struggle?"

"I shy from no man. But I am cautious, as I told you. That is why I am still alive. I have no reservations about being involved in the larger battle as you say, although I'm not sure it is more important than my struggle against the apostates of our religion. But I don't want to put myself in the position of becoming another victim of a problem that seems to exist in your organization."

"There are flaws in all organizations, nothing is perfect. I have watched you. You seem to be disorganized. You sow confusion in your own ranks. It rankles your followers and makes you inefficient."

"You have studied me closely."

Rashid nodded.

"Since my disorganization, as you call it, seems so obvious, do you wonder why I am so?"

"It has crossed my mind. Maybe you are not so good at planning, so you have to constantly revise, change direction."

Muntaqim smiled. "It goes deeper than that."

He paused to take a bite of some hummus and bread.

"You see, I have also watched you. Studied you, especially since the phone call. That is why I know of your plans being defeated so many times."

He hunched himself forward in his seat as if warming to his theme. Rashid watched with interest. He was coming to an important point.

"You say you have no security leaks. If you believe that, and I don't really doubt you, then you must ask yourself what else is happening. The list of foiled attacks, deaths of your fighters, is not random. Something else is at work."

"And you know what that is?"

Muntaqim shook his head. "I have a theory only. But it shapes my thinking and my actions. What if there were people who could see what has not yet happened? Who could divine intent? People who had what might be called special sight?"

"That sounds blasphemous."

"Maybe. But there are stories, legends of such people. They were often considered prophets or oracles, or witches in league with the devil. Such stories may have a basis of truth to them."

"Are you saying that this is the cause of some of my setbacks?"

Rashid's voice sharpened; his eyes narrowed.

"That is a theory that one cannot test. And one that I couldn't change. So, it is not useful to me. I don't operate on fantasy or children's stories."

Muntaqim, instead of being taken aback by Rashid's sharp retort, only smiled. "Here is my point. I don't know if such people exist. But I have chosen to act as if they do."

He sat back on his couch, his smile broadened as much as his sharp face could permit.

"Now you understand why I seem so disorganized?"

"Explain yourself."

"If such a person or persons exist, then my only defense is to continually change my pace, my direction. All the while, keeping my goals the same. I become unpredictable, confusing." He paused and looked thoughtful for a moment. "If such people exist, then I must confuse them, take them by surprise."

"And you're saying that if you were to fight with me, with my plans and goals, you would continue to use these steps. And these steps are purposely done as a way to confuse an unknown and possibly non-existent enemy of our jihad?"

"Yes. You understand. You can rely on me to disrupt the best-laid time schedules, change intermediate steps, but keep the end goals of any fight. It will be less efficient, but, in the end, safer and more successful."

Rashid now smiled. His face relaxed. He stood up and shook the warrior's hand. "You are my new general."

Chapter 8

U ri watched the news that night, showing the devastation of the explosion. His anger rose. Early the next morning, the news announced who the targets might have been and the count of the killed and wounded. He heard the name of his old friend Ariel Weiss.

Ariel was a gentle man, but nobody's fool. He was the perfect negotiator, always cordial and polite but with a sharp sense of other's bluster and misdirection. It enabled him to shut down those who would try to lead him astray. He would gently but persistently steer his opposite, he never considered them his opponents, back to the issues at hand and force the other party to address them.

Uri got dressed and headed to METSAD headquarters in Tel Aviv. He stormed through the offices and multiple desks designed to keep interlopers from interrupting important people like Eitan Malka, the head of METSADA. Finally, after much noise and threatening speeches, word reached Eitan of this wild man, Uri Dayan, who would not go away until he talked to his old boss.

Eitan sighed and ordered him brought up to his office.

"What do you know?" Uri asked as he burst into the room.

"How are you?"

"Cut the crap. I'm not good. My old friend, Ariel was killed. It was on the news. He was working on something important? That's what I think. And someone didn't want it to happen, so they killed him along with a lot of others. If he was the target, then they assassinated him in a way designed to send a message. What's the message?"

Eitan shook his head. "Can't say."

He glared at Uri but kept his voice even.

"Look, I'm busy. What do you want besides to rant about your friend? Lots of us knew Ariel and Natan. You're not the only one."

"I want you to put me on this."

Eitan stared at him. Uri had done well on the major assignment he had given him. The one that had taken him to Yemen. But he had also been badly wounded and had to be rescued. He had become a liability on that mission.

"You know I can't do that."

"You can and you will. I'm going to dig into this on my own if I have to. You know me well enough to understand that. Make me official, in your undercover way. That's what we do. It'll work better for both of us. I'm going to see those who did this brought down. With or without you."

"Uri. Go home. Let me gather more information. I'll talk with you later."

He held up his hand as Uri was about to object.

"Don't. I'm not saying no. Just let me get a better understanding of what happened, then I can see how you might help. Do that for me. I've helped you out of your retirement blues once before."

Uri stood there, his face flush with anger, his body tense with bottled-up energy. He was in his fifties, having lived a hard life, which his body evidenced. But his experiences in Yemen had re-ignited his desire for action, and Eitan had given him some assignments since then. They had provided the incentive to take better care of himself to not become a liability. Now, he had to bottle up that desire and wait for his marching orders. It was necessary, but it didn't sit well with him.

"Okay. But don't leave me hanging. If I don't hear from you shortly, I'll do this on my own."

He turned to go and, at the door, spun around.

"And don't try to stop me."

† † †

After they had driven the sketch artist back to Langley, Jane and Dan went down to her offices.

"Too soon to see what Fred and Warren have come up with?"

Jane shook her head. "Let's give them the rest of the night. We'll get together in the morning."

"If I'm right, these guys are gone. They'll probably exfiltrate across the southern border, meet with the cartel that helped them into the country and head back to wherever they came from, probably the Mideast."

"You sound sure of yourself."

"Most probable scenario."

"What do you think of what Geoffrey said?" Jane asked.

"If he's right, we may have a problem. Watchers have been incredibly helpful. Partly because the enemy doesn't know about them."

"They are not a recent phenomenon. They have a history going back hundreds of years."

"Maybe thousands, who knows? In the past they might have been labeled as witches or seers. It was too much to hope that our enemy wouldn't think about their involvement at some point."

Dan looked across the room in thought.

"It doesn't change things. We may just have to accelerate our attacks on targets. The more disruption we can sow, the more they become unsettled. If they're thinking about a group like the Watchers, our attacks can make them think more about survival than countering any advantage the Watchers bring."

"You've got it figured out?"

Dan shook his head. "Far from it. But this seems the only way to go forward."

He looked up at Jane.

"If this is Rashid's work, then he's got another fighter to lead his cause. One that may be more attuned to our advantage than the Scorpion was."

Just then, Jane's phone rang. It was Eitan, her contact in METSADA.

"You're working late," Jane said when she answered. "I'm putting you on speakerphone. Dan's here."

"Yes. Working late," Eitan said. "Everyone here's in an uproar. There're voices clamoring for a counter strike, although we haven't yet identified the perpetrators, and no one has come forward to claim responsibility."

"How did such a bomb get into Israel without anyone knowing?" Dan asked.

"Also, a mystery we're working on."

He paused for a moment.

"The target seems to have been two of our diplomats, both working on the Abraham Accords. They received a letter that morning requesting that the two of them meet at this restaurant. An unknown Saudi diplomat wanted to have a private discussion about some critical issue that had come up. It was very enticing. We had security all around the area, but it didn't prevent a bomb-laden van from driving up and a terrorist from setting it off and killing himself in the act.

"The first guess is that the bomb was combined with some accelerants to increase its explosive effect. Have you any ideas about the composition of the explosion in D.C.?"

"I hope we'll have some information tomorrow. We'll share with you when we know."

"And the same here."

"Do you think this might have been an operation that developed over some time?"

"At this point, who knows? We're working to identify the van, which was pretty much destroyed and trace that back to where it might have come into the country."

Dan turned to Jane. "I've got to get overseas. These bombings are linked. They have the imprint of Rashid on them—large, multi-country attacks. That means the ones responsible are over there, not here."

"If you do come over," Eitan said, "I want to team an agent up with you. Someone who can help you here in the Mideast."

"You know that's not my style," Dan said.

"I know. But I think you can work with who I have in mind."

"And who is that?"

"Uri."

Eitan went on to explain how Uri had stormed into his office the morning after the bombing and insisted he put him to work.

"Ariel Weiss was killed in the explosion. Uri and Ariel were old friends from way back. He's now on fire and I can only use him undercover. He could work with you, if you're coming here."

"He got himself shot in Yemen. Became a liability."

"But he helped. He's actually in better condition now. I've kept him working, small stuff, but it's given him a purpose besides drinking."

"You say he's stopped drinking?"

"No. That will never happen. But he's in better shape now. He can help. You saw that before he got shot."

"All right. I'll think about it." Dan's voice evidenced his reluctance.

"Let's not get ahead of ourselves," Jane said. "We still need hard data that links these attacks. And we need a clue to point us in the right direction."

"Agreed," said Eitan. "But it won't come from sitting around waiting for it."

"Don't worry," Jane replied. "We're hard at work, as I know your agency is. Let's talk tomorrow and see what we have found out."

After Jane ended the call, Dan spoke up.

"I've got to go hunting."

Jane nodded, her face grim. "But let's find a target to hunt."

Chapter 9

Rashid watched the television feeds that brought him the latest news from around the world. The nearly simultaneous bombings in Jerusalem and Washington, D.C., were the leads on all the channels. He smiled as he savored his morning coffee. He had received a cryptic message last night from Muntaqim that the job was complete. Now, he watched the news channels show him the images of the completed missions. In D.C., they reported twenty-eight people dead and thirty-five wounded, some seriously. The death count was expected to rise. The Jerusalem explosion had killed nineteen people outright and injured thirty-eight others. Some of those were also not expected to survive.

Muntaqim seemed disorganized, unplanned, confusing. But it was precisely what he had told Rashid would be his style. Despite that, or maybe because of that, he had been spectacularly successful. The U.S. stock market had dropped a thousand points in one day. The trading had ended just before the exchange was about to halt it to avoid a total collapse. Who knew what the next day would bring? The same was true for the Israeli stock market in Tel Aviv. Civic life was disrupted in both countries. Not to the extent of the 9-11 attacks, but second only to that day.

Now, to follow up with more disruption. Rashid's mind began to imagine the next move. A discordant thought intruded on his reverie. What would be the fallout? He could see the disruption he had caused, which would lead to a pause, if not a cessation of progress in the Accords. But what would the retaliation look like? It would come. Rashid had no doubt. It had taken the form of an assassin or team of assassins who had tracked down his best fighter and killed him somewhere in Yemen. Would Muntaqim be able to withstand this counter-offensive? Had he hidden his trail well enough? Rashid didn't believe in Muntaqim's theory about people with special sight who could look into their plans. It was mind-reading at a distance. It was too preposterous to believe. He let the man indulge himself with his disorganization as long as he could bring the results Rashid saw this morning. The idea, however, remained a fantasy in Rashid's mind.

† † †

The men involved in the D.C. bombing switched cars at a warehouse in Fairfax County south of the capitol. Now, in a passenger van, the six men drove south on I95. Below Richmond, they headed west to connect to I81, running the length of the Shenandoah Valley. In Knoxville, they joined I40 for the long drive to Little Rock and then to Dallas. They would stay in the mosque, hidden by the imam, until the cartel arranged for them to cross the border and travel deep into Mexico before departing, one at a time, on separate flights to separate cities in the Mideast.

Muntaqim was not with them but had sent one of his most trusted fighters, Jamal Almasi, to lead the attack. They had spent little time in the U.S. Muntaqim felt the more time spent there, the greater the chance of exposure.

He wanted his men to get in, do their final preparations of putting the components together, and execute the attack. The warehouse had been rented for four months through a shell corporation that Rashid had set up. He had set the timeline up so it wouldn't appear as a recent rental just before the bombing. Assembling the bomb was not complex and required only a day, two at the most, after the compounds arrived.

Speed had been the primary operating principle. That, and no outside contact with the general public. The men stayed in separate motels that catered to traveling workers where they could blend in. They were picked up in the van that, after the attack, would drive them to Dallas. With only five days spent in the area, they didn't attract any noticeable attention. There were no clues for anyone to connect them to the explosion, so there were no reports to the authorities investigating the attack.

† † †

Information had started to come in from the investigation. Two days after the blast, the forensics team in the U.S. had identified the chemical residue as coming from SEMTEX, a version of C-4 made in Slovakia. There was also evidence that diesel fuel and, most likely, propane had been used to enhance the blast. Israel intelligence confirmed that the bomb used in the Jerusalem explosion was of a similar makeup. The probability that the same group coordinated the two attacks was now firmly established as the working hypothesis. It would direct the ongoing investigation.

Dan and Jane were sitting in her office when the call came in. It was from Geoffrey.

"We've located the driver," he said. His voice carried a tone of excitement and satisfaction.

"Tell me," Jane said.

"His name is Bilal Hamid. He comes from a town in northern Syria near the Turkish border. It's called Al Qamishli." He paused for a moment. "It's odd because there are a lot of Shiites in that area."

"So?"

"One of our people from the Mideast, says that the man is Sunni and has roots in Mosul. We're not sure what he was doing in Al Qamishli."

"That's not important. What is important is where did he go after the bombing," Dan said.

"People are on the lookout for him. If he goes back to his own area, we'll see him."

"Do we know how he got in?" Jane asked. "I assume that all involved would follow a similar path."

"I can't see that clearly. My sense is that he came over the southern border. There were meetings between Rashid and the man that runs the Sinaloa cartel."

"Probably infiltrated by them," Dan said.

"I have my people searching all relevant airports using the image you helped create," Jane said. "We're going back through time from the day before the blast. We'll find him, if he flew into the U.S."

"I think I should get ready to head over to the Mideast," Dan said. "We have a lead and a direction. Our best chance is to find this Hamid guy and see how much he knows."

"Let's reach out to Eitan. I want you to work with Uri."

Dan started to object, but the look on Jane's face stopped him. She was in charge. He had decided that he should accept that reality for both of their sakes. She had good instincts. Her insistence on Uri in his earlier mission had paid off, even though the man had gotten badly injured. He would not have found the Scorpion without him.

Dan nodded. "Agreed."

Chapter 10

The phone rang, dragging him out of a heavy sleep. The man shrugged off his bed cover and rolled over on his side with a heavy sigh. His head hurt, and the early morning light piercing his eyes only worsened the pain. It had been a boisterous night. A naked female lay sprawled on the other side of the bed, face down. Jetmir patted her ample bottom, heaved himself into a sitting position, and picked up the phone.

"*Po?*" Yes? His voice was still thick with sleep.

"You have seen the news?" The caller did not identify himself, but Jetmir knew the voice. It was a man who called himself Muntaqim.

"*Jo.*" No. "I just woke up. What is so important to disturb me at this early hour?"

"It is not early. And it is important."

"What is it?"

"Just look at your TV. We will not discuss it over the phone. Then, you must stay quiet. Lie low for a while. I will inform you when you can party again. Take a vacation, only stay out of sight."

"I don't know what has happened, but I do know you don't order my life."

"Do not disregard me. You are a link in a chain. You will understand when you see the news. Then I expect you to do what I say. If not, I may have to eliminate the link."

Jetmir, now fully awake, started to get angry. "I do not take orders from you. Do not threaten me. You are a customer, nothing more. If you want to take your business somewhere else in the future, that is up to you. But you do not tell me how to live."

There was a pause. "Forgive me, my friend. I did not mean to order you around. But what I say is for your benefit as well as mine. The things you will see should convince you of that. The world has been shaken up and now we must be cautious."

"You mean lie in a hole or under a rock. Cower like a rabbit? That's not my style. I enjoy the benefits of my work...as do the ladies I play with."

Muntaqim sighed. Jetmir could hear it over the phone. "It sounds like you have had a busy night. Perhaps you could take a few nights off, as a favor to me. Let me ask that much of you."

"I will look at the news. After I get up. Then I will decide. Just remember who you deal with."

He ended the call and lay back on the bed. He looked over at the sleeping figure. Last night's lust now seemed misplaced as he viewed the young woman's somnolent form. He lurched to his feet.

Jetmir was not tall but heavily muscled, with a thick body that was getting thicker over the years. His eyes were dark, almost black, set deep in his face, with a thick crop of black hair on top. He had a long nose, flattened by many fights. No one would consider his face handsome; brutal was the word that came to mind. He had a thick neck, and his shoulders were broad and sloping. His long arms ended in thick hands that could form powerful fists. Everything about him indicated he was not a man to mess with or cross.

He had grown up fighting his way to dominance on the streets during the rule of Hoxha. The dictator's control over society and paranoia later in life created a dangerous environment for someone who occasionally operated outside the law. With the end of the Hoxha rule, the country, which had been sealed away from the rest of the world for so long, began to open up to the West, and chaos emerged at the end of strict authoritarian discipline. This environment allowed Jetmir, like the mafia in Russia, to take advantage of the disintegration of civic order. Jetmir rose to some level of power in the gangs but stepped aside and entered arms dealing. He set himself up as an independent, leaving the constant struggle over turf to the other gangsters. He had created a lucrative niche for himself and was not going to abdicate any of his power and freedom to a customer. Even one as well-funded and powerful as Muntaqim.

Jetmir worked out of a fortified warehouse in the industrial section of Tirana, where he often slept in an inner room well-protected from any external assaults. He walked to his small kitchen, put a packet of coffee into his machine, and turned it on. He then turned on the television and flicked around some channels until he came to a news outlet. It had images of a bombed building in Jerusalem.

Jetmir watched in fascination. The brewing finished, and he poured the coffee into a cup. The broadcast then switched to the U.S. capital. Images of a bombed building were also displayed. The newsreader droned on with a serious face, wondering if the two incidents were connected and what purpose they might have had. Other commentators chimed in to opine that this might be the first of a new wave of terror that would sweep through Europe. The show moved on to talk about the economic impact of the events on the stock markets, not only in the countries where they had occurred but also in the larger European markets.

Jetmir smiled. He had most of his assets in gold and diamonds—easy to transport, easy to hide, and not affected by the market swings. He also included choice parcels of real estate in his holdings.

He sat back and thought about what Muntaqim had said. Now he understood his concern. While he would not allow anyone to force him to obey orders from anyone, he could understand the man's point. He made a decision.

Jetmir got up and went back into the bedroom. He pulled the covers off the sleeping girl and gave her a sharp slap on the butt. She squealed and rolled over.

"What did you do that for? I want to sleep in."

"Get up. It's time for you to go. I have some things I have to do."

"Can't I just stay here? I'll make some dinner for us tonight." She gave him a sly smile. "We can enjoy ourselves again, like last night."

Jetmir shook his head. "Sorry. I'm too busy. Something's come up."

He threw her clothes at her.

"Now get dressed and get going. I'll call a car for you."

The girl got out of bed and stretched enticingly in front of Jetmir. He appreciated her attempt to lure him into changing his mind, but she was of no consequence to him. There were many more where she came from.

Getting no reaction, she pouted and walked off to the bathroom, flouncing her breasts with each step.

A half-hour later, she was gone, and Jetmir was packing. He would spend a few days, maybe a week, in a secluded cabin he owned in the Oafe Bushi Forest east of the capital. It had been a hunting cabin owned by one of Hoxha's ministers. It was luxurious for its time, and Jetmir had further improved it since his acquisition. If there was a problem, he would not be where anyone would think to look. He could operate for a short time from there. Better to leave Tirana quickly. There was no telling how soon authorities would come looking once they had identified the SEMTEX he had sold to Muntaqim.

David Nees

Chapter 11

On the third day after the two explosions, Jane was called into a meeting with the upper-level management of the CIA. Her boss, Henry Mason, was there, as was Henry's boss, Roger Abrams. Roger was head of SAD, the darker side of CIA operations. It surprised her that Garrett Easton, the DDO, was also there. Easton was a political figure, like his boss, William Gardner, the Director, who didn't want to know too much about clandestine ops, especially the dark kind. Jane wondered about that fact and why she had been included in such a meeting. There were other people from the SIGINT side and one lone member from the legal department.

Jane took her seat, a bit nervous and uncomfortable. She didn't like being on anyone's radar, especially those at such a high level. She preferred to toil away in the basement, pursuing the fight she had dedicated herself to years ago. A fight that shaped her life outside of her work. Normal relationships were impossible in her position. She had tried them, and they had all come undone. There was too much that couldn't be shared, too many secrets, and too many odd hours. Jane had long ago resigned herself to that fact.

She stayed dedicated to this fight she had adopted as her own. To beat back the forces of those who wanted to undermine and destabilize her country. She had joined the CIA after the 9-11 attack as a young woman just out of college. Quickly, she gravitated to the operations side of the organization, where Henry discovered her. Once offered, she jumped at the chance to operate in the field, and when Henry was tasked with setting up a black op mission to strike back at the enemies of the U.S. before they could strike us, he asked Jane to join him.

Now she sat in a meeting room with the powerful, uncomfortable, as if naked and exposed.

"Ms. Tanner," Garrett said when they assembled, "I asked Roger to bring someone to this meeting who has direct involvement in kinetic operations. Henry suggested you should attend."

He paused to look around the room.

"As you know," he continued, "the President has called on all agencies to work together. We need to find those involved and strike back."

He turned back to Jane, "Now we have many operations going on overseas. We need to utilize those connections to hunt down the perpetrators."

"There are some in Congress already talking about domestic terrorists, right-wing groups that want to sabotage the peace efforts in the Mideast," Roger said. "They're making a twisted argument that conservatives somehow want to keep the Mideast in turmoil, so we can keep intervening."

"I know," Garrett replied, "it's already become politicized."

"Sir," Jane said. "I'm not sure why I'm here. What do you need from me?"

"In short, your view on where we should look, to start with."

Jane thought about that for a moment. The DDO wanting to know from her where to start. It seemed preposterous. But Henry had warned her that the agency was marshaling all areas. Garrett wanted to hear from the people on the ground, not filtered through their supervisors. She was one of several such meetings he was having. Once he felt he had a good sample of the on-ground operations and capabilities, he would return to giving high-level direction.

Meanwhile, Roger, Henry's boss, had told her she should continue to dig deep and see what she could uncover and pursue. He knew of her secret weapon and knew she would see to its deployment in the most effective manner possible.

"Well," Jane said, hesitating. There were many potential minefields to navigate in her reply, but she had to push forward. She had been called upon to give her views; that was what she would do. "This is definitely not domestic. I don't have hard evidence for that, but my years of fieldwork say this is the work of Muslim fundamentalists. Ones who don't want to see the Israelis and Saudis develop closer ties."

She continued with growing assurance.

"The place to look is the Mideast." Jane took out copies of a lifelike drawing of a Middle Eastern man and passed them around the table. "We found an eyewitness. He gave us this image. We're distributing it to our operatives and see if anyone knows who this is."

The group studied the drawing.

"This is incredible. So realistic," Roger said.

"Have you shared this with the FBI?" Garrett asked.

Henry shook his head. "I told Ms. Tanner to hold off until we met. If this picture is leaked, it could alert the perpetrators to go deeper underground. Right now, they think they are anonymous."

"Still," Garrett said, "it could get the public looking."

"Sir," Jane said, "that wouldn't be much help if the man's in the middle east."

Garrett paused. "I see your point. But we could use this to find out how he came into the country."

"We're already working on that," Jane said. "But our suspicion is that the terrorists came across the southern border."

"You have intel on that?"

"It's a developing situation," Jane replied.

Garrett shook his head. "That's going to be a problem. The President already said he didn't want to hear about the bombers coming over the border from Mexico."

Jane just looked at him without replying.

"So, that will be the official line?" Henry asked.

"For now."

"And when we get hard intel otherwise? What do we do with that?"

"Use it, but don't publicize it."

The meeting continued for another fifteen minutes, after which Garrett thanked Jane and Henry. He dismissed them to finish up with Roger and the others.

"Politics rears its ugly head again," Jane said as they walked down the hallway.

"It always does. That's why Roger allowed me to set up our ops. He plays the game with Garrett and William, but he also knows we need to strike back. He's betting we'll be able to identify a target and go after it. If the public never knows how they came into the country, it won't derail our efforts."

"I get that, but it's lying to the public. They don't know how dangerous that open border is. We don't fully know how dangerous it is."

Henry shrugged. They got to the elevator and stopped.

"Just don't let it throw you off. If you uncover who did it, take them out. We can't have them brought back here for trial. That will just give them a forum to attack and recruit from. I just want you to dole out some rough justice."

Jane nodded as the doors opened. "Is that the official word?"

"Official enough."

Chapter 12

Dan and Uri sat in an empty building in Al Qamishli, watching a block of rundown brick-and-mortar houses located in the northeast quadrant of the city. The neighborhood showed evidence of past conflict, with pock-marked walls, some houses abandoned like the one they were in, and some homes that had been reduced to rubble. They took turns watching the neighborhood. Dan had his favorite sniper rifle, a Sako TRG 42 chambered for the .338 Lapua Magnum. The magazine held five rounds. It was bolt action but with a 60-degree bolt for rapid re-chambering. Dan had it fitted with a Schmidt and Bender 3-27 x 56 scope and a suppressor. The rifle lay on a table set up behind the opening deep enough inside the room so it could not be seen from the outside. The two men took turns watching from a chair closer to the window with binoculars.

Bilal Hamid, the driver Geoffrey had identified, was reported to be staying in the city, specifically in this area. Dan and Uri had set up their observation post two days ago after arriving by car. Dan had documents indicating he was with UNESCO and headed to Mosul to work on preserving the antiquities in that area. Uri was his driver, interpreter, and fixer. The documentation was enough to get them from Jordan into Syria. However, it would not, if discovered, explain why they had stopped in Al Qamishli.

Both men knew that running afoul of the army or police would be disastrous for them and cause more than a minor incident. Still, capturing the only hard lead they had was worth the risk.

Earlier in the week, Dan had arrived in Tel Aviv by private jet, courtesy of Jane. He had used a diplomatic passport in the name of Victor James, and his luggage, which contained his favorite weapons, was not subject to search. Upon exiting the airport, he was picked up by a Land Rover SUV and whisked to METSADA headquarters. He entered an upper office and was greeted with a big bear hug.

"My favorite American," Uri exclaimed as he hugged Dan. "You look a lot better than when I last saw you."

"As do you." Dan smiled. "Are you up for this new mission?"

Uri's welcoming face turned serious. "They killed a good friend and mentor of mine in the blast. I'm definitely up for this."

"You look like you've been keeping yourself in good shape."

Uri's smile returned. "Never felt better." He patted his stomach. "Especially after losing forty pounds."

"That'll help you keep up."

"Keeping up with you was never a problem."

Dan smiled. He deposited his gear on the floor and sat down.

"You want something to eat, drink?"

"Coffee would be nice. Lunch later. How soon do we get going?"

"Eitan is meeting us in a few minutes. He has all the info."

"The sooner the better."

"Agreed."

Uri went to the side table and poured Dan a cup of strong, black coffee. Just then, Eitan entered.

"Welcome to Israel," he said. "I wish it was under better circumstances."

He went over to Dan and shook his hand warmly.

"I hope you don't mind Uri going with you. He would not be denied. I figured it was better the two of you team up than have him out there alone, wreaking havoc."

"We'll wreak more together," Uri replied.

"How long before we can set out?" Dan asked.

"Two days. This was put together quickly. I have to get an SUV modified to smuggle your weapons. And my team is finishing your IDs. Relax, get over your jet lag. Once you set out, things won't be easy."

"I doubt it will be harder than Yemen, especially for Uri." Dan looked over at the man.

"I don't plan on getting shot this time. It will be me doing the shooting."

"I want...Jane wants information. First information, then do what you need to do," Eitan said as he sat down at the table with the two men. "Uri knows this, but the word's come down that all those involved...all of them are to be eliminated."

"That could be a lot of people," Dan said.

"Think of it as similar to the '72 Olympic team massacre in Munich. All the terrorists involved were assassinated. It took years, but it was done." He leaned forward towards Dan. "We Jews are very good at vengeance when the reason for it arises."

Two days later, as promised, the men were off, crossing into Jordan on their way to Syria. They drove a run-down-looking Toyota Land Cruiser with a hidden compartment for weapons and, unlike its appearance, was in good mechanical condition.

"We're going to try to capture and interrogate this guy, right?" Uri asked. He was lounging on a mattress in the corner of the room.

"We get all the info out of him we can."

"He won't know much."

"Probably right. But all we need is a name. We use him to find the next link in the chain. He's got to have a connection to others no matter how compartmentalized they are. We move from him to the next. Keep working our way up."

"Eventually we get to the top, to those who directed the attacks."

"I think Rashid, the wealthy Saudi is the one at the top," Dan said.

"What's he get out of this?"

"He's working to take down the U.S. The Saudis are warming to the U.S. It's an on-again, off-again relationship. They need us, we need them, but their doctrines get in the way. We're often the enemy of Islam—"

"And they're the keepers of the faith."

"Bingo! Give that man a prize."

"That still doesn't explain Rashid.

"They walk a tightrope...the government. That makes Rashid have to walk a tightrope. My guess is some in the government don't mind his forays into jihad, but others don't like it and certainly don't want him to be too successful."

"So, you think this wasn't officially sanctioned."

Dan shrugged. "Who the hell knows? The Saudi government may not even know who did the bombings. But they have to react."

"Decry it, and pull back."

"That's it. If Rashid's behind this, then he accomplished one goal of slowing down the progress."

He turned away from watching and back to Uri.

"He's also accomplished another goal. The financial markets are in disarray since the bombing. Everyone is worried about a new wave of terror violence."

"It's in the news each day. Everyone's on edge," Uri said.

"Even in Europe."

Dan turned back to the window.

"I see him!"

Chapter 13

B oth men watched Bilal emerge from a building and enter a rundown Nissan pickup truck. They grabbed their gear and rushed down the stairs to get into their Toyota. Uri swung it around the corner of the alley and into the dusty street. He slowed as the pickup pulled away.

"Won't be easy to not get spotted," Uri said.

"Hopefully he'll get into a bit of traffic and then we won't be so conspicuous."

"In this town?"

Thankfully, the man turned onto one of the main roads and headed towards the center of town. Uri followed, now a few cars behind.

Before reaching the downtown area, he turned right and crossed the bridge that connected an island in the river to the city. Dan and Uri followed. There, the traffic thinned. The pickup made a couple of turns and stopped at an unused warehouse. Uri turned the other direction when he came to the intersection. He slowed as he drove down the side street while Dan watched.

"He's gone into the warehouse."

"Got it."

Uri turned into an alley, reversed the SUV, and stopped.

"We'll go on foot. Bring the M4s," Dan said.

Both Uri and Dan carried suppressed M4 carbines. The sound would not be heard from a block away and would help them remain undetected when shooting.

"There'll be more inside. What's the plan?" Uri asked.

"We get in, find the driver, take him, and get out of town."

"If a shootout starts, it'll bring others. We'll be outnumbered and not in a good position."

Uri grabbed Dan as he was about to exit the SUV. He pulled him back inside.

"Let's just reconnoiter. Watch what's going on and maybe learn something," Uri said. "I want to take out these assholes as much as you do, maybe more. But we need a quieter way to kidnap this guy."

He looked over at Dan intently.

Dan nodded his head. His face dark with anger and determination. "Okay. We'll do it more subtly."

Uri slapped his shoulder. They both got out of the vehicle and walked down the side street with their carbines down by their side, trying not to be too conspicuous. The two men wore communication devices, short-range transmitters with earpieces and throat mics.

"You check the windows at the front, I'll go around back," Dan said. His voice was quiet and firm. He was now in action mode.

Uri nodded, and they split up. Dan paused when he reached the back corner and crouched down to peer around it. There was no one in sight. He turned the corner and went to the first window. It was about six feet off the ground. Dan stood on his toes and peaked over the edge. There were four men inside. One of them was the targeted driver identified by Geoffrey. There was no way to know if the others were connected to the bombings or just local supporters of the driver, helping him hide out. Probably been told to lie low for a few weeks.

He could hear the conversation, but he could not follow the Arabic. *I hope Uri can hear. He'll be able to interpret.*

Near the front, Uri could also see the men assembled towards the rear of the building. He caught some of the conversation. The driver was complaining about having to sit tight in the place Muntaqim had chosen. He wanted to go home to more comfortable surroundings. The other three men were telling him, with increasing intensity, that he needed to obey Muntaqim. Uri registered the name in his head. He knew what it meant, avenger or revenger. He wondered if it could be the *nom de guerre* for the leader of the bombings.

Uri backed away from the window. The four men didn't look ready to wrap up their conversation any time soon.

"I can hear most of the conversation," Uri said quietly into the mic.

"What are they saying?"

"They're arguing with the driver. He wants to go to his home. He was told by someone called Muntaqim to stay hiding where we saw him and these guys are trying to convince him to obey the boss. I'm guessing this Muntaqim is the one who organized the bombings."

"We have a name now. That's a big step forward."

"What do you want to do?"

"Let's go in, you from the front me from the back. Eliminate the three and take the driver."

"You can get in from the back?"

"Yeah. There's a door partially opened. It may be stuck, but I can get through it."

"Got to be quick and then we get the hell out of town."

"Roger that. And let's not shoot each other."

"Stay to your right after you go in, I'll stay to the same side as you. We'll both be shooting away from each other."

"Got it. Go on my signal."

Dan crept to the partially opened door. He checked his carbine, making sure the safety was off and that it was chambered and ready to fire.

"You in position?"

"Yeah," Uri replied.

"Go."

Both men suddenly appeared in the dim light of the warehouse. At first, the four men didn't see them; it took another moment for them to react. They had weapons, but they were leaning against the chairs placed around the area. Their pause proved their undoing.

Dan fired at the one on the right side of the group, and Uri fired on the man to the left. Both rounds struck the men in the chest, and they went to the ground writhing. The driver and the fourth men dove for their weapons by the chairs. Two rounds tore into the third local, and he rolled to one side.

Dan fired another round, hitting the chair that the driver was reaching towards. It splintered; the rifle went spinning.

Just then, Uri shouted in Arabic, "Stop! We won't kill you!"

The man hesitated and looked at Uri. After his shot into the chair, Dan dropped his carbine and took off towards the driver. He covered the ten yards in less than two seconds. Before the man could react to Uri's command or reach for another weapon, Dan launched himself at him. He slammed into his back, and they both went to the floor. The man gasped, the air driven out of him by Dan's impact. They hit the ground with Dan on top. He immediately swung his fist down low on the back of the man's head. The blow stunned him. He was still, and Dan drove his next punch hard into the side of his head. The man went limp.

Uri ran up. "Quite a flying tackle."

"I used to play football."

"You didn't kill him, I hope."

Dan shook his head. He'll be out for a while, which is good."

"Let's get out of here, then."

"You get the SUV. I'll clean up."

Uri gave Dan a serious look. He understood what "clean up" meant. Then he turned and ran towards the front door.

A minute later, he pulled up. Dan was dragging the driver by his arms to the door. Uri helped load him into the back cargo space. They tied his hands and feet and gagged him.

"All done inside?"

Dan nodded. "Let's go."

Chapter 14

With Bilal bound and gagged and stuffed under a blanket on the floor, Dan and Uri drove to the northeast. They would cross the Tigris River and into Iraq at Piri Semalka. Shortly before reaching the border, they stopped, and Dan injected Bilal with a sedative, ensuring he would remain quiet and still.

Uri had a thousand U.S. dollars to bribe the border officials so they wouldn't look too hard in the back area where they had packed Bilal. On the Iraq side of the river, the land became hillier. It was Kurdish country. The Kurds had re-emerged as a regional force with the destruction of ISIS. Dan had contacts among the people, fighters who had worked with the CIA trying to defeat first Saddam, then ISIS. Now, these fighters, when not arguing among themselves, worked to stem the influence of the Shiites who ran the country from Baghdad.

They drove east and then north, heading deeper into the Kurdish territory. They had not been stopped since the border crossing. Their captive was beginning to come around. They could hear him starting to thrash and try to shout, his voice muffled by the gag.

"He's going to need another shot," Uri said.

"Not sure that's healthy."

"I'm not concerned about his health, only ours."

Uri scanned the countryside around them. It had a wild look. Cultivated fields were interspersed with scrub forests and steep hillsides that could not be planted. They passed only the occasional farmstead, usually a small house and barn with goats and sheep in pens, surrounded by fields either planted with crops or grasses for grazing.

"I've got some contacts here. Names I can drop when we're stopped," Dan said.

"You can count on that happening."

It was a half hour later when they came to a checkpoint. The Kurdish flag was flying over the barricade. There were two pickup trucks with machine guns mounted in the beds. Five men stood around with carbines slung over their shoulders.

"Here we go," Uri said. "Let's hope someone speaks Arabic."

"Many do along with their native Kurdish, Turkish and Persian."

"True multi-linguals."

Uri rolled down the window and smiled. The man approaching him did not smile.

"You have papers? What are you doing here?"

"We are here to look for Zerya Barzani. Do you know of him?" Dan asked, leaning across the center console.

"Papers," the man repeated.

Both men produced passports and documents showing their assignment to work in Mosul. The man studied them as another walked up. All five men were now looking at the Toyota. Not much seemed to happen at this checkpoint, and Uri and Dan's arrival was a break in the dull routine.

"This is not the way to Mosul. What are you doing here?"

Uri spoke up in Arabic. "We are taking a side trip to visit his old friend, Zerya Barzani." He repeated the name. "Do you know of him? Where we can find him?"

The man looked at Uri, then turned to the others. "Barzani?" he asked.

Two of the men shook their heads. An older fighter spoke up.

"I know him. He lives north of here."

"They say they are friends," the man at the window said.

"Do they work for the U.S.? Barzani worked with some agents. They helped arm many militia during Saddam's time."

Uri followed the conversation as best he could. But when it shifted into Kurdish, he could not follow. Dan looked at him, but Uri only shrugged.

Finally, the man turned back to Uri. "You work for the U.S.? Barzani worked with the U.S."

Uri pointed to Dan. "He worked with Zerya. That was before. Now he works with the U.N."

"What is in your vehicle?" The man looked at the covered lump in the back of the SUV.

"We have someone that Zerya needs to speak with. Someone who may be able to help both him...your people, and others with information."

The man stepped back and grabbed his carbine. His movement caused the rest to bring their weapons up.

"You have someone back there? Tied up? Get out of the truck and raise your hands."

Uri translated to Dan, adding, "I think this is going to get worse."

"Position him as an enemy of the U.S. and the Kurdish people. Someone Zerya would want to talk to."

The man motioned Uri to walk around back and open the rear cargo door. He then told him to pull off the cover. They looked at the groggy, bound, and gagged man.

"Where did you get this man?"

"Al Qamishli"

"Syria? How did you bring him across the border? Why take him to this Barzani?"

"We bribed the border guards. He is not a friend of the Kurds. We think he has information useful to both the U.S. and to your people. This man," Uri pointed to Dan, "knows Zerya Barzani and wants to help his friend."

He waited for the man to digest what he said.

"We can offer you a payment for helping us find Zerya. You will be helping your cause. This man," he pointed back to the captive, "is not a friend of the Kurds. He may say so, but he lies. It is up to Zerya to get the truth from him. That is why we go there."

After a few words in Kurdish to one of the men, he reached into the SUV and pulled off the man's gag.

"Help me!" the man called out. "They killed my friends and kidnapped me." He spoke in Arabic.

The border guard turned to Uri. "Is this true?"

Uri shrugged. "They attacked us when we went to capture this man. Tried to kill us. We defended ourselves. He is not truthful. I told you. We know Zerya Barzani and he," Uri pointed to Dan, "is friends with Zerya."

The man stepped back and talked with one of the other guards who knew Barzani. Meanwhile, the captive glared at Uri.

"You will not get away with this. I will see you killed. These men will set me free."

"You are a lying dog," Uri replied. "We will see what our friend says after he interrogates you."

Uri turned to the two men.

"We have come openly to you. We did not try to hide this man. We're trying to bring him to Zerya Barzani. He would not like it if you freed him or detained us. Dan," Uri again pointed to his partner, "is his friend. Show us the way and I can pay you for your help."

The man in charge looked at Uri. "How much do you pay?"

"Two thousand U.S. dollars."

The man's eyes got wide. He turned to the other man, and they hurriedly conversed in Kurdish. Finally, he turned back to Uri. "We will show you. Pay the money first."

Uri turned to Dan. "Two thousand. Don't show him the rest of the money."

Dan carefully took a small wad of one-hundred-dollar bills from his pocket and counted out twenty. He passed them to Uri, who passed them to the guard. The guard nodded to the rest of the bills in Dan's hand. There were eight more of them. He handed them to the guard, who put them in his pocket.

"For the extra money, you draw us a map and write a note so we can go through other checkpoints," Uri said. He now acted more forcefully since he had paid the man. They were now working for him, and he pressed that advantage.

Chapter 15

Dan and Uri drove off with a crude map. They re-gagged their captive while he shouted that the guards were cowardly dogs, letting these two men kidnap him. His ranting did nothing to sway them, only to make them happier to see him gone and for them to split up the cash windfall that had just come into their lives.

Four hours of driving and passing another checkpoint. This time, more easily with the note, the map, and their captive again sedated. Later, they arrived at a compound on the top of a steep slope. As they pulled up, multiple armed men surrounded them. They were instructed to exit the vehicle with their hands in the air.

Dan shouted Zerya Barzani's name, and Uri filled in the rest of the information. After checking them for weapons, the guards escorted them into the house.

Inside, they were met by a bear of a man. He stood just short of six feet and had a large barrel chest. His thick arms ended in large, calloused hands. He had a full, black beard on his broad face. His eyes were dark and lit up when he smiled.

He was smiling as he came forward.

"Is it really you? It seems like many years ago."

Dan smiled. "Zerya, you look great. Life is treating you well?"

Zerya's smile broadened. "I have done well. The money your agency paid me helped expand my influence and authority. And I have managed the complicated Kurdish politics since."

He pointed to some chairs in the room.

"Come sit down. You must tell me why you are here. Although I enjoy seeing a ghost from the past, I wonder what you bring with you. Not trouble, I hope."

He clapped his hands, and a servant brought a tea serving to the table between them.

"Before we get comfortable, there's something I have to tell you," Dan said.

Zerya gave him a grave look. "I should have known, trouble follows you, or you bring it."

"Not so much trouble as inconvenience. We have a prisoner in the back of the SUV. We need to debrief him." Dan paused for a moment. "He's tied up in the back of our SUV. He's not in danger of suffocating...or going anywhere."

"Then let him stay. We will relax, talk, and you can tell me the rest of your story."

Tea was poured. Dan introduced Uri as his interpreter, and the three men sat back. Zerya looked carefully at Uri.

"Your accent is strange. What part of the Mideast do you come from?"

"An unusual part," Uri replied. "I'm Israeli."

Zerya smiled and clapped his large hands. "I knew it! Your Arabic is good, but your accent raised questions."

"It has served me well when I'm undercover in Arab countries."

"You must not run across many astute people."

"I admit to being a bit out of practice."

Zerya leaned forward, "Tell me, do you work for Mossad?"

Uri smiled and shook his head. "No. But if I did, I couldn't tell you."

"Even though our two peoples are friendly with one another?" He turned back to Dan. "And what do you have to do with this? Running around here in northern Iraq with an Israeli agent and a captive in your backseat? There must be quite a story behind all of this."

Dan told Zerya that the man they held had been positively identified as one of those involved in the D.C. bombing.

"We have so few clues. We're stuck with this guy as our best lead."

"He won't know anything. If I know my terrorists, they have become very compartmentalized. It limits damage for something just like this, your capture of the driver."

"It's a start. We'll keep pulling threads until we get to the top."

"Have you heard of someone called Muntaqim? This person might be the leader," Uri asked.

Zerya looked thoughtful for a moment and then shook his head. "We have defeated *Daesh*, and they are no longer a power up here in the north." He paused and raised his cup to Dan, "With the help of you and your fellow fighters."

Dan noted how Zerya used the pejorative acronym for ISIS or ISIL. The abbreviation has an unpleasant sound to an Arabic speaker's ear and is similar to the word to trample down or to crush something.

"We are always struggling with the Shiites, especially now that they control Baghdad, but we continue pursuit of our goals, an independent state." He paused to think for a moment. "There are areas where the Sunni and Shia conflict is more intense. Someone must be driving it, but I don't have much knowledge of that."

"That is okay. We will find what we can from our driver and move on from there." Dan put his cup on the table. "Zerya, you are helping us a great deal. Tell me what you need and I'll relay it to Washington and try to help."

Zerya smiled. "Your fellow fighters and advisors up here were of great help. Now they don't seem to be so interested in us. We can always use ammunition. We need 7.62 rounds and rockets would be useful, the MK153."

"I'll call back later on my satellite phone and get the process started. The same channels as used before still work?"

Zerya nodded.

"As much as I enjoy this relaxing time," Uri said, "I would like to start interrogating our prisoner. Is there someplace quiet and discreet to work?"

"There will be much noise?"

"Only if the subject does not want to talk with me."

"There is a special building at the far end of the compound. It is secure and not much sound gets out. I will have your prisoner placed there. Let him sit for a while and imagine what is going to happen to him. It helps. One's imagination can be a powerful weapon for you to use. It is late. We will eat and talk more and then you can start your questioning tomorrow. I assure you, your captive will be more receptive to your questions after twelve hours in that room."

Chapter 16

Back in D.C., Jane checked in with her boss, Henry Mason. He was at his desk with his head in a stack of papers when she knocked and entered his office. He looked up. "How is Dan doing? Any progress?"

"They've captured the driver and are taking him to a safe place where they can interrogate him."

"I'm going to pass the second image over to the FBI, so they can work on it."

Jane shook her head. "It won't help. He's left the country just like the driver. It will only alert him. Give Dan a day to find out what the driver knows. He's trying to work his way up the chain of command."

Henry sighed. "I'd like to report some progress."

"Patience, boss. We work in the dark and generally only report after the mission is over. Even then it's never publicized."

She changed the subject.

"The President is still going with the charade that the bombers came through one of our ports of entry?"

Henry nodded. "It creates an awkward situation when he can't be found on any security cameras."

"So, they'll just show a likely image and ruin some poor guy's life? Just to avoid the uncomfortable truth that our southern border is wide open?"

"Afraid so. Politics trumps the truth. Let's find the bastards and get their testimony. That will change the lie that's being told."

"If the media will publicize it. I'll tell Dan to include how they entered the country in his questioning."

Jane was back in her office when Fred entered.

"Don't you knock?" She snapped at him, venting her frustration about D.C. politics.

"Sorry." He approached her desk and laid a paper on it.

"This is the Imam of the mosque in Dallas. He's the one we suspected of harboring the anthrax terrorists. Warren picked up some communications after the bombing. It suggests the perpetrators drove there and were hidden in the mosque until the cartel came to take them back over the border."

Jane looked up with an angry expression on her face. "It's like a damned sieve, just stroll in and out of the country whenever you like. I assume they're all gone by now?"

Fred nodded. "From the communications, they departed two days after arriving in Dallas. They're long gone. That's reinforced by the driver being found in Syria."

† † †

Jetmir was growing stir-crazy. It was now a week since he had departed Tirana. He chastised himself for not bringing one of his women with him. She would have been a good distraction. His reluctance to let anyone know of this hideaway had overruled his desire for company, and now he was growing ever ill at ease. Being sequestered, away from action, was not to his liking.

"Fuck it," he said to himself. A part of him noted that he had begun to talk out loud, and no one was around to hear. "I can be safe enough back in the capital. And it's easier to do business there."

Cell reception was spotty in his mountain hideaway.

"No one will connect me to the SEMTEX. I used two middlemen, one in Tirana and one in Slovakia. The second one doesn't have any idea who brokered the purchase and the one here in Tirana would give me up only on pain of death." He smiled. "Doing so would result in a painful death from me."

A decision made, Jetmir packed up his clothes and headed out to his car. He drove a BMW 8 Series Gran Coupé in the sporty M version. It was a quarter of a million Euros, but Jetmir could afford it, and he enjoyed not only the power of the car but its effect on the women he encountered. Three hours later, he arrived at his home in the capital city.

It was a walled villa just south of the center of town, one of the few houses left on the lakefront of the Grand Park. After he had purchased it, he set about improving its security features. In his business, he had to make sure his home and base of operations were secure. Sometimes, customers tried to strike back, or rivals sought to remove the competition.

Cameras ranged along each wall, giving him a full view in all directions. The ones on the waterside were aimed at the dock and yard. There was a security room with a wall of screens showing each camera. The images could be enlarged, paused, or rewound as needed. Jetmir did not employ a security staff to monitor the room, preferring to do that himself. He had guards who came on duty each evening and patrolled through the night.

He felt safe in this fortress of a house. Even if anyone discovered his connection to the bombing, they would not be able to prove it, and he had paid off enough important people that he would not be arrested.

It was time to get back to work, doing what he did best: arm people, good or bad, whatever their ideology or aims, at a price that made him ever richer.

Chapter 17

T he next morning, Dan, Uri, and their host, Zerya,
met for breakfast.
"I want to do the interrogation," Uri said to Dan.
Dan gave him a long look.

"It's personal," Uri said.

Dan looked as if he was going to object but said, "Just remember, we need to keep him alive."

Uri gave Dan a slight smile. "I've done this before."

Bilal sat and waited in the closed shed that acted as a jail. The sun broke over the hills to the east, and he knew that someone would be coming soon to interrogate him. He understood that it was going to be about the bombings. He also understood that the tactics would be brutal and would not stop until he had told them everything. Luckily, he didn't know much, but Bilal doubted that would help him.

He sighed. He knew that his life might be over at this point. Only Allah knew. He just had to submit. Still, a tear formed in his eye when he thought about his family and how he might never see them again.

Uri stepped into the room. The door closed behind him with a loud clank of a locking bolt being slid into its receiver. The floor was concrete, the walls made of concrete blocks. There was a table and two chairs but no bed or mattress. The only light was a single, powerful bulb hanging from the ceiling. On the walls and ceiling were mounting points for ropes or chains. Their meaning was unmistakable.

Bilal had spent the night on the bare floor with no blanket to fend off the mountain chill. His hands were still tied behind him. Uri hoped the man had spent some time thinking about what the room's equipment might mean for him.

He stepped over to Bilal and yanked him to his feet. He pointed to a chair and indicated he was to sit down. After Bilal sat down, Uri took the chair opposite him with the table in between. He stared at the man for a long moment.

"I can make this easy or very painful." He spoke in Arabic. "You have no position from which to bargain. You have only to tell me what you know. I will start by telling you what I know."

He paused for a moment.

"A witness saw you driving the BMW away from the bombing in Washington, D.C. It was a positive ID."

Uri slid a lifelike drawing of him across the table to Bilal.

"I want names. I'll start with the passenger, the man who drove the van."

Bilal stayed silent. Uri looked at him, his face darkening with growing anger.

"A very good friend of mine, an old friend of many years, was killed in the bombing in Jerusalem. The two bombings were part of the same operation."

He glanced at the rings and chains arranged around the room.

"You know what these are for. I have used them in the past and will use them today on you. Only it will be personal for me this time and I will enjoy your pain and suffering. This is my next step if you say nothing to me."

Bilal stayed silent. Uri could see his growing fear, fighting his resolve to not betray his fellow jihadists. Uri allowed himself an inward sigh, one Bilal could not see. It was going to take some pain. Only then could Bilal justify his talking. Uri understood. He had to be tested before giving in. To talk now would be considered an act of cowardice. Only after enduring some pain could he feel that he had not betrayed his comrades.

"We will do it the painful way."

Uri got up and knocked on the door. It opened, and he left the room.

"Is he going to talk?" Dan asked as he met Uri outside the shed.

Uri shook his head. "But they all do in the end. It is just a matter of time."

"What next?" Zerya asked.

Uri explained to their host what he needed, and when it was ready, he went back into the room with two of Zerya's men. They brought in an electrical box with dials and a receptacle with a cord plugged into it. The cord ended in two clamps. An extension line ran from the box out of the door, probably to an electrical outlet. The men lifted Bilal out of the chair and uncuffed him. They put his arms up and locked them to a chain. They pulled the chain, raising Bilal to his toes to keep pressure off his wrists and arms. A water bowl was put on the table next to a long, sharp knife.

Once done, the men left without a word. Bilal watched Uri with his eyes full of fear and his breath coming in short pants.

"I'm not going to beat you. That is a waste of time and energy. These probes," Uri pointed to the clamps, "are wired to a direct current with a great deal of voltage. It won't kill you but will cause much pain. How much is up to you.'

He struck the two clamps across one another, causing a loud snap and sparks to fly. Uri picked up the knife.

"If this does not cause you to tell me what I want to know, I will castrate you. I can cauterize the wound so you won't bleed to death...or I can let you bleed out. In any case you will go to your paradise as a eunuch, unable to enjoy all your virgins."

He took the knife and began to cut Bilal's clothes. Without a word, Uri jammed the clamps into the man's groin and attached them to his testicles. Bilal jumped and twisted but could not escape the painful grip of the clamps. Uri went to the control box and turned the dial part of the way up.

"This dial controls the voltage and therefore the strength of the current. It's directly connected to the pain you feel."

He flipped the switch, and a cry escaped Bilal's mouth before he could stop himself. There followed painful grunts and twisting to no avail. Uri flipped the switch off. Just as Bilal began to recover his breath, Uri increased the voltage and flipped the switch back on. The process went on for another ten minutes until Bilal was nearly unconscious.

Two hours later, Uri stepped out of the room. He met Dan in the courtyard.

"Did you get what we wanted?"

Uri shook his head. "He does not know much, but he is ready to talk. I can sense it. I'm giving him a few moments to recover and then I'll go back in."

Dan stared at the man. He could see that Uri, despite wanting to be the interrogator, did not derive any pleasure from it. Killing enemy combatants was one thing; torturing helpless captives was another. It was distasteful for both men.

Uri turned back and stepped inside the shed.

"Time to tell me what you know." Uri's voice was now comforting as he helped Bilal to a chair. "You have done well. Better than most jihadists I have interrogated. You tell me now, what you know, and I'll let you die quickly without more pain. I will also not go after your family."

The man looked up at his captor and tormentor. He felt a slight sense of relief creeping in. He sensed from the start that he would not escape alive, but now a way out was offered. One that would protect his family. He would trade his knowledge for their security. It was a noble way to go.

"You promise this?" His words were slurred and barely audible.

"Yes. Unless we find later that you have deceived me. I must say that before you tell me anything."

Bilal hesitated.

"You have nothing to be ashamed of. You did well and showed your bravery. Now save your family."

"I will tell you what I know. But I'm sorry, it is not so much."

"I understand."

Again, Uri's voice was gentle, almost friendly.

"Just what you know."

"I, and the others, knew it was to stop the peace talks between the Jews and Saudis. Why, I do not know."

Uri nodded. "Who was the man with you?"

Bilal gave him a name, and Uri wrote it down.

"Where does he live?"

Bilal described a little house just north of the small town of Tall 'Afar.

"Who gave you orders? Did you get them from the leader? From Muntaqim?"

Bilal looked surprised. "You know of him?"

Uri nodded. "But we don't know who he is."

"I do not know either. It is his fighting name, his name for jihad. The man that led us was Jamal."

"His family name?"

"Almasi...I think."

"Where is he?"

"I don't know for sure. We were brought together for this mission. I did not know him before. I think he's an Iraqi."

"Like you."

"Yes. He is from Ramadi. He works in the large recycling center...junkyard to you."

"And the name of the man who supplied the bomb material."

"I do not know. No one below Muntaqim and the two men who led the attacks know. We were not told, but I think he was from the Balkans."

Uri patted the man gently. "You have done well." He got up to leave.

"What happens to me now?"

Uri turned to him with a sad smile on his face. "I will be back...soon."

He turned and left the room.

Chapter 18

They buried Bilal in the hills outside of Zerya's compound. The same afternoon, Dan and Uri set out heading south. They would spend time in Mosul where Uri said he had a contact. They wanted to get more information about the leader of the U.S. bombing.

"This man will help us find Almasi?" Dan asked.

Uri nodded. "And from him, the name of his counterpart for the Jerusalem operation. We still have many to pursue."

"Or at least identify so others can pursue them. I'm more interested in the arms dealer and this Muntaqim. Do you think he's a replacement for Scorpion?"

"Maybe. If he's running operations for Rashid, that could be the reason for their lack of complexity. They've simplified and gotten more lethal."

"I'm worried that they have figured out a way to neutralize our intelligence."

"Moving faster."

Dan nodded, deep in thought. *And also guessing we may have some special insight.*

Once in Mosul, Uri drove them into an older part of town.

"We will go see Dozan. He passes us information from time to time and we augment his income so that he is comfortable, but not ostentatious. He is a Kurd and so wants to help us as we have helped his people."

They parked the Toyota in an alley and walked to a door further down the narrow passage. It was old, with faded paint, but still solid. Uri knocked and stepped back to wait. Nothing. He knocked again. A moment later, the latch let out a scraping sound and turned. The door opened a crack, held by a strong chain. A face appeared.

"We are friends looking for Dozan," Uri said.

"*Aintazar*," Wait, came the reply, and the door closed.

"He is a cautious man," Uri said.

A moment later, the door cracked open again. "Who is looking for this man?"

"Tell him, Uri."

The door closed again. They heard a chain rattle, and then it opened wide.

An old man motioned for them to hurry inside. He peaked out and then closed and bolted the door. At that moment, another younger man came into the front room.

"Uri!" he called out, opening his arms wide.

"Dozan! I am happy to see you. See you alive and well."

"I work at it. One can't be too careful."

They spoke in Arabic. Dan could only catch a few phrases as they exchanged greetings.

"Are we keeping you busy? Well paid?"

"Enough."

"You are safe? No one suspects you help us?"

Dozan shook his head. "I am very careful. I go by Farid in public. It means 'unique' which I am. It is better than using my Kurdish name. Most can tell I'm a Kurd, but my name makes them less concerned about me."

He led them into a back room. A woman with a head scarf brought tea and cups to the table and left them alone. The old man who manned the door sat outside in the front room.

"Why are you here? It is not so safe for you. Especially after the bombing," Dozan said.

"That is why we are here."

He introduced Dan as Victor.

"We are hunting the men involved. We have the names of two of them. One is from Ramadi. We hope you can help us locate him."

"And the other?"

"We know where he is. He is not as important as the man from Ramadi. That man is Jamal Almasi."

"You can pay for my help?"

"We can pay you well. I will see to it. Have I ever let you down?"

Dozan shook his head. He stood up.

"We must get your truck off the streets. Does Victor speak Arabic?"

"Not so well."

"Then you take the truck. My uncle will go with you and show you a garage. Then you come back and wait here. I will work to find this man."

Everyone jumped into action except Dan. He felt useless but understood the need to remain quiet and unnoticed. It was better than having to explain who they were. Their covers would only hold up for a short time, even here in Mosul. A quick check with UNESCO officials and they would have to rely on convincing the authorities that UNESCO made mistakes and some of the people involved did not know of others. Dan didn't want to have that conversation.

He felt a knot in his stomach. Iraq was a country where one could not relax. Threats seemed to be everywhere. The factions were still antagonistic to one another, and that occasionally broke out into violence. If caught, an American and an Israeli would only wind up in prison and brought to trial for spying.

Dan and Uri waited for three days. During that time, they never left the back alley house. Dozan had insisted on their confinement.

"I do not wish to die or end up in prison because you need to exercise your legs or go sightseeing."

On the third day, Dozan came back after being out for hours. "I have found your man, this Jamal Almasi. He is still in Ramadi. I can show you on your computer."

Dan opened his Panasonic Toughbook and logged in. His satellite phone gave him an uplink.

Almasi lived on a busy street lined with small, rundown houses packed together. It was five blocks from the Euphrates River. But Dozan pointed out that the man worked at a massive junkyard in an industrial section of town. The area was much less populated.

"We can take him there," Dan said when he saw the area on his mapping program.

Uri nodded. He turned to Dozan. "You have done well. I will make a call and see that you are well-paid for your help."

"One appreciates being appreciated," Dozan said with a smile. He did what he did to help his people. The Shiites were no friend of the Kurds, but neither were the Sunnis. He liked working among them and stirring up trouble when he could, along with passing information, usually of little importance, for money. He hid most of what he received, converting it to more portable gold. It would help protect his family when they had to leave and go north into more friendly territory. Meanwhile, Dozan was happy to make good money and help his cause.

Chapter 19

D o we head south to Ramadi or go west to Tall 'Afar?" Uri asked as they climbed into the Land Cruiser.

"I think we should take down the driver of the van first. I can do it quickly, once we identify him. Then we concentrate on our more important target."

"If we do that, we have to move fast. After Tall 'Afar, the word will get out and others will go under cover."

"We'll be quick. Once we get Almasi, we'll want to take time with him. There's a lot to learn, a lot he'll have to tell us." Dan turned to Uri, "I'm thinking that we may want to take him out of the country, to your people, to interrogate him."

"That will be hard. I think we're going to have to do it ourselves."

"He'll be a tougher nut to crack."

Uri gave Dan a wicked smile. "They all crack in the end."

They drove out of Mosul on Highway 1, heading west towards Tall 'Afar. The day was hot. An oppressive blanket of heat weighing them down. A haze from the ever-present dust hung in the air. At the intersection with Route 715, a more minor road that led into the town, traffic was funneled off the divided highway to a checkpoint, not using the elaborate interchange that had been constructed but never fully completed. Uri navigated the checkpoint using their UNESCO identity cards and the story that they had to pick up a local worker in Tall 'Afar.

Once past the checkpoint, Dan relaxed. When they got to the town, Uri would turn north and park somewhere well off the road, out of sight. Bilal had described the road and farmhouse well. The plan was to locate the target, drive past it, park, and hike to the house to wait and watch. It was a well-practiced routine; Dan was used to waiting.

After turning north, both men scanned the surroundings intently. It was vital that they find the exact location of the house. Bilal's description, while complete, fit many dwellings in the area.

"We could be watching for a long time if we don't get this right," Uri said.

"Or shoot the wrong person."

"Neither option appeals to me."

Uri slowed as they scanned the buildings to the right of the road. Bilal said the van driver lived in a small cottage located a quarter mile behind a large estate with a perimeter wall near the road. Just past the large house was a dirt road leading to six houses. The driver's house was the first one on the road.

Sure enough, after twenty minutes of slow driving, Dan spoke up. "That looks like the estate Bilal described."

Uri grunted.

"Just keep going slow, don't stop." Dan examined the house as they drove past. "Now we'll see if there's a dirt road and other buildings as Bilal described."

He stared intently as Uri drove slowly onward. The dirt road appeared just as described.

"I see the houses. This looks like the place."

"I'll keep going to make sure. If there's nothing ahead, we'll come back and stop before we get to the side road. We need to find a good place to hide the truck."

"Agreed. Keeping the Toyota out of sight takes precedence over being close." He turned back to Uri, "That is if you're not too old to do some hiking."

"No problem if I only have to keep up with you.

Dan kept watching. They drove for another ten minutes without finding any other buildings that fit Bilal's description.

"I think that was the right spot," Dan said.

"I agree."

Uri swung the Land Cruiser around and headed back down the road. When they came to some hills, he turned off the road, and they worked their way up a small dry riverbed that led into the higher ground. Once into the surrounding hills, the vehicle was hidden from the road.

"This is a good place to park," Uri said. He turned the Toyota around and positioned it for departure.

"Now we hoof it," Dan said as he got out. He went to the back and pulled back the padding in the rear. On one side, there was a hidden latch that opened a compartment. He took out his Sako, packed in its case, and unloaded it. After assembling and checking the rifle, he shouldered it. Uri loaded a small backpack with energy bars and water along with ammunition. Both men strapped sidearms to their belts, and Uri shouldered his M4.

They looked at each other.

"Guess we're ready," Dan said.

They started around the hill towards the houses to the south of them.

Both men hiked with a careful eye to the road on their right and the buildings ahead. The ground was a combination of sand and gravel, with larger boulders and bedrock protruding from the sandy base. The irregular terrain consisted of hills of varying heights, all of which helped screen them from either the road or buildings.

After a half hour, they stopped. Both men were sweating through their dusty clothing. They lay on the brow of a hill and looked at the target house to the south. Dan sighted the distance with his range finder.

"Looks like 520 yards. Not a difficult shot."

He busied himself adjusting the scope for the distance.

"So, we don't go any closer?"

"We're good."

"Great. It would be hard to go farther without being seen."

The terrain flattened out as it got closer to the collection of houses.

"Now we wait," Dan said. "Always the waiting. That's a big part of the story of my life."

"Jane make you wait?"

"Don't talk about her."

"Hmmm. Getting protective, are we? Sounds like you've got a serious thing going."

"I'm serious, Uri. I don't want to talk about it."

Dan's voice now carried an edge to it.

"Take it easy. I kid you, because I envy you. I lost my wife and then my family because of this work. You and Jane, you could make it. You're both involved in this crazy world. It probably only works that way, although two people in this arena finding one another is as remote as a unicorn."

Dan was settling down in his shooting position, shuffling his body to nestle into the dirt and sand. He made sure he was comfortable and that his Sako properly supported. Once he felt stable, he took a kerchief out and laid it on the ground in front of the barrel.

Uri looked at him.

"Keeps the dirt from puffing up from the muzzle blast and giving us away."

Uri nodded.

"And I don't mean to snap at you. What you say is true. I've experienced it with someone before Jane. I realized we lived in different worlds. What was worse was when those worlds collided. I knew then that a relationship with someone outside this world would only endanger them and make me vulnerable."

He turned back to stare at the house.

"You don't mind spotting, do you? It'll help me from having to stare through this scope for hours."

"That's what I thought I was here for...that and getting us through checkpoints."

"You *are* useful for that."

They settled down in silence. Unlike more urban areas, there was no traffic noise. Few vehicles moved on the road. The sun grew low in the sky, and the silence seemed to increase, damping the urge to talk, and when they did, it was in hushed tones even though there was no ear nearby to hear.

Chapter 20

W e're losing the day," Uri whispered.
"Yeah. I'm hoping we don't have to lie here all
night."

"We've both done worse, you know that."

"He can't be out working somewhere. I'm betting all
those involved have been told to lie low. We just need him
to come out to stretch or get a breath of air."

"Better just before dark, it will mask our departure," Uri said.

"We can't go back the same way we came. If the guards haven't changed, they'll wonder where the man we came to get is."

"I thought of that. There are some very poor roads going south from Tall 'Afar. But we should be able to take them and connect with better ones heading towards Baghdad. We have to drive towards the capital before heading off to Ramadi."

"Don't want to go into Baghdad. Too many checkpoints and our cover won't hold up, going the wrong way from where we're supposed to be working."

"We'll work it out on the map. Let's get this job done first."

"If he shows."

Lights went on in the house even though the sun was not quite below the hills in the distance. Suddenly, light spilled out on the front step as the door opened. A man stepped through the light and into the softer evening glow. Uri and Dan could see the sharp light of a match as he lit a cigarette. Dan studied the man's face through his scope.

"It's our guy."

He watched the smoke through his scope to check on the windage around the target. Uri scanned the distance between them, also looking for evidence of wind.

"Looks pretty calm tonight."

"Lucky me," Dan said as he nestled back down into his shooting position. "No talking now."

He settled into that familiar concentration where everything outside of him and the target faded away. The old imaginary thread formed, connecting his rifle to the target. The bullet would drop 47 inches, just under four feet, as it covered the distance. It always felt to Dan like he was lobbing his round at the target. It didn't matter; he had dialed the scope in to compensate for the distance. He could now place the reticle directly on his target. The bullet would do its job. When it arrived at the man's head, it would be traveling at just over 2,300 feet per second or just above Mach 2. Well beyond the speed of sound. But he would never hear the shot that would take his life.

Dan's breathing slowed. His heart rate followed. He lay poised but relaxed, motionless. The rifle was unwavering, with his reticle settled on the man's head as he stood there, savoring the coming evening, enjoying what would be his last smoke. *The man who drove the van that killed over thirty people.*

That was Dan's last thought as his finger tightened gently on the trigger in between heartbeats. The rifle gave a muffled *whomp* and kicked solidly against Dan's shoulder. A moment later, the man's head exploded, and his body collapsed like a rag doll with no frame to support it.

"Done," Uri said in a quiet voice. "Good shot."

Dan was already sliding back from his position. He retrieved his kerchief and tucked it away. The two men crawled back down the slope and, when low enough, stood up. Without a word, they turned to retrace their steps to the waiting Toyota.

The woman inside the house heard the thump as the man collapsed. The crack of the round's sonic boom followed instantly. She did not know what it was but went to the door and opened it. There lay the man with the back of his head blown away. She began screaming and dropped to the body.

Uri and Dan could hear the screams; they easily carried through the evening air.

"Sow the wind, reap the whirlwind," Uri said half under his breath as they hurried back to the truck.

"Leave the headlights off until we get back on the road. We should have enough light to drive by."

When they reached the Toyota, Dan packed away his Sako and jumped in the front with Uri. They both took long drinks from their water bottles.

"That went well," Uri said.

"Better than having to wait through the night. He stepped outside and met his destiny. Being a jihadist comes with a price. That's what we're all about. Making sure those who engage in it, know what is in store for them."

"I'm not sure how strong a message Bilal will send by just disappearing. Zerya was quite adamant that neither he nor us were going to take his body back and dump it so others could see what had happened."

"They will suspect, since he just disappeared, never to be seen again."

"But this," Uri gestured with one hand while the other wrestled the steering wheel over the uneven ground, "everyone will know why he met this fate. It will make them pause."

"Let's hope so."

When they got to the road, Uri turned on the headlights and pointed the truck south towards Ramadi. There was nothing to see as they drove past the houses set back off the dirt road.

Chapter 21

The two men headed south from Tall' Afar on a paved road that ran south for miles, only to turn back north towards Mosul. It was like a loop encompassing a portion of the desert and linking it to the large city. The road was paved and in reasonable condition. They met no one on it as they drove through the night. When the road turned back north, Uri looked for any travel way off to the east. They were trying to connect with Route 1, the Mosul-Baghdad Highway, which ran south from Mosul to the capital. The road generally followed the Tigris River and went past Tikrit, which was not a place Dan and Uri wanted to go through.

They worked their way along a series of back roads, some little better than driving through the roadless desert, always heading eastward, changing paths when the one they were on turned in a different direction. It was slow going as night fell. The headlights illuminated what passed for roads but hid some of the ruts and potholes, causing them to go slower to avoid damage to their vehicle.

Finally, they came to Route 1 as dawn approached. Dan, now driving, turned south, and they went on in silence, each man lost in his own thoughts. A passing truck occasionally punctuated the desert stillness.

Uri yawned and stretched his arms as he woke from a nap.

"We got to get off this before Tikrit," Dan said.

"I know." Uri pulled out his map and studied it for a moment. "I sure could use a cup of coffee right now."

"We both could, but we'll have to do without. We're not stopping anywhere. It'll raise too many questions."

Uri looked up from the map. "There's what looks like a paved road going off to the right, just before Bayji. It's where this arrow-straight road makes a right turn to run alongside the river. The new road will take us west of both Baghdad and Ramadi. We'll cross the Euphrates River and then head back east into the city."

Dan thought for a moment as they drove along.

"There'll probably be a checkpoint on or near the bridge. Maybe we should look for a way to drive on the north side of the river until we're closer to our target.

"Got to cross sooner or later."

"I know. How about we scope it out and if we see a problem, go somewhere else. There's got to be a lot of bridges across the river. They can't put checkpoints on all of them."

"They could, but you make a point. There might be a few that are not secured. Worth a try."

He looked back to the map.

It was full daylight when they approached the river and the first bridge. They could see a building before the bridge, and vehicles lined up.

"That's a checkpoint," Dan said. He turned off onto a side road. They drove southeast for a few miles before stopping.

"Okay, where do we go now?" They were just to the south of Lake Qadisiyah, formed by a dam on the Euphrates.

Uri's head was down in the map. "I can't be sure which of these small roads we're on, but just keep heading southeast. We'll just have to wing it until I find a landmark I can locate on the map."

"Southeast keeps us on the right track…and out of trouble?"

"As much as we can be in the middle of Iraq with a pretty lousy cover story."

Dan gave his partner a grim smile through his dust-laden face. "Yeah. Hard to explain how we wind up wandering around in the desert down here when we're supposed to be digging around in Mosul for artifacts."

"Always try to explain before shooting our way out."

They drove on through the desert.

"How much gas do we have?" Uri asked.

"A little more than half a tank."

They had filled up in Mosul and had five jerry cans with them.

"That should be enough to get us to Ramadi. We should fill up before we snatch this guy. Then we disappear into the desert."

"If it's like this, it shouldn't be a problem."

They were navigating their way through almost a maze of tracks and trails. Some better than others, some rough and barely used. The ground was hilly, and the trails wound around the hillocks, taking the easy way but making the path torturous and seemingly aimless. They could see no houses or villages. The desert was empty except for the tracks.

"Why all these paths? They twist and turn, intersect every mile or two. I wonder who made them."

"Centuries of wandering, camels, and herders. When you're on foot, the twists and turns don't seem so unusual. Speed it up, and it looks chaotic."

They drove on in silence until Dan stopped beside a hill that offered a bit of shade. He got out to relieve himself.

"You drive for a while," I need to stretch out and relax."

The two men sat back in the Toyota and ate an MRE along with some water.

"The joys of living on the road," Uri said. They munched their way through the meal, washing it down with their bottled water.

"I guess I've had worse fare."

"Or no fare. That's definitely worse."

They relaxed in silence for a few minutes. Listening to the stillness of the desert.

"It's like we're the only ones left in the world."

"Yeah. A bit different without the noise. I've been to Baghdad once before and it's noisy. Worse than Jerusalem."

Dan looked at his watch.

"What time do you think we'll get to Ramadi?"

"Who the hell knows? If we find something better than these trails, we'll make better time. My guess is it will be night and we'll have to wait until tomorrow to snatch our guy."

"Another night sleeping in the Land Cruiser."

"If we have the luxury of getting any sleep."

Chapter 22

Late that night, they could see the lights of Ramadi in the distance. Before they reached the built-up area, the two men stopped where they couldn't be seen from the road and slept until the dawn's light shone through the windshield, rudely awakening them from exhausted sleep.

"That's like a laser in the eye," Dan said as he got up and pulled down the visor in an attempt to keep the low sun out of his eyes.

"Not like the gentle shake of a woman lying next to you," Uri said.

"When was the last time you experienced that, old man?"

"Fuck you. I'll bet you've not been doing any better. I still get around. Who showed you all the hot spots in Tel Aviv?"

"I'll admit you got me there. But didn't you realize that neither of us fitted in?"

Uri smiled. "Yeah. I told you that I went there to suck up the energy. Who cares what others thought?"

"Okay, hot shot. How do we get across the river and find Almasi?"

Uri was looking at the map. "I'm betting the larger bridges will have checkpoints on them. In order to keep traffic moving, they may allow local plates to just drive across. Unfortunately, that doesn't include us. We'll have to navigate our way to the smaller roads and bridges."

"So, we go along and if we see signs of a checkpoint we bail out and try another one."

Uri looked over at Dan. "That's about it. Patience is the key. We'll find at least one bridge without a checkpoint."

After another MRE and bottle of water, they drove off towards the city. Uri took over the driving, and Dan slouched down in the passenger seat to minimize his unmistakable Western look, even with a keffiyeh pulled over his face. After an hour working their way around the crowded roads, some large and busy and some small side streets where the Land Cruiser stood out, they found a narrow road leading to an older bridge. The neighborhood was rundown, and suspicious glances cast their way as they drove towards the bridge.

"I don't see any checkpoint," Uri said. "The traffic is moving steady if slow."

"Let's go then. We have to get to the other side."

They crept along with the traffic, amid the never-ending horns honking, successfully crossing the river, and turned south only to come to a smaller branch of water after a mile.

"Damn," Uri exclaimed. "I didn't realize we had this in our way."

Dan looked up. He took out his binoculars and studied the bridge.

"Don't use those too long. You'll attract the wrong attention."

"Try another bridge, maybe go to the left. It looks congested on this one. I can't tell if it's a checkpoint or just a backup."

Uri turned and they drove on. He stopped or slowed down at each intersection, and both men looked to see if there was a bridge down the road. Finally, they found one. Uri turned, and Dan risked using his binoculars again.

"This one looks okay. Let's do it."

With both men on edge, glancing around them, Uri drove over the bridge. He gave out a sigh after they got across.

"Now on to Almasi," Uri said.

"First gas," Dan said.

He pointed to a gas station. "Stop here. I'll stay in the truck, you do the pumping and paying."

"I get to do all the work and pay for it. Some deal."

"You blend in better than I do. That's my story and I'm sticking to it."

Dan smiled and hunkered down in the seat.

After, they drove south until they found the junkyard. It sprawled over four acres with winding dirt paths through it. They were irregular, not laid out on a neat grid. Dan noticed the limited sight lines due to the winding paths. *Harder to find someone, but better to ambush them.*

"We need a way to identify Jamal," Dan said. "There're probably more than one worker here."

"Yeah. We can watch this evening to see how many people leave. Then we'll know what we're up against."

"Hang out near the entrance?"

Uri nodded. They were driving past the south or back end of the lot. The offices were on a connecting road on the other side, closer to the river.

"We go up that side road and wait a couple of hundred meters from the office. All we need to do at that point is count heads."

"We still have to ID him."

"I can do that tomorrow."

Dan gave Uri a questioning look.

"I'll go up and pretend he's my cousin and I need to find him. They should be able to tell me where he is in the yard."

"What if he's not in the yard? What if he's in the office?"

Uri scowled as he thought about the problem Dan brought up.

"We watch and see how many come out of the yard today and go in tomorrow. That will let us know how many are in the office. If there are only a few, I can shoot the ones who aren't Jamal and then we take him."

Dan thought for a moment. "I don't like it. Don't like starting a gun fight here."

"I'm open to suggestions."

"I'll let you know when I have a better one...but I still don't like it."

Uri parked along the street with the entrance and office ahead of them, farther down the road. Late in the day, five men trickled out of the junkyard. Three came from the yard itself. One walked down the street, away from Uri and Dan; two got into an old pickup and drove off. The two that came out of the office headed in different directions. One rode off on a motorcycle, and the other got in a car and drove past Uri and Dan.

They kept watching for another hour and a half until they were sure no one else was in the yard.

"Let's find a place to spend the night," Uri said.

He turned around, drove back to the road they had come in on, and headed past the south side of the yard. Uri found a dirt track that led to some empty buildings a quarter of a mile off the road. He backed the Toyota along one side, out of sight of the road, and shut it off.

"One more night in Hotel Land Cruiser," he said.

Chapter 23

D an called Jane on their satellite phone as they
settled down for the night.
"Tell me what's going on," she said after they
connected.

"The two directly involved in the D.C. bombing are no
more. We have the name of the leader of the attack. We're
going to snatch him tomorrow."

"Where are you?"

"Ramadi."

There was silence on the line.

"Damn. Be careful. We don't have any assets to help
there since we've pulled out."

"I know, neither does Uri. Another thing. This
mastermind seems to be someone called Muntaqim. It
means avenger or revenger. It's his *nom de guerre*. Put
Fred and Warren on it and see if they can come up with
anything. This is the guy we need to find."

"Will do. Anything else?"

"The explosives were supplied by someone from the
Balkans or Caucasus we're trying to pin that down. I want
that guy as well."

"I'll get Fred and Warren to look at that. They've
confirmed that the Imam in the Dallas area harbored the
bombers until they left. The official word, however, is that
they didn't come over the southern border."

"Politics."

"Yeah. But we can still do our job."

"Need to do something about that Imam," Dan said after a pause.

"I don't disagree, but not you. You stay the course and deliver these bastards some rough justice."

"Yes ma'am. Happy to help."

"And Dan...take care of yourself."

The line went dead. Dan sighed and sat back.

"Everything okay back home?"

"Okay except for politics hiding the truth of what happened."

He shook his head as if to clear it.

"Doesn't change what we have to do."

The two men settled down, scrunched under their jackets as the desert air turned colder.

With the first light, the men awoke. The air was cold. They got out of the Land Cruiser and stretched their limbs. Both shuffled around in the morning chill, trying to loosen the kinks from an uncomfortable night in the SUV.

"Not the best night I've ever had," Uri said.

"Huh." Dan looked over at the man. "A fucking bad night, if you ask me. Be glad when we can snatch this guy and get out of here. Speaking of which, can we turn him over to your team after we interrogate him?"

"Not sure. We'll use that phone of yours and call Eitan after we secure the target. He'll let us know."

They ate a few power bars and drank some of their water.

"Let's get back to the junkyard," Dan said. "I'm anxious to get this done and get out of here."

"You feel what I feel? Like we're on borrowed time?"

Dan nodded. "I keep getting more and more antsy. The sooner we snatch Jamal and get lost in the desert, the better I'll feel."

Dan drove up and parked on the street. This time closer to the office entrance. Both men slouched down and watched, just peering over the dashboard. Within an hour, the workers started to arrive. Three of them went into the office. Five minutes later, another group of men entered the office.

"Hell, are they all hanging out in the office?" Dan asked.

"Probably to start the day. They may go out into the yard by a back door. I doubt they'd go out the front door and then re-enter the yard."

When no more men showed up, Uri raised up in his seat. "I'm going in. I'll ask for Jamal. Pretend I'm a distant relative from the north looking for work and was told to see him."

"Sounds a bit doubtful."

"You got a better idea?"

Dan shook his head. "Just bring your sidearm. If I hear any gunshots, I'll come running."

"If you hear gunshots, bring the truck up and then come in." Uri smiled at Dan and got out. "Here we go."

He closed the door of the vehicle and walked to the office.

When Uri stepped inside, the conversation that had been going on stopped. There were three men in the office area. They all turned to look at him.

"My name is Fadil. I'm looking for Jamal."

One of the men spoke up. "I am Jamal. What do you want?"

"I'm from up north, near Tall 'Afar. I'm looking for work and was told to find you."

"Who told you to find me?"

With no good answer, Uri pulled out his 10mm Sig Sauer P220. The three men froze.

"Who are you? What do you want," one of the other men spoke up.

"Who I am is not important. What I want is to talk with Jamal for a while. He and I are going to leave and have a conversation."

"I'm not going anywhere with you," Jamal said.

As if on cue, the other two men reached under their shirts to pull out weapons. Uri's first shot hit one of them center mass; he swung his aim slightly to the left and shot the second man as he brought his gun up towards Uri. Jamal had already pulled out his pistol, and Uri dove behind a desk as he fired at him. It was just the two of them now. Uri's problem was that he needed Jamal alive. Jamal, however, did not need Uri alive. In fact, he probably wanted him dead.

When he heard the shots, Dan drove up to the door and swung the Toyota around. He sprinted to the office and burst through the door, body bent low to the ground, eyes up for targets. He saw a man with a pistol. Dan fired. The man dove for cover.

"Don't kill him, that's Jamal!" Uri shouted from behind a desk.

In mid-stride, Dan planted his right foot and drove to his left, closing the gap between him and Jamal as the man dove behind a couch. Dan hit it in full stride, slamming into the back of the sofa. The couch tipped over on Jamal, pinning him down. Dan jumped on the man's back as Uri ran up. Uri wrenched the weapon from Jamal's hand. Dan grabbed a floor lamp and pulled the wire from it. He used the cord to tie Jamal's hands behind him.

Just then, the men from the yard burst through the back door. One of them had a pistol in his hand. They shouted out in Arabic, asking what was going on. One of them saw the two dead men on the floor and reached down to pick up his weapon. Uri fired, and the man dropped to the floor alongside the dead man. The other one shot at Uri. The bullet whistled close to his ear. Uri swung his pistol over and shot him in the chest. The third man ran out the back door. Uri jumped up and started after him. He opened the door to the yard. There was no one to see and no sound of anyone fleeing.

"Let's get out of here," Dan called. "Others may have heard the shooting."

"The last guy has gotten away."

"Doesn't matter. We have Jamal. Let's go!"

Uri stepped back into the office. Dan had pulled Jamal upright. His eyes were dark with anger.

"You won't get out of here alive."

Uri glared at him. "Watch us."

They hustled Jamal out of the office and into the Toyota. Dan started the engine. Men had begun to assemble down the street and walk their way. Dan accelerated the Land Cruiser away from them in a burst of sand and dirt. They careened around the corner and down the road that paralleled the train tracks. As they turned the corner, two pickups came around the bend by the junkyard and stopped at the men. Some of them jumped in the back, and within a minute, the pickups set out after the departing Land Cruiser.

Chapter 24

When he could, Dan crossed the rail tracks and turned west again. They needed to escape the city before their actions ignited a significant uproar. He got onto a paved road that paralleled the major highway, Route 1. When the road turned back north, Dan left it to race down another dirt road and through some outlying villages without slowing down. They passed through an agricultural section with irrigated fields. After crossing a built-up causeway over swampy ground, they drove through some ancient ruins and into the empty desert. The road got rougher, and Dan had to slow down.

"Can't keep up a fast pace, but we're getting farther away from civilization."

"They're still following," Uri said. He was looking back the way they had come. A dust trail rose in the air, fresher than their older one that marked their passing.

"We get out further, I'll find a place to pull over and we'll ambush them."

"Deeper into the desert," Uri said.

"Roger that."

They spoke in English.

"You won't get away," Jamal said in English.

"What do you know? He can speak multiple languages."

Dan spoke as he kept wrestling with the steering. Uri twisted around in the seat again, looking down at Jamal bouncing on the back seat floor.

"Not so comfortable. Don't worry. We'll deal with your friends. After that we're going to deal with you." He smiled as Jamal glared up at him. "This will seem like an easy trip compared to what I've got in mind for you."

"Who are you? What do you want?"

"All in due time, all in due time." Uri turned to look out the back window. "They seem to be closing."

"That's because we had to slow down. They'll soon have to do the same. I'm betting this Land Cruiser can go as fast as their shitty pickups."

"I think one of them has a machine gun mounted on it. That could be a problem."

Now, past the ruins, the desert seemed to be empty. The road deteriorated into a rough, two-track.

"Looking better and better," Dan said. His breathing evidenced the effort he was making to keep the Toyota's speed up yet not break anything or turn it over.

"Hillier to the north," Uri said. "Let's head there."

Dan began to work the intersecting paths, turning more and more north towards the hills. Both men knew they would find a place to stop and go on the offensive with their pursuers. The following pickup trucks were barely in sight. From the dust cloud, it looked like there were more than two vehicles.

"The numbers have grown," Uri said.

"We'll deal with it."

Dan turned off the two-track, now barely noticeable, and drove up an empty wadi. The floor of the ravine was reasonably flat, so he could accelerate.

"We'll go up a ways and find a good outcropping to get behind."

"We should protect the truck. It's our way out, assuming we deal with these bastards."

"We'll deal with them."

Dan's voice was grim. He had to keep sawing away at the wheel as he forced the Land Cruiser faster than it was comfortable going. He had turned off the air conditioning to ease the burden on the engine, and, with the windows lowered, the men were being caked in a thick film of dust.

"Found it," Dan yelled. "Up to the right."

Ahead were the remains of an ancient wall. It looked to be a part of what might have been an outpost or some defensive position. It took advantage of the natural rise of rocks and faced south towards the opening of the wadi into the flatter desert.

As they passed the wall, Dan slowed, and the truck crawled forward on the rising ground. The surface was rockier but provided decent traction, but he worked his way around the larger rocks and boulders, which could damage the undercarriage of the Toyota.

Finally, he stopped. The two men jumped out and went to the back to get their weapons. Dan grabbed his Sako and Uri his AK. They both grabbed packs with extra ammunition and ran to the remains of the wall. Dan found a spot where he could slip the Sako through a notch and fire with some protection. Uri moved down-slope to his right so they would create separate firing positions and separate targets.

"Check on our guest," Dan said as he laid out his five-shot cartridges. He had ten of them loaded and ready to go. That was fifty rounds before he would have to stop to reload. He hoped that would be enough.

Uri got up and ran back to the Toyota. When he opened the door, he found Jamal struggling to get himself untied.

"Can't have that," Uri said. He yanked the man out of the back seat and dragged him around to the rear of the truck. There, he pulled out a coil of tactical cord and added it to Jamal's tied wrists. Next, Uri took some duct tape and taped Jamal's hands together so he could not work on his bonds. With that done, he sat Jamal down on the rear passenger door and tied his feet together. Last, he secured a length of rope around the man's neck and the door handle. Jamal could not get his hands free or slither away from the truck.

"Don't go anywhere," Uri said with a wink.

Jamal glared at him. As an afterthought, Uri put a strip of duct tape over the man's mouth.

"Don't want you yelling anything out to your buddies."

He put away the tape and cord and ran back to his rifle.

"Going to have a firefight shortly," Uri said.

"I'm looking forward to it," Dan replied.

Chapter 25

They watched and waited. The dust cloud grew, and soon they could make out three pickup trucks, their beds filled with men. The lead truck had a machine gun attached to the bed. Uri scanned the oncoming vehicles with his binoculars. Dan kept watch through his scope.

"Damn!" Uri exclaimed. "Is that an M2 on the truck?"

"Looks like it. That's not good. Fifty cal and 500 rounds per minute. That could decimate our protection. Literally blow these walls apart."

"I know. Can you take it out?"

"Gonna try."

Dan settled back to his rifle and scope. He planned to stop the advancing trucks while they were too far away to be effective with their AK carbines. The M2 was a different story, however.

"Uri, spot me. I'm going to try to stop the first truck."

When they were about 600 yards away, Dan fired.

"Short and to the right," Uri said.

The truck didn't slow down.

Dan started firing repeatedly, working the bolt as fast as he could. He "walked" his shots forward as the truck also approached. When the first mag emptied, he quickly ejected it and shoved a new one in. The next rounds hit the vehicle, with one shattering the windshield. The truck swerved and almost tipped over before the driver regained control. Dan's next shots went into the cab. He changed mags again.

The truck stopped. It was just under 500 yards out. The man in the back at the machine gun opened fire on the wall that hid Dan and Uri. His shots hit below. He brought them upward, and in a moment Dan and Uri could hear the impact of the .50 caliber rounds hitting the ancient stone and mortar wall and the native rocks. Stone chips flew everywhere. The two men hunkered down as the bullets kept slamming into the wall or flying overhead with their deadly whistles. When he chanced a look, he saw that the other two pickups had swerved around the stalled machine gun truck and were coming.

"Start firing on the pickups!" Dan shouted. "I'll try to neutralize the machine gun."

Uri opened fire with his AK-47. His rounds initially fell short, but he quickly zeroed in, and they began to have an effect. That brought intense return fire, which pinned both men down.

"You got to get that machine gun," Uri said as he hunkered behind the wall.

"Trying," Dan said as he squeezed off another round and worked the bolt.

The machine gun had a shield mounted to it. Dan's rounds were pinging off of them, unable to reach the gunner. Even the .338 Lapua round would not penetrate the armor plate.

Some of Dan's shots went between the plates but didn't hit the gunner. His shots, however, kept the gunner from firing accurately. He risked his life to put himself directly behind the barrel of the gun. One of the other men looked like he was shouting at him, which helped the gunner to take better aim. Dan turned his attention to the spotter, and his next shot hit him in the chest. His body flew backward from the bullet's impact and crashed into another fighter before landing in a heap in the bed. Then Dan saw the machine gunner's head behind the barrel. He squeezed off a round, and the gunner's head exploded.

"Got him."

Uri risked a glance through the growing rubble of their wall. He kept sending rounds down on the pickups. They were still coming, although more slowly. Dan switched over to the advancing trucks, and, along with Uri's accurate fire, they stopped them about 200 yards out. The men took cover behind the trucks.

"We have to conserve ammunition. Don't know how much they have, but this could be a drawn-out battle," Dan said.

The two men settled down. Uri switched to single-fire mode, only firing when they had a clear target. For a few minutes it looked like a stalemate.

"What do you think?" Uri asked.

"It looks like they've got about six men left. No one's manning the M2 right now which is good for us. Everyone's behind the trucks. Seems like someone passed the word to not be trigger-happy."

Only sporadic shots came at them from the three trucks. Dan and Uri had the advantage of the high ground, so anyone trying to carefully aim was in jeopardy of getting killed. The attackers understood this and kept their heads down.

"If you can disable their trucks with that Sako, maybe we could make a run for it and leave them here."

Dan thought for a moment as he maintained watch through his scope.

"We might need to do that. They may be waiting for dark to advance."

Uri looked over at Dan. "How do we do this and not get us or our truck all shot up? We're going to need the truck."

Dan studied the field. The attackers were below them in elevation and about 200 yards from their position. If they tried to drive away, they would have to go downhill, bringing them closer, before turning west to put some distance between them. Once they had enough separation, they could double back on the far side of the wadi and get back out into the open desert. The danger lay in the first quarter mile. He looked back at the truck and Jamal still held captive, tied to the door handle.

"If we can move a bit more west, away from them before going back downhill. That doesn't eliminate the danger, but decreases it."

"Staying here isn't much of an option," Uri said. "If it were just us, we could move back into the rocks and head for even higher ground. Pick them off when they come up to the wall. But we've got Jamal. He's not going to help."

"And when it gets dark, they could use the M4. If they've got tracer rounds in their belts, they can easily zero in on us and keep us pinned down while the others advance."

Dan sat with his back to the wall while Uri watched. With a sigh, he turned around to look through his scope. He spoke while sighting the two trucks.

"We have two options. Get the hell out with the Toyota, or move back into the rocks and wait to counter attack."

"First option," Uri said, "could get us or the Toyota shot up. Second one could also see us and the truck shot up, especially with Jamal as baggage."

"Plus, we have no night vision goggles. That was a big advantage in Yemen."

"Speaking of Yemen, why do I always wind up in these precarious firefights with you?"

"I'm the guy your momma told you to not hang around with."

"Funny, that's what all my friends said about me growing up," Uri replied. "This time though I'm going to try not to get shot."

Dan reached into his backpack and took out a power bar and water. "Food and fuel. Keep your energy up, old man."

Uri smiled and gave him the middle finger salute.

Chapter 26

Muntaqim sat in his modest home south of Rutba, a small village west of Baghdad and Ramadi. The village was located on Highway 10, which ran from Baghdad through Ramadi, west across the desert and into Jordan. The region was mostly empty but fully Sunni in its sectarian makeup. His place was in a rare area where water came near the surface, which resulted in acres of low desert scrub and brush, enough to hide his two-story house from ground-level view. There was a long dirt road leading to his compound. It wasn't a fortress but an unassuming goat farm along with some chickens and other livestock and a grove of date palms. Muntaqim had family members who worked the farm. They didn't know all that he was involved in and didn't care. That he paid them to work his farm was enough. It gave them a stable and decent living. Muntaqim liked having family around him. It made for a loyal and protective group of men.

If anyone tried to attack him, his relatives would defend their compound along with him. All the men could handle weapons; Muntaqim had seen to that. He also had established multiple escape routes going into the desert. In effect, he could leave and go in any direction. His perimeter defense consisted of a network of surveillance cameras that would alert him to anyone approaching within a half mile from any direction. With such advance warning, he could mount a defense, a counter offense, or make his getaway.

From what Muntaqim had learned of the Scorpion, the man had found himself trapped in his own fortress. Muntaqim wanted no part of that. Open spaces and hiding in sight with the anonymity of a goat farm worked best for him. The lack of luxury didn't bother him. Muntaqim had no need for luxury. That was for soft men...or fools. His arms dealer, Jetmir, seemed to be a man of foolish appetites. They would eventually get him killed despite Muntaqim's efforts to caution him.

Word had just come to Muntaqim that the man who had driven the truck in D.C. had been killed at his home in Tall 'Afar. It was apparent from the description that reached Muntaqim that a sniper had struck. No one had seen or heard the shot, and the man had his head blown apart on his front porch. In addition, the driver of the getaway car had disappeared. He had been told to hide out in Al Qamishli in Syria. Muntaqim had people there and had arranged what he felt was a safe place, not even allowing him to live at home. Yet someone had taken him. He had disappeared, and the men assigned to watch him were dead.

It was clear that these two men had been somehow identified and tracked down. Again, his worries about the all-seeing ability of the U.S. came to the forefront of his mind. The other possibility of something beyond advanced technology also lurked in the corner of his mind. He had no better place to hide. His only defense was to remain silent. Whether advanced technology was at work or something more extraordinary, harder to defend against, the best path for him was to stay quiet.

He felt trapped by his inability to communicate with the men involved in the bombings. He hoped word would get around. When he was informed, that had been his response. He told the man who brought him the news to alert everyone to continue to lie low. But that man did not know how to contact all involved in the missions. And, others actively looking for him, Muntaqim would not expose himself by sending messages. Everyone would have to wait out events, as would he. There were still more places to retreat to if needed until his trail grew cold. One was Saudi Arabia; even though his employer and benefactor would not like his presence in the kingdom, he kept it as a last resort...and knew the route there, south through the desert.

† † †

Dan thought about their situation while keeping watch through his scope. Occasionally, one of the attackers would raise his head to study the wall, looking for a target to shoot at. When one man rose up, he had the misfortune of Dan aiming his Sako in the man's direction. In a moment, Dan squeezed off a round, and the man fell back with blood spraying from the back of his head.

"What are they down to?" Uri asked after Dan had taken his shot.

"Can't be sure. I'm going to still call it six."

He turned away from his watch for a moment to study the sun.

"You know if we decide to run and time it right, they'll be shooting into the sun. That gives us a better than even chance of making it out intact."

Uri turned to look. "Got about an hour to go. Let me scout a route down this slope further away. You keep watch."

"Don't go getting yourself shot again."

"Don't worry. I'm going to stay high up, away from the direct line of fire. I'll just hike west from the truck for a bit and see what the downslope looks like. Better to know before we set out. Once they hear the truck start, they may charge."

Dan turned back to the two pickups while Uri headed back to the Toyota in a crouch.

Twenty minutes later, he returned. "We can go across the slope about 200 hundred yards. It's slow going as we have to cross ditches, smaller washes running down the hill. But I think we can make it. The route down is no worse than what we navigated coming up. You might have to risk going faster, but we'll increase our separation significantly. That, and the sun should help."

"Can you stuff our guy in the back? I'll keep watch and before we go. Put some rounds into the pickups to make sure they can't follow."

"That Sako can damage an engine?"

"Not like a .50 cal, but if I can hit some ignition part or the fuel system, they won't run or won't run well."

"Put a few rounds in the radiators. Then they won't go far."

"You want fries with that order?"

Uri gave him a questioning look.

"Never mind, it's an American thing. Go get our prisoner ready."

Chapter 27

It had been five hours since Dan and Uri had driven up the side of the wadi to hold off the men chasing them. Since the initial gun battle, things had settled down. Their pursuers didn't seem to be in a hurry to engage them, which only convinced both men that they planned to sneak up on them at night. Fighting now or directly assaulting their superior position might get the attackers killed. At night, well-spaced from one another, the odds would be better. For now, with Dan and Uri having decimated their ranks, they were wary of a direct confrontation.

When the sun had sunk far enough to get in the eyes of anyone looking west, Dan got up and headed back to the Toyota in a crouch. Without a word, Uri followed. While they had waited, Dan had put multiple rounds into the engine and radiator of both pickups. He didn't bother with the machine gun truck further back. That seemed to be fully disabled.

They got in the truck. Uri checked his AK and loaded a fresh 30-round magazine.

"Ready?" Dan asked.

Uri nodded. He turned to allow himself to shoot to the rear.

"Keep your head down when we come into their field of fire. They won't fully understand what's going on until they see us coming down the hill," Dan said.

"Then all hell will break loose."

"Right. And you do what you can to suppress their fire until I can get us further west."

He turned the key, and the Toyota came to life. They turned west, and Dan worked his way across the dips and ditches, careful to not jam the front bumper into any steep side walls of the depressions. Uri glanced at their progress, and when they reached the place he had scouted, he called out.

"Here's where you can turn downhill."

Dan stopped and examined the route while Uri crawled into the backseat.

"Looks as good as any place."

"It gets rougher further on."

"I'll take it."

He put the Toyota in low gear and spun the wheel, turning the SUV down the hill. The speed picked up even without using the throttle. Dan reached down with his left hand and pulled the parking brake release, steering with only one hand. He used his left foot on the parking brake, assured that the brake would release when he took his foot off. This allowed him to brake with only the rear wheels, keeping the front wheels rolling and steering. Though imprecise, the method kept the speed somewhat in check, but, more importantly, the vehicle aimed down the hill, not slewing sideways and in danger of rolling.

As soon as they came into view of the attackers, still less than 300 yards away, they could hear gunfire. The shots hit in a scatter pattern, not too close. Uri rolled down the window and started sending rounds back at the trucks. Dan let the Toyota go faster as they got further down the slope. A shot hit the farthest rear window on the driver's side and shattered it with a shower of safety glass fragments.

"Keep your head down!" Dan shouted. He abandoned his rear brake technique and now was busy with both hands on the steering wheel.

Uri fired more rounds, quickly zeroing in on the trucks. Dan scrunched down in the driver's seat, peering over the dashboard. His vision was obscured, and the Toyota took some sharp hits on rocks that he couldn't avoid.

He cursed under his breath. The truck was slewing and sliding, bouncing and pounding over the rocks and sand of the desert ground. When he could see a way to the west, Dan turned and accelerated into the sun even before they reached the flat bottom.

"It's working!" Uri shouted. "They're blinded."

The rounds were landing all around them, but mainly behind the receding Toyota.

"A little further and we'll be clear," he said.

Dan now raised himself higher and could immediately guide the truck more smoothly. He kept accelerating, pushing the Toyota closer to its limits, willing it to melt into the sun and away from the pursuing bullets.

Finally, the shooting seemed to stop.

"One shot-out window, probably some rounds in the side of the truck as well. We got off pretty good," Uri said.

He climbed back into the passenger seat.

"The bullet holes could be a problem at a checkpoint."

"Let's worry about that later. I'm glad we got through this part," Uri said.

They drove two miles to the west while angling downhill until they reached the wadi floor. Here, the ground was flatter and sandier, allowing Dan to maintain a good pace without risking the Toyota.

"The wadi will close up further west," Uri said. "We need to turn around."

"I got it. We'll have to go past Jamal's buddies. They'll know we have to turn around. They could spread out across the floor to try to stop us."

"Can't be helped. It's the only way out." Uri thought for a moment. "How about I drive? I'm good at desert driving and you're the sniper. We'll have to drive through as fast as we can with guns blazing."

"As good a plan as any."

Dan pulled over, and the two men switched positions, with Dan sitting in the back seat. He loaded a fresh magazine into the AK and then filled up the partially emptied one Uri had just used.

"Two full mags. Sixty rounds. That should be enough to get us through."

"If it isn't, we're in trouble," Uri said.

He turned the truck around and headed back down the wadi, all the while tracking towards the south wall, *away from the attackers*.

Chapter 28

H enry knocked on Jane's door and opened it without waiting for a response. Jane looked up from her work.

"What brings you down here?"

Henry went over to her desk and sat down in a chair. He sighed; his body slumped in the seat.

"You look terrible,' Jane said. "What's up?"

"I got the word to slow down this investigation. More like orders."

"What? What's going on? Who told you this?"

The questions came tumbling out of her mouth.

"I got the word from Roger. He got it from the top—"

"The Director or the DDO?"

Henry nodded.

Jane looked at him, her face showing disbelief. "What's the explanation? We've got two significant terror attacks. One on an ally of ours. These are the largest attacks since the twin towers. And we're supposed to stand down? My team is making progress, you know that."

"Not actually stand down as in stop the investigation. But slow down. It seems that the powers above only want us to find and kill the low-level operators."

"They don't want us to work out way up to the people who organized this? The people who financed these attacks?"

Henry shook his head.

Jane slammed her fist down on her desk. Her empty coffee cup jumped.

"That doesn't make any sense. Does it to you?"

"In a way...yes."

"Want to explain that? Because I don't see it." Jane sat back in her seat and glared at Henry.

He sighed again. "You got any coffee down here? Any that's drinkable?"

Without a word, Jane went outside to grab a cup from the ever-full pot in the outer office. She returned and placed a cup in front of Henry, then sat back at her desk and waited. Henry took a sip and set it down.

"You say you don't see it, but you probably do. You just don't think what I'm about to say goes on much here."

He took another sip and continued.

"There's a confluence of interests, at the highest levels of power, that distort things. They make things murky, so one doesn't always know the right path to take. What's the truth? What's good for our country? What's the proper course of action, the patriotic way, so to speak."

Jane continued to stare at her boss. He looked older, sadder. Less the man who hired her, the man who still had the fire in him. The warrior who became a bureaucrat but still wanted to fight the bad guys. Now, he almost looked defeated.

"Henry, you're speaking in riddles. Just tell me what the hell's going on here."

"I'm surprised you don't know, but I'll walk you through it, as far as I understand the situation."

He sipped his coffee again.

"Way back in World War Two, we were overly scared about the possibility of Nazi spies in the U.S. They were here, but the threat was actually overblown. People in government, in the intelligence arena, people who became part of the OSS, which became the CIA after the war, teamed up with organized crime, to ferret out the spies. The mafia hated the Nazis as much as many of the politicians, despite our government's isolationist posture.

"After the war, the CIA, still had these connections and used them to work against the leftist, communist threats." He paused for a moment. "You know the cold war started almost immediately after World War Two."

"I know my history."

"What you probably don't know is that the CIA had these ties that they maintained. They included ties to Israeli intelligence. After all there was a large collection of Jews working with organized crime. That connection goes back to the bootleg days."

"So, you're saying there's all these unsavory bedfellows connected to our organization. Connections that are best left undiscussed. Okay, I get that, but what does that have to do with what you just told me?"

"I'm getting to that. A little history first."

He straightened up in his chair as if pulling himself back into action.

"These connections continued. Think Bay of Pigs. A disaster, but one that the mafia was involved in along with the CIA.

"Now our organization needs covert banking, covert transportation, along with its covert agents to operate. So, we wind up using banks that can maintain secrets. These banks generally are of use to the underworld as well. And Mossad uses the same organizations."

"We bank where the mafia banks?"

"As I said, we use banks that can hide depositor's money. They have to be big enough to handle large sums of money. For that reason, they're often used by criminals, drug dealers, arms dealers along with intelligence agencies. So, yes.

"We don't interconnect much beyond that until we get to operations like the Iran-Contra mess that Oliver North was a big part of. But we do have this nexus. Currently, it involves not only mafia money, but Israeli and Saudi money."

Henry paused and took another sip of coffee. Jane could not resist the urge to interrupt with more questions.

"There's a lot those banks around the world. Why would we have to overlap with the criminal groups?"

Henry shook his head. "The ones that are well-placed, able to provide not only the top levels of security and anonymity but have the connections to move money, large amounts, around when asked is a much smaller group. They're in different parts of the world, including Switzerland and the other usual suspect places.

"Now the Saudis do not want it publically known how closely they were working with the Israelis. It could ignite a great deal of opposition both in their country and around the Mideast. The Israelis don't disagree."

"I can understand that. But what the hell does that have to do with this banking stuff you're telling me about?"

"That banking stuff, to make this a shorter lecture, involves money that is going to groups involved in drug and arms smuggling. So, to track this attack to its highest levels and track the money flow, like your two geeks out there can do," Henry pointed over his shoulder to the outer room where Fred and Warren worked, "would expose us, this organization, to some very bad publicity."

"What are you saying?"

"We are sometimes in bed with some bad actors, you know that. We therefore allow some bad things to go on...for the greater good."

Jane looked at her boss in amazement. She knew her agency was not squeaky clean, but she had always admired how Henry could stay away from those issues and fight the good fight.

"So, we let those involved get away with this? Innocent people, civilians, got killed. That needs to be punished, made right."

"I agree. I want you to find the ones involved. Your team has a good start, but don't go too high. The ones who perpetrated these attacks should be killed."

"But not...say, Rashid. The man who we think may be behind all of this. The one who may have financed it. It took a lot of money to do this. He has the money and the motivation, we know that."

Henry nodded. "Agreed. But he has powerful friends in the Saudi government. They allow him to operate but try to keep him from being too disruptive."

"But, if Rashid was involved, then he was working at cross purposes to his own government."

"That would be so. But that is for the Saudis to handle, not us."

"We have to trust that they'll rein him in? He's been responsible for many other attacks, and they didn't seem to have a problem with them. Yet a lot of people got killed."

"Again, I agree. But in this case, it will unmask too much that would embarrass too many in power. Our own organization and with it, the administration, the Israeli government, and the Saudi government. There's too much at stake. Just find and kill the operatives."

"And that'll put a lid on it. I get it now. Kill them so they can't testify."

Jane gave Henry a sour look.

"Hell, I wanted to kill them so they couldn't take advantage of our court system," she said, "bring them rough and swift justice. Now I realize I'm just playing into the puppet master's hands."

"It's still the right thing to do."

"But don't go too far. That's what you came down here to tell me with this long lecture."

"What I told you is accurate. You knew there was corruption. It exists in all organizations. I just wanted to make sure you know how deep it goes, how entrenched. Yet, even with its existence we can still do our jobs. It's one of the reasons I wanted to set up shop with this operation. To sidestep all of the compromises that face us working through the regular bureaucracy."

He got up and, with a last, tired look at Jane, exited her office.

Chapter 29

Quickly, the stalled-out trucks came into view to their left. They were a good half-mile away, just over 800 yards. That distance was beyond the capabilities of the AK 47. Neither Dan nor the attackers could successfully fire at one another.

Suddenly, the M2 machine gun opened up.

"Shit!" Dan exclaimed. "The M2. It can reach us and I can't fire back. Step on the gas. Our only hope is to create a difficult target until we get out of range."

He could see the rounds working their way towards them. The gunner was not making corrections fast enough to get zeroed in, which helped. He was also behind in tracking their lateral movement.

"Keep accelerating. He's having a hard time getting his rounds close."

"I go too much faster, we might crash."

"Got to risk it. Those rounds'll tear us up. They can penetrate the engine and stop us cold."

Uri accelerated the Toyota. It was now bouncing and lurching over the uneven terrain. The rounds were coming closer. Both men heard a burst go screaming over the truck. Another group struck just behind them.

"He's having trouble staying with our motion."

Dan felt like a target in a carnival shooting gallery. Eventually, the gunner would get lucky. That was all he needed to stop them, possibly killing one or more of them at the same time. The truck continued on, slamming and jumping over the rough ground. Dan held on as best he could. He looked in the rear area. Their captive was rolling around, slamming into the sides of the compartment. *He'll be bruised up pretty bad*, Dan thought.

He could hardly make out the trucks. That didn't mean the rounds couldn't reach them. The M2 had a range of over 7,000 yards or four miles. *We're screwed if that gunner gets his shit together.*

Suddenly, there was a pause in the firing.

"What's happening?" Uri said.

He didn't turn his head but continued looking forward, trying to keep the Toyota going as fast as possible. They were now receding down the wadi to the east. The sun had dropped behind the hills in the west, and the shadows were lengthening.

"We can't be out of range yet."

"We aren't. He probably has to cool his barrel. He's been putting a lot of rounds through it. Maybe they don't have a second barrel to change out."

"That helps." His voice shook from the motion of the truck.

"Helps that it's getting darker as well." Dan paused to look back. He now couldn't see the truck. "We might get out of this alive."

"Can you see them?"

"Negative," Dan said.

"That means they can't see us either."

"Only the dust we raise, which won't give them an exact location. Keep at it. We've got a chance. Zig zag if you can. If he's smart, he'll shoot over the dust cloud. Just don't set up a pattern that he can anticipate."

Uri swung the truck to the left, throwing Dan across the seat.

"Shit, give me some warning before you do that."

"Sorry. I've just got this itch in my back, waiting for a .50 caliber round to smash into me. It makes me antsy."

"I hear you."

Uri continued to drive as fast as he could as the evening darkened. He didn't turn on the headlights and finally had to slow down. Sporadic rounds had started again. This time, the gunner was throwing his rounds further down range from the dust signature, just as Dan had predicted. Uri's more erratic path kept them from coming too close, and finally, he stopped firing. It was now dark enough that the dust cloud was no longer visible. In addition, the slower pace created less of a trail to see.

"I think we made it," Dan said.

Uri sighed. *You didn't get me death. Not today.*

Back on the paved road, the men headed for Ramadi with their prisoner. It was night. Both men were now more alert and tense. They had relaxed after getting past the machine gun but now were heading towards dangerous territory again.

"There was no cell reception back out there in the desert, but they probably called people here when they set out after us," Uri said.

They used their lights and blended into the light traffic along the paved road.

"I don't think we want to try to enter Ramadi and cross where we did before," Dan said. "Who knows how far the word went out, how many are looking for us, for this Land Cruiser."

"I agree. But there're few bridges across the Euphrates. And some of them are still damaged."

"So they can man a bunch of the rest."

"Especially if they're looking for us."

Iraq seemed like a maze with lethal traps randomly placed along the pathways. It was a crapshoot, with them being the rats trying to figure the way out.

"So how do we get out of this hell hole?"

Uri looked over at Dan.

"We can't use our cover. We're too far from where we're supposed to be." He paused for a moment. "And we've got this extra piece of baggage named Jamal. That doesn't help."

"You are the master of the obvious, aren't you?"

"I'm thinking out loud. We need to go north, before Ramadi. South won't help us. But going north takes us close to the Syria border, which will make crossing the river harder."

"We need to get back to Zerya. He can hide us, and we can debrief our captive."

"That's a lot of Iraq to get through unnoticed."

"I don't mind being noticed, just not by the terrorists or the government."

They were driving along Route 1, heading towards Ramadi. Suddenly, Uri braked and turned the Toyota around and accelerated.

"What are you doing?"

"We passed a road going north back a few miles. It'll take us near Syria, but I looked at it earlier on the map, thinking about our retreat. There's not much along the road, so no checkpoints."

"But we can't use the bridges there."

"Right. We'll have to dump the Toyota and make it across the river on our own. On the other side, we steal a vehicle and head north."

"That's a crazy plan."

"But one that has a chance to work. Better than wandering around in Ramadi waiting to be spotted, looking for a bridge without a checkpoint. That way makes me feel too trapped."

Uri came to the intersection and turned to the north. They drove on, now in silence.

Chapter 30

T he men had to admit defeat. Many of their fighters were dead, and the infidels had escaped. Plus, they had Jamal Almasi, an important man who knew many things. All this had to be reported to Muntaqim, something no one was looking forward to doing.

Muntaqim did not treat failure with much sympathy. He dealt out harsh punishments and discipline when his plans were not carried out correctly. What had happened to Jamal was a failure, not part of his plans. The men wondered how the kidnappers had discovered Jamal. It couldn't have been by chance. They had to know of his participation in the bombings. After the attacks, everyone was told to blend back into civilian life until the furor died. All involved had done that, but it hadn't helped Jamal.

They chose Esad to go to his farm and to report what had happened, thereby violating Muntaqim's orders to remain separate from one another. He was the only one who had seen and heard the kidnappers escaping from the junkyard after they had attacked the office. Although his name meant "lucky," he didn't feel that way when the others chose him to deliver the message. They decided that a visit was better than contacting Muntaqim by phone, something he did not like in the best of times, and certainly not right after these two devastating bombings.

Esad took his old Nissan sedan and headed out of Ramadi, following the same route as the kidnappers. He turned off to the south at a small intersection. There were a few houses where the roads crossed, not really qualifying as even a village. The road south was dirt. The surrounding land was planted and dotted with trees, and bushes were not cultivated. This was due to the higher water table, which farmers generations ago had discovered and took advantage of.

As he approached the farm, Esad slowed. He knew he was being captured by the cameras. He also knew that his old sedan would not seem to be a threat, but Muntaqim would not take any chances. Sure enough, armed men in a pickup truck intercepted him as he turned onto the long dirt drive to the farmhouse.

He stopped and got out, raising his hands. Two of the men approached, carbines held ready to shoot. They spoke in Arabic. "What are you doing here?" one of them asked.

Esad replied, "I have a message to deliver to Muntaqim. It is important and he does not want us to call or use the internet. So, I come in person."

The man who asked spoke into a radio he had clipped to his belt. When finished, he turned to Esad. "Put your hands on the car. We must search you."

Esad did as he was told. After a pat down, they directed him to follow them in his car. They pulled up at the small farmhouse, and the men motioned for Esad to go inside. At the front door was another armed man, much larger than the others. He patted Esad down for a second time and then, satisfied, let him enter.

He directed Esad to a large room while staying close behind him. Once inside, the guard gestured for Esad to sit on a cushion. After he sat down, a fully veiled woman came in and served him tea. She then left while the guard remained, standing behind and to one side.

The young man picked up his tea and noticed his hands shaking. He had never been in the leader's house, much less violated his orders. Now, as the deliverer of bad news, things could get very unpleasant for him. Muntaqim had a fierce reputation, rightfully earned.

After a few minutes, a large man entered through a curtain at the back of the room. He had a dark, full beard and sharp, black eyes sunk deeply in his head. They pierced you with their glare. Esad scrambled to his feet and bowed. He had never met Muntaqim, but he instantly knew this was their leader, so powerful was his presence. When he got to his feet, the guard started forward, but a small gesture from his leader stopped him.

Muntaqim stared hard at his visitor. When Esad completed his bow, Muntaqim gestured for him to sit again. He then went to his own cushion on the other side of a low table and lowered himself onto it. The man and the cushion on which he sat were higher than Esad, making him look up at his leader. The fully covered woman quietly entered and placed a cup of tea and a plate of dates on the table in front of Muntaqim. She retreated without any acknowledgment from the warrior.

Muntaqim sipped his tea and then put a date into his mouth. After swallowing, he spoke.

"You have disobeyed my orders to come here. I hope you have something important to tell me...for your sake."

"Yes, *zaeim*." Esad used the word for leader.

Muntaqim nodded and waited.

"Jamal Almasi was kidnapped yesterday. From his work in Ramadi...at the recycle yard."

"Kidnapped? By who?"

Esad swallowed. "Two men. One spoke Arabic. I heard it. The other one looked western and yelled something in English."

"And you did not recapture him? They got away?"

Esad could only nod his head.

Muntaqim stared at the young man. His eyes penetrating as if looking for signs of deceit or weakness. Esad's face only showed fear. The fear of a powerful chief, the fear of one who did not suffer defeat well.

"They were very good shooters. One, I think the westerner, had a long-range rifle. It could strike us before our AKs could reach them."

"That's all you had to fight with? All you brought to rescue Jamal?" Esad could feel the increased intensity in his questions. He shook his head.

"We had a machine gun in one of the pickups, but the long-range shooter, he was able to stop the gun far away."

"The machine gun. What caliber is it?"

"Fifty caliber, *zaeim*."

"It shoots farther than any rifle."

"Yes, zaeim, but the man shooting killed the one operating the machine gun. He was deadly. If anyone poked their head up, they were shot."

Muntaqim was silent for some time before he spoke.

"They had stopped running. Why didn't you assault them?"

"They were on high ground, with good defenses. An old wall from ancient times. We were waiting for night, when we could spread out and creep up on them."

"But you didn't."

Esad shook his head. "They left, headed into the sun which blinded us. We tried to stop them."

"But you chased them."

The statement hung in the air like a question.

Esad swallowed again. Sweat was dripping down his face. "The shooter had disabled our remaining two trucks. We were stranded."

Muntaqim's face grew darker, more dangerous. He leaned forward on his cushion, his stare pinning the young man to his seat. "You violate my rule to come here to tell me that you let one of my men get kidnapped and failed to rescue him? Do you want me to take you out back to be shot?"

Esad shook his head violently. "No *zaeim*. It is to warn you." He took a breath and then continued. "Jamal knows where you live...here. He also knows how you stay hidden. I don't know all these things, the details, but I am sure Jamal does. He may talk and that could endanger you. That is why we decided that we had to contact you. And why I was chosen."

Esad could say no more. He could not tell how Muntaqim would react. He could only hope that his *zaeim* would see the value in his visit.

Chapter 31

After turning north off the Ramadi highway, Dan turned on his satellite phone and called Jane.

"Are you okay?" she asked after answering.

"Uri and I are fine. As fine as can be expected in the middle of Iraq. We have a captive. It's the guy who led the D.C. bombing. We're trying to get north to meet up with Zerya Barzani. You need to send him some money. He's been very helpful."

"I remember him. He worked with us a few years ago when ISIS was still in power up there."

"That's the guy. Get some funds on their way to him. We're going to need his help to get our asses out of here."

"Will do. Who's your guest?"

"His name is Jamal Almasi. I'll take a picture of him and send it to you when we get some cell signal. Get Fred and Warren on this guy. Find out as much as you can. Everyone connected to him, is probably connected to the bombings."

"This is good work," Jane said.

She almost told Dan about Henry's visit but held back. The news would set him off, and there was no telling what he might do. Such corruption, allowing evil people to get away with crimes, especially crimes against civilians, could trigger something in him. She guessed it was a holdover of his experiences with the mafia in Brooklyn and their killing of his wife and child.

"I'll be in touch," Dan said, ending the call.

Hours later, Uri slowed. They were approaching the T intersection where the road met Highway 12. Dawn was breaking. There were more houses now, along with circular fields created by irrigation from the Euphrates.

"There'll be some sort of truck depot, maybe more than one, for refueling and getting something to eat. Going west, towards the border they'll be a checkpoint. Going east, none. That's what the map shows."

"Let's hope you're right. I don't want to have come all this way to get stopped at a checkpoint."

"If there is?"

Uri shrugged. "We turn the hell around and try somewhere else."

They reached the intersection, and, as Uri predicted, there was a truck depot on the right servicing eastbound trucks. Uri pulled the Toyota into the area and parked along the edge, out of the way. The open space was unpaved with the dirt packed down from years of saturation from fuel and oil, along with constant pressure from heavily laden trucks. There was a run-down, one-story building set back from the fuel pumps.

Dan took out his binoculars and scanned the road east. "Nothing showing. Just the highway."

He turned around and looked west, where there was an apparent checkpoint a few miles from the intersection with commercial and passenger vehicles backed up waiting to go through.

"We don't need gas if we're going to ditch the Toyota," Uri said. He started the engine, and they set out going east.

"Check the map for where we can get close to the river without being seen," Uri said.

An hour down the highway, Dan told Uri to turn onto a dirt road going left towards the river. They were back into the desert with its interlacing tracks and trails.

"Just keep working north and avoid farm houses," Dan said. "Don't go fast and raise a lot of dust. We can't cross until nightfall anyway."

Uri merely grunted as he worked the Toyota over the rough two-track. After nearly an hour of travel in a very irregular path northward, Uri drove them up a shallow wadi. Here, there was no road. The hills along each side were not steep but high enough to shield them from view.

"No one's going to find us here," Uri announced as he pulled the Toyota over and turned off the engine. He got out and stretched.

"Damn, I'm tired. Stiff as well."

"You're just old," Dan said.

"I can still keep up with you. When I can't, that's when I know I'm over the hill."

Dan got out and went to the back. He lifted the lid and pulled Jamal out to sit on the tail of the truck.

"Our guest looks a little beaten up. I don't think he enjoyed the ride."

Uri was relieving himself in the sand at the front of the Land Cruiser.

"Looks like he pissed himself along the way as well."

Uri came back and pulled the duct tape off of Jamal's mouth. The man let out a string of curses in Arabic. Dan had gone off to one side to relieve himself.

"What's he saying?"

"Just the usual about we're sons of dogs, our mothers were whores, Arabic insults. Not very creative, if you ask me."

Dan came back and stared at their captive. He grabbed a bottle of water, untied Jamal's hands, and gave him the bottle. Jamal was still sitting on the truck with his feet tied together. Dan untied Jamal's feet and pulled him off of the SUV. He made him sit on the ground.

"Tell him if he tries to run, I'll break one of his legs."

Dan and Uri sat on the tail of the Land Cruiser with Jamal in the dirt. They passed him a power bar and some more water. All three men ate and drank in silence.

"How do we get him across?" Uri asked.

"I'll get him across. Hopefully we can wade, but if it's too deep, I'll swim him over. You bring some of the gear. One of us will probably have to go back for the rest of it."

"The river will be high. It's spring and the snowmelt from the highlands will feed it."

"Turkey has a dam, don't they? That should control it."

"They've got a power dam, but the average flow will still be greater than in the summer."

Dan shrugged. "Doesn't matter. I'll get his ass across one way or another. I just want to get out of this shithole and to the north."

"And some safety."

"Some safety. It's all relative, but Zerya represents a safe haven compared to being out here on our own."

The two lapsed back into silence. Jamal, after his outburst, remained quiet. It seemed as though he didn't want to trigger his captors into duct-taping his mouth again.

Chapter 32

The two men took turns sleeping in the truck while one kept watch. Dan re-tied Jamal and put him back into the rear. The heat became more oppressive as the day progressed, making sleeping harder. Dan finally got out and lay down on the sand and dirt in the shade of the Land Cruiser. After hours of stifling heat, the sun neared the western hills, and the temperature began to moderate.

"A couple of hours to go and then we can try to cross," Dan said. "We hike to the river and then scout along it for a good place."

"Got to tape Jamal's mouth again. We can't have him trying to give away our position.

After the sun disappeared, the night was dark, with no city lights to relieve the black sky. There was a new moon, so it would not shine at night but rise in the morning and set in the afternoon not able to be seen in the bright light of the sun.

"Time to go," Dan said.

The two men got up. They pulled Jamal out of the truck and untied him. They placed a backpack on him with much of their food and water. After, they re-tied his wrists in front. Uri shouldered his pack with his weapons tied to it, as did Dan, and the three set out towards the river.

"If you try to run away," Uri whispered to Jamal, "one of us will take you down and hurt you. Just walk quietly and don't try to cause trouble. There's no one out here to help you."

A half-hour of walking brought them to a dirt road running along the river. They squatted behind some brush and watched for any movement or lights.

Nothing.

They crossed the road and entered the scrub growing near the river's edge.

"Wait here," Dan said. "I'm going to scout farther down the river."

He started downstream, scanning the shoreline, looking for an easy entry into the water. Trying to guess the depth was impossible in the dark of the night. Ahead, Dan could make out a darker shape in the black. He stopped and crouched down. It appeared to be some type of building, a small house or storage barn. He watched patiently. There was no sign of life. Nothing moved outside. No animals in the yard, no car, no equipment, anything that would indicate someone living in the building.

Recently, after the Iraq war, much of the population had begun to accept dogs. Markets had grown up in the larger cities. It was unusual since many Muslims believed dogs were unclean. Those who considered the phenomenon thought it might be due to the need for increased security. Small shopkeepers purchased many of the dogs to protect their businesses. The Iraqi's experience with American bomb-sniffing dogs may also have led to the recent interest.

Here, there seemed to be no dogs or other animals. After watching for some time, Dan approached the building. It was an old farmhouse. He crept up to a window and peered inside. There was nothing to see, only a deeper darkness than the night surrounding him. A circumnavigation of the structure revealed no footprints or other evidence of anyone's presence.

Dan readied his carbine and pulled on the front door. It scraped and ground on the threshold but succumbed to his efforts. He dropped to one knee, aiming his rifle inside, looking for any threat. There was nothing. Nothing moved in the dark. After a moment, he stepped forward. It was a single room with what seemed to be a kitchen on one side. There was no furniture left, only a counter, which Dan assumed was the kitchen area, along with some cabinets, their open doors showing they were empty.

Satisfied there was no one on the property, Dan went back out and headed to the river. There on the bank was a rowboat. It was wide-beamed, crudely built, and had some oars in the bottom. The paint had long since worn off, leaving a spotted residue and graying wood. Gaps showed between the planks. It wouldn't be watertight, but Dan guessed it was better than swimming. He turned and headed back to Uri and their captive.

"Found a place to cross. There's an abandoned rowboat. It's in lousy condition, but it's better than swimming."

"And if it sinks halfway across? What do we do?" Uri nodded to their captive. "We can't just let him swim away."

"I'll keep him tied to me."

"And if he drowns you?"

"He can try. I doubt he can even swim. If we go down, you'll take my backpack with you. The Sako will get wet, but I can dry it out. Our friend will have a pack on, and I won't. He'll most likely want me to keep him afloat rather than try to swim away or drown me. Anyway, swimming halfway is better than swimming all the way."

Uri shrugged as if he remained unconvinced. The three men got up and headed to the shack and the rowboat.

They alternately poled and paddled the leaking boat as they progressed across the river. The water seeped in through the planking in multiple rivulets, and the small craft rode lower and lower in the water.

"We going to make it?" Uri asked.

"It'll be close. As we get more water inside, the boat rides lower, and we go slower."

"I noticed."

Uri was puffing from the exertion as both men pushed and pulled on the oars, trying to force their unwieldy craft across the river.

Before reaching the opposite shore, about fifty yards out, The boat ground against the bottom and refused to go forward.

"Time to leave," Dan said. "We should be able to wade from here."

Dan tied a line around Jamal's neck and held it as a leash. They shouldered their packs and climbed out into the water, which was knee-deep.

"Not too bad, if this is as deep as it gets," Uri said.

They began to slog forward. Jamal trailed behind but kept pace by the loop tied around his neck. As they closed in on the shore, Uri stepped into deeper water. He fell forward with a shout and surfaced, flailing around to get his feet under him. The water was chest-deep. As Uri went down, Dan also fell into the deeper channel, dragging Jamal after him. Jamal shouted in alarm as he disappeared underwater. With much splashing and sputtering of water, he emerged, arms flailing.

"You're okay," Dan said. "Stand up!"

Jamal got his feet under him and began to calm down. The current tugged at the men but was not strong enough to pull them off their feet.

"Let's go," Uri said.

He began to march forward. Dan followed, pulling Jamal along at the rear. After going ten more yards, Uri again sank. He didn't go under but now had to swim. It was awkward with his backpack on, but he kept at it.

Jamal stopped. Dan tugged at his leash, but the man resisted.

"You don't come along, I'm going to shove you into the water."

Jamal seemed to understand but shook his head.

"Look around," Dan swung his hand around him at the expanse of the dark river. "You can't stay here. We get to the shore, you'll be out of the water."

Jamal just looked at him.

"Uri, tell this son-of-a-bitch to get going."

Uri spoke in Arabic to Jamal, and after a moment, the man began to move forward.

When he and Dan got to the deeper area, Dan grabbed Jamal's arm and shoved him forward with himself alongside. They immediately went under the water. Dan kicked his legs to move forward and pushed Jamal with his arm. The man tried to grab him, but Dan kept him facing the shore, away from his body. After much thrashing, kicking, and Jamal spluttering and coughing up river water, their feet found purchase, and the two men stepped up into shallower water. Now the water went from chest to knee deep.

While not deep, the going was hard. Their boots sank in the mud and it took an effort to pull them free of the suction so they could take another step. Each step required extra effort. Ten minutes later, they climbed onto the bank, and all three men lay down in the scrub growing at the water's edge.

"That was fucking hard," Dan said.

"Even for a tough guy like you?" Uri asked.

"Even me. It must have been overwhelming for an old, out-of-shape fart like yourself."

Uri took a swig from a water bottle while giving Dan the finger. He passed the bottle to Jamal, who drank deeply.

"Better on dry land, no?" Dan asked.

Jamal just looked at him.

"Think he doesn't understand English?"

"Probably more than you guess," Uri said. "I'd remember that."

He translated what Dan had said into Arabic. Jamal nodded enthusiastically.

Uri turned to Dan. "What's next?"

Chapter 33

S teal a car."

Dan got up from the grass. He gestured to Jamal to get on his feet. Dan took a roll of duct tape from his backpack and put a strip across Jamal's mouth. He got an angry glare back.

"He doesn't like me taping his mouth."

"I don't blame him. Makes it hard to breathe."

"*Macht nichts.* Let's get out of here. I'm tired of moving around with a target on my back."

The three walked through cultivated fields, moving away from the river and westward to connect with a road Uri had noted on the map. Unlike before, they had to head towards inhabited areas to find a vehicle to steal.

The fields were soft, which made the going harder. They moved to the edges to avoid the loose, plowed ground. After an hour, they reached the dirt road. It ran north, away from the river. Unfortunately, there were no buildings in the immediate area, so no vehicles.

"North?" Dan asked.

Uri took out his map and searched it using his shielded flashlight. "Nothing back towards the river...no village or town. There's one about five miles north. It looks like just a small cluster of buildings at a crossroads." He looked up. "If we hurry, we can make it before daylight."

"Sounds good. Stealing a car isn't a good idea in the daylight and don't want to spend another day hiding out in this heat, waiting for night."

Without another word, the men set out at a brisk pace that approached a jog. They needed to cover the five miles in about four hours, which would leave them a small piece of the night to hide their attempts to locate and steal a vehicle.

After an hour, Jamal began to lag, and Dan had to repeatedly shove him forward. After numerous tries at hurrying him along, he stopped. Dan took water and power bars from Jamal's pack and passed them around.

"Tell Jamal in no uncertain terms that I'm going to cripple him and leave him behind if he doesn't keep up."

"He may like that. I'll try it a bit differently."

Uri turned to Jamal. He pulled the tape from his mouth and spoke in Arabic, "This man," he pointed to Dan, "will break both of your legs, badly, if you don't keep up. You will not be able to walk. We'll tie you up so you can't crawl and leave you hidden. We will come back and then take you away to torture you. It will be more painful for you."

He smiled at Jamal, who stared at him intently.

"If you keep up, we will spare you the broken bones, the pain. We only want to talk with you and need to go to a safe place to do that. If you cooperate, it will be better for you in the end."

Uri stared at Jamal as the man digested what he had said.

"You will kill me in the end," Jamal finally said. "Why should I help you do that?"

"Because we may not, if your help is useful to us. And if we do, it will be quick. If not, it will be long and drawn out." He paused for a moment. "I am very good at long and drawn out."

Uri stood up.

"Time to go. It is your choice how we proceed."

This time Jamal kept a better pace, although not as quick as Dan would have liked. Still, the sun had not yet risen when they could see buildings ahead. The intense blackness of night was now beginning to dissolve into a dark gray, indicating the coming dawn. In the east, the sky was turning a deep blue from its previous black.

"Not a moment too soon," Dan said in a low voice.

The men moved slower now, careful to not make any excess noise. They could see no vehicles on the road. At the intersection, there was a building to their right that looked like a repair shop. In the soft, pre-dawn light, they could see two cars and a truck parked in the yard, along with two tractors.

"Wonder if any of them work?" Uri said under his breath.

"Let's take a look."

They walked to the yard. As they got close, they could see one car blocked up with a wheel off of it. The other sat there with the hood partly open.

"Both of these look like they're being worked on," Dan whispered.

He walked forward to the pickup truck. It had a welded derrick in the bed to convert it into a tow truck. Dan opened the driver's door and slipped inside. There was a hole in the dash where a radio had once been. Loose wires were dangling from under the dash. The heat controls looked like they probably didn't work. Dan pressed the brake and found pressure. He moved the gear shift from park to reverse and drive. There were distinct indents as he pushed the lever, which indicated the shift mechanism was working.

He got out and huddled with Uri.

"This one looks like it can run. It's the shop tow truck. We need to drain any gas out of the other two and take it with us. No way of knowing right now how much gas is in the truck. Let's look around and see if we can find any cans and tubing."

"Siphon the gas?"

"If we can."

A search around the building uncovered two 20-liter cans. One had a top, the other didn't. Uri found a flat piece of wood that could be placed over the open can to stop gas from sloshing out. The search didn't turn up any hose.

"Option B," Dan said. He took one can and crawled under the rear of the first vehicle. Using his knife, he stabbed a hole in the gas tank and jammed the can under it. The liquid splashed noisily into the container.

"Hand me the other can," Dan said. He didn't want to waste any of the gas if there was more in the tank than one can could hold.

When the first can overflowed, Dan pulled it away and jammed the second can into the stream. A few moments later, the fuel stopped splashing out. Dan waited and then shoved both cans out from under the car.

"Put that into the truck. Might as well fill it while I'm getting more."

He went to the second car and crawled under. He stabbed the gas tank, and the fuel began to flow into the second can. While it was draining, Uri finished pouring the first can into the pickup and brought the now-empty back to Dan. When the can was filled, Dan slid it out. Gas poured onto the dirt as Dan shoved the empty can under the slit in the tank. The second can only filled about halfway before the fuel ran out.

Dan brought it over to the pickup and poured the gas into the truck. From the sound, he could tell it was close to full.

"Got a full tank and one spare can of gas out of that. Time to try to start her up."

"Hot wire it?"

Dan shook his head. "I can jam my knife into the ignition and turn it. This is an older pickup, and that should unlock the steering and operate the starter.

"Just so it starts. If it doesn't, we don't have a backup plan. It'll be daylight soon."

Dan looked at the sky. "It'll start. I'm just hoping this guy doesn't get up at the crack of dawn and we can get a couple of hours head start."

"If the truck doesn't make too much noise."

Dan smiled and climbed into the cab. Uri shoved Jamal up into the bed and climbed up after him.

Chapter 34

T hey were four hours down the dirt road, heading north. They had connected to a paved road, which had some truck traffic on it. The road ran west of Tall 'Afar but turned back to the east north of the town on its way to Al Ya'rubiyan.

"We'll be able to get to Zerya tonight," Dan said. For the first time, he began to smile.

"We'll need to find gas. Either buy it or steal it."

"I don't think we have to worry about a car theft report. And this far away, no one will recognize the truck. We just have to keep Jamal from doing anything to cause trouble."

"Keeping Jamal from trying to alert someone could be difficult."

"Agreed." Dan thought for a moment. "When we find a place to get gas, we'll drive past it. We stop where I can keep myself and Jamal hidden. You go back and fill up. Then pick us up and off we go again."

Two hours later, halfway to Al Ya'rubiyan, they found a truck stop with diesel and gasoline.

"Good thing this showed up," Dan said. "We're almost empty."

He drove past the turnoff and stopped a mile up the road. There was no cover along the flat, straight desert road.

"Not much place to hide," Uri said.

"I know, but we don't have much choice. It looks like the same scene all the way to the horizon. "We'll just walk back about a hundred yards and sit down quietly. Maybe no one will notice." He turned to their prisoner. "Jamal here will behave. You tell him I'll stab him with my knife if he causes any trouble. He's seen it work on the gas tanks."

Uri repeated Dan's words in Arabic just in case Jamal could not fully understand their English. The two men walked into the desert, away from the road, and Uri turned around.

Twenty minutes later, he came back. During that time, three vehicles had passed. None of them seemed to notice the two men hunkered down in the sand and rocks. When they returned to the truck, Dan got out water for him and Jamal.

"It's no fun just sitting in the sun. It's a good way to get heat exhaustion or sun stroke."

They drove off.

"We'll be passing through some towns ahead," Dan said, "but I'm glad we stopped. I just want to navigate quietly through these places. The less we interact, the better."

Before getting to the towns, Dan re-taped Jamal's mouth and crammed him into the footwell and under his feet. The man protested through his closed lips to no avail.

"Got to keep him out of sight and quiet as we go through the towns."

From Tall 'Afar, they retraced their earlier steps north into Kurdish country and Zerya's protection.

"Seems like a long time ago we were here," Uri said.

"Stress does that to you."

It was getting dark, which wasn't a problem since the men knew the route. When they got close, they ran into a checkpoint and stopped. Five rough men, all with headscarves wound around their heads and faces, approached the pickup. They all had Kalashnikovs slung over their shoulders, hands close to the triggers.

"We are friends with Zerya Barzani. Let us through and call him. Tell him Victor is returning," Dan yelled through the window. Uri repeated the words in Arabic.

Two men talked with one another while the others kept watch. One of them looked inside to find Jamal curled up in the footwell. He shouted something in Arabic to the others who came crowding around.

"Our prisoner. Zerya will want to talk to this man," Uri said.

Both Uri and Dan spoke with authority.

The two men talking now approached the truck. They spoke to Uri in Arabic.

"How do you know Zerya? How do you know where he lives? And who is this man?"

"We don't tell you this information. It is enough for you to know that we are friends with Zerya and he will not be pleased if you stop us from meeting with him."

Uri pointed to Jamal.

"He will want to talk with this man."

Uri motioned for the men to get going.

"Make the call. You can call Zerya? Do it."

The men talked to themselves again. There seemed to be an argument going on. Dan looked at Uri.

"They are discussing the dangers of ignoring what I told them as opposed to protecting Zerya from any unwelcome guests. We just need to act confident. I told them to call him, but I doubt they have his number."

"Clever man."

Uri held back a smile and leaned out of the window. "Go ahead. Call Zerya Barzani. Call him or let us through. We don't have all night to wait here. It is important for Zerya to interrogate this man."

Finally, one man seemed to prevail. He ordered one of the vehicles pulled back and waved them through.

Without a "thank you," Uri drove through the checkpoint as if he were late for an important meeting.

"Well played," Dan said. "We probably have only an hour to go."

He reached down and helped Jamal get back onto the seat.

"He can be a little more comfortable for this last part of his journey."

The old pickup droned on. No one talked. The men were hot, dusty, and fatigued. Jamal sat as comfortably as he could in the middle of the front bench seat. He seemed to want to avoid antagonizing either captor and getting shoved back down on the floor where it was not only more bruising but hotter and dustier.

Chapter 35

D an took out his satellite phone and called Jane. "There you go again, waking me up in the middle of the night."

"My only form of recreation these days."

"Where are you?"

"We have our package, the man who—"

"Hold that thought," Jane said, cutting him off. "I need to use another phone. The battery is running out and I can't find the charger. I'll call you back."

The connection went dead. A few moments later, Dan's phone rang.

"What's up?" Dan said. "That doesn't sound like you, letting your phone die. Is this line secure?"

"Not sure. Just listen, don't talk." She explained her conversation with Henry.

"What the hell?" Dan said.

"Don't editorialize. Just listen."

Jane went on to explain the new rules. How they were not to get too high on the chain of command in the bombings, and if the trail led to Rashid, he was off limits. Dan tried to interject along the way, but Jane cut him off. Her voice sounded more severe than he had heard in a long time.

"I'll call you tomorrow," Jane said. "When my phone situation is better. Do you have another phone to use? As a backup?"

"Only Uri's cell phone."

"How about your host?"

"I can ask him when we get there."

"Do that. I'll see if we have a number for him as well."

"Zey—"

"Stop! I know who you're with. If I can, I'll reach out to you through him."

She ended the call abruptly.

"What was that all about?" Uri asked.

Dan shook his head. "Something's up. She didn't want me to give out any info on the call, like her line was tapped. But it's a secure line."

He went on to explain what Jane had told him. Uri whistled in amazement.

"Your government is going off in the wrong direction. What you told me, to stand down, not find everyone involved and take them out, protect politicians at the expense of security? That's crazy. All those civilians killed and no one in authority cares? They will actually cover it up?"

"Seems like it. Maybe you should call Eitan and see if he's on the same page."

"Not a chance in hell. This is going to be like the Olympics in '72. We're going to find them all and kill them. We have a backbone unlike your politicians."

"I don't disagree with you. We'll see what tomorrow brings."

He looked at his phone.

"I have her number, so if Barzani has a phone and reception, I can call her tomorrow. Maybe I'll find out more then."

"For now, we have our friend Jamal to deal with. Does that phone call change anything?"

Dan shook his head. "Not in the least."

When they arrived at Zerya's compound, he stepped out of the main building and welcomed them.

"My friend!" Zerya exclaimed as he wrapped his arms around Dan. "You come back. And, again, you bring a prisoner. You are busy men. Am I to become your dumping ground?"

Dan smiled at their host.

"No, my friend. But again, we need your help. You know we operate without any support. Did you receive a payment?"

Zerya beamed at him. "It's on its way. I was told it will be quite generous, helpful to our cause. You have powerful friends in Washington."

He pointed to Jamal, who was standing bruised and disheveled with a scowl on his face at the back of the truck.

"Who is this unfortunate?"

"I'll tell you later. For now, can you secure him for us? Maybe give him a little water?"

Zerya gave some orders in Kurdish, which neither Dan nor Uri could understand, and two of his men took Jamal off to the secure shed.

"Now come. I don't want to be rude, but the two of you do not look very good. And you do not smell so good. I think you need to refresh yourselves and eat something."

After cleaning up, a feast of a meal was laid out for Dan and Uri. It consisted of lamb, roasted, then simmered in a tomato and yogurt sauce, and served over bulgur pilaf. There was a large plate of dolma, vegetables stuffed in grape leaves, along with the ever-present flatbread. Strong black tea with generous amounts of sugar was served along with the meal. The quantities were large, and Dan and Uri ate until they were stuffed.

After the meal, the men sat back against the cushions placed on the floor. Dan related what had transpired. He didn't withhold any details. Zerya was a sympathetic host. He had no love for those who would try to harm Israel and his benefactor, the U.S.

"So, you will interrogate this man tomorrow? Find out who should be next on your list and go after them? You know you can't keep going around Iraq assassinating or kidnapping people without running into trouble. When you are in the south, I can't help you."

"We know that. This man led the attack in Washington. We expect to find out who led the attack in Jerusalem from him. Where that man is, we have no idea, but I don't think I can convince Uri here to go back to Israel with nothing to show for it. We had some images to help us identify those in the U.S., Uri's people have nothing to go on."

Zerya shrugged. "It is dangerous."

"Everything I do is dangerous," Uri said, finally speaking up. "I will tell my people of your generosity. Maybe we can cement closer ties. That could only increase your influence among your people."

Zerya smiled at him. "You don't need to point out the advantages of such friendship. We are a people in need of friends abroad. Our fight is against many countries, sometimes even yours," he looked at Dan. "But we take help where we can. Someday we will achieve our dream. For now, we make alliances where and when we can."

He paused to sip some tea.

"When you decide you must leave, I suppose you will want my help? Getting in, you could use your cover and, later my name. Getting out, may be harder to do."

"That might be prudent. If it is within your power."

Zerya smiled. "Much is within my power if I am careful."

The men continued late into the night, talking and drinking tea. Finally, Dan was openly yawning from their previous lack of sleep, and Zerya sent them off to comfortable beds.

In the prison shed, Jamal, locked in a small room, curled on the floor in the corner under a thin blanket, trying to not think of what the morning might bring.

Chapter 36

The following morning, Dan borrowed Zeyra's phone and called the number from Jane's earlier call.

"Jane here," came the familiar voice, now sounding guarded.

"Dan here. I'm on my host's phone. Are we okay to talk?"

"I'm going to switch phones again and call you right back."

The line went dead. A minute later, Zeyra's phone rang. Dan answered it.

"That's a lot of precautions. Has security been breached?"

"What I told you yesterday is being reinforced with increased surveillance. Fred and Warren alerted me to it two days ago. Their phones are being monitored."

"The powers that be will know you're hiding calls from them."

"Let them. What they don't know, they can't use. If I'm using my tradecraft to protect the integrity of my clandestine operation, I can make a strong case for that being legitimate."

"You're just being a good agent, that it?"

"That's it. Now tell me what you've got."

Dan brought Jane up to speed regarding their activities since entering Iraq.

"You think this Jamal will give you his counterpart in the Jerusalem explosion?"

"We think he probably knows. He may know of the other low-level operators as well."

"So, Uri gets the targets he and Eitan want. What's your next step?"

"Try to get more information about this Revenger character. I want to find him."

"And if you can't?"

"I also want the arms dealer. We have one tiny lead. He may be from the Balkans. We're hoping our guy, Jamal, can give us more."

Jane had no doubt that between Dan and Uri, the two could get their prisoner to talk. The only questions were how long it would take and how damaging it would be to Jamal. With so little regard for human life and so many civilians killed or injured, she had no sympathy for whatever techniques the two might use. Uri, she felt, would be the more aggressive.

"What will you do with him after you get the info you need?"

"You have to ask?"

"Not really. I just needed to confirm that you aren't going to try to bring him out."

"He's not coming out. His time is over. He made his choice and now pays the price."

Dan paused for a moment.

"It seems as though we're playing into the politicians' hands. Leave no one alive to bring embarrassing testimony to the public."

"For the moment. What you should do is record the prisoner. That tape could be leverage. Then ignore the directive I've been given. Go as high as you can, recording everything along the way."

"That's a good idea, I can do that."

"It's going to be hard to communicate. Those above me and Henry want nothing more than to monitor your activities. While they don't know exactly who you are, they do know that I run the most effective, deadly agent in the field. They're smart enough to have figured out what went on behind the public scenes from that last attack."

"Where I went too far according to you?"

Jane ignored the barb. "You can bet the DDO and Director understood what, if not who, was behind Congressman Greely's resignation. These are not stupid people."

"No. Just compromised, part of the system, part of the elite which it seems wants to preserve their position at the expense of everything else."

"Kind of like most human beings."

"It's just that they wield so much power, it affects us all."

"Stay abroad. Get this done. We'll figure out things later."

"Will do. Just don't hold it against me if I don't communicate much from here on."

"You've got my number. I'll keep this phone alive. If you can call, I'll always have a second phone to switch to and call you back."

"Copy that. I'll be in touch."

"Just take care of yourself."

"I always do, ma'am."

Dan smiled and ended the call. It was time to talk with their prisoner.

Waterboarding was a very old technique used for hundreds of years. It mimicked the experience of drowning, which created almost instant panic in the victim. One of the horrors for those on the receiving end was that, if done carefully, it could be repeated many times. The victim would inhale only a little water, which they could cough out, and vomit whatever was swallowed. One could not underestimate the extreme discomfort and stress of being unable to breathe, of being underwater, even if it was simulated.

Uri and Dan had a long discussion regarding which technique to use. Uri's desire for payback led him to favor cutting off fingers. Dan's argument about the efficacy of the waterboarding approach and how it left the victim in better shape to give them helpful information eventually won the point.

"They don't hold out for long," Dan said. "Three or four rounds at the most. I think then they feel they've withstood enough to allow them to capitulate without feeling like they've betrayed their cause."

"Do we keep him alive long enough to check out the info he gives us?"

Dan shook his head. "We can tell him that, but I can't impose on Zerya that much. We dispatch him when we're done. But if he thinks we'll check on his story and then come back, if he's misled us...well, that could be a deterrent against lying."

The men explained to Zerya what they were going to do. They needed some wood to construct a ramp that they could tie Jamal to, head down. It was this helpless and downward position that formed the basis for the experience he would suffer.

They constructed the waterboarding frame just outside the door to the room holding Jamal. He could hear the pounding of the nails and ponder what was in store for him. The experience only increased his dread even though he tried to remain calm and keep his panic under control.

When the frame was ready, they pulled Jamal out of the room. He stared at the ramp with wide eyes, unsure how it would be used.

At Dan's insistence, no one spoke. They forced Jamal onto the ramp, head down, tying his ankles to the top of the frame. He began to squirm around. Still, no one spoke. With quiet efficiency, Uri and Dan secured Jamal's arms to the sides of the ramp. They nailed small wooden blocks along each side of his head so he could not turn away. Lastly, they ran a strap over his mid-section, not too tight, but enough to further limit his movements.

Now Dan and Uri squatted down on each side of Jamal. Dan spoke, and Uri translated.

"I'm going to waterboard you. I haven't done this before." Dan was lying, but Jamal would not know. "If it goes right, you won't drown. If it goes wrong, you'll drown as if I had thrown you into a river with a concrete block tied around your legs. I will continue until you are ready to talk."

Jamal glared at Dan. He seemed to be suppressing his fright. "I have nothing to tell you, infidel. We were never told anything and don't know who was involved. Even if I did, I wouldn't tell you."

Dan listened to the short diatribe and gave Jamal an evil-looking smile.

"We shall see. We shall see how brave you are. I'm told that the most seasoned fighters cannot withstand more than four rounds."

With that, he got up.

Chapter 37

J amal made it to round four. After he came up spluttering and coughing the fourth time, he gasped out a plea to stop. Dan squatted down next to Jamal, who was still strapped to the board. He set his phone to record their words. With Uri translating, he spoke.

"I am surprised. You did as well as any other fighter. Are you ready to talk to us, tell us what you know?"

Jamal nodded as best he could while still immobilized by the platform. Dan stood, and the two men raised Jamal up, still tied to the plank. They took out the blocks holding his head in place.

"In case you decide you're tough enough to go another four rounds with me, we'll keep you strapped to the board."

"First," Uri said, "we want to know who led the Jerusalem operation. You were probably both trained together before splitting up."

Jamal quieted his coughing and tried to settle himself as best he could while still tied down.

"Usair Bashara."

"Where do we find Usair?"

"In Syria."

"More specific. He lives in what town? He has family there?"

"Just south of Aleppo, at the edge of a small village named Az Zarbah."

Uri looked at Dan, who gave him a shrug. Both men understood that this was not enough information. They could not go around Syria asking questions or directions. It was hostile territory for them, as dangerous as Iraq.

"Can you draw us a map?" Uri asked.

"*Balaa*," yeah.

"We will do that later," Uri said.

"What will you do with me? Later?"

"That depends on how helpful you are. You will be held here until your story checks out. If you have misled us, we will come back, and you will die slowly and painfully. We will find your family and kill them as well. We struck down one of your men on his front porch. That's where his wife found him with his brains lying on the floor."

Jamal looked at Uri with dead eyes. Dan could tell he believed the threat, but the man seemingly did not want to ask the ultimate question regarding his fate. *Our tendency to self-deceive goes deep*, he thought.

"What about Muntaqim?" Dan asked.

Jamal turned to him.

"You will not find him."

"We will try...and you will help us," Dan replied.

Jamal gave him a slight smile.

"You were close after you took me. He lives in a small farmhouse south of the road you took out of Ramadi. You passed right by him."

Dan looked at Uri.

"It will do you no good to go back there, even if I draw you a map. It is a well-guarded fortress. But hidden. You can't tell anyone important lives there. And to make it harder he moves around. He has heard of my capture by now and by the time you go back, he'll be somewhere else. He has places in Mosul, Al Qamishli, where you took my bomber. You may have crossed paths with him and didn't even know it."

His smile increased.

"He is not predictable. He moves around like a ghost, like the wind. You cannot guess or know. That is why no one can find him. He finds you."

"No man is impossible to find," Dan said. "Let's try the arms dealer. Who sold you the SEMTEX?"

"His name is Jetmir. That is all I know. He's from the Balkans."

"You did not meet with him?"

Jamal shook his head. "Muntaqim did. We just received the package and made the bomb.

Dan hid his frustration. More waterboarding would not cause the man to remember what he did not know.

"How did you get yourselves and the bomb into the U.S.?"

"We crossed the river from Mexico. We assembled the bomb in the U.S."

"The cartels helped?"

Jamal nodded. "Just to get us across."

Both men left Jamal alone and went outside to talk.

"Looks like we can't pin this Muntaqim down," Dan said.

"Agreed. Let's work on the rest of Jamal's team. We still have to go after them."

"Maybe he can give me a description of Muntaqim. We'll have it on tape, and I can have a forensic artist draw him. It may help us."

"Sounds like a, what do you call it, a wild-goose chase?"

"It could be. But I'll try anything. This is the guy at the top, next to Rashid. Maybe we can't get to Rashid, but we can get to his hit men, like we did with Scorpion."

The two went back inside and continued to interrogate their prisoner. When they were done, they stepped back outside.

"We got the names and towns for Jamal's team," Uri said. "I can set Eitan after them. It will take some time, but our intelligence will uncover them eventually. Time to send Jamal to his reward?"

"I have a question for him before we do."

They went back inside.

"Jamal," Dan said with Uri translating, "you've been helpful. We'll be holding you until we can check out your story."

"What will you do to me after you find I'm telling the truth?"

"What will you do if we set you free?"

Jamal looked at Dan. Both men could see he was considering his answer.

"I must remain true to myself, to my religion."

"And that means?"

"I will go back to jihad. It is my calling, my life."

"I understand. It is what I expected," Dan said.

He stepped around behind Jamal, pulled out his Sig Sauer P320, and shot him in the back of the head. It was over in a second. Jamal died instantly.

"Quick and clean," Uri said.

Dan nodded. "No way we could release him, even after cooperating."

"And remember what he helped plan and carry out."

Dan shook his head as he put his pistol back under his belt. "No end to the fight, it seems. No converting these guys."

"Maybe someday, when and if Islam goes through a reformation."

"That's a low probability considering all the reactionary forces pushing and pulling the religion," Dan said.

"Ours is not to solve the problem. Ours is to defend our people against the onslaught."

The two men left the shed, and Zerya's men came in to take Jamal's body away.

Chapter 38

With a description of Muntaqim, the name and location of Usair Bashara and his team, the place where the U.S. bomb had been assembled, and lastly, the name of the arms dealer, Dan and Uri were stuffed into a truck of produce and driven into northern Syria. Uri had called Eitan from Zerya's compound to tell him they would be crossing into Lebanon late that night, somewhere south of Homs. When the driver dropped them off, he would transmit the coordinates.

From Aleppo, they headed south. The neighborhoods were not friendly, with few Kurds living in the region. The truck bounced on through the night. Dan and Uri wedged themselves in between crates, trying to not get thrown around. It was hours of jarring and bruising until, south of Homs, the truck stopped.

They were on a back road with no town or houses in sight. The driver was at the rear as Uri and Dan untangled themselves from the crates of produce. They jumped off the back with their gear bags in hand.

"The border is on your right. You cross a small stream and cut the fence."

He handed Uri a pair of wire cutters and shook the men's hands.

"*Adhhabmae Allah*," Go with God. He turned, climbed back into the truck, and drove off, leaving a cloud of oil smoke behind.

Dan and Uri quickly stepped off the road and disappeared into the tall grass near the creek. They crouched down and waited, each man listening for any sounds that would indicate someone alerted to their presence. The night remained dark and still. After listening for a full five minutes, Uri took out his phone and called Eitan. With no greeting, he quietly spoke the coordinates into the phone and hung up.

"Now we wait," he whispered.

Dan nodded.

Two hours later, with dawn getting uncomfortably close, they heard an engine and saw headlights across the creek. A vehicle was slowly lumbering down what was probably a barely used path towards the stream. The beam from the headlights bounced up and down as the machine went through the potholes. As it got closer, the lights were extinguished. Both men listened; they could not see the vehicle anymore.

Then everything went quiet. The engine had shut off. After a minute, the headlights flashed twice and then went dark again. Uri nodded to Dan, and the two got up and pushed through the tall grass. They waded into the creek, which was only knee-deep. On the other side, they got to the fence; Uri took out the cutters and clipped the barbed wire. Once through, they headed south towards where they had last seen the headlights, keeping to the cover of the tall grasses near the creek.

When they reached a dirt trail, they could see the shadow of a vehicle parked fifty yards away from the border. Uri smiled in the dark and immediately started towards it. Dan followed with some worries of an ambush. In a minute, they were at the truck. Uri shook hands with the four men who got out, speaking quietly in Hebrew. The six of them crowded into the older SUV, with Dan and Uri stuffed into the third seat. The truck turned around and headed away from the border.

"What is next?" Uri asked in Hebrew.

"We head for the coast. Near the Turkish border," one of the men said. "We drop you off. A boat will pick you up on the beach. You must move fast and keep low. Get into the dunes quickly. You have towns on either side, but where we let you off, there is nothing but farm fields on the land side and dunes and beach on the seaside."

"If the surf is high?" Uri asked.

The man turned and gave him a smile. "You swim."

No one spoke anymore as the older SUV drove east towards the sea.

The man who had spoken to Uri now told them to get ready. They were on the Sea Road heading towards the border. They had passed a small airport and were now in an empty, unlit stretch of road.

"We stop at any moment now. When you get through the dunes to the beach, flash your light three times out to sea. You'll get two flashes back. Go up or down the beach if they are not in front of you. The boat will come ashore if the surf is not high. If it is, you go in and swim out to the boat."

He gripped Uri's hand.

"Good luck."

The SUV slowed and then stopped. Without another word, Uri and Dan grabbed their gear and slipped out of the rear seats onto the pavement. The vehicle immediately drove off; the two men crouched low and ran towards the dunes. Shortly, the dunes hid them from view, and they slowed their pace. They could hear the surf ahead and smell the salt water. Dan breathed deeply the wet, salty air, full of the aroma of seaweed and fish. It was the smell of freedom, extraction from enemy territory, and an opportunity, after so many days, to let his guard down.

When they got to the beach, they stood looking out to sea. Uri flashed his light three times and waited. Within moments, two flashes came back a couple of hundred yards to the north, out in the water. The two men set out on a jog up the beach. When they thought they were far enough, they stopped and watched.

"Doesn't look too rough," Dan remarked. The waves were about two feet high and breaking regularly at the shore. "Maybe we won't have to get wet."

They kept scanning the water and finally noticed a dark hull coming towards them, still to the north. The two adjusted their position. Soon, they could hear the outboard motor pushing the boat along. Just before reaching the beach, the operator cut the engine and pulled it up. The boat was now shoved forward by the waves and crunched on the shore. Two men got out and kept it from being turned sideways to the surf.

"*Maher*," one of the men said. "Quickly."

Dan and Uri splashed into the water, jumped over the gunnels, and sat in the bottom of the boat. The two men pushed the boat back to deeper water and then jumped in as the third man got the engine going in reverse. The whole maneuver took less than a minute, and they had backed clear of the surf line, turned around, and were motoring into the ocean and out of sight of the shore.

It took ten minutes of motoring to reach a fishing boat. The men climbed aboard, and the boat was hoisted out of the water on the stern davits. They then set farther out to sea before heading down the coast. Dan and Uri went below and hid in a small space that would not be discovered if any Lebanese agents stopped the local fishing boat.

Dawn brought them to Israeli waters, and everyone relaxed. Four hours later, they docked in Haifa. There, an official SUV met them, and they were off to Tel Aviv at high speed.

Chapter 39

It was just after noon when Dan and Uri were ushered into Eitan's office in the nondescript building in Tel Aviv. Both men were exhausted. Food and drink were laid out on a table; it looked like they'd get no sleep until they were debriefed.

Dan used Eitan's encrypted cell phone to call Jane. She answered and, after hearing it was Dan, hung up and called Eitan's number back.

"You're back in Tel Aviv. Good."

"Made it out alive. You using a burner phone? Do you want to further explain what's going on over there?"

"Are you alone?"

"Negative on that."

"I better wait. As much as I like Eitan, I don't want to share my dirty laundry with him. I'll catch you up later. You should not come back to the U.S. for a while."

"No problem with that. It's not what I wanted to do anyway. Let me give you some of what we learned. Write it down, but you may not want to share...yet."

Dan told Jane all they had learned from Jamal, including the fate of the three men they had encountered.

"We left a hard-to-follow trail, but everyone will know what happened to Jamal. We had a serious gunfight with his supporters and left many of them out in the desert dead or wounded and without transportation. If any get back, they'll have quite a tale to tell, especially to Muntaqim. Though our captive said he probably already knows what happened."

"After you debrief, you'll go back to Venice?"

"Yeah. Then I'm going after the arms dealer, Jetmir."

"He'll be hard to find."

"I have my sources."

"Gaspard?"

"Probably not. More likely my friend in Moscow, Kusnetsov."

"The gangster. Some friend."

"I saved his life, and the life of his wife and daughter. I think I can rely on that. Unless he has a financial stake in this guy, he'll tell me what he knows."

"I hope you're right. Call me when you get to Venice."

Jane ended the call.

Two grueling hours later, Eitan finished picking their brains about the terrorists and how they could locate them.

"Both of you have done well. You've brought honor on METSADA. Again, we justify our existence and budget. I will bring Mossad into the effort now that we have a direction. Do not worry, Uri, we will find the rest of them and eliminate them."

He turned to Dan.

"Thank you for your help. How can I repay you?"

"Let me get some rest, then I need you to fly me back to Milan. I left my car there it seems like ages ago. My gear bag has my weapons so you will have to get that through customs as your diplomatic property."

"That is no problem. Where will you go after that?"

Dan smiled and shook his head. "Somewhere. It's not for you to know."

"How do we get in touch with you? If we need to?"

"You can't. I'll check in with Uri. If you need me, you tell Uri. But I'm heading out on my own. You have your list to go after, I have mine. And I've got resources to track them down."

Eitan smiled and nodded. "You want to keep your moves secret? Don't worry. We won't interfere. If you need our services or support, call Uri. We have safe houses in various countries. They could be helpful to you. I can also send Uri if you need him."

"I want to stay here, boss," Uri said. "See this through. If we eliminate these guys quickly, it will strike fear in their hearts. We can sow seeds of reluctance for future missions of this type."

"We can only hope," Eitan said with a sad look.

Uri went over to the bar and poured three glasses of brandy. He handed them around.

"Here's to a successful mission. May all terrorists die quickly and violently."

"May they not sleep well at night before they do," Dan added.

The three men downed the strong liquor. Then Dan and Uri headed off to rest and sleep in the rooms provided.

Five hours later, there was a knock on Dan's door. He opened it to find Uri standing there, still dressed in his dirty clothes.

Uri looked at Dan, who was also dressed. "Can't sleep either?"

"I did for a while, but the mission isn't done yet...at least for me."

"I feel the same. Seems like I'm wasting time napping here in Eitan's 'fortress'. Let's go out."

Dan grabbed his jacket, and the two men descended the stairs and into the streets.

"We can't hit any posh spots, dressed like this. We have to take our business to the less reputable places," Uri said.

"As long as they have good food and drink."

Uri winked. "I won't let you down."

Uri led them to a bar called Uganda on the southern end of Tel Aviv's south side. It combined a café, bar, book, and record store. Along with these offerings, something else was usually going on: an art or comic book exhibit or an experimental band playing. The format was informal, which meant Dan and Uri didn't stand out too badly in their soiled clothes.

After ordering two craft beers and a shot of vodka each, they looked at the menu. Dan could not help scanning the crowd to note exits and danger points, along with anyone giving them too much attention.

"Good beer," Dan said after taking a sip. He lifted his glass to Uri. "Here's to a successful mission."

Uri responded and took a long drink from his glass. He smacked his lips after.

"That tastes good." He picked up his shot glass and downed the vodka in one gulp. "Work's not finished, though."

Dan nodded as he downed his vodka shot. They began to peruse the menu when a band started up. The sound was cacophonous, loud, and full of discord.

"Fuck," Dan shouted across the small table to Uri. "Can't talk. Can hardly hear myself."

"You're right." He put down the menu. "Luckily we have more choices."

Uri put down some bills for the shots and beers, drained his glass, and stood up.

"Let's go."

Chapter 40

The men walked outside and savored the moment. The street wasn't quiet but seemed so compared to the raucous noise coming from inside the club.

"I must be getting old," Dan said.

Uri laughed. "I know I am. But that was just abusive. We're going to have a generation with hearing issues."

"Listen to us. We sound like some old farts for sure."

Uri called for an Uber car. Ten minutes later, they were on their way to Allenby Street.

"Lots of bars and clubs here, so if we don't like one, we can just walk to the next."

"Sounds like you're planning on keeping me out late tonight."

Uri turned to Dan with a sly grin on his face. "You've had enough rest. It's time to enjoy that fact that we're still alive, not like the other bastards we encountered."

The driver dropped them off in front of Lucifer.

"Quite a name for a bar," Dan remarked.

"Hard liquor and smoke is their motto. I like that."

The bar was dark and smoky, just as the motto indicated. Dan figured they'd find out about the hard liquor soon enough. The music was rock with an underground flavor but listenable, unlike the experimental band that had started up in Uganda.

Another round of craft beers followed by Uri's favorite chaser, Tubi 60, a potent liquor that many felt produced effects similar to ecstasy.

"L'chaim," Uri said.

"I'm going light on this. I remember the last time."

Uri winked at him. "Such an old man."

After another round of drinks, they ordered some food. Uri looked around. The clientele seemed to be wide-ranging in age.

"We don't stand out. I see people from their twenties to their sixties here."

"Except for our dirty and stink-laden clothes."

"Who cares? As I said, tonight is for celebrating. Tomorrow, we go back to hunting."

Dan raised his glass. Soon, the food arrived, and the two men mixed eating and talking about what the future might bring either of them. It was past midnight when Uri ordered two double expressos to go with some brandies. After finishing the drinks, he grabbed the waiter and gave him his credit card.

"Put a big tip on this for me. My employer is paying."

The man grinned and thanked him. After paying the bill, they got up and walked out onto Allenby Street. The pedestrian traffic, even at that late hour, was heavy. Many people in various stages of inebriation or general partying mode strode past them.

"Come on," Uri said, taking Dan's arm. The two men walked down the block.

"Where to now?" Dan asked.

"Sputnik. It's a good place to wind up the evening. I'm going to need something more to eat soon."

They walked down the street. Uri turned into a narrow alley off the road. At the end was a graffiti-laden door that led into a sunken outdoor garden space. The walls were done in an old abandoned factory look. Farther inside, the décor was defiantly non-décor with interesting art inter-spaced with funky adornments. The atmosphere was dark, punctuated by bright lights dominated in red. There was a crowd, even at this late hour. Dan noticed the sound system, which was deep and pervasive. The music was loud, but not to the point of being unable to talk. Most patrons looked to be in their twenties and thirties, with some older hipster-style people sprinkled in.

They found a table in a corner, and Uri ordered pizza slices for the two of them, something Sputnik was noted for, along with two draft beers.

"The carbs help soak up the alcohol," Uri said as he stuffed a slice into his mouth.

"Or so you're told."

After finishing their pizza and beer, Uri ordered a round of brandies and more coffee. They then relocated to a quieter table. It was getting to be early morning, and only the serious night owls were still out.

"The casual pub crawlers have long gone home and are safe asleep in their beds," Uri said. "They have to get up this morning and go to work. We, however, have already completed our work...or at least a good part of it."

He paused to examine Dan's face.

"Something is bothering you, my friend. We should be celebrating a successful mission including getting out of Iraq alive. Yet you seem distracted, worried even. What's up?"

Dan shrugged.

"No, you don't get off that easily," Uri said. "We risked death together, now more than once. You're my partner. Someone whose hands I'd put my life in. I want to know what's bothering you and a shrug for an answer won't do it."

Dan sighed and leaned back in his chair. He took a sip of his brandy and then coffee. Then, he poured the brandy into the cup.

"Easier that way," he remarked. "It's just that we both have unfinished business and I'm anxious to get about it. Mine involves digging through the Balkans to find some fucking arms dealer. When I find him, killing him will be easy. But keeping him alive will be the challenge. I need him to lead me to Muntaqim."

Uri's smile faded. "He may not shed much light on our Revenger. If the guy is as smart as I think he is, then the arms dealer won't know any more than Jamal did."

He leaned forward to stare into Dan's face.

"Muntaqim will be a hard SOB to find. It may take years, but we won't stop looking, I can promise you that. I won't let Eitan, or anyone else that may fill his shoes forget."

"Your government is good at that. Mine seems to want to cover this up. Take care of the low-level operators and don't look too deep. It might disturb money relationships."

Dan shook his head as if to clear it.

"That's just fucked up. I sometimes wonder why I risk my life."

"Because someone has to stop them," Uri said in a quiet voice.

"Yeah. But they keep on coming and my government seems to not want to know or support what we do."

"They keep on coming, so we keep on killing. Sooner or later, we'll slow things down. The word is already out about you. Of course, no one knows who you are, but the jihadists certainly know someone is killing them...and very effectively, I should add."

Uri paused while staring at his friend.

"I could go with you, if that will help. I can get Eitan to approve the mission."

Dan shook his head. "No, you stay here. Find Usair, Jamal's counterpart, and the rest of his men. That will make your government happy."

"And me."

Dan nodded. "This is my mission. I need to go it alone."

Uri pondered Dan's words. After a few moments, he looked up.

"I will have Eitan give you a list of safe houses and contacts he mentioned. We have some in the Balkans. I know your people do also, but it doesn't hurt to have options."

Dan raised his cup. "Thanks. I appreciate that."

Uri raised his glass. "I appreciate your saving my life, in more ways than one."

Chapter 41

Rashid had thought long and hard about the death of Scorpion and the disruption of so many of his plots, unlike the success of these most recent attacks. He knew that the man, or men that had killed Scorpion were probably American. The ones who killed his assassin seemed to have access to superior intelligence. He needed to find this man or these men.

It would be a long, expensive, and possibly futile search. Could he find this needle in the haystack? Rashid had a research team begin looking for all Americans living in European cities. The number would be huge, but Rashid had significant resources and, by necessity, much patience. He instructed the team to start with cities around the Mediterranean. The search would spread out from there if he got no hits.

They were to look for males, single or in a group. Not married men or men with families. This assassin was probably not a family man. He hoped that, eventually, he would uncover this ghost that many considered a jinn or supernatural creature in Arab lore.

His satisfaction at two successful missions was diminished by news of the deaths and disappearance of many of the men involved. Muntaqim had informed him of three men involved in the U.S. attack who had been killed or had disappeared. It reminded Rashid again of the intelligence capabilities of the U.S. Someone had seen one or more of the men, had identified them somehow, and then had found them in Syria and Iraq.

But to Muntaqim's credit, the man's tactic of being unpredictable and using simple, speedy plans seemed to have worked. If this was how his war would go, he was pleased. *Simple is better.* Muntaqim's slogan ran through his head.

The ringing of his private cell phone interrupted his thoughts. Only a small few had access to this number, and no one called it without serious reason.

"*Marhaba,*" Hello, Rashid said as he picked up his phone.

"It is your general," Muntaqim said. "I need to speak with you in person. Let us meet tomorrow at the usual time and place."

It was a cryptic call, giving no information to anyone listening. The two men had established a meeting spot in Sakakah, Saudi Arabia. The town was northwest of Riyadh and about 100 miles from the Iraq border. It was nearly 400 driving miles from Muntaqim's house near Ramadi. Muntaqim could make the drive overnight to meet Rashid at 11:00 a.m., their prearranged hour. For Rashid, the journey from his offices in the capital would take only an hour by private jet.

"What is it that calls for us to meet?" Rashid asked when they were together. "We do not want to do this frequently."

"You know," Muntaqim said, "that two men from the operation have disappeared. I can only assume they were killed. Now a third, the man who was in charge of the U.S. operation has been captured. He knows much, including my location. I will have to leave my home and stay on the move. It is more exposure, but better than sitting still waiting for an attack."

"You can be attacked? In Iraq where you live?"

"The Americans can do much—"

"But surely they would not try to mount an operation in Iraq."

"No, but their intelligence is very good and they are not afraid to use drones. But they might choose to help the Israelis, who could and would mount such an operation."

Rashid was silent for a moment. The men were seated in a private compound located amid irrigated fields full of olive trees. Rashid had acquired the property years ago. It produced a nice profit and gave him a quiet, secluded location to meet warriors like Muntaqim, men whom he could not host in his offices in the capital.

"I am beginning a search for these Americans. The one, or ones, who have been disrupting my plans. They could not foil this latest attack, but seem to be able to get on your trail. Much too quickly for my comfort."

"And mine as well. Something more is going on. I can feel it."

"What you spoke of earlier?"

Muntaqim nodded.

Rashid didn't comment on Muntaqim's theory. He did not believe such tales, but if his general kept being effective, he was happy to allow him to operate in his disorganized manner. Rashid went on to describe the search he had begun.

"It is like looking for a particular rock in a desert full of rocks," Muntaqim said.

"It may be, but with enough resources and patience, it can be accomplished."

"You have the resources, but how much damage will occur while you are being patient?"

Rashid gave Muntaqim a sharp look. "Do you offer a better path?"

"No *zaeim*. It is only that I will have to be very careful until you are fortunate enough to unearth who is chasing us." He took a sip of his tea. "And if you find out who, let me be the one to kill him."

Rashid gave his general a grim smile. "I would not have it any other way."

Chapter 42

When Dan got home, he carefully inspected the threads he had strung across the doors and frames as a low-tech backup to his hi-tech surveillance system. Nothing had been disturbed. He walked through the large house, checking the windows as well. The design of the house had always pleased him, an excellent sampling of European luxury tucked into a forgotten neighborhood outside of Venice.

He checked his security cameras, not only around the inside of the house, but throughout the large lot. They were hidden in the trees and shrubs as well as mounted on the building. They would capture anyone coming onto the property well before they attempted entry to the house. With the cameras hidden, there were no clues that this home had exceptional levels of security, which would have heightened the interest of anyone trying to locate him. Nothing showed up on the videos.

After a fitful night, Dan got up and stretched. He decided to not take a long bike ride but loosen up and work out at home. He was feeling protective and would be leaving shortly, so he wanted to maximize his time in his house.

The search for the arms dealer necessitated a visit to an old enemy and now, hopefully, a friend, Yevgeni Kusnetsov.

He knew where to find him. It involved traveling to Moscow, something Dan didn't relish, especially with the current regime and the war in Ukraine. The President had become more dictatorial since the war had started, and not gone so well. Dissident voices were stilled quickly and, sometimes, brutally.

Jane was working to fast-track his visa to enter Russia, using his "Official" level passport indicating he was a security consultant for their embassy. This passport gave him certain privileges, including getting a visa in days rather than weeks or months.

I wonder what Zhenya is doing through all of this? Dan knew the gangster would find a way to make money out of the situation, no matter the outcome.

He spent the day puttering around the house, trying to think and act domestically. Still, his mind kept wandering back to preparations for his trip. He would need to get some leads from Kusnetsov to follow. From there, it would be a matter of tracking his quarry. Dan felt the familiar sense of confidence and a growing excitement over the chase and the ultimate capture of his prey. The feeling kept crowding out his domestic thoughts until, with a sigh, he gave it up and began to check the weapons he would take with him. The Range Rover was his choice of vehicle. It was comfortable, versatile on different roads, and had much more room for his weapons and ammunition in its hidden compartment.

Dan included his Sako TRG 42. He spent some time cleaning and checking the rifle and then took it apart and packed it away for the trip. His choice of weapons also included the familiar M4 carbine, a better weapon for close-in fighting. Next, he picked out a Sig Sauer P320 9mm from his pistol collection. As a last thought, he added his suppressed Ruger Mark IV .22 semi-automatic pistol.

It was an up-close killing machine, as quiet as a BB gun, giving off a soft, short puff of sound with each shot.

With weapons selected and packed away, Dan sat down after a quick meal to savor one of his favorite whiskeys, Jefferson's Ocean. A bourbon sent to sea in casks. The changing temperatures and constant motion aged the bourbon in ways a rickhouse could not. It might have been his imagination, but Dan always thought he could detect a bit of sea salt in the finish.

Three days later, Dan got a message that his visa had arrived at the consulate in Milan. Per Dan's emphatic instructions, nothing was sent to his home or even a post office box near Venice. He wanted to leave no trail that could create any undue interest in the area where he lived. This meant a drive in his modified Peugeot along the semi-anarchic roads of Italy, playing with all the expensive super-sedans that flew down the roadways, flaunting speed limits.

When Dan returned home, he packed and set out early the next day. The fastest way to Russia was to drive northeast along the Adriatic coast, through Austria, Slovakia, and to Brest in Belarus. At Brest, he picked up a major highway that took him south of Minsk and on to Smolensk in Russia. From there, it was a straight drive into Moscow, where he hoped to find Kuznetsov.

David Nees

Chapter 43

The Wild Nights Club was located in an upscale area with expensive restaurants and stores, but it was also known as a neighborhood populated by the *bratva*, or brotherhood. The club fit in well with its surroundings, being upscale as well as large. Inside, it had three separate bars. They ranged from the expensive and classy to the noisy and touristy. There was a quiet bar with posh décor where important people could meet and talk business. They were safe from the possibility of being interrupted by inquisitive reporters or lesser people who were politely but firmly turned away. There was a noisy disco-themed bar that also sported a dance floor complete with flashing lights. Farther back in the large building was a strip bar where girls, all young and all with exquisite bodies, pole danced and gyrated. They spent the night getting their thongs stuffed with money—Euros and dollars being most appreciated. For extra money, they would also perform the standard lap dance. For even more money, some would take a patron upstairs to one of the private rooms for an intimate session of sexual activity. The police didn't interfere since the mafia kept things well under control.

In the past, the bar had made enormous profits. The liquor was watered down in the disco bar. The girls in the strip bar were adept at working the patrons into buying overpriced, diluted drinks, plus they had to hand over a percentage of their tips to the management. Tales of severe punishment floated among them about girls who tried to scam the managers. Few who heard the stories disbelieved them. As a result, there was little non-compliance in sharing their earnings. Some of the girls were introduced into more regular sexual activities, winding up in a more controlled and desperate life as a prostitute.

All the girls were housed in dorms owned by Kuznetsov and charged rent for the privilege. In a sense, the gangster had a captive workforce from which he could continuously extract money. Some girls bought into the system and rose to management positions when they got tired or too old to dance and attract large tips. Some helped recruit new blood to keep the system going.

When Dan arrived in Moscow, he checked into a small hotel. It was outside the main tourist district and catered to Russians rather than tourists. Still, Dan was cautious of hidden cameras. One could never be sure in Russia, especially Moscow, whether or not one was being monitored by the authorities.

After unpacking, he put on a light sweatshirt and went down to the lobby and out onto the sidewalk. He started to jog down the city streets. It was a good way to get to know a neighborhood and also an excellent technique to get privacy for a phone call. After about a mile, Dan started to walk and cool down.

He stopped at a small park. It was empty. The pale afternoon sun shone through the trees, creating dappled shadows on the walkway. Dan punched in the last number he had for Kuznetsov. The phone rang five times, and then someone picked up.

"Da?"

It was a woman's voice.

"I'm looking for Yevgeny Kuznetsov, this is a friend calling."

"Who is this?"

"Victor, Victor James."

"Victor!" The woman's voice was now filled with enthusiasm. "This is Duscha, Zhenya's wife."

"Duscha. It is good to hear your voice. Can you tell me how to reach Yevgeny?"

"Certainly."

She proceeded to give Dan a number.

"He will be surprised to hear from you."

Dan gave her his best wishes and hung up. *Off to a good start*. If Yevgeny felt about him like his wife did, he'd have no problem getting his help, even in these tumultuous times.

After glancing around to make sure no one was watching him, Dan called Yevgeny. A gruff voice that Dan recognized answered the call.

"Yevgeny, this is Victor James calling."

There was a moment of silence on the other end.

"Victor? Is it really you? Tell me where we met."

"At your dacha. You were in a bit of trouble. I took care of the problem. After, we had a bit of an adventure."

"Adventure, indeed. How did you get this number? And where are you?"

"I called your old number and your wife answered. I'm in Moscow."

"Duscha. I told her not to save those phones. She is always wanting to be frugal. I will have to dispose of them myself."

"You change phones often?"

"One must be very careful, especially these days. It is a small price to pay for security." He paused momentarily and yelled something in Russian to someone in the room.

"It is hard to find good help these days. Why are you here? There is something you want, *da*?"

"Yes. I need your help, but not on the phone."

"Of course. You come to the club. You remember where it is?"

"Yes."

"Come tonight. Someone will meet you at the door. We'll have dinner here and talk about old times and why you think you need me to help you."

"I can be there in an hour."

"Otlichno." Excellent. "Don't bring any weapons into the club. My men will frisk you and they may not like finding a gun, in spite of what I tell them."

Chapter 44

An hour later, a cab dropped Dan off at the Wild Nights Club. Dan dressed in casual slacks, a pullover shirt and jacket. He wore sturdy shoes that had nearly the support of boots yet didn't look out of place in a bar.

Upon entering, a large man who looked like a bouncer greeted him just inside the main door. The man eyed him, and Dan stepped forward.

"Ya khochuuvidet' Yevgeny Kuznetsov." I want to see Yevgeny Kuznetsov.

The man gestured for him to follow and turned away from the lobby. In a side hallway, he motioned for Dan to spread his arms. He then patted him down. Satisfied, he turned again, without a word, and led Dan up the main staircase. On the second floor, they walked down a hallway with multiple doors, which Dan guessed were offices. At one, the man knocked and then opened the door.

"Voyti," enter, came a voice. He opened the door and gestured for Dan to go inside.

The door closed behind Dan, and a large, bear-like man stood up from behind an enormous desk.

"Victor!" Yevgeny spread his arms in welcome.

"Yevgeny," Dan said. He stepped forward.

Kuznetsov stepped out from behind the desk. A dark look flashed across his face. "You didn't come here to kill me, did you?"

Dan stopped, surprised by such a question. "Zhenya, I gave you life, saved you and put my life back in your hands. Why would I come now to harm you?" His voice carried a mix of hurt and questioning in it.

Yevgeny's smile reappeared, and he stepped forward, grabbing Dan in his large arms. "I am just kidding you. Making fun." He clamped him tight and thumped him soundly on his back.

Yevgeny stood back and eyed Dan. "You have not aged much since we last met. I thought you might be dead now with the life you lead."

"It wasn't all that long ago. But you're right, maybe I should be."

"Come, sit down," Yevgeny gestured towards two stuffed leather chairs with a table between them. "We must talk. About what you are doing here, what you are involved in, and what you want from me."

He picked up his desk phone and spoke into it. A minute later, a scantily clad woman entered with a tray of caviar, thinly sliced black bread, two glasses, and a bottle of vodka. She set it on the table and left without a word. Yevgeny's eyes followed her as she left the room with her bottom swaying in a tantalizing manner.

He sighed. "It's nice to be around such beauty, but tiresome as well. One is always tempted and the objects are willing. Still, one has work to do, businesses to run."

He sighed, leaned forward, and poured each of them a half-glass of vodka. Then he loaded a piece of bread with caviar and took a large bite, followed by a big swallow of vodka.

"Ah," he said and settled back into his chair. "Victor, if that is your real name, eat. It is the finest Caspian caviar available."

Dan followed suit and savored the salty fish eggs spread on the robust bread. "It's very good," he remarked.

"Da." Yevgeny repeated the process and then looked directly at Dan. "You must need something. Tell me what it is. I'm not sure I can help you since we work on different sides of the law. I am respected for my power, not for my citizenship qualities."

"We live in much the same world. One of dark people with dark motives, so I think you will be able to help."

"The same world, but on different sides of the fence that runs through it."

Dan took a detour in the conversation. "Before I get to my request, tell me how things are in Russia and more to the point, here in Moscow?"

Yevgeny shook his head and poured himself another half-glass of vodka. "It is a bad time with the war in Ukraine. Many young people, especially the males, have fled or are trying to flee. Everyone is more tense. You can feel it on the streets. I see it here in the club. Not so many people come now and almost no tourists.

"Some young people demonstrate in the streets." He paused as if to think. "They are brave...but stupid. Most are arrested and if not put away, given a bad experience."

He held out his hands.

"The result is I am losing money, but what can I do? The police still require the same level of bribes, even if business is suffering."

Dan smiled. "Zhenya, I can't believe you are losing money. I am sure you have figured out how to make money out of this war."

Yevgeny smiled back at him. "I have ways, other avenues. One must be flexible and creative. Be important to those in power. Important enough for them to pay you for your services."

"Are you supplying arms?"

Kuznetsov smiled again. "It would not be prudent for me to answer that question. Are you working for Interpol, trying to trap me?"

Dan shook his head. "No. I have my thoughts on this war, especially what it is doing to civilians, but there are other things on my mind."

Yevgeny looked across the room, seeming to stare at nothing. "Yes, that *is* sad. Little people always get hurt by these things." He looked back at Dan. "That is why I decided early in life to never be one of the 'little people'."

He grabbed another slice of bread and slathered it with caviar.

"Tell me what you need. Later we will have a great meal in honor of your visit and I will think about what you ask of me."

Dan paused for a moment. How much would Yevgeny help? Dan had ended the man's desire to avenge his son's death by killing him. He had placed his life in Yevgeny's hands when the gangster was in his control after saving his life. With that gesture, he had managed to break the cycle of distrust and vengeance. But in the end, they worked towards different goals, which someday could conflict. Dan hoped that time would not come too soon.

"You heard about the bombings in Washington and Jerusalem?"

"*Da.*"

"I'm trying to find those responsible for them."

"So you can bring your vengeance to them?"

Dan nodded. "It is important to my country and to me personally to strike back. The terrorists must know that the arm of the U.S. is long and can reach them wherever they hide."

"But they will not stop. You cannot make them fear you that much. They invite death. They long for paradise."

"Maybe. The ones higher up may not have such a martyr's view. You and I both know many of them are corrupt. They do not practice what they preach."

The conversation had been going on in a mix of Russian and English, which worked well for both men, neither being especially fluent in each other's language.

"You need help? Or just information?"

"I need to know who supplied the bombers with SEMTEX. They used a lot of it. All I know is that his name is Jetmir and he comes from the Balkans."

Chapter 45

The two men moved to a private dining room on the mezzanine level of the club. It was a weekday, and the crowd was thin. True to his word, Yevgeny had a grand selection of food brought for them to savor and enjoy.

With a clap of his hands, the meal began. Yevgeny smiled as the servers marched in with much ceremony. The meal started with a bowl of borscht. Following this course, a platter of roast duck made its entrance. After placing it on the table, the chef dramatically and expertly carved the duck. He arranged the slices of meat with careful precision on the platter. Fresh potatoes were gently placed around the platter, forming a border to the cuts. Selections of red and white wines were on the table, along with the ever-present bottle of vodka.

The two men ate in silence. Dan marveled at the effort Yevgeny went to. Was he aping the grandness of the czarist era?

When they had finished and drunk some wine, there was another ceremonious process as the chef entered proudly carrying a platter of sliced boar accompanied by garden vegetables. The platter was almost a work of art, beautifully arranged with vegetables of contrasting colors and textures forming a colorful border around the main course. Following the platter came a selection of small gravy boats with *au jus* and various mustards, jellies, and other condiments to go with the roast.

After an hour of eating with only small conversation, the meal finished with blinis served with honey, a dollop of fresh whipped cream, and fruit compote. With the dessert came strong black coffee and brandy.

"You've made quite a feast for me. But don't you include Duscha in such meals? I would think she'd get mad at you for not bringing her here," Dan said.

"She knows I'm working late because of your visit. So, in a sense, it's your fault." Yevgeny gave Dan an evil-looking grin. "But I had a selection of all of this," his arm swept over the table, "sent over to our house so she and my daughter are well-fed and happy."

"Duscha knows of your work, right? I mean that you are a gangster and head of a major organization of gangsters."

Yevgeny gave Dan a critical look. "You are direct, are you not? Yes, Duscha knows. She understands this is our life. She knew before marrying me, so there was no misunderstanding. My wife appreciates the luxuries my work provides as well as the protection against the disasters that seem to afflict Russia."

His face grew more serious.

"How about you? You have not kept up with Christina?"

Christina was an internationally known concert pianist whom Dan had fallen in love with and now could not see.

"She is playing this weekend in St. Petersburg. We could go, you and I. She has gotten much more dynamic and expressive in her playing since the two of you were together. Exotic rumors still float around the music community of how a mysterious man, a spy or assassin, opened her heart to play with more feeling. They are never spoken openly, only in hushed tones."

He took a sip of his brandy and coffee.

"I am still a great fan of hers. Especially when she plays Rachmaninov—"

He stopped abruptly. Dan's face reflected intense pain as a wave of grief swept over him. It came unexpectedly, without warning.

"Is something wrong my friend?" Yevgeny asked. His voice now full of concern.

Dan shook his head. His stomach spasmed as he fought to catch his breath and get control over his body. He saw Yevgeny watching him closely.

"You still have feelings for her, *da*? There is still a place for her in your heart."

Dan shook his head without answering.

"I don't believe you, my friend. You act so noble, so much the warrior, unreachable, unaffected by love and emotion, but I see through you. You are grieving, still sad about your self-inflicted loss."

Dan got himself under control, and his anger began to rise. "It was you that broke into our world. You who sent men to kill me, bring danger to her."

Yevgeny gave Dan a cautious look. "That was when I thought you were responsible for my son's death. I did not know then what I was to learn later, including how you would save my life."

"While you ruined mine."

"No. Your life was ruined when you recovered your memory. The world was always going to find you. And when it did, you knew the only way to protect Christina was to confront it. That is why you came to Moscow."

He paused as Dan digested what he said.

"And it was Lecha that attacked Christina." He paused before adding, "And you took care of him."

Dan nodded, now feeling a bit calmer. "I'm sure my killing him increased your business as well."

Yevgeny gave him a broad smile. "It did. Another competitor, and one who tried to kill me, gone from the business." He tipped his brandy to Dan. "I have much to thank you for."

Dan didn't return his smile or toast.

"I did not mean to make this evening unpleasant for you," Yevgeny continued.

Dan shook his head. "It is just that the loss comes to me at times and is overwhelming."

"You could not stay with her? Run off to do your assassinating and then go back to hide out with your love?"

"The worlds collide. Lecha showing up was proof of that." Dan paused for a moment. "And the look on her face..."

"She was there? When you killed Lecha?"

Dan nodded. His voice was strained as he continued. "It was a look...a look of horror. It made me feel dirty, somehow wrong, even though I had just saved our lives. What happened was so foreign to her. I could not live with that look, live with her now that she saw firsthand the violence of my world."

Dan took a gulp of his brandy.

"Enough, Zhenya. Let's not talk of this anymore. Will you help me find this Jetmir?"

"I know of him. Give me a few days and I will track him down. From what I know, he is a capable man and takes much caution in his work. He will be hard to get to"

Yevgeny looked at Dan's hard, determined face. "But of course, you will be able to reach him. Do you kill him or take him prisoner?"

"There is much I want to learn from him, but in the end, he will die for his involvement."

"I hope we do not find ourselves up against each other."

Dan looked at his host for a long time, thinking about what the man had just said. "We have trust between us now, hard-earned. That could change. Things never stay the same forever. Your business, running your enterprises, making your bribes, maybe killing your rivals, is none of my business. You are not a terrorist trying to attack my country, trying to kill our people."

"But I could be arming those who do." Yevgeny took a sip of his brandy. "What if I had sold the SEMTEX?"

Dan stared hard at the gangster. "It is useless for us to go down that path. Let us be thankful that such an issue did not come up between us."

Yevgeny scowled back at Dan's glare. After a long moment, his face softened. He raised his glass of brandy *"Vashezdorov'ye!"* To your health.

Dan slowly smiled and returned the salute.

Later, Dan walked out into the chilly late spring air of the Moscow night. He refused Yevgeny's car and started off on foot. The pain of loss started creeping back into him. Moscow was an integral part of the web of events that led to his break with Christina and the loss of their relationship. He felt the burden of his isolation. The responsibility of who he was and how he could not ask anyone to become part of his world which was so dangerous.

Still, he was tempted. To see her again, even from afar—unseen... He shook his head. It would only open the wound in his heart. And making his presence known to her...to what end? It would probably cause her much stress. Sadly, he let the thought go. *She probably has someone by now.*

Then he smiled at a sudden thought that broke into his mind. Kuznetsov spoke about him awakening the emotions in Christina, melting the Ice Queen, but he realized that she had also taught him about love. It was painful, especially in the parting, but what she gave back to him opened him up to allow Jane deeper into his life. While Christina left a void that would remain, she helped him find someone who had become his lifeline to sanity.

His mind drifted back to his training days shortly after Jane had recruited him. During that time, Dan had begun to understand the world he was entering. A world where there was no exit. A world where one could not go home at night to the everyday life of a private citizen. Now this was the reality of his life. He chastised himself for feeling pity.

Take what she gave you, what you had together and be grateful. Feeling sorry will only make you weak. Let it go.

Chapter 46

Two days later, days during which Dan spent his time visiting the museums in Moscow, trying not to think about Christina, playing a concert only seven hours away by car, he received a message from Yevgeny asking him to come to the club that same day. Upon arriving, someone again escorted Dan to Yevgeny's office on the mezzanine level.

"I have information for you," Yevgeny said with a satisfied smile when Dan entered the office. "This Jetmir lives in Tirana. But he disappeared for about a week right after the bombings. Then he showed up again back in the capital. The man lives and operates out of that city. I could not confirm that he dealt the SEMTEX, but you already have come to that conclusion."

"I've gone through the information. He's the ultimate source. You have an address?"

"I do. But he is not easily captured. His office area could be better described as a fortress. And his home is also well-secured. Cameras and guards in both places. Plus, he has the support of the local police who he pays off."

"I think I can get around those issues."

Yevgeny shrugged. "Not so easily if you want to capture him. Killing from a distance would be easier, but I don't think that is what you're after."

"You guessed correctly." Dan paused for a moment, not wanting to be impolite. "I want to thank you for the wonderful dinner, but I have to go now. I need to get this mission done quickly. It has been too long."

"That means you won't stay for the concert in St. Petersburg?"

Dan shook his head. His emotions were now under better control. "That would not be wise, for either her *or* me."

Yevgeny sighed. "I'm sorry about that. I know what comfort a good woman can be, especially in our business."

"Zhenya, we are not in the same business. But you are correct. It is just not meant to be with Christina."

An hour later, Dan was checked out of his hotel and on his way back to Europe. His trip would take two days. He would retrace his route back through Belarus and into Poland before heading south. The more direct route through Ukraine was impossible with the war going on. On his way to Belgrade, Serbia, the roads through Slovakia and Hungary gave him ample opportunity to exercise the Range Rover while making him wish he had brought his Peugeot.

From Belgrade, Dan made his way west towards the Adriatic coast, entering Montenegro before turning back south and into Albania. When near towns or cities, Dan carefully watched his speed, not wanting to be arrested and extorted for a bribe.

At the Albanian border, his Official-level passport raised eyebrows. The border guard had to consult with his superior officer, who made a phone call. Once the information regarding the passport reached higher-level officials, he was quickly passed through without any further search or examination.

The drive from the border to Tirana took three hours. Dan arrived in the early evening and drove around the capital for another hour, looking for a suitable nondescript hotel. He found one on the east side of the city center. It provided off-street parking, which was a plus.

Once checked in, Dan, following Yevgeny's directions, drove out of town on the autostrada heading northwest. Less than a mile out, he exited to a local road that turned north from the highway. He was now in a warehouse area. After passing an abandoned ruin of a factory located in a large field with other smaller buildings left abandoned, he drove past a dirt lot with packing and shipping crates stacked haphazardly. Behind the yard was a rundown, concrete warehouse that had seen better days. It almost looked abandoned.

Dan slowed, and his eye caught the cameras arranged on the building, indicating something more than an abandoned or failing business inside. He continued on, not wanting to draw attention to himself. *Have to come back at night and check this out more closely.* After a mile, he turned back towards the central part of the city.

Close into the city center, just south of Skanderbeg Square, was *Leginii Tiranës*, or Lake Tirana. It was a large park with the Presidential Palace on its east side. A few legacy mansions scattered around the shore remained in private hands, and Jetmir's home was one of them. From Yevgeny's description, Dan located the arms merchant's house on a small peninsula surrounded on three sides by water. There was one long drive up to the mansion. It would be hard to reconnoiter as any vehicle would stand out and, if not known, immediately become a cause for suspicion and further investigation. Dan knew he would have to be creative if he had to capture Jetmir at his home.

Late that evening, well after dinner in a local restaurant near his hotel, Dan changed into dark clothes. He carried a black knit watch cap but didn't wear it. It was not the sort of look one expected of a tourist. He set out in the Range Rover towards the warehouse. When he got on the frontage road, Dan found a place to pull off and parked on the side of a closed warehouse, one of several in the rough industrial complex. The SUV was in the shadows, partially blocked from view by any passing vehicles. From his duffle bag, Dan took out his night vision goggles. He exited the Range Rover and began to walk towards the target warehouse.

Crossing the empty field with the abandoned buildings was easy. There were no street or lot lights, but the NVG made it easy to navigate in the dark. When he reached the edge of the target lot, Dan stopped to scan the grounds. *Need to know if any guards are patrolling.* He patiently waited and watched. Nothing stirred. *Relying on the security cameras. Anyone inside overnight?*

Dan could not imagine leaving the warehouse unmanned, even for a night, especially if there was any significant inventory of arms. It would be too easy a target for thieves. Local criminals had to know something of Jetmir's operations and might want to take advantage of any unguarded moments.

As he was waiting, a police car drove up and pulled into the lot. Someone in the vehicle shone a spotlight around the compound as the car drove up. After scanning the front lot, the patrol car proceeded around the side to the rear. Two minutes later, it reemerged and exited the yard.

That's how he arranges overnight surveillance. His friendly, local police. Still, Dan felt there had to be someone inside.

Under the cover of the shrubs between the lots, Dan worked his way around towards the rear of the building.

In the back were two loading docks with a man door between them and one ground-level garage-type opening that a truck could drive into. He was looking for any additional entrance points. Along one side of building, there was an additional door.

More cameras. Dan noted the multiple cameras mounted high on the top edge of the wall. He guessed these were not motion-driven but recorded continuously all night. *Probably checked throughout the night or first thing in the morning, then erased for a new 24-hour period.* While the doors would not be a problem, the warehouse looked impossible to access without being seen or recorded.

Having learned as much as he could, Dan made his way back to his vehicle. He got back to his hotel and thought about his situation. Jetmir had disappeared. That was what Yevgeny said. Where did he go? Did he have a hideaway outside of the city? If that were so, it might be easier to capture him there. A remote hideout, somewhere in a forest, in the mountains, would let Dan make an assault without worrying about the police intervening. Then it would be a matter of overcoming Jetmir's defenses, whatever he had set up, killing any guards he had, and taking him prisoner. *Hell, I could even stay there and use his own hideout to interrogate him.*

The challenge would be how to flush Jetmir from the city since he had returned. Tomorrow, he would go swimming and check out the man's home. *Can't just drive by and check it out. Have to find a dive shop. Someplace that sold snorkeling gear.* That was not going to be easy, even here in the capital.

Chapter 47

Jetmir was pleased to be back in Tirana. Here, he had power and influence. The criminal gangs to whom he provided weapons respected him. He paid the police and prosecutors enough to be let alone and had a bevy of girls to please his every whim. Then Rashid called again.

"Where are you?" The Saudi asked after Jetmir answered.

"I'm in Tirana. Doing business."

"That isn't wise."

"I can't hide out forever. I have people here who can protect me and I have a business to operate."

"Let me tell you what has happened since you went away," Rashid said. "Two of the men involved in our mission have gone missing. Another was shot, at great range, on his doorstep. And a third, the leader of one of the operations was kidnapped."

Rashid paused to let that sink in.

"This last man. He knows much. He will give up all he knows. No one resists torture for too long."

"He doesn't know who I am, or where I am."

"Do not be so sure. If he knows your name, he may know where you are located. That is enough for anyone to find you, let alone the ones who search for us."

"They search for you, not me. I'm a side issue for them. You should fear for your own life."

"I take proper precautions. No one can reach me in my country. For you, it is not so hard."

"You've seen my operations. It's impossible for anyone to get into the building without being seen and intercepted by my guards. Plus, I have a safe room to retreat to."

Rashid didn't answer. Jetmir was being obstinate and foolish. He didn't understand what they were up against. This man or team of men was diligent, deadly, and effective. They didn't stop. He couldn't insist, but if Jetmir became a casualty of those pursuing him, Rashid would lose another vital link in his jihad.

"If you won't take my advice and disappear, then put on extra security. If those taking down my men go after you, you'll need them."

Rashid didn't wait for an answer but hung up the phone.

Jetmir pocketed his cell phone. *Rashid's afraid? He's getting nervous just because some of his men were careless and got captured or killed.* He got up. *That won't happen to me.* He put the thought out of his mind and went downstairs to observe the packing of 200 AK-47 Kalashnikov rifles and 10,000 rounds of ammunition bound for a warlord in the Congo.

Later, when the shipment was packed, a truck drove it to the coast to be loaded on a small freighter in the port of Durrës. The ship was bound for Matadi, located approximately one hundred miles up the Congo River from the Atlantic Ocean. It was the main port for shipping, handling about 350 ships yearly. From there, the weapons would travel by private plane to Goma in the east and then be delivered to the warlord who led a small army of rebels. It was good business with a never-ending need for more ammunition, replacement rifles, and various other military-grade munitions.

Jetmir had his modest empire to grow. He could not stop because Rashid was paranoid about the response to his bombings.

That day, Dan spent searching Tirana for snorkeling gear. He finally was able to purchase a mask and snorkel along with a pair of kid's swim fins. Back at the hotel, he took his knife and cut away the front of the shoe part on the fins to make room for his larger feet. When he put them on, his toes stretched over the fin. It was not ideal, but the fins still would work and help propel him through the water.

That night, he drove to the lake. Before reaching the cleared and groomed promenade, which ran along one side of the lake, he parked. With his swimming gear, he slipped out of his SUV and made his way through the bushes to the lake's edge. It was past midnight. Thankfully, there was a crescent moon low on the horizon. A half or full moon would shine too brightly on the water, making it much easier to see someone swimming in the dark. Tonight would be sufficiently dark to allow him to cross the lake unnoticed.

It was a weekday, with little traffic and no pedestrians along the promenade. Dan silently slid into the water and began to breaststroke the quarter mile across the lake. Before entering, he had noted the heading of the peninsula with Jetmir's house on his wrist compass. With just his head barely showing, he slowly worked his way across the open water. There was a slight breeze, which helped to mask any wake he left behind. He moved quietly, avoiding any splashing, using his snorkel and mask to keep most of his head submerged.

It took just over a half-hour with pauses to correct his course to reach the other side. Dan aimed for a reed bed on one side of the house. The house was oriented towards the lake. Large doors opened onto a patio edged with a low wall. There were tables and chairs with folded umbrellas placed around the space. From there, a carefully groomed lawn stretched to the shore with a long dock extending out into the water. As he got closer, Dan could see the side yard was also neatly trimmed. The plantings were all arranged in an orderly fashion, evidencing the work of a professional landscaper. The result was not only attractive grounds but also few places to hide and not be observed by security cameras.

Once in the reed bed, Dan stopped. The water was waist-deep. He knelt on the hard mud bottom and raised his head. The reeds shielded him and allowed him to scan the grounds. He noted a full array of cameras on each wall. A careful look did not reveal any black areas, places which didn't get coverage.

Lights were shining through the windows facing the lake. Dan could see figures moving inside. *Someone's home.*

Along the side yard was a tall elm tree nearly 100 feet high, with a collection of grasses and bushes planted in an arrangement underneath. It might be possible to crawl from the woods beyond the property to the tree using the shrubbery to block a camera view. The tree would shield him. The problem would be how to cross the remaining thirty yards of open grass to the walls of the house.

If I can get to a wall, I'll probably be inside the camera's view. It won't see me. They look to be aimed out into the yard. But the open area looked impossible to cross. It was well-mowed, and even crawling, his figure would stand out. *Is anyone monitoring the cameras?* That was the question. If there was no one, then Jetmir would be relying on motion detectors. He could fool them with patience in his approach.

He sank back down into the water and began to swim around to the other side of the house. He went under the long pier. There were rocks lining the shore on the far side. Water grasses grew amidst the rip rap on the bank, which provided some cover but less than the reeds. Dan crawled through the shallow water until he reached the bank, close to the high grasses. He lifted himself and peered through the vegetation. This side of the yard was narrower. Part of the way between the house and the un-landscaped brush was a grouping of rose bushes. These would also provide cover, and the open distances to cross were shorter. Still, they were rose bushes. Dan didn't relish crawling through them.

He moved back into the water from the rocks and sat on the bottom. *It's a crap shoot. How do I tell if the cameras are monitored?* As he pondered his dilemma, lights on the side of the house flashed on, illuminating the yard. Dan slunk down into the water and crawled back to the grasses for cover. He peered out. A small group of deer had wandered into the yard to graze on the freshly mowed grass.

The odds of no live monitoring just went up in his mind. It was not definitive, but now more probable. He would still be taking a risk. Once at the wall, he had to remain tight up against it to keep out of view of the cameras or trigger the motion detectors on the lights. Then he had to get into the house. Then, he had to find Jetmir and gain control over him.

When the lights went out, he slipped back into the water and headed out into the lake. After reaching the far side, Dan dried off, changed, and returned to his hotel. Later in his room, he sat in thought. *Easier to just kill him. If I could get some explosives, I could blow up the warehouse and destroy his operations. Take him out, blow up the place, and leave town. If done quickly, no one would find me.* A deadly ghost. He liked that. It preyed on the terrorist's superstitions.

Chapter 48

U ri lay on the ground outside of a nondescript house on the outskirts of a small village in Syria just south of Aleppo. His infiltration had followed the same pattern as his earlier exfil with Dan. Two special operation commandos, Meni and Tevel, accompanied him. Eitan had reluctantly allowed Uri to go on this mission. Uri had made a strong case for how well his efforts had paid off when working in Iraq with Dan.

"Syria is dangerous, but not as dangerous as Iraq. We did okay there, a lot due to my abilities. Ariel was my friend. I need to avenge his death. I uncovered this guy with Dan. You cannot deny me the opportunity to bring our vengeance to him."

The argument had some merit, and Eitan knew that Uri would never forgive him if he deprived the man of this moment. The two men with Uri were members of Sayeret Maglan, a commando unit also known as Unit 212. They were trained to operate deep inside enemy territory.

Now, the three of them huddled amidst the scrub of the surrounding desert, watching the house of Usair Beshara. The information from Jamal indicated this was the house. Jamal had even given them a description of the man, which Israeli intelligence had fleshed out, even providing a picture of the terrorist. He had come onto the Israeli's radar some years earlier. They had been on-site since the night before. There had been no activity.

Uri was concerned that word had gotten to Usair, causing him to flee to another location and be lost to them. The only thing they could do was wait. Uri remembered what Dan had said, "there's always the waiting." He had experienced it himself throughout his undercover time, spying in enemy territory.

"You think we have the wrong place?" One of the two younger men asked in a whisper.

"No. The intel is good. It also aligns with what our prisoner told us."

"But if he got wind of us coming after him? He'd run and we'll be waiting here for nothing."

"We wait." Uri's grim look silenced the man from further questioning. "If he doesn't show up, we burn the house and leave. It will only delay his ultimate fate." He turned back to the house.

A dust cloud previewed a car driving up to the home. It stopped near the front door. Three men got out. The Israelis all watched with their binoculars as they walked to the door and entered.

"It's Usair," Uri whispered. "We got him."

"They may be getting some gear to run off and hide. We must take them now," Meni said.

"You're right, they can't leave," Uri answered.

They were about 100 yards from the house.

"Like we planned," Uri said. "We split up, Tevel covers the rear, me and Meni go to the front. We take out the car if necessary. No one leaves. No one comes out alive."

The men nodded without a word. They checked their weapons and reserve magazines. Each man carried a TAR-21 assault rifle. It was a compact, bullpup design firing a 5.56mm NATO round from a 30-round magazine. The rifle's rotating bolt system allowed for 900 rounds per minute in automatic mode. It had an effective range of 1,800 feet. In addition to the TAR-21, the men carried the standard Glock sidearm with extra 9mm magazines.

Uri headed towards the front door with Meni. Tevel started towards the rear of the house. There was no cover between the scrub in which the men were hiding and the home. If seen, they would be easy targets out in the open. Uri and Meni aimed for the car, which would provide some shelter. Tevel headed towards a wall enclosing a compound at the back of the building. From there, he could fire at anyone trying to leave while using the wall for protection.

Someone inside the house noticed an armed man heading to the rear. He alerted the others, and they grabbed their weapons.

"Go to the back. Don't let him in. Kill him," Usair shouted.

He and the other man went to the front windows. There, they saw a man duck behind their car.

"We're surrounded," Usair's partner said.

Without replying, Usair stuck his AK out of the window and aimed at the car. At the rear, he heard the third man start firing. Usair let loose a volley at the car, shooting through the cabin windows to try to hit the person hiding behind it.

"Don't shoot the car. Then we can't get away!" One of the men shouted.

"We can't get away while there is someone at our car. Call for help."

"We can't take too long," Uri said as the two crouched behind the car. They huddled behind the engine at the front. Rounds shattered glass as they whistled through the cab. "They'll call for help. Hell, the whole village could be coming."

He started for the rear of the vehicle.

"You keep them pinned down," Uri said.

"What are you going to do?"

"Get to the wall, throw a flash-bang inside and go through the door. When it goes off, you come running. We don't have any time to waste."

Meni gave Uri a grave look and nodded. He turned back and crawled to the front wheel. When he started firing, Uri sprinted to the front wall. He plastered himself against it next to the door, on the far side of the window where the shots came from. He pulled a grenade from his tactical vest and shuffled to a window. Taking a deep breath, he pulled the pin and tossed it inside.

A moment later, a blast erupted from inside the house. A bright light, along with debris, flashed through the open window. Uri turned and drove his shoulder against the door while Meni came running. The latch splintered, and Uri dove low through the opening. Dust and smoke hung in the air. As he crossed the threshold, he heard shots to his left and rounds slammed into the wall over his head. Uri brought his TAR-21 up and swept the space with automatic fire. He saw a figure fall.

At nearly the same moment, Meni came through the doorway, looking to the right. More shots rang out, and Uri felt a round tear through his upper right arm. The force spun him to the right and to the floor. Meni fired on automatic at the figure that had raised itself from behind a tipped-over table. He missed. The table was solid oak, but Meni let off a full auto burst into the wood before running forward. A man's head appeared from behind the overturned table, as his body fell to the floor. He lay on the ground, groaning from multiple wounds where the rounds had penetrated the table and hit him. Meni aimed at his head and fired two single rounds, silencing him.

At that moment, the third man came into the room. He took a fraction of a second to absorb the scene. That proved to be fatal. Uri had shifted his TAR-21 to his left hand and shot him before he could react and fire. At the sound of Uri's carbine, Meni swung towards the other side of the room.

"All clear," Uri shouted. "They're all down. Call Tevel to come inside."

When all three commandos were in the room, Tevel looked at Uri's wound. He cut off his sleeve.

"We can do this later," Uri said. "We have to leave. Quick, take photos of the dead men and let's get out of here."

Tevel let his arm go. "The round went through pretty cleanly. You're lucky. I can clean it quickly." He reached for some antiseptic.

Uri shook his head. "We have to get out of here," Uri said. "Even if they didn't call for help, others heard the gunfire and will be coming."

The men got up and, after making sure all three terrorists were dead, ran to the car and drove off.

"Drive like hell was after you," Uri said. "Our best hope is to put distance between us and the house."

Meni drove wildly through the streets, heading outside of town. The car swerved down the narrow roads, dodging parked vehicles, sliding around corners, and raising large dust clouds. They drew looks, but no one followed. Once clear of the village, Meni accelerated to even greater speed.

"Head to the river. We need to get into Lebanon. We'll follow the same path as we took to enter."

He took out his cell phone and winced as he tried to punch the keys with his right hand.

"Operations," came a voice as the call connected.

"Mission accomplished. We collected three trophies. Now headed back the way we came."

"We can meet you tonight. Same time, same place."

"Let's meet earlier. We have no time to waste."

"Negative. We can't get there sooner. Do your best."

The phone went dead.

"Fuck!"

"What's wrong?" Tevel asked.

"They can't pick us up until tonight."

Tevel looked over his shoulder to check whether they were being followed. "I don't like that. They'll start a search. They'll be looking for this car."

"How far from the river are we?" Meni asked. He kept his eyes forward as the car sped down the dirt road, occasionally shouldering the traffic aside. Meni tried to not slow down for more than a moment.

Uri got out his map. "Two miles to our left."

They were headed north towards Homs.

"We don't want to go too far north," Uri said. "Look for a place to dump the car and we go on foot to the river."

"Hide out there." Tevel said.

"It's the best we can do."

Chapter 49

Having decided to gather more information on his prey, Dan began to stalk Jetmir to learn his habits and where he might intercept him between the fortresses of work and home. A kidnapping *en route* would be easier than trying to penetrate his security.

A week passed. Dan rented a car in the middle of the stretch, worried that his Range Rover might begin to draw too much attention. Jetmir traveled in a large BMW sedan. He always had at least one bodyguard with him, armed with both a sidearm and a semi-automatic carbine. Taking Jetmir would mean killing the guard. The whole episode would be noticed, making it more difficult for Dan to secure his prisoner and get out of Tirana quickly.

No easy choices. Dan sighed to himself as he sat in his hotel room. He had to make a decision. He couldn't just keep following the man. There was little left to know about his routine. He didn't go partying. He had plenty of girls who made visits to his home. Dan assumed he had access to plenty of drugs and liquor to make his own party. Still, he had hoped the man was attracted to the frenetic world of clubs, the ones with the driving techno-rock music and lots of ecstasy. It would be easy to capture or kill him in such a loud, chaotic environment. But at the moment, Jetmir seemed not to be interested in such pastimes.

The next day, Bekim, Jetmir's security chief, came to him at work. "Boss, I think we may have a problem."

Jetmir looked up from his paperwork.

"I noticed something odd. Your bodyguard said he thinks someone has been following you for more than a few days. He's spotted a Range Rover. That vehicle disappeared, but another one, a regular car has been showing up behind you for the last three days."

"Same car?"

Bekim nodded. "He checked the plate. It's a rental. I tracked it down. Rented to a Victor James. He's a security consultant to international businesses."

Jetmir thought for a moment. "I don't know any Victor James. Why would he be interested in me?"

Bekim shrugged. "I decided to take a close look at the home videos for the last two weeks, since I was told of the surveillance."

"You found something?"

"I'm not sure." He took a couple of USB sticks from his pocket and walked to a computer. "Take a look at this."

Bekim inserted one and fast-forwarded the video file. "Watch carefully." The video flashed when the deer triggered the lights. At that moment, Bekim paused the recording. "Look carefully at the grasses on at the edge of the lake." He pointed to the spot. There was a large shadow behind the grass. "Watch it." Bekim started the recording, and the shadow disappeared.

"What is that?"

"It's not an animal. Only beaver or otter move around near the shore. This is too large."

"A person?" Jetmir tensed up.

"That's only a guess, but I can't think of a better one." He fast-forwarded again. "This camera points out to the lake. Look carefully at the water."

Bekim pointed to the screen. Jetmir squinted at the video. Sure enough, something was moving slowly and quietly through the water. Something round. It could have been a beaver or muskrat. Jetmir wanted to think that, but it was too round. And after seeing the shadow at the shore, he could only imagine a head. A human head.

"This is the stalker?"

Bekim looked at him. His face was dark and serious. "Would you dismiss this? What would be the consequences? You are in a dangerous business. Maybe something happened earlier that made it more dangerous. All I know is that this looks like serious, professional surveillance...of the most dangerous kind."

Jetmir was quiet. He was not afraid, but if his security chief was right, this was a very high level of probing into his defenses.

"Check the cameras at the warehouse. Let's see if whoever this is has been there."

"I already did that. I couldn't see anyone, but later I hacked into other cameras in the area and saw what looks like the same Range Rover on the road. Someone drove by and, later, parked nearby. We can assume this person surveilled the warehouse."

"So, they know where I run my operations and where I live."

"We have to conclude that."

"I can't just go on as if nothing has happened. Eventually, there will be a problem."

"Correct again."

Jetmir was silent. What could he do? This was what Rashid had warned him about.

"We have to lure whoever this is out into the open. Then we can take care of him," he said.

"I was thinking the same thing. Only we don't want to act at your home, or even here at the warehouse. Too much at risk."

"I could make a point of going out of town, not try to sneak away. Act like I don't know someone is watching. Get this person into an environment where I can control the situation with no interference."

Jetmir's security chief smiled. "We have good security at your lodge. It's isolated. We could set up an ambush for whoever follows you."

Jetmir returned the smile. "No one to interfere out there. We can observe this person as he approaches, even through the forest."

"And eliminate him."

Chapter 50

U ri watched the roadside as Meni kept up a furious pace in the sedan. When he spotted a bombed-out building on the right side of the road, he told Meni to pull off.

The car slewed sideways as Meni yanked the steering wheel while braking hard to slow down.

"Be careful!" Tevel shouted. "You'll get us killed."

Meni got the car under control and pulled it around behind the ruins of the building. The men got out. Uri moved slowly, favoring his right arm.

"Let me bandage that wound," Tevel said. "You're bleeding. We need to stop that."

Uri sat down with some reluctance, worried about pursuers catching up to them.

"It won't do us any good to have you become a liability because you lost too much blood."

He poured some antiseptic on the wound. Uri grimaced but didn't say anything. Then Tevel wrapped a cauterizing bandage tight around Uri's upper arm.

"That should work for now."

Uri stood. The three scanned the road before crossing to the west side. Without further delay, they hiked off through the fields towards a distant scrub line that marked a lot boundary. They moved as fast as Uri could go. To be caught out in the open would mean a shootout and probable death.

Once in the cover of the brush and trees, they stopped. Tevel checked Uri's bandage, which was holding tight.

"You good to go?" Meni asked.

Uri nodded. "Just let me rest a moment. Then let's get the hell out of here. We've got a couple of miles to hike before we reach the river."

"A couple of miles without being seen," Meni said.

"It's farm country. We can detour around farm houses. Keep to the fields. We'll be alright," Uri said. His voice did not convey a great deal of confidence. *I've been in worse situations*, he kept telling himself. While well-trained, Meni and Tevel had never been this far inside enemy territory on such a mission. They knew the stakes were high. Capture would mean certain torture and death.

The sun was getting low in the sky when the men reached the river. It shone through layers of haze that had risen from the desert floor during the day. Along the way, they had stopped when necessary to avoid people, waiting for anyone they spotted to move on or go inside a building before skirting around them. Now, in the dense brush at the water's edge, they began to relax.

"I'm betting no one has discovered the car yet," Meni said. "If it had, they'd be able to track us heading west. It wouldn't take a genius to guess we were making for the border."

"Don't get too comfortable, they still could find it and figure things out. They could be here in twenty minutes."

"And our ride out doesn't come for another four hours," Tevel said.

The men sat quietly and pondered their situation. They dared not cross in daylight, and even after the sun set, the west side did not provide the cover the Syrian side did, which made them reluctant to move.

As night fell, they heard a truck coming from the south.

"Moving slowly from the sound of it," Uri said. "Quick. Into the water."

The men slipped through the brush, trying to not push the vegetation down and leave a trail. They slid into the stream. It was waist deep, even near the shore, and flowing quickly.

"Down there," Uri said. He pointed downstream towards the approaching truck. But there, reeds were growing into the water from the river bank. "We get inside the reed bed."

They let the current pull them downstream and then settled into the reeds. They sat on the bottom with their heads and shoulders sticking out of the water.

"When they get close, slink down so only your face is showing. Don't move. Don't even breathe loudly," Uri said.

The two nodded with no response. As the truck approached, they understood why it was going so slowly. A spotlight shone from it, aimed at the scrub growing along the bank and flashing across the water to the other side. Two men on foot were walking through the brush, communicating with those in the truck. They were shouting and passing instructions back and forth in Arabic. Uri listened but only got bits of the conversation. It was a mix of encouragement and anger. The terrorists were sure that the ones who killed Usair and the other two men were foreign commandos sent to wreak revenge for the Jerusalem bombing. One of them expressed the thought that Muntaqim, Uri heard the name clearly, would not be happy if they let the killers get away.

As the men approached, Uri and his team slid farther down into the water. Now, they could not hear but only stare at the sky as they tilted their faces up, barely out of the water, and tried to breathe quietly. Uri calmed his heart rate so he could slow down his breathing. He hadn't heard any dogs, which could have proven fatal. If the men moved past, they had a chance. Maybe the search would head back away from the border. They still had more than two hours to go.

After five minutes, Uri raised his head. He resisted the urge to shake it and clear his ears; instead, waited patiently for the water to drain and his hearing to return. The truck had moved farther north from their position. He nudged his companions, and they sat up.

"We made it through this round. Let's get farther south. From my reckoning we're too far north. We can let the current take us downstream."

The men half floated, half walked, letting the current do the work. Uri tried to keep his upper arm out of the water, which he guessed was filled with a toxic stew of pathogens. An hour later, Uri figured they were close enough to wait for the pickup. The signal would be the same that they used when he and Dan exfiltrated. Once across into Lebanon, he could begin to relax. And once on the fishing boat, they could all declare the mission a success.

Chapter 51

They set a plan. Jetmir would make preparations as if he were going to leave the city. He would do it in an open and conspicuous manner. Anyone watching him would understand what he was planning to do. Both men thought that there would not be another surveillance attempt at Jetmir's home since that involved a swim across the lake. It would be easier to spy on the arms dealer at work. Jetmir was betting that his enemy would spend more time watching him at the warehouse, looking for a place to...what? Attack and kill him?

One night, Dan did another swim across the lake. This time, he went around to the front of the house, moving through the woods, keeping out of view of the cameras. Once at the front, he studied the ground. Jetmir's BMW was parked in the circular driveway near the front door. There was an island of ornamental shrubs in the center of the circle.

If I can get there, I can crawl to the car without triggering the cameras at the front. It was a risk, but one he needed to take. He had a magnetic tracking device to plant on Jetmir's car. He had noticed what seemed to be preparations for the arms dealer leaving town. If Jetmir was departing for a hideaway, that would play into Dan's hands, but he needed to follow the man; well behind him so he would not be discovered. He could not remain in visual contact down various back roads without being noticed.

He maneuvered as far from the house as possible, keeping the car in front, between him and the building. *Got to try*. With a deep breath, Dan crawled out from the cover of the woods, across the drive, and into the shrubs in the center island. *Made it*. He maneuvered until he could look out at the car, now much closer, and get a read on how much interference it created. Thankfully, the vehicle blocked most of the camera views. The issue would be to move slowly and not trigger any motion sensors.

It took twenty minutes to cross the thirty feet separating the plantings from the car. Once at the BMW, Dan relaxed. He took out the tracker and slid it under the frame. He put it inside a channel of the side frame. *If they check the car, wheel wells will be the obvious place to look. It won't be there. Hopefully, they won't look further.* Job done; Dan crawled back to the woods and swam across the lake.

Jetmir's team took a few days to let a routine develop before making the preparations. During this time, the security chief noticed an odd thing. Whoever was watching Jetmir had stopped trying so hard to disguise the fact. Men he had placed in and around the warehouse noticed a figure, easy to see but not easy to identify, lurking around Jetmir's business. It caused some confusion. While they were trying to let the intruder know Jetmir was planning to leave town, the intruder seemed to be letting them know he was watching him.

"Maybe he's trying to scare you out of the city. Get you away from your security so he can strike," Bekim said.

"Possibly. What he won't know is that we're setting our own ambush for him."

When Jetmir finally left, he made it very clear. He said goodbye to his security chief and took one of his mistresses with him in his BMW. With a jaunty wave, he drove out of town, hoping whoever was spying on him would follow. Sure enough, Bekim called him *en route* to his hunting lodge deep in the Oafe Bushi Forest. The Range Rover was heading out of town on the same road.

Once he had departed, Bekim called his men and began to put his plan into action. He got in his car and sped out of town towards the camp, taking a faster, less scenic route. He wanted to get there and finalize the preparations.

On the way, he called Jetmir. "He's way behind you. I checked your car for tracking devices, but he must have hidden one somewhere. I didn't find it."

Jetmir held his tongue. That was a potentially dangerous miss by his security chief, but it would make little difference.

"We know it now, so let's use it to our advantage. It gives him a beacon to home in on and us the ability to know where he's aiming."

"Right," Bekim said. His voice could not disguise his relief at not being called out for his miss. "Park your car near the outbuilding when you arrive. It will divert the man's initial focus away from you."

Without comment, Jetmir ended the call. He sped up, now not worried about his pursuer keeping up. Better to put distance between himself and whoever was following him.

Dan followed at his own pace without hurrying. From what he could tell, Jetmir did not know he was being tracked, so changing vehicles to avoid discovery would not be an issue. If the arms dealer was going to hide out for a while, evidenced by the supplies he had packed and the woman he had brought, Dan could take his time. It would be better for the man to settle into a routine and begin to let his guard down. He'd watch and wait. Then he would strike.

Chapter 52

D an followed the BMW, miles behind, as it wound through the mountains, now enveloped by the forest. The ping finally stopped, seemingly in the middle of the woods. Dan guessed it was parked at Jetmir's hideaway, probably at the end of a long, private road that didn't appear on a map. He watched carefully as he approached the signal. The road he was on would take him past, but he could locate the driveway. Sure enough, a mile later, there was a graded, gravel road going off to the left with signs marking it as private property. Dan kept going.

After unloading the car, Jetmir drove over to the barn, where the security team had set up monitors for the surveillance cameras. Bekim was already there, watching the various feeds.

"There!" he shouted, pointing to one of the screens. He paused, then backed up the video, and Jetmir saw the Range Rover drive slowly past the entrance.

"He's followed you here, just like we wanted," Bekim said.

"You can take care of him? He'll try to penetrate, to reach the lodge. His aim must be to capture or kill me."

"We will take care of him. I have cameras set up all through the woods between the road and the lodge."

"But you can't cover every part of the woods. He could get past."

"The cameras near the lodge provide an unbroken field of coverage. If we miss him early on, we'll see him as he gets closer. My men will take him out."

Bekim had brought ten men with him who were also housed in the barn. The building usually held maintenance equipment, which they had moved outside to provide room for the men and security equipment. They would set up a round-the-clock vigil, working in shifts.

"Can you take out his SUV? Then he can't get away. We'll have him trapped."

"Already planned on that," Bekim said.

He had a renewed pride in his voice. He may have missed the tracker, but he had elaborate plans, even though hurriedly made, to kill or capture this intruder.

"Leave it to me. Go and enjoy yourself."

Jetmir paused for a moment. There was nothing he could do to add to his security. He had set the idea in motion; now it was up to Bekim to execute the plans. Jetmir left the barn and walked back to the lodge. He would finish unpacking, eat, drink, and enjoy the woman he had brought. But first, he would make sure his personal weapons, an AK-47 and his 9mm pistol, were loaded and close at hand.

Dan drove along the mountain road. There were few places to pull off of the narrow mountain road. Finally, two miles farther, there was a scenic turnout overlooking a valley.

He turned off and immediately went to the back of the SUV. He opened the hidden compartment and took out his 9mm and Sako TRG 42. The rifle was fully disassembled and in a padded carry bag. He shoved the bag into his backpack, already loaded with water, power bar-type snacks, and ammunition. Then Dan paused for a moment, looking at his M4 carbine. He wanted the Sako for long-range shooting, but if he got into a firefight, the M4 was the weapon he needed. He decided to be greedy and grabbed both weapons.

As he closed the rear hatch, he heard a faint whine above him. Without looking up, he knew what that sound meant: a drone. It could be spying on him or loaded with an explosive to take him out. Dan snatched up his carbine and backpack and jumped over the guard rail, sliding and falling down the cleared hillside. As his body dropped below the level of the pullout, he heard the blast, and metal bits flew above him and out into the space beyond the hill. He lost his footing and control, bouncing down the rough ground, twisting and turning, and banging off tree stumps. His backpack and carbine were ripped from his hands.

As he careened downward, Dan wildly grasped at anything trying to stop his descent. His body slammed into the stumps that littered the cleared slope. Each hit was a massive blow, like someone kicking his torso. He kept reaching for something, anything to grab to slow or control his fall, as he twisted and rolled downward. It was hundreds of feet to the bottom, where a river had cut through the mountain. Sky and dirt flashed through his blurred vision; his arms flailed wildly in an effort to grab something to slow or stop himself. Then he slammed into a large bush, which broke his fall. His hands grasped the vegetation, and he lay tangled, gasping for breath. Slowly, he began to take inventory of his body. There were no broken limbs, but he felt bruised all over. A groan escaped him as he tried to move.

He looked back up the slope. He could barely see the guardrail protecting the edge about a hundred feet above him. With great effort, Dan shifted his position until he could look around. Where were his backpack and carbine?

He was lost, ineffective without them. *God, I hope they're not at the bottom of the slope.* The thought of getting to the bottom without injury and then getting back up seemed impossible from his current position.

He scanned the hillside, above and below, and saw the backpack hooked into a low bush. It was twenty feet down and to the right of him. Dan took a deep breath and started to crawl on his belly, using his body as friction to avoid another free fall. The slope forced some sideways slipping, which he could limit. The effect was to get him down to the bush holding the pack as he crossed the lateral distance.

Once reaching the pack, Dan rested. His body ached all over like he'd been beaten in an alley with a baseball bat. The bush that stopped the backpack felt insecure to Dan as he rested against it. He needed to get back to the more substantial growth that had stopped his fall. He forced his arms to twist through the pack's loops, groaning as his joints protested. With the pack on, he had to be more careful crossing back to the larger bush. He was now projecting more weight above the ground, which could stabilize him, plus he had to go uphill.

Panting with pain and exertion, Dan began to crawl at an angle up the slope. His progress was slow, with moments of slipping back downhill. When that happened, he dug his fingers into the dirt, grass, weeds; anything to keep him from accelerating into another disastrous plummet.

When he reached the lower side of the large bush, he heard the vehicle on the road above. It seemed to slow down, and then he heard the crunch of gravel as it pulled off onto the overlook. Dan pulled himself up close to the bush. He was on the downhill side and hoped no one could see him from above. *If they think I'm dead, that gives me an advantage.* He watched through the foliage.

There was talking from above, indistinct, undecipherable. Two men peered over the edge, looking down the hillside. Dan lay still against the hillside. *Trying to see if I survived the attack.* It looked like an animated discussion was going on. Maybe a difference of opinion as to whether or not he had been killed by his fall. They couldn't find a body in the ruins of the Range Rover. One man tossed a rock down the hillside. It bounced and accelerated until lost to sight as it plummeted to the river below. The man then picked up a larger piece of metal from the SUV and tossed it after the rock. It also accelerated down. Dan risked turning to look over his shoulder to see it careen off the uneven ground, not slowing until it got too low for him to see.

The discussion seemed to be resolved, and the men turned away from the edge. The vehicle started, and Dan could hear it drive away in the direction from which it came. *Let's hope they decided I'm dead or dying at the bottom, near the river.*

He pulled himself more upright to scan the hillside again. He needed to find the M4. It was going to be necessary. There was a group of men surrounding Jetmir that had to be taken out before he could capture his target.

Chapter 53

J etmir and Bekim had a heated discussion when Bekim returned. He reported the vehicle destroyed, but no body was found.

"How can that be? Even if he was blown to bits, there would be parts. You'd see something."

"I agree. My guess is that he jumped over the guardrail. He may have heard the drone and knew what that meant. He's experienced."

"But you didn't see him. You looked."

Bekim nodded. "That's right. But the hillside is so steep you can't walk down it. We threw some pieces of the wreckage over and they bounced down, accelerating as they went. A body would do the same. If he jumped, he would be tumbling right away. All the way to the bottom."

"But you didn't see him down there."

"The vegetation at the bottom is thick. Plus, it's hundreds of meters down. He would be badly wounded with broken bones, even if he were alive. He's either dead, or will die soon, crippled at the bottom of the gorge."

Jetmir looked long and hard at Bekim. "I wish I could share your conviction. No body tells me the threat might still be out there."

"You want to stay here? On high alert just in case?"

"I'm here. I'll stay the week as planned. I can work, although it's not so convenient as the internet connection goes out sometimes. You maintain the vigil we set up."

Bekim shook his head as if exasperated. "It's all for nothing. I'm telling you he's dead or unable to function. Certainly not able to climb back up that hill."

Jetmir's eyes flashed in anger. "You will do as I say. It is not you who has your life on the line. He's targeting me."

He started to leave the barn. At the door, he turned. "Just do as you're told."

† † †

Dan took some time after the car drove off. He used the bush to bolster him against sliding down. From a more solid position, he began a thorough scan of the slope from side to side, then moved his gaze lower on the hill to repeat the process. Fifty feet below, he could see the straight barrel of his carbine sticking out of a low bush. It didn't look too secure.

Dan carefully jammed his backpack into the bush, making sure it would not accidentally dislodge. Retrieval of the M4 could take some time. Again, he lay face down and crawled sideways along the hillside until he was directly uphill of the rifle. He had dropped about twenty feet in the process but now had to go straight downhill.

Can't do this head first. The idea of ramming his head into a stump caused him to shudder. He turned to face uphill, sighted a mark to keep him on track, and began to let himself go down in a controlled slip. When his speed picked up, Dan dug his toes and fingers into the hillside to slow himself. It was painful on his hands but less painful than what had occurred earlier. After a few minutes of slipping, he peaked over his shoulder to get his bearings. *Need to go right some.* He made the adjustments and reached the bush in a few more minutes. Careful to not dislodge the weapon and send it skittering down towards the river, he reached out and secured the sling. With the webbed sling tight in his fist, Dan gently pulled the rifle free and was rewarded by sliding another ten feet downward. He dug into the hillside to stop himself, the carbine draped over his elbow.

When he was under control again, He slipped the sling over his shoulder and let the carbine settle on his back. Now, he began the long struggle back up the slope. It was far too steep to attempt to walk, let alone crawl on hands and knees. The effort required belly-flat-to-the-ground crawling. Even then, he slipped backwards at times while grasping at grass, roots, rocks, anything that would halt his slide.

A half-hour later, he had made it to the large bush. Dan reached the uphill side and lay back against the vegetation holding him from tumbling down. He breathed deeply, letting his body relax. Looking up from where he lay, he could barely see the guardrail, still about one hundred feet above.

Got to go. If I stay here too long, I'll stiffen up and then won't be able to make it. Don't want to spend the night here. He took out some water and a power bar from his pack and ate and drank. He tied the M4 to the backpack. Then, with a deep breath, he shouldered the pack and pushed off from the bush that had saved him. Again, it was belly crawling with fingers and toes digging in to push upward and keep himself from sliding back down. He resisted the temptation to raise his body up to go faster. He needed the friction of his body against the ground to help keep him from sliding backwards.

It took an hour to reach the top, with many stops along the way to rest. Once he got his hands on the guard rail and levered himself over it, Dan sighed and lay flat on his back on level ground for the first time in nearly three hours.

Finally, Dan got to his feet. It felt good to stand on level ground and not feel like a snake clinging to the hillside on his belly. He looked at his Range Rover, now a burned shell with doors blown off and a large hole in the roof. *Really liked that ride.*

He sighed, shouldered his pack, and started back up the road. He walked for about a quarter mile and then went into the woods. Here, the hill was less steep, and he could hike it. He kept just far enough into the tree line to avoid being seen from the road if anyone came looking for him again. Dan's mind raced with thoughts about how to recover and gain the upper hand with this setback.

Chapter 54

B ack in the lodge, Jetmir made a call to Manhar Sula. He was head of the dominant criminal gang in Tirana and most of Albania. He was even better connected to the authorities than was Jetmir, who had always tried to remain allied with this influential gangster, being careful to not engage in anything that the man would see as threatening his interests.

"Jetmir, how are you doing? It there anything you need?"

Manhar was not one for small talk, always wanting to get to the point. And Jetmir only called if he needed something from the influential gang leader.

"I am sorry to call you only when I am in need—"

"Do not let it worry you. You provide me with help through your business. For that I am happy to provide you with any help in yours."

"I am under attack. There is someone, at least I think it's just one person, who is trying to kill me."

"Who is this? And why is he trying to get rid of you?"

"I don't know who it is, but I think it has to do with the recent bombings in Washington, D.C. and Jerusalem."

There was a moment of silence.

"Ah...you had something to do with those events. No need to confirm or deny. You think certain agencies are out for revenge. Is it MOSSAD or CIA?"

"I can't tell. It really makes no difference."

"If this man is unsuccessful, will others come? What can you do if they know who you are and where you live? Remember the Black Septemberists were all killed eventually by Israel."

Manhar paused for a moment.

"You have a serious problem that may not go away."

"That may be so, but my more serious problem is immediate threat. I'm at my country lodge and the man has tracked me here."

"Your security has not dealt with him. That is not a good thing. Do you want me to deal with him?"

The question sounded to Jetmir like Manhar was thinking his answer would be an admission of weakness. In his profession, weakness was not something one wanted to project. It invited trouble from competitors and opportunists.

"I know for sure he followed me here. I've blown up his vehicle with a drone. The problem is we can't find the body. He parked near a cliff and may have fallen over, down to a river deep in a gorge."

"But no body. Did you go down and search?"

"I haven't done that yet."

"I think you should do that. But in the meantime, assume this person is not dead."

"That's what I'm doing. My security chief thinks he's dead, at the bottom of the gorge."

"But you don't."

"I don't think it's wise to assume that much."

There was a long silence. Jetmir waited. Manhar often took time to gather his thoughts. He didn't want to waste words.

"That is the correct assumption. You want me to send you some men? To help defend you? Or to find this body?"

"I'd like you to send men to help defend while I search out where this person is, dead or alive."

"Give me the directions. I will send ten men. In the meantime, arm yourself. Don't put your faith in your security. You are a fighter. I know your past. Be ready to fight whoever this is yourself. You must never get soft and rely on others. That is how one gets taken out."

Jetmir hung up the phone with a strong "thank you." He knew that this aid would come with a price. One he would be asked to pay in the future. It was worth it...to have a future.

After ending the call, Jetmir went back to the barn. Bekim was monitoring the multiple camera feeds. Jetmir felt it was like a blind man looking for a light. Only the light would not help him.

"Bekim. Send two men to the overlook and have them go down into the gorge. Use ropes if necessary. I want to find the body. If, as I think, it is not there, then we will know for sure that he's not dead. Meanwhile, beyond watching these screens, send teams of two men each out to do a search. Search the forest on the left side of the drive, the side nearer the overlook. If this person is coming, we know he hasn't crossed the drive. The monitors would have recorded that. If he's alive, he's out there. In the woods. He's coming. Find him and kill him."

"But what about your security?"

"My security depends on killing this intruder. Send two to search the gorge and two teams of two to search the woods. That leaves two men behind...plus you."

"You want me to send men out now? It's going to get dark soon."

"Now. I don't wait for the enemy to attack. I act now."

He walked back to the lodge, where he had his AK-47 and pistol. The woman Jetmir had brought with him looked at him with some trepidation in her face.

"Is there a problem? Why are you pulling out these guns? I thought we were going to enjoy a quiet week in the country."

"We are," Jetmir replied without looking up from checking his rifle. "But someone is out there, coming to kill me, so I have to be prepared."

The woman gasped. "Oh no!"

Jetmir looked at her. "Do not fear, my love. He won't shoot you, unless you get in front of me. But you must do as I say, when I say, without question. You understand?"

Her eyes were wide with fright, but she nodded her head.

"Now go make some food, if you know how to do it. I'm hungry."

† † †

Dan hiked slowly, trying to not aggravate what he had realized was a sprained left ankle. He felt safer in the forest. No drones could see him under the canopy. He aimed towards the drive while slowly working his way up the slope. He assumed the roadway ended at Jetmir's lodge, which was most likely perched on the top of the hill. The approach had to be in the woods. The drive would be monitored.

Night was falling, and it would get very dark under the trees, with little illumination penetrating from moonlight. He worried that stopping for the night would leave him too stiff to move the next morning, but there seemed to be no alternative. NVGs would not help much inside the dark cover of the trees, and if he reached Jetmir's hideout, he would still need to monitor it to learn more about it before attacking. That meant time spent being still, time spent getting stiff.

Chapter 55

A fter getting across the river and being picked up,
Uri and his team were driven to the same beach he
and Dan used. The surf was higher this time and
the men got a thorough dunking before getting into the
boat.

When Uri returned to Tel Aviv, he was immediately
taken to a private clinic to have his wounds cleaned and
dressed. Then it was on to METSADA headquarters to
debrief with Eitan. After the pictures of the dead men in
the Syrian house were developed, it was confirmed that
the assassination team had killed Usiar, the man who ran
the bombing attack in Jerusalem. The other two men were
being run through the terrorist database to see who they
were. From the remains of the van, the investigation had
determined the identity of the vehicle and when it came
over the border. The terrorist must have assembled the
bomb in less than twenty-four hours, so more people must
have been involved. Identifying others involved in the
chain of events would prove almost impossible since Uri
had not been able to capture Usair alive. Still, Eitan and
the others considered the raid a success and took
satisfaction in the quick delivery of retribution.

As he went home to recover from his wound, Uri
thought about Dan. He wondered how his friend was
doing in his search for the arms dealer. As important as

that was, Uri felt it detracted from the central thrust to find their way to this mysterious Muntaqim.

† † †

Dan lay on the forest floor with his left ankle elevated on his backpack. After a few minutes, the throbbing diminished, which was a good sign. Then he heard the sounds of someone moving through the brush accompanied by muffled voices.

He immediately got up, strapped on his pack, and grabbed his M4. After listening, Dan guessed it was two people. *Searching for me. Stupid to do at night.* Still, he'd have to deal with the threat. If they flooded the woods with searchers, he'd have difficulty remaining hidden.

Decision made: Dan started to maneuver to avoid being in the path of the searchers. He moved carefully in the dark. The men searching had lights but still made noise. Dan needed to be stealthy. As he was working his way out of their path, his left foot caught a root and twisted. The pain shot up his leg, and he went down, grunting in agony. Dried sticks on the forest floor cracked as he fell to the ground.

The talking among the two searchers stopped. Dan could see the flashlights turning towards where he lay. Without waiting for them to get closer, he twisted his body around to bring the suppressed M4 to bear. He would not be able to see the men until they were nearly on him. *Maybe they'll be stupid enough to hold the light in front of them. The body will be directly behind the beam.* He figured it was a good bet and lined up one of the lights. The M4 spit out two quick rounds with muffled bursts. Dan didn't wait to see the results and quickly swung his aim to the other light and shot.

The first man lurched backward; his light flashed up in the air as he fell. The man next to him stopped in shock, and before he could react and dive for cover, two more shots came from ahead and tore into his torso, flinging him backwards.

Dan watched both lights fly off in different directions. He used the butt of the carbine to help lever himself back up and limped towards the two men, now lying on the ground. Both men were gasping for breath.

"How many of you are there? Dan asked, kneeling down.

Neither man could speak English, and they were beginning to choke from internal bleeding. *Nothing to be gained.* Dan stood up and quickly dispatched each man with a shot to the head. He retrieved the flashlights and turned them off. *Have to assume there are more teams out here. If they're using lights, I'll see them before they see me.*

He decided to get closer, which meant going uphill. *Can't fall again. My ankle won't take much more.* He started moving up the slope, going slowly and lifting his feet carefully with each step. He scanned the surrounding forest with its dim shadows of trees for any signs of light.

When he got close to the edge of the woods, Dan sought some dense undergrowth to hide in. He found a tangle of vines and understory plants and burrowed into them. Ignoring his pain, Dan squirmed around until he felt planted inside the cover, yet able to see out. For now, he was not interested in the cleared ground leading to the two buildings, just what was happening in the woods. If there were additional search teams, that was the direction they would come from. By now, his ankle was steadily throbbing. *It'll swell if I take off my boot.* Dan sighed and relegated himself to leaving his boot on as a wrapping for the ankle. He didn't know when he'd have time to ice and elevate it.

He saw it before he heard any sounds. The sudden flash of a light as someone swept a beam back and forth. It came from deeper in the forest, to his right, closer to the long entrance drive.

Need to intercept them. They're probably headed back to the compound. A plan had begun to form in Dan's mind. Take out any search teams as quietly as he could. That would reduce Jetmir's defenses and delay his reaction to Dan's evident presence. If the teams didn't come back or check in, it left room for doubt as to what was going on and where Dan might be if they concluded he was alive.

He pushed out of the thick cover. Now, with a target to aim for, he set out, limping deeper into the woods. Finally, he turned on his flashlight, acting like he was one of the search parties. One of the other two men blinked their light twice. Dan returned the signal. He could see the lights of the two men approaching. Dan switched off his own light, which triggered more signaling from the other two. He didn't respond, letting the mystery remain.

As the other team came closer, Dan took up a position behind a large tree and sighted his M4. With the other team thinking they were approaching their fellow guards, it was going to be easy for Dan to strike them. He waited until they got within twenty yards and then fired as before. The first two rounds took out one man. The other one, quicker to react, dropped to the ground, and Dan's shots flew overhead. His flashlight went out. Now, neither man could see the other. Dan stood still and listened while his eyes searched the dark.

He heard the vegetation cracking and crunching. The guard was on the move, crawling. Dan had no shot. Then, a dark shadow, barely seen, arose and began running towards the drive. As Dan brought the M4 to bear, the shadow disappeared. He fired a few rounds at where he felt it would go but heard no indication that he had hit anything.

"Damn," he muttered out loud. Now, the others would be alerted. Dan started back to the compound. He'd have to ambush any search parties as they returned. *They'll regroup. They know it's senseless to hunt for me in the dark. Better to wait until light when the odds will be in their favor.* He would have to eliminate as many as possible before daylight and then deal with the rest. The need to capture Jetmir alive was still uppermost in his mind. He could kill him from a distance, but taking him alive was more difficult and dangerous. He turned back towards the clearing and limped as fast as he dared.

Chapter 56

B ekim's radio crackled to life.
    "We're under attack!" one of the searchers yelled.
    They spoke in Albanian. "He killed Leka. I'm coming
in. I think the other team was killed. They haven't responded
to our calls."

Bekim resisted the impulse to tell his guard to stay out.
No matter what Jetmir said, three men out of the four he
sent out being killed was not a good outcome for the search.

"Come in. We'll wait until daylight. It seems as though
our assassin is alive. We'll find him with the day."

"I'm heading to the drive. Out of the woods."

When his man was on the way back, Bekim called
Jetmir. He didn't want to, but Jetmir needed to be told.
The danger was imminent, even though Bekim felt he
could eliminate it come daylight.

"So, he is alive. Call back the two men you sent to the
gorge. There's no reason to check it now."

"If I can. There won't be any reception when they're at
the bottom."

Jetmir let out an expletive. "We need them here, not
wandering around at the river."

Bekim was silent. He'd do what he could but could not
work magic.

"Do you want me to bring the men to the lodge?" he
asked after a moment.

"No. Keep them at the barn and maintain watch. He can't get to us without exposing himself. We have more firepower than he does."

Jetmir's girl looked at him. Her eyes wide with fright. "Someone's coming? Coming to kill us?"

Jetmir turned to her. "Not us, me."

"But you'll stop them? Oh god. It's so scary! Why didn't you tell me someone was after you? Is this why you came here? Why did you bring me?"

She wandered around the room, muttering to herself, clasping and unclasping her hands. Jetmir looked at her with disdain, yet he had to concede that she must feel powerless and unable to think how to protect herself.

"Whoever is out there. First, we will kill him. Second, he is not interested in you. If things get busy, you just stay out of the way and you'll be safe."

She looked at Jetmir. He could tell she didn't believe a word he said. She had heard too many stories about wives and girlfriends being killed along with the targeted males by gangs. She probably felt she would be a victim if Jetmir died.

He grabbed her to stop her frantic pacing. "Whatever you do, stay out of my way. I'm going to defend myself and that is how I defend you." He held her firmly and forced her to stare at him. "Do you understand?"

She nodded mutely.

Dan reached the edge of the woods again. The house was situated on a half-saddle, facing east, with the ground sloping away in that direction to where Dan hid. The slope was steep enough to provide satisfying views into the valley below that had almost swallowed Dan. To the west, there were similarly grand views of the mountains fading into the distance.

The sky was now beginning to turn from a deep black to a blue. Dawn was coming. With the additional light, Dan could get a better look at the compound. He could see the drive, which came out into the open area. It swung to the right, towards a sizeable barn-like outbuilding, then circled left to curl around the front of a grand-looking, two-story lodge made of logs. Jetmir's car sat in front. There were lights on in the barn and a van parked out front.

Dan noticed the hill climbing higher to the north with a few rocky outcroppings along its steeper slope. It provided shelter from the winter storms coming down from the north. Dan also noticed that the rocky sections would provide cover for him to control the compound with his Sako rifle. He would be in his comfort zone. It would be hard to assault his position, and he could turn the open ground into a killing zone.

Decision made, he turned to his right and started for the north slope. It would not be easy to climb with his ankle, but it would be worth the effort. He needed to get settled into a sniper hide before dawn. With the light, Jetmir might be tempted to make his escape after sending his men out to sweep the woods. How many men he had at his disposal was still a question for Dan. He limped along inside the tree line as fast as he could.

An hour's struggle brought Dan almost to the outcropping as the sun, still hiding behind the hills to the east, began to light up the sky ever more completely. Twenty minutes later, sweating and panting from the exertion, his left ankle throbbing like a bass drum, Dan slipped into the rocks and crawled around to find a suitable shooting position. Only then did he take out a water bottle and drink. Next, he took the Sako out of his pack and carefully assembled it, carefully checking the mounting of the sight to be sure it had not shifted. Through his range scope, he determined the distance to the front of the compound was 500 yards, far enough to be out of range of the AK-47 carbines but easily within range of the Sako. Having hit targets out to over 1,000 yards, any shots he needed to make would not be a significant challenge.

During his climb, the fourth man from the woods returned to check in with Bekim.

"Did you see who shot the others?" Bekim asked.

The man shook his head. "No. He shot at our flashlights. We held them in front of us, giving him an easy target. When Ermal got shot, I dropped to the ground. I heard a round go over my head. I shut off my light and crawled away."

Bekim ignored his man's admission of cowardness. "It was one man?"

"Po," yes, the man replied. "Only one shooter."

"And you think this same man took out the other two?"

Ermal shrugged. "Who else? They haven't checked in." He looked around. "Where are they?"

"But you didn't hear the shots."

"He was firing a silenced weapon. I could tell from the sound."

Bekim thought about what his man had said. Jetmir should be told, but with the growing light, Bekim was suddenly uncomfortable about going out into the compound. Someone was out there. Someone deadly. Someone watching.

Chapter 57

Bekim used his phone to call Jetmir. He explained the situation to him.

"So, I'm a prisoner in my house. This is worse than when I was back in the city. And you can't stop a single man from killing my men, trapping me here? I should just get in my car and leave. Let you deal with him. He's got no vehicle after all."

"I think it would be dangerous to go outside."

Jetmir's voice was near to exploding. "I can't get the twenty feet from my door to my car?"

"I can't guarantee it. Plus, you have the woman and luggage. That will slow you down."

"Luggage, woman. Hell, I can leave them. He's after me, not my women. And screw the luggage, I can buy more clothes."

Jetmir paused to catch his breath and get himself under control.

"You lay down suppressing fire. You have enough men. Then I can get to the car and go."

"That's a good idea," Bekim said. He needed to calm his boss down and correct him without making him angrier. "The problem is we don't know where he's hiding in the woods. I can shoot up the forest, but I don't know if I'll even be shooting in the right direction." He paused for a moment. "And this man knows what he is doing. He's a good shot and has already killed three of our men."

Jetmir swore for the next minute while Bekim stayed quiet. When he had regained some control, Bekim spoke again.

"Let me think about how to do this. I may be able to get to the van and shield you from any shots. But only if I can determine where the shooter is."

"Call me back when you have a plan. I have to get out of this trap."

After the call, Jetmir thought about the help on its way. *Ten people. No more. Can they help? Or will the sniper take them out as well?*

Up amid the rocks, Dan watched. His Sako was lying beside him. There was a notch in the outcropping for him to slide the barrel through when the time came. He could sight the compound and anything in it without being seen. The suppressor would also make it harder for anyone to locate where the shots were coming from. He had laid out six five-round magazines, all loaded with the .338 Lapua Magnum cartridge. When the shooting started, he had rapid access to thirty rounds before he would need to spend time reloading. Because of his distance from the compound, an assault on his position would be necessary before anyone could effectively return fire. Even if they had a shoulder-fired rocket launcher, he would be out at the end of its effective range.

Dan smiled at the thought.

As he watched, Dan saw a man run out of the barn. Quickly, he slipped his Sako through the notch and took aim. Before he could center on the target, the man dove around to the front of the van, cutting himself off from

Dan's view. The driver-side door opened. A moment later, the van started to move. Dan fired a round into the right-side rear tire. He followed that up with another round into the left. Still, the van moved forward, now on two flat tires.

What's he up to? He can't leave like that.

When the van got to the front of the lodge, it turned sideways and stopped. *He's making a shield for the BMW. Jetmir's going to try to flee.* Dan switched his sights to the front door. *Don't want to kill him. But I can't let him get away.* As Dan pondered his dilemma, Jetmir dashed out of the door for the cover of the van. From there, he could get to the car without Dan having a clear shot. *Disable the BMW?* In the back of his mind, he thought the BMW could be used for his own getaway, but if he had to disable it... he'd figure something else out.

Dan could not get a clear shot at the car with the van shielding it. He could put rounds into the roof but not the tires or engine. *Maybe the dashboard.* However, that came with a high probability of hitting Jetmir. He waited. With each round fired, those in the barn would have an opportunity to pinpoint his position. Then, he might have to worry about men coming through the woods from different directions. Better they stayed cooped up in the barn.

The BMW started to move. Jetmir had crawled into the driver's seat. Dan paused. To shoot through the roof now might mean killing Jetmir. As the car turned, Dan led the machine and emptied his five-round magazine at the front of it. At 500 yards, the rounds took just over a half-second to reach the target. The rounds hit the engine bay and the left front tire, flattening it. The engine seemed to splutter, and the car stopped short of the exit to the main drive.

Dan jammed a new magazine into the rifle. While there was a pause, he took the opportunity to reload the spent magazine, giving him thirty more rounds to shoot. As he loaded his mag, Jetmir slipped out of the passenger-side door and hid behind the car. The van now started to move towards Jetmir. Dan let it continue. *Better to have him back in the house or barn than running through the woods.* He watched as Jetmir slipped into the van when it got close, and then the machine limped back towards the lodge on its flat rear tires. *He's got a loyal guy driving that van.*

Now, shots rang out from the barn. The rounds hit well below Dan's position. During the volley, Jetmir dashed back into the house. Dan let him go. He watched the barn. He could tell that the shooters had a general idea of where he was and, once looking in the right direction, would assume the rocks as the perfect place for a sniper to hide, just as Dan had decided. *Not good. Have to watch for an assault.*

He took aim at one of the windows. When he saw a barrel stick out, he fired two rounds. One straight over the barrel and one to the right of it. The barrel flipped upwards and disappeared. *One down. How many to go?* So far, no one was trying to get from the barn to cross the open ground in an attempt to reach the woods. Taking out the one shooter seemed to have stopped the firing coming from the barn. *They either know they can't reach me, or they're scared of exposing themselves.* Firing blind, even if they were in range, would be almost useless at any distance.

As Dan focused on the shooters, the van backed up to the barn. A large door swung open to cover the rear of the vehicle. The passenger door opened, and a figure dove through it to the cover of the barn door. Dan fired one shot, which he knew would penetrate the wood, letting them know it was of little use as protection.

The compound went silent. No shots came from the barn. No one tried to leave either the barn or the lodge.

From his elevated position, Dan could see anyone making for the woods. *What next?* Dan was patient, but nightfall gave his enemy opportunities he didn't want to allow or deal with.

David Nees

Chapter 58

D an drank some water and ate a power bar from his backpack. He thought about his position. He had the compound under his control, but that would either diminish or cease with the dark. The situation called for him to act soon, which meant giving up his position to engage at close range.

As Dan reviewed his options, he heard the sound of approaching vehicles on the drive. He quickly brought his rifle up to the ready. Two vans came into sight and started around the circle. They stopped at the barn. The side doors opened, and two men started out. Dan fired two shots in rapid succession, and both men went down. Two more men tumbled out of the other side of the vehicles. Dan started firing into the vans, hoping to do as much damage as possible.

Both vehicles started up and drove around to the south side of the barn, shielding themselves from Dan's line of fire.

Damn! Dan stopped and quickly reloaded his magazines. *What next?* He watched, but no one made a break for the woods. *They've gone inside. That's good for now.* He knew that he would have to abandon his position, as dominant as it was, by nightfall. The larger number of fighters meant he had to become a shadow, unable to be found and pinned down. If he could take out more before he gave up this advantage, so much the better, but Dan didn't hold out much hope that the enemy would expose themselves easily.

He watched the compound intermittently as he made sure his mags were fully loaded. He also checked his M4, which he would need if he had to engage at close range. Suddenly, a shot rang out, and almost simultaneously, he heard the round chip the rocks to his left. *Damn! They brought a high-powered rifle.* Now they could reach him. The game just got more intense. Dan watched the barn carefully, trying to locate the shooter. He focused on the rear of the building. From the front came a burst as someone fired a rocket at the rocks. It hit just below his position with a loud explosion and a shower of dirt and stone. Even out near the end of its range, the explosive warhead could be devastating. *They could bang away at my cover until I'm exposed.* Dan realized he would have to move much sooner than he thought.

He gathered his gear and crawled forward, using the rock cover. It gave out, leaving him twenty yards to the trees and the deeper woods. Dan stopped. He knew he'd be exposed to the high-powered rifle getting across this open area. *Can't jump up and run.* That option was too risky. One, because he couldn't run well due to his ankle injury, and two, because he would present too easy a target for anyone with sniper skills.

He waited. Another shot rang out, hitting the rocks closer to where he had been lying. This time, Dan saw that the shooter was behind a concrete rain catchment container. He was adept enough to not spend much time exposed before sending a round at the outcropping. Dan swung his Sako around to bear on the place where the shooter would appear. He waited.

Two minutes later, the rifle poked back around the edge of the concrete. Just before the shooter fired, Dan sent a round down-range. It hit the corner of the concrete just above the barrel. The rifle pulled back, and Dan, without hesitation, got up and hobbled towards the safety of the trees. He only breathed after entering the cover and moved farther into the woods.

My NVG gives me an advantage if they move out against this position come nightfall. He would go down the slope to engage the opposition before they expected him. It was one against ten plus. Not impossible, but not great odds.

Once the team sent by Manhar got inside the barn, the leader, Ferid, called Jetmir on the phone.

"You called us into an ambush?"

He shouted into the phone as Jetmir answered.

"You're from Manhar? I didn't send you into an ambush. There is someone after me, that's why I called Manhar." Jetmir recognized Ferid's voice.

"Why didn't you let me know you were under attack? I've got two men already killed."

"It wasn't my fault. I couldn't call you. I don't know your number."

"This will cost you dearly. We lose men to save you. You will owe Manhar much."

"Get this man. Kill him. Then I will talk with Manhar. You have the weapons to get to him?"

"I have enough."

"Good. Take care of things. He's already killed too many of my men." Jetmir hung up.

"What do you want to do?" Bekim asked after Ferid pocketed his phone.

"Get my sharpshooter on this man's position. Show me where he is."

Bekim took him to a window, and they both peeked around the edges of it.

"It is that rocky part up the hill."

Ferid studied the rocks. "Your AKs probably don't reach up there."

Bekim shook his head.

"I have a shooter that can reach him and a rocket launcher as well." Ferid began to issue orders, sending the man with the rifle out towards the rear and the man with the rocket launcher to the front of the building.

"We will assault the position. Keep him pinned down. You send men into the woods to form separate teams and climb through the woods. They can attack from the side. He'll be defenseless."

"Should we wait for night?"

"Can your men see in the woods at night?"

Bekim looked doubtful.

"That's your answer. In daylight we can be seen, but we can also see him. At night, who knows?"

Chapter 59

fter packing away his Sako and shouldering his M4, Dan worked his way down the hill, all the while favoring his left ankle. He angled to his right, not wanting to run directly into any group ascending the slope. He moved slowly to protect his injured limb but also so he could listen. Dan expected to hear the men coming for him before they could hear or see him.

It wasn't long before he heard the crack and crunch of people moving through the woods, stepping on branches and other ground litter. He could detect no talking, but they were making enough noise to give away their position.

Dan moved sideways and found a good-sized tree for cover. He had a clear view for twenty yards across the path of the oncoming men. Laying down, he aimed his carbine along the field of fire. Four men appeared, trudging forward up the slope.

Dan opened fire on automatic, taking down the first two. The third man dropped to the ground and turned to return fire. Dan's next burst ended his efforts. The fourth man dove back into cover and now was silent. Two of the men were still alive; Dan could hear them groaning. *Got to get that fourth man.* He did not want him reporting back to the barn. Better to keep them in the dark. Would they send out more? Dan didn't know, but he needed to be ready. *Thin the ranks first, then to attack the barn.* In the end, these fighters didn't matter. They were just in the way of him getting to Jetmir.

Dan picked his path carefully and began to crawl forward and to his right. He needed to close on the fourth man to ensure he didn't make it back to the barn. Every few seconds, he paused to listen, but no sound came from the direction where he thought the man was hiding.

When he had closed half the distance, he stopped behind a larger tree and lay still, waiting and listening. Usually, the enemy showed their hand first. They panicked and began to move, giving themselves away.

Suddenly, there was a burst of sound. Someone was crashing through the undergrowth, away from Dan. The quarry was flushed, but Dan didn't have a shot. And with his ankle, he couldn't pursue. He searched the undergrowth but only caught a fleeting glimpse of a figure moving away at speed, lurching right and left, dodging trees and bushes. Soon, there were only the sounds.

Damn! The curse exploded from his lips. Even with a good ankle, he might not have caught the fleeing man, but at least he would have had a chance. Now, he would get back to the barn and report that Dan was out in the nearby woods, waiting.

Dan limped up to the fallen men. One had died in the burst of gunfire, the other two had been mortally injured. One of those had expired. The last remaining man lay on the ground wheezing with blood frothing at his mouth, indicating a damaged lung. Dan rolled him on his side so he could clear his airway.

"How many in the barn?"

The man looked up at Dan, seeming to not comprehend.

"How many?"

Dan held up five fingers, then five more gesturing, which was more accurate. The man focused on the ten fingers but could not say anything. Dan asked again and then watched as the man's eyes went blank.

He sat back in frustration. *So, the two vans. Eight to ten people.* Dan began to go through the math. Ten people, two he took out immediately, now three more. Then, the shooter at the window and a second one. But how many men were in the barn to begin with? *Too many unknowns.* A quick calculation gave him twelve to fifteen men he was up against. *It doesn't matter. Just have to take them out. They're in the way of me getting to Jetmir.* He sat back for a moment and thought about doing an end run around the defenders. Just work his way to the lodge and capture Jetmir. But how to escape? Defending himself against the others would only be more complicated if he had to keep control over Jetmir. No, he needed to go through the ones protecting the arms dealer.

His next thought was of Jane. She came unbidden into his mind. *What was she doing now? How was she handling the increased surveillance?* He shook his head. "These thoughts will get you killed." He spoke out loud to himself. *Think about her after the mission.* The memory of Christina brought up in Moscow had proven to be unsettling. He didn't need to have his mind subvert him again. *Compartmentalize.* He admonished himself. Save the indulgent thoughts for later.

It was time to move. He wanted to be positioned to deal with any other combatants entering the woods. The more he could take out without attacking the barn, their "fortress," the better for him. Leaving the three men where they had fallen, Dan made his way further down, moving roughly parallel to the barn. He was about seventy yards into the woods from the clearing. When the ground flattened out, he guessed he was down to the level of the compound.

After some searching, he found a place to position himself that hid him well but had some visibility to anyone coming from the buildings. He relaxed and waited. The bugs soon found him. It was late spring, and they were becoming a nuisance. Dan had a long experience managing them, built chiefly on the learned ability to cover as much of himself as possible and tolerate the assault on the parts he could not cover. Silence, lying motionless, was critical, no matter what. The wrong move could prove fatal, as many he had fought learned too late.

He knew he was up against city gangsters. They were brutal, violent, and often deadly, but they had no sniper skills and probably little experience in the woods. That lack would be to Dan's advantage. But would they send anyone out? The man who got away would report a deadly ambush by someone unseen. He would enhance the tale so that he would not seem cowardly, thus creating an exaggerated picture of how the attack in the woods went. *Might be hard to get volunteers.*

Having given up his oversight from the rocks for mobility in attacking and counter-attacking, Dan knew he was vulnerable to Jetmir being rounded up in one of the vans he hadn't disabled and driven away. He knew he could not lie in wait too long. The fight might not come to him; they would just leave. And he would have to start all over only with Jetmir on high alert. Dan sighed in frustration. Again, circumstances dictated his tactics.

Chapter 60

D an got up. *If the fight won't come to me, I'll have to take it to them.* He began a careful advance through the woods, keeping silent and protecting his ankle, which had not stopped throbbing despite elevating it every time he stopped.

As he neared the edge of the woods, the underlying brush grew thicker, getting more sunlight from the clearing ahead. This gave Dan more cover. He found places where he could get a glimpse of the compound and adjusted his course to come out near the barn. He positioned himself on the south side, where the two vans were parked.

After some thought, Dan decided to shoot out the tires on one van. He could only hit the tires on one side, but taking both front and rear out should cripple the van enough so no one would use it. That would leave only one vehicle capable of leaving. *And I'm going to need it.*

In single-shot mode, Dan punctured both left-side tires on the rear van. After taking his shots, he rolled behind a large tree. The barn opened up with multiple volleys of fire from differing points. The shooters did not know precisely where Dan had fired from, so they sent rounds in a broad pattern. Dan sighted one shooter at a window and fired. The shot hit him in the head, and he flopped back out of sight. The shooting stopped as the men pulled back from the windows and door openings.

Dan thought about his next move. He had one grenade and one flash-bang. These could be used to assault the barn and give him a short advantage in the face of greater numbers. *I'd like to save the flash-bang for Jetmir.* Dan figured this would be the best way to get control over the arms dealer without having to shoot him.

During daylight, there was no way for Dan to cover the open distance between the woods and the barn. The ones inside might not come out to engage him in the forest, but they certainly were going to make sure he could not approach and attack them in the barn. *If they're not coming out in the day, they probably won't come out at night. Unless they have night vision goggles.* NVGs would give them an advantage or at least put them on par with Dan if they thought he might have some.

Stalemate. I can keep watch on one van. They can't leave and evacuate Jetmir. If they remain in the barn, I can't get to them. How long will Jetmir allow this to go on?

While watching the barn closely, Dan went through the scenarios and outcomes. He concluded it would be Jetmir who would trigger some action. The man would not be happy with any stand-off. He wasn't going to wait days for Dan to run out of food or water. No one knew how much he had in the way of supplies.

Inside the barn, that exact conversation was taking place between Jetmir in the lodge and Bekim and Ferid in the barn.

"You want to wait him out?" Jetmir asked. His voice dripped with disdain and incredulity. "You think he'll just go away? Or simply starve to death?"

"Nothing that simple," Ferid said. "His capabilities will degrade before ours. He's out there, unprotected from the weather and bugs. He can't have the food and water we have here in the barn and you have in the lodge."

"And what makes you think he won't just move over to the lodge and come after me? He can work around you. If you remain pinned down, afraid to move, he's won and I'm on my own."

"*Shef,*" boss, Bekim said, "have you considered he might want to capture you alive? Not kill you? It seems he didn't shoot to kill when you tried to escape in the car."

"That gives me little encouragement. He may want some information from me. Then he'll kill me. Hell," his voice began to rise, "he could get in here and do just that while you cowards huddle in the barn."

"If he moves against the lodge," Ferid said, "call us and we'll come over."

A string of profanities followed Ferid's comments.

"Get the fuck out into the woods and kill him. You outnumber him. He can't shoot all of you before you take him."

"But—"

"No buts. Go do it. I'm not going to sit here and wait for him to move on me while my security is thirty meters away sitting like cowards. Go out and kill him now!"

Ferid and Bekim looked at each other as the phone went dead. No one spoke. The men who had been listening didn't say a word. Silence reigned in the barn. Finally, Bekim grabbed Ferid and led him to one corner, out of hearing of the rest of the men.

"I can't just sit here when my boss demands action," Bekim said. "I know it's risky, but he has a point. If this man goes to the lodge and captures Jetmir, he could kill him before we get there. He may want information, but he'd never let us capture him and free my boss. He's very purposeful...and deadly. You didn't see the hill he fell down after we blew up his SUV. He's tough."

"I know he's tough...and dangerous. I have five dead men to prove it. Six now with that last round of shooting."

"If we send all our men out, we *can* overwhelm him."

"And how many men die?"

Bekim thought for a moment. He had fewer men to offer than Ferid. But he had already lost men.

"What do you tell your boss if this man is successful and kills Jetmir? Won't he think of you as a failure?"

Ferid snorted. "He'd probably take over Jetmir's business. He might not be disappointed."

Bekim shook his head. "There is someone from the Middle-East. Someone connected to Jetmir. Someone who can tell him what to do. That someone will come here, to us, and demand answers. From what I hear, we don't want that person coming here. Not you, not me, not your boss."

"Who is this dangerous person who we should be afraid of?"

Bekim shook his head. "I have never met him. Jetmir calls him Muntaqim. It means Revenger. He's very dangerous and backed by a very rich and powerful person. That is all I know."

Now Ferid looked less disdainful. Doubt seemed to have crept into his face. "And Jetmir listens to this person?"

Bekim nodded. "He ordered Jetmir out of town earlier and told him to stay there. Jetmir came back and then this assassin showed up." He paused for a moment. "I don't think you or I, or your boss would be safe from him."

"Hah. He can't touch us. In Tirana we rule."

"He would not come in trying to defeat you or put your boss in place. He would just come in and kill everyone involved. All of us."

"How would he know?"

Bekim just shook his head. "I don't know, but he would know, and act."

"We send our men, some to certain death? Now against this assassin?"

"Better than having the other one come here."

Chapter 61

Dan was contemplating the stand-off when eight men burst from the barn and started running towards the trees. They were indiscriminately firing their carbines as they ran. Dan sighted the men closest to him and dropped two of them. Before the others could zero in on his position, he backed away and turned to run further into the woods. Shots followed, but not coming close.

Once he had gained some distance, he stopped and found some dense cover to hide in. His ankle throbbed from the running, but he ignored it. The game was on now. They were going to try to overwhelm him with the remaining men. The noise of the men crashing through the woods diminished as they slowed. *Now they have to hunt for me*. Dan smiled. This was the fight he was looking for.

He scanned the surrounding area, noting the larger trees, swales, and rocks sticking out that could provide cover and a retreat path. A gully ran off to his left, taking water across the saddle and down towards the western slope. It would provide cover for a fast crawl, but he would be exposed if he tried to run.

He crawled back to the depression and slid in. The sounds of the men grew closer. They were taking more time, being careful to watch for an ambush. *The guy who got away must have warned them.* From the sounds, Dan guessed they had formed a rough line, staying in sight of each other. They were turning to the north to work the woods back to the slope where Dan had first set up. *Want to pin me down, not let me escape to the side and attack from there.* He had a momentary feeling of being a stag driven by hunters. Only this stag could counterattack.

He crawled forward in the swale, moving sideways to the approaching men. When he felt he was close to one side of the line of search, Dan stopped and waited. They would soon be in sight. A figure appeared fifteen yards ahead and to his right. Then another further right. The men walked tentatively. Dan could see their nervousness. They knew his attack could come at any moment.

He aimed for the nearest man, The one at the end of the line. His shot hit him in the head, and his hat flew off with a spattering of brain and blood as his limp body collapsed to the ground. Without waiting, Dan swung his rifle to the next man and hit him in the chest as he was dropping to the ground. Men were now shouting, and the line seemed to swing towards Dan. Shots rang out. This time close to where Dan was lying. He started a fast crawl away from the closing shooters. Rounds flew overhead with their deadly whistle; others gave a solid *thunk* as they slammed into trunks.

When Dan reached a low rock outcropping, he crawled out of the depression. Now rocks chipped as the shooters honed in on him. He could hear them start forward with blood-curdling shouts. Dan scrambled on his belly to a nearby tree and turned, flat on the ground, to watch the approaching men. *Have to wait and take out as many as I can in an automatic burst.* Picking off one or more would only increase the possibility of getting trapped.

One of the approaching men appeared ahead. The brush moved with others coming up on his flank. There was only a brief glimpse of them as they pushed through the undergrowth. Dan fired, and the shot hit the first man in the chest. He staggered back, sank to his knees, and opened up on full auto in Dan's direction. Shots flew overhead and slammed into the tree. One grazed Dan's upper arm, spinning him sideways. *Damn!*

He spun around to the other side of the tree. The man was still kneeling, trying to keep his rifle aimed. He fumbled for another magazine. One he was not going to get to use. Dan's next shot hit him in the side of the head, and he flopped over, lifeless.

He didn't watch but lifted his aim as two more men appeared beyond the dead shooter. Dan flipped his fire control to auto and opened up, sending thirty rounds towards the men still partly obscured by the brush. The mag emptied, and Dan quickly changed it out. He noticed blood on his right hand, running down from his upper arm. *It still works. Got to move.* He dropped his backpack, which was a liability, and, ignoring the pain, started forward, crawling towards a tree closer to the man he had shot. The other attackers closed in and fired at the tree where they had seen Dan. But he had another position and waited.

They would come again. He'd be ready. Dan did a quick mental count. Eight entered the woods. *I killed two in the first encounter. Two more while I was in the swale, now another. That leaves three, and some of those might have been hit. Time to finish this.* He picked his next cover position, another rock outcropping just past the fallen shooter.

He started crawling. His right shoulder protested in a wave of pain as he worked forward with his elbows on the ground, cradling his carbine. He could hear a man breathing heavily somewhere ahead. *He's hit and out of the fight. Where are the others?* By Dan's count, two more might be waiting for him ahead.

When he reached the outcropping, he stopped. He searched the brush ahead and to either side while listening intently. The enemy often gave themselves away by sound before they could be seen.

There was only silence.

No one's moving. They figured out that to move is to get shot. It was back to a waiting game. Dan was now positioned roughly between the remaining men and the barn. Then he heard it. A soft crunch. Behind him. Coming from the direction of the barn. Dan's back tingled. He kept motionless. To turn would make too much noise. The rocks he lay behind covered him only from the opposite direction. *They held someone back? Their sharpshooter?* Whoever it was, he was being careful and quiet.

Chapter 62

O ne of the men Dan was moving towards called out. He had heard something as well. Dan couldn't understand the Albanian, but there was no answer. *He's not the fool the others are.* Dan had to get to some cover before this new guy came upon him. He wore fatigue-style clothing in earth tones but was not camouflaged and could be easily seen by someone looking closely.

He began a careful, slow turn, wincing from the pain but not making any sound as he inched around to face the oncoming threat. He could crawl to the other side of the rocks, but there was another shooter somewhere on that side, and he didn't sound injured. From where he lay, he could see a tree ahead, but that was in the direction of the new combatant. Dan needed to retreat and go back to where he had come from. He hoped that would put him to one side of this new fighter.

He began to crawl back to his earlier position, forcing himself to move slowly, not make a sound. The man who had called out did so again. And, again, no sound came from the other. *Too smart. He's looking for me.* The first man said something. A long string of words Dan didn't understand. It sounded like a set of directions. *Maybe he's telling the new guy where I am. Better be somewhere else.*

Dan had switched his carbine to shoot left-handed. He kept crawling slowly while scanning in the direction of the new intruder. Then, he saw the outline of a body through the dense brush.

Dan shouldered his M4 and fired. The outline dropped, then a burst of shots rang out, peppering the ground near him. Dan scrambled to his feet and dashed for the cover of the tree ahead. Rounds whistled near him, Some flying overhead and some hitting the dirt or trees. In a last effort to get to cover, he dove headlong towards the tree as the bullets flew. He hit the ground face first and slid forward before twisting around to hide behind the trunk. The rounds continued to fly past. He could feel blood starting to flow down his face and over his eyes. His right arm soaked his sleeve in blood, and his left ankle throbbed in his boot as if trying to burst free of its containment.

There were shouts in Albanian between the two men. *I might have hit him, but I didn't kill him or take him out of action.* When he had caught his breath, Dan peeked around the tree. After a minute, he saw one of the men from the original group, the one who had been trying to call out to the intruder. He was flitting from tree to tree, moving towards the rocks where Dan had lain. *Maybe a shot here.* Dan watched, rifle at ready. He waited until he could anticipate the next tree the man might dart to. When he started, Dan fired, and the man stumbled forward, seemingly hit, only to reach the cover of the tree.

At that point, Dan heard an engine start up back at the barn. *Someone's leaving! Jetmir! They're going to make a run for it while I'm pinned down in the woods.* Without hesitation, he stood up and tore off towards the barn, moving to the side of the new combatant. He ignored his ankle, which screamed in pain, and moved as fast as he could.

Shots flew after him but were ineffective. *They're wounded, so they won't be able to follow quickly*. As he reached the edge of the woods, he saw Jetmir opening the passenger door after stuffing his girlfriend in the rear seats. Dan stopped and fired, hitting him in the right shoulder. The impact spun him against the side of the van, and he slid to the ground. Dan's next shot was through the windshield. The round hit the driver somewhere on his torso. The van stopped. Dan ran forward. He reached the van as the driver brought his sidearm up to shoot. Dan fired through the passenger door. His shot hit the driver in the side of his head. He slammed sideways against the door as brain and blood splashed on the window.

Dan dropped to Jetmir to grab his pistol as he was trying to pull it from his pants. That move saved his life as a shot from the barn flew over his head. Without hesitation, like a whirlwind, Dan spun around and slithered to the front of the van. *Someone left behind in the barn!* Dan didn't hesitate. There was no more time for standoffs or letting the enemy regroup. The wounded men might come out of the woods at any moment to attack from the rear. He moved to the driver's side of the van and unhooked a grenade from his vest. He pulled the pin and threw it at the window.

The blast was satisfying. No one could have survived it. Still, Dan ran, hobbling to the window, and peeked inside. Amidst the ruin was a limp body. He limped back to the van and grabbed Jetmir, who was trying to crawl away. He dragged him back and jammed him into the van. Then he went to the driver's side and pulled out the dead driver, who looked like Jetmir's security chief. He found some cord in the back and tied Jetmir's arms behind his back. The man cried out from pain as Dan forced his wounded arm to impinge on the shoulder injury. He opened the side door and grabbed Jetmir's sobbing girlfriend. He tied her arms as well.

When both were tied, he looped a line around each of their necks and tied it to a seat mount. They could not free themselves, and they could not run.

"Wait here. I have to finish some business in the woods," Dan said to a scowling Jetmir.

Back in the woods, the two men called out to one another. Both were wounded.

"Shots back at the barn. He's gone back there. I think Jetmir was going to leave while we had him engaged here."

"Yeah. Run away while we deal with the devil. How bad are you hurt?"

"Hit in the leg." It was the new man speaking. "I tied it off, but I can hardly walk."

"I got hit in the butt." It's bleeding and painful. I can limp around a bit."

"He'll come back. We need to do something."

"Not me. I'm getting out of here, while I can still move."

"You leave me? When I came into the woods to help you?"

"We'll both die if we stay here. You think we can defeat him? Wounded like this?"

A string of swearing came from the sharpshooter ending in *"tehangertdreqi"* may the devil eat you. Without a reply, the man moved away, down towards the western slope of the saddle.

A few minutes later, the wounded fighter heard Dan's approach. He brought his AK-47 up to shoot. A shot rang out, and the carbine flew from his grip, shattering his left hand. Dan stepped out into the clearing and limped forward.

"Who are you?" the sharpshooter asked in broken English.

"You speak English. Good. I am the one who brings retribution. Someone once called me the Angel of Death."

"Hah! You no angel."

"No but I bring death."

"You're wounded, but still alive, still fight and kill."

Dan ignored the remark. The man was stating the obvious.

"You're the sharpshooter? The one who could hit the rocks above?"

The wounded man nodded.

"You shot well. I congratulate you."

"So, you kill me now?"

Dan paused for a moment. "I should. But there has been much killing today. And there may be more before it's over. Maybe not for you though."

"You leave me, you kill me anyway. I die here."

"I will take you back to the barn. There's food, water, shelter. You can call for help when I'm gone." Dan looked at the man's leg. "Keep that strap tied tight so you don't bleed out."

"Why you do this?"

"I don't know. You're a worthy fighter. Smart. The others were just fools, gangsters. Not warriors. Maybe I respect that, so you get to live."

He stepped forward and pulled the man to his feet. After disarming him, Dan led him forward. Along the way, he stopped to pick up his backpack, which held his beloved Sako. They got back to the van, where Jetmir and his girlfriend waited, still tied tight.

Jetmir rattled off a rapid message in Albanian as the two approached.

"What's he saying."

"I should throw you down and kill you. He thinks I am superman type. Not wounded cripple with bad leg and broken hand."

Dan smiled and led the man past the van into the garage. Upon seeing his boss, Ferid, lying in pieces on the floor near the window, the sharpshooter let out a string of curses. Dan didn't ask for an explanation.

"You are on your own now," Dan said, letting the man down to the ground. "Remember if we meet again, I gave you life today. Take care of it."

"Faleminderit," thank you, the man replied.

Dan turned and walked away.

Chapter 63

At the van, Dan untied the woman and sent her into the barn. She was so terrified that she didn't represent a threat. Then he climbed into the driver's seat and drove off.

"Are you going to kill me?" Jetmir asked.

"Not unless you make me. I need information. You give me what I want, I may let you live. You don't, I can make you die slowly and painfully. I have done it before and will happily do it again to you."

They drove in silence. When they were miles from the lodge heading away from Tirana, Dan pulled off the road and followed a trail into the woods. He drove down the path until they were hidden from the road. After stopping, Dan untied Jetmir from the seat.

"Out," he said.

Jetmir didn't budge. Dan walked around the van and yanked him out of the passenger door. Jetmir yelled out in pain. Dan dragged him to his feet and walked him over to a tree. He returned to the van, brought over a length of cord, and tied Jetmir to the trunk. Then he stood back and watched him.

"What are you going to do?" Dan didn't answer but just stared at his captive. He was in hardly better condition than Jetmir with his throbbing ankle and grazed shoulder. *We both look pretty bad.*

"I need some information that I think you can supply."

"I didn't know what the SEMTEX was going to be used for. It was just one group of Arabs killing another as far as I was concerned. That goes on in Iraq in case you didn't notice. I don't take sides. I just sell my weapons."

"I think you knew more than that. This was a large order. Probably the largest you've ever done. It was so large, It got on the radar of some people I know in Russia. That's how I found you."

"So, they wanted a lot. That doesn't mean I knew what it was for."

"Tell me who 'they' is. That's a start."

"My arm is killing me. Untie me and let me sit."

Dan shook his head. "Talk first. Then maybe I'll let you sit. Who contacted you?"

Jetmir paused. Dan could tell he was weighing his options. Risking retribution by giving out a name or trying to save his skin by spilling his guts.

"I don't know his real name. He goes by Muntaqim."

"That's right," Dan said.

"You know? Then why ask?"

"Let's see how honest your story is. You don't know all that I know. Lie to me, and I'll take one of your fingers. Lie twice, I'll take a hand." Dan took out his tactical knife and examined the blade. "It's quite sharp. I can leave you pretty well mutilated, but alive, if you make it hard for me. It's your choice."

He could see Jetmir shiver.

"You have his number?"

Jetmir nodded.

"Where is your phone?"

"In my pocket." Jetmir inclined his head to his left pocket.

Dan replaced the knife in its sheath and pulled the phone free.

"Access code?"

Jetmir shook his head. "Fingerprint." Dan turned on the phone and held it to Jetmir's hand. He found Muntaqim's number, which he wrote down on a scrap of paper and stuffed into his pocket.

"I want you to call him. Tell him you survived an attack by me and you need to meet with him. You want his protection and more info about me. You can tell him I almost got to you and you can't just sit here and wait for me to try again."

"He won't believe me."

Dan smiled. "You better hope he does. Otherwise, I have no use for you and you can imagine what that means."

Without waiting for a reply, Dan punched in the number and put the speaker on as he brought it close to Jetmir.

It rang for some time, and then someone answered. *"Marhaba,"* hello, the voice said.

"I need to speak with Muntaqim, tell him it's Jetmir."

"He cannot speak with you. You should not call."

"Don't tell me that. This is an emergency. I was attacked!"

Jetmir's voice rose. Dan's threat seemed to fuel his anger.

"He will be not happy if we don't talk."

"Aintazar," wait.

The phone went silent.

A few moments later, a voice came on the line.

"What is it that you break my order to not call me?"

Dan looked at Jetmir with a question in his eyes. Jetmir nodded as if to say it was him.

"An assassin attacked me. I barely escaped. He killed a lot of my men and wounded me. Who is this person? I'm not safe around here. I can't sit around waiting for him to try again."

"Slow down. Tell me what happened."

Jetmir repeated the highlights of the story, leaving out Dan's ultimate victory. His emotion and the pain in his voice made his tale convincing. Dan nodded in encouragement.

"So, what do you want from me?" Muntaqim asked after Jetmir was done.

"I'm coming to see you. I have to get out of here. You have much protection. I need that. He's killed many of my men. I'm not safe in Tirana."

"Then go somewhere else. You cannot come here."

"He can find me here in Europe. He won't be able to find me in Iraq, or wherever you are now."

"And where I am now must remain a secret."

Muntaqim, I've done good work for you—"

"And I paid you well for it."

"I can do more good work for you. But I need to be protected until you can find this man and kill him. What do you think will happen if he captures me? I will wind up telling him everything and that will tie you to the bombings."

"You do not know much."

"I know enough to make the focus on you tighter and more intense. I would not want that, but no one can survive torture and not tell everything in the end."

There was silence on the line.

Finally, Muntaqim spoke. "All right. You will come to Iraq." Muntaqim gave him the name of a shop in Fallujah and the man who ran it.

"You will contact him and he will tell you where to go. When can you get here?"

Jetmir looked at Dan, who shook his head.

"I...I'm...not sure. I have to arrange things and make sure I can get away without being followed. I will call you back."

"Just leave word with whoever answers. You will not talk to me again before we meet."

The phone went dead.

Jetmir looked cautiously at Dan. "I got a meeting. But you didn't think he would meet with me directly? He has run me through a secondary. That man will make sure it is me and not someone else trying to ambush him."

Dan stared at Jetmir for a long moment. He understood the arms dealer was making a case for keeping him alive.

"We could go to Fallujah together. I can get us past this hurdle. Then you would learn where Muntaqim is."

"I have to think on that."

Dan turned to go back to the van.

"Can you untie me? My shoulder aches bad. I need to bandage it."

Dan went back to the tree. "If you try to run, I'll just shoot you and be done with it."

"I won't run. Do you have any first aid in your pack?"

Dan nodded. He untied the line around Jetmir, holding him to the tree, and then pointed to the van. Jetmir started to walk but began to falter. Dan took his good arm and held him steady.

"Not sure I can make it. I think I'm losing too much blood."

Jetmir's legs began to wobble, and he slid down despite Dan holding him.

"Sit here. I'll get the pack and some water."

Dan released his hold on the prisoner and started to the van. As he walked, he heard rustling from behind. Dan turned, and Jetmir, with his hands tied in front of him, had twisted his body around and pulled up his pants. Jetmir pulled out a small revolver and brought it up to bear on Dan. Without hesitation, Dan dove sideways, pulling his 9mm out of his holster simultaneously. The first bullet whistled past him. A second one slammed into his vest, hitting one of his spent magazines. Dan grunted as the force of the impact twisted him around. He rolled on the ground and fired four rounds at the sitting figure.

Jetmir slumped over. The revolver in his hand fell free. Dan struggled to regain his breath. His chest felt like a concrete wrecking ball had slammed into him. He struggled to his feet, grunting in pain with each movement of his torso, and then walked over to the arms dealer. He pushed the gun away with the toe of his boot and looked at Jetmir. The arms dealer looked back at him with lifeless eyes. Three of the four rounds had hit him in different parts of his chest. One looked like it had penetrated his heart. Dan picked up the gun. It was a .32 caliber, hammerless revolver often used as a backup gun. It was designed for concealment in an ankle-type holster. Dan cursed himself for not checking his captive more thoroughly. Such mistakes often had severe consequences. *Got to be more careful.*

He stared at the man. His life now revolved around so much death. He had witnessed more than he cared to count, either caused by him or by those he fought. It still seemed odd to him how one could easily tell lifeless eyes from ones where the person was still alive. Was that a measure of the soul? Some part of a human that shines through and then disappears when life is gone? He shook his head. He didn't know. The reflective moment passed. His chest brought pain with each breath he took. His arm was still oozing blood, and his ankle still called out for relief.

The loss of Jetmir was not a catastrophe. Dan knew it would have been almost impossible to take him into Iraq and keep him under control. He knew the name of the shopkeeper and where he worked. It was all he needed to take the next step up the ladder leading to his final prey, the Revenger.

Chapter 64

Leaving Jetmir where he had fallen, Dan drove off in the van. After consulting a map, he headed south, away from Tirana, before turning west. Along the way, he called Jane. She answered and then switched phones to call him back.

"Still have the same problem, I see."

"Yep. Still being careful. What can you tell me?"

"Mission accomplished and another link in the chain uncovered. I'm heading to the Semanit River. Look it up. I'll steal a small boat and float down to the mouth. I'll need to be picked up."

"Why the river?"

"It gets me off the road. The police will soon be looking for what I'm driving. And the river gets me to the Adriatic and out of the country."

"I'll need some lead time. Say, two days."

"When I reach the river, I'll call, I can spend two days floating down to the sea. It doesn't go through any major cities, just farm fields."

"Are you okay?"

Dan guessed Jane could hear the pain in his voice. "Pretty banged up but intact. I think I need hazardous duty pay."

"Your whole job is hazardous duty."

"Just so you recognize it. What I suffer for you."

"For *our* cause, for *our* battle. Call me when you get to the river. I'll make something happen."

He drove along, trying to put Jetmir out of his mind. Dan had taken everything he needed from the man. The response to the bombings continued with its count of bodies growing. Hopefully, it would send a message to those who contemplated such actions. It would not deter the ones directly responsible, as Uri had said sometime earlier in one of their conversations. But Jetmir's fate might create some reluctance for those who helped them. *Can only hope that's the case.*

That night, after taking a long, circuitous route that kept him far away from Tirana, Dan arrived at the river. He slipped across to the south side at the village of Rreth-Liboshi, where one of the few bridges that spanned the slow-moving waterway existed. The road took him roughly along the river, going generally westward. When the river made its serpentine curves to the north, the separation between the river and the road increased. When the river curved back, Dan could tell the gap between the two closed down. Still, he needed to get closer.

He turned off on a dirt road that promised to follow the stream more closely. He drove along, looking with no success for an isolated farm or place that might have a rowboat he could steal. Finally, late that night, he came to a group of concrete piers jutting out into the water. They were empty and seemed to have no use except for, perhaps, loading barges of farm produce to take to the sea.

Dan stopped to inspect the structures and discovered a small wooden boat pulled up on the shore, almost under one of the piers. *That'll do.* Dan figured it probably leaked, but if it would float for the night, he would pull it up at daylight and hide out for the day. Drifting and paddling downstream at night seemed to be the safest plan.

After some time of pulling, he wrestled the boat free from under the dock, Dan was pleased to find a broken oar inside. It would provide some additional power to move him along what seemed to be a very polluted and turbid stream. *Still, going with the current is better than going against* it. As sore as Dan was, every bit helped. He took his satellite phone out and called Jane. After she answered, he just said he was on the river. She would know what to do with the information.

Then he pushed the boat into the water and waded out with it. When the water got knee-deep, Dan rolled into the hull, gritting his teeth at the pain in his chest and arm. After catching his breath, he took the oar and paddled into the slow current of the dark, snaking water. Once heading downstream, Dan let the current drift him along. The progress was slow, but he was happy to lie back against his pack and try to rest his body. The river was about 150 yards wide. There were no lights along the banks, which were lined with a thicket of brush and trees shielding the farm fields just beyond the water. This was a fertile, flat land, so the river moved slowly. It also drained away much of the pesticides and fertilizers used on the crops. Dan could smell the agricultural pollution. *Don't want to go swimming in that.* He drifted into an intermittent sleep. The row boat's motion was quiet. There were no waves or rapids to disturb the water.

Sometime later, Dan was wakened by a crunch, and the boat pivoted in slow motion. He sat up and looked around. It was still dark. Moonlight glowed on the eastern horizon, indicating it would soon show itself. The stars shone sharply, with no city or even village lights nearby to compete with their sparkling brilliance.

Looking around, Dan figured out that the rowboat had grounded on a sand bank where the river made one of its curves. He was on the outside of the curve where the silt would ground and stick near the shore and left behind to grow into a shallow bar as more and more suspended dirt was deposited.

He poked the oar down. The water was inches deep. With a tired sigh, Dan climbed out and began to shove the boat back into the stream. After twenty yards of pushing, the water began to deepen. Once over his knees, he swung a leg up and rolled back into the boat. Again, waves of pain swept over him from his injuries. He paddled forward, putting some distance between himself and the bar. When past the curve and back into the center of the stream, Dan sat back again and tried to relax. The water was now about three inches deep in the bottom of the hull, so it would be a wet night.

Despite the wet boat, Dan drifted off again. The pattern continued for the rest of the night, with Dan falling asleep, sometimes only for minutes, to be awakened by some out-of-place sound. He ran aground two more times before the night was over. As daylight grew, he looked for a suitable place to pull up to the shore. When he found a thick stand of brush with a flat bank, he paddled the leaking boat to the river's edge. He pulled it up onto the sand and, with some effort, turned the weathered hull over. Then he lay down behind it, shielding himself from anyone looking across the water. All they would see was an abandoned boat washed up on the bank.

Two days later, Dan drifted into the mouth of the river. Here, the tide overruled the current. Dan paddled as hard as he could with the broken oar and his injuries to escape the incoming tide's suck. Once away from the river's mouth, he set out away from the shore. About a mile out, he could see a small fishing boat sitting at anchor. No sign came from the vessel. Dan trusted that the vessel was waiting for him. He started for it. Exhaustion was growing as his injuries sapped his strength. His shoulder wound was now feeling infected, making it harder to concentrate, let alone expend the energy to move the heavy, waterlogged boat forward.

As he got closer, he saw a small dinghy with an outboard motor drop into the water and head towards him. It pulled up to the old rowboat. Dan's head hung down in fatigue.

"Need a ride?"

David Nees

Chapter 65

The voice was cheerful and American. Dan looked up.

"Marcus? What the hell are you doing here?"

The large ex-Delta Force soldier smiled broadly. "Jane thought you could use a friendly face, along with some help. You sounded pretty banged up when she last talked to you."

Dan tried to smile and only nodded.

"Here, get in the dinghy. We'll let this old hulk drift away. I don't think it'll be floating for too much longer."

When they got back to the fishing boat, hands helped Dan onto the vessel with much painful grunting on his part. Two people helped him into the cuddy cabin, where he sat down, and someone offered him a cup of coffee.

"You are a mess," Marcus stated after looking him over.

"Thanks. I feel like it as well. Where are we going? This is a pretty small boat to voyage to Italy or anywhere else."

"You got that right. Roly little fucker she is. I'd hate to be out in a storm on her. Still, she was close by and available."

The three other men had gone back out of the cabin. Dan heard the engine start, and the boat began to move.

"So, where *are* we going?"

"We, my friend, are going to meet up with a luxury motor yacht that Jane has rented or appropriated, not sure which. It's about a half day's motoring away. These intrepid Albanian fishermen will be generously paid off and then they will go about their normal business of smuggling immigrants into Italy, along with the occasional fishing."

He turned Dan sideways.

"Let me look at this shoulder."

Hours later, they pulled up next to the large motor yacht. The crew held the small fishing boat close to the stern of the larger vessel as many hands helped Dan onto the swim platform. From there, he climbed the steps to the rear deck and then inside.

Everything happened in a fog as a fever gripped Dan. He did not register on the doctor attending him, cutting away his clothes, cleaning his wound, and examining the massive bruise on his chest. There was only the fog, which approached a delirious state...and the pain. After checking him out, the doctor gave Dan a shot, and he fell blissfully asleep on a clean, comfortable bed.

That night, Marcus made a call to Jane. Marcus and his best friend, Roland, also an ex-Delta Force soldier, had been recruited by Jane. They had worked with Dan on many of his missions. At first, Dan had chafed under Jane's orders to include the two fighters, but soon the three of them had developed a close bond. One only brothers-in-arms can build over the years of intense and deadly combat. Both Marcus and Roland were large men, not really able to blend in with the general population. Their military bearing, coupled with their sizeable, fit bodies, meant people noticed them and gave them space. As a result, although deadly in their own right, it was hard to use them in the covert missions involving Dan. That said, when the chips were down and fighting needed to be done, he wanted no one else by his side.

"How is he?" Jane asked.

"Pretty banged up. His shoulder got gouged, pretty deep by a bullet and it got infected. The doctor had to dig out some of the infection. He also took a round in the chest—"

"Oh no!"

"It's okay. It was a small caliber gun and a magazine took the impact, so there was no penetration. Kind of like body armor, but he's got a hell of a bruised chest. He's sleeping now. The doc says he might be out for a day or more, given what he's been through and the sedative. He's got an IV in him to keep him hydrated."

"Thank God for that. I'm glad you're there with him."

"Always happy to bail out our boy. You do know we rescue his ass more often than not, don't you? I think you should give Roland and I a bonus."

"Bonus, my ass," Jane replied, "that's why I hired you."

"May I quote you on that? When he gets back to the land of the awake, I'll tell him that is our official role, rescuing his ass. He keeps denying it."

Jane chuckled.

"I'm happy to make you laugh. You relax now. I'll get our boy safely back to Israel."

"Good. I'll be flying there in two days for a debrief."

"You bringing Roland?"

"You think I should?"

"He'll be pissed if you don't."

Jane laughed again. "Don't worry. He'll be on the plane, telling me how all the ladies are sad he's leaving on another adventure. I don't know exactly where we go from here. Much will depend on Dan's information, but I think we may need both of you for whatever comes next."

She ended the call, and Marcus went out on the stern deck to watch the wake shimmering in the moonlight.

It was a day and a half later when Dan woke up. The nurse called Marcus, and he came down to the bedroom.

"Back in the land of the living, I see," Marcus said as he entered the room.

Dan was sitting up in the bed. The IV was still plugged into his left arm. His right upper arm was cleanly bandaged.

"So, it really is you. I thought I was dreaming, or delirious."

"No dream. Yours truly in the flesh." Marcus stepped forward. "You look a lot better than when you came in."

"I feel better, but I don't remember much. What happened?"

"We picked you up from the rowboat, remember that?"

"Vaguely. How long have I been out?"

"Thirty-six hours. You're on a fancy yacht that Jane commandeered. She put a doctor and nurse aboard. She was worried about you from your last conversation. Good thing. You had a nasty infection growing on that arm from the bullet wound. What the hell did you do? Roll around in pig shit?"

"I think I fell into the river. Stumbled. Maybe a couple of times. It's very polluted."

"Anyway, the doc got it cleaned out and you're on some serious antibiotics."

Dan looked around. The room was luxury-yacht plush, richly paneled in light-colored wood with a gleaming, deep glass-like finish, all accented in stainless steel. Clever built-in cabinetry was everywhere you looked. A flat-screen TV hung on the wall opposite the bed.

"Pretty nice digs," Dan said. "I'm hungry. Any chance of getting something to eat?"

"That's my guy. You can almost kill him but when he comes to, he's hungry. We have a chef and good-looking serving girls—"

"I think they're called ship's mates," Dan said.

"Call them what you will, they're beautiful."

"I'm sure you've gotten to know them."

"I'm working on it," Marcus said with a wink.

"What about your helicopter pilot? You get tired of her?"

Marcus shook his head. "No, my friend. But she's back at Fort Bragg...and I'm stuck here with you." He lifted his hands as if to say, what's a guy to do? "She's still the special one, but our lives are not going in similar directions right now...we'll see." He turned to go, "I'll go have the chef rustle something up for a recovering warrior."

Two days later, the yacht arrived at Marina Herzliya just north of Tel Aviv. From there, the two men got into an SUV and were driven to METSADA headquarters, where Dan's long adventure had begun.

Chapter 66

fter Dan had finished recounting events, Eitan sat with a thoughtful look on his face. Uri was at the table, along with Jane and both Marcus and Roland. The room was quiet. Dan sat uncomfortably, still aching from the bullet impact to his chest and his sprained ankle.

"You have an impressive array of contacts," Eitan said after a long pause. "Not many people are almost blood brothers with a notorious Russian mobster. He's been on our radar for years since he deals in both drugs and arms. I don't understand how you can be close to someone like that."

"I don't think that's important right now," Jane said.

Dan's face showed some irritation. He didn't like her to run interference for him.

"It's a long story and not relevant to our current situation," Dan said. "And, it really doesn't matter a whole lot to me what you think about my contacts. You know that we have to operate in a world of compromised individuals and unsavory characters. As far as this man is concerned, he has quite a strong internal sense of morality."

"His own morality," Eitan said.

"Agreed. But at least it's consistent. One can rely on it, unlike most politicians I know."

"Let's get back to the mission," Uri said. "I don't give a fuck about Dan's relationship with a Russian mobster. He got what he needed and he's got a name which may be the path to the next player, this Muntaqim."

"And he's eliminated one of the responsible parties in the chain leading to these attacks," Jane said.

Eitan threw up his hands in defeat. "I don't mean to argue with you or minimize your incredible results. I only state my reservations openly since I've been burned by sources of so-called help in the past."

"Judge your own, not mine," Dan said.

"The question now is how do we proceed against this target." Jane said. "We have to get back into Iraq, to Fallujah and who knows where else. It's again undercover deep into enemy territory. A place you can't openly go." She directed this last to Eitan.

"But you can," he replied.

"The country has a Level 4 advisory, so no one can travel easily," Jane said.

"Okay. It's undercover. Like the last time," Uri said. "Dan and I did all right on that mission. We can do it again. There's a renewal of archeological interest, not just in the Mosul area, but all over Iraq. We need to set up another cover. One that lets us range farther afield. Dan and I couldn't use our cover story very far out of Mosul. But a different setup would let us operate in the area around Fallujah and Ramadi."

"Uri has it right," Dan said. "If we can create a new cover story, we don't have to worry about being caught by random checkpoints. It got to be very nerve-wracking because we were out of the area for our previous story. It wouldn't have held up if we had been stopped so far from Mosul."

"This is all fascinating," Marcus said, "hearing Dan's mission debrief and plans to get back into Iraq, but where do Roland and I fit in?"

"We don't blend in very well," Roland said. "A point you made quite clear before." He pointed to Jane.

"Dan can speak Italian well enough to pass. Certainly, to any Iraqi listening," Jane said. "He can be head of an Italian archeological expedition to map out potential sites for future excavations. Then there's no need for permits and approvals from the state. It's just a preliminary search with a report to be made up for the Iraqi government to review. Something for the future."

She leaned forward, propelled by the idea. "Uri is the fixer again. He can pass for an Iraqi and speaks Arabic."

Jane paused and looked over at the two imposing Delta Force men.

"You two are grad students working with Dan. You're American. No sense trying to hide it. You are just on the mission to do what your boss, Dan, tells you to do. It's part of your grad work."

"Big, dumb, and clueless. That it?" Marcus asked.

"I wouldn't put it quite like that," Jane said. "But the role does allow for how you stand out. I brought you over here so Dan would have more backup. This Muntaqim, the Revenger, is not one to take lightly. Even if you can get to him, he will have many people around him. They will protect him with their lives. I feel better with you two in addition to Dan and Uri."

"Just like when we went after Scorpion," Uri said. "The old gang gets together again."

"Speak for yourself, old man," Roland said with a wink.

"Okay," Eitan said. "Let's think about this. Is it viable? Is it the best cover? Would it be better to have the group be doing an arms deal with the government? Or be an engineering group proposing some new infrastructure project?"

The discussion went on for another hour, with variations of cover stories being offered. In the end, the group came back to the archeological idea. It was the least political and probably of little interest to any local police or military personnel they would come into contact with. They just needed the proper visa stamps and letters of approval from certain government agencies, none of which would be checked by the locals and all of which could be forged by the Israelis.

"I'll need a few days to put together all the documentation," Eitan said as the meeting ended. "I'll get someone to start tutoring all of you regarding the relevant archeological information you'll need to convince non-experts. There will be some learning to do."

"I'm taking Dan with me," Uri said. He needs some R & R before we begin. Get me a packet on the background that has to be learned and we'll work on it."

"Going off with mama. That sounds like special treatment. I think I'm jealous," Roland said.

"I'm sure you'll be able to deal with it," Jane said with a smile. She added a sharp look to indicate he was treading on thin ice.

Dan had said little during the meeting after recounting his operations. He was sore, still tired, still fighting the infection, and was happy to let Jane make the decision for him to just take some time off. He knew this mission would be no cakewalk. The most difficult part was yet to come.

Chapter 67

The Gulfstream 550 landed in Eilat, the southern city in Israel on the Red Sea at the head of the Gulf of Aqaba. Jane and Dan were hustled into a waiting SUV and driven south. They turned away from the gulf into the hills to a private luxury compound owned by the Israeli government. The main house was seven thousand feet of open floor plan luxury with windowed walls that opened to let in the cooling breezes and provide long views of the surrounding hills above and the sea below. There was a private pool along with a discrete chef and maid who provided all the support they could ask for and knew when to vanish, leaving the two of them alone.

"What a place," Dan said as they investigated the retreat. "Eitan has access to some fine assets."

"You deserve the best," Jane said. She walked close to him as they toured the grounds.

"I could stay here for a long time."

"It is a nice piece of luxury living. At least we get to sample it for a while."

"How long is a while?" Dan asked. He stopped and turned to Jane.

"I told Eitan we needed a week."

"So long? Is that wise?"

"You said yourself, that Jetmir set it up with this Muntaqim that it would take him some time to get to his man in Fallujah."

"Just don't want to be late. He'll get suspicious."

"You have Jetmir's phone. You can text him later when the four of you head out. He'll not be suspicious of a text since he didn't want Jetmir calling him."

She moved against him, pressing her body gently up against his bruises.

"But let's not talk about him. They'll send down the study materials in a day, so we have some time with nothing to do but relax and enjoy one another's company."

Jane raised her head to this scarred, wounded warrior that she loved. There was no dancing around the fact in her head anymore. Dan bent down and met her lips in a long, tender kiss. Their bodies flowed against one another, almost melting together.

"You do know how to kiss," Dan said as their lips parted.

"I can say the same about you."

She could feel the heat rising in her. He was still recovering, but her arousal was strong and powerful. She had to temper it to his condition. Usually, he would be the aggressor when their passions rose up. An aggressor that she welcomed and met with equal parts of sexual energy. Now, her instinct told her to be gentle, soft, and tender. There would be time for full-blown passion later, even in this short week. Rest, comfort, good food, and light exercise would quickly restore her warrior, her lover. That afternoon, they had a lazy lunch feast of local seafood, a vegetable salad from locally grown produce, and fresh fruits consisting of orange slices, dates, and strawberries in a sweet cream sauce.

Dan fell asleep while Jane watched over him. After ensuring he was comfortable in their airy bedroom, she went into the living room and opened her laptop. She sent off an encrypted message to Henry outlining the plans. Warren had changed the encryption level on her computer and, with her insistence, on Henry's. They could openly communicate with one another without anyone looking in. Henry warned her not to overuse it as the sophisticated level of protection would eventually make someone in the agency or the NSA suspicious. Jane understood, but Henry had to know where they were and what they were about to embark on.

Later, when Dan woke up, he and Jane took a short walk in the dry hills surrounding the compound, being careful of Dan's ankle. An armed Israeli military guard followed discreetly behind.

"This feels good," Dan said as he tentatively moved his stiff body. "The inflammation seems to be going down and my chest is not hurting as much as earlier. The ankle is still tender though."

"Rest and quiet will help. I've also hired a personal trainer to work with you."

Dan smiled and took her hand. They walked in silence, with Dan moving more easily as they continued. Jane thought back to the time they had spent in the mountain cabin before she had dropped him off at Camp Perry. She suspected her feelings then; now they had become a reality. *We've come a long way*, she thought. A smile spread on her face.

"What are you thinking?" Dan looked at her.

"How our relationship has progressed since I first met you. I like where it's gone."

"We get to carve out a few moments of peace and passion in the midst of all this mayhem. It keeps *me* sane."

He sighed and upped his pace.

"But I have to get back in shape for this next round."

"Gently. We have a week. Let's make the most of it."

Dan stopped and put his arms around her. "I plan to."

The week went by too fast for both Jane and Dan. Days were for rehabilitation as Dan healed; nights were for loving. His passion grew fiercer as his body recovered. Jane absorbed it and fed it back to him. They were both glad the help slept in a separate building, as they gave little thought to the noise they made.

The days were spent in ever-increasing intensity of activity as Dan drove his body back into action. Jane had thought their days would be lazy, filled with relaxation and time to hold one another close. There were those moments, but Dan filled most of the days with studying his role as an archeologist and increasing his physical activity, which included swimming in the pool, now that his wound was not infected.

Late in the week, they took a day off to go on a snorkeling outing in the coral reef off the beaches. Always present but always unobtrusive were the guards who kept vigil. Jane watched as Dan would dive down twenty or more feet to check out some details in the coral. She could swim well but preferred to stay on the surface, scanning the strange world beneath her as she floated above it. Dan's muscular body moved with surprising efficiency through the water. He did not try to shove it aside, expending extra energy needlessly, but seemed to flow through it, more like an aquatic animal.

"How did you get so good at swimming?"

They were sitting in an outdoor café overlooking the beach after rinsing off from their snorkeling.

"I added some water workouts, something like the SEALS do, during my Army time. I thought it would be a good addition to my repertoire. I don't want to be in a situation where I don't feel I can fully operate."

"Yet you wind up in many of those."

"That's how it goes, in combat. Especially the type of unscripted combat we engage in. We go find the target, but, as Roland and Marcus always give me crap about, I often don't have a plan." He thought for a moment. "Or I may have a plan but that goes out the window after first contact. Then we have to operate on instinct and be able to function in the face of whatever challenge comes our way."

He reached up to touch her face.

"You are so beautiful. How did I get so lucky to have a boss so good looking, so smart, and who loves me?"

Jane smiled and kissed his hand. "You *are* a lucky man."

She leaned over and kissed his lips.

"And I'm a lucky woman."

The week ended all too soon, and they were back in the Gulfstream on the short flight to Tel Aviv.

Dan looked out the window as the jet climbed into the sky. "I'd love to come back here some time with you. Actually, I'd love to go anywhere with you." He paused for a moment as he stared out of the window. "Just savoring this last peaceful moment. Then we go to work."

Chapter 68

Two days after returning, the four men, Dan, Uri, Marcus, and Roland, were on a commercial airline to Baghdad airport. Customs searched their bags diligently, not dissuaded by their passports and letters of permission pertaining to their archeological activity.

After clearing customs, they took a taxi to the US embassy and consulate. There, they received a used, slightly beaten-up Toyota SUV. It was nondescript on purpose and had a clever, hidden compartment built into the rear, taking up some of the gas tank space. There was a crate brought down to the garage earlier. It contained the arms they would need to secure their mission. The men unpacked the weapons and put them into the hidden compartment with copious amounts of ammunition. There were M4 carbines for all, along with 9mm Sig Sauer pistols. In addition to these were both flash-bang and explosive grenades. Once unloaded, they packed the crate with various archeological tools and instruments.

The trip was about fifty miles, but they could expect road checkpoints along the way. Uri elected to drive as he was the fixer of the group. The others were to play naïve and dumb, especially Marcus and Roland, who would pose as students working for Dan.

After loading everything, the men climbed into the SUV. The station chief bid them a farewell. After getting

Jane's message and the sealed crate, he knew better than to ask about the mission. He was happy to see them off, and only worried about the blowback that would come from any fuckup by them along the way in carrying out whatever mission they had been assigned.

"Play dumb," Dan said, looking over his shoulder at Marcus and Roland as they drove off. "That's an easy role for you guys."

"Fuck off," Roland said. "I didn't come all the way here, leaving behind weeping women, just to get insulted by some Army puke."

"Top graduate of the US Army Sniper School, I'll have you know."

Roland gave him the middle finger with a smile on his face. "Jesus. It's good to be back in action. You chased that arms dealer all around the Balkans and didn't let us in on that."

"Wasn't my call," Dan said. "Jane felt a smaller team would be more successful."

"But now she thinks you need our help," Marcus said.

Dan shrugged. "She's getting an idea that this Muntaqim is quite a deadly fellow."

"Not as deadly as Scorpion, I'll bet," Uri said.

"Maybe. Muntaqim's certainly cautious. Seems to change up his routine and doesn't have a permanent hideaway, a lair like Scorpion. That was *his* downfall," Dan replied.

Marcus stared out of the window as Uri negotiated the turbulent traffic in Baghdad. "Yemen was pretty bad, but somehow, this place seems more dangerous. I'll be glad to get out of the city."

"I don't disagree," Dan said. "After two weeks here, I could hardly sleep. Every day I felt the growing pressure. That at some point the hammer was going to drop and we were going to be stopped with our cover story useless."

"This one hold up?" Marcus asked.

"It should. At least for a while. The letters of permission were purposely written by someone who's not in the government any more. He recently passed away. They're dated while he was still in office."

"So, they can't check with him."

"Right. They can revoke our permissions, but can't actually show our docs are phony."

"Clever, these spies," Roland said. "I say it's best we do this quick and clean. Get the location, go in hard, kill this fucker and then get the hell out of Dodge."

"We'll play it by ear, one step at a time," Dan said.

Roland put a hand on Dan's shoulder. "Does that mean you don't have a plan? All we talked about the week you were gone revolved around perfecting our cover. I assume you were doing the same, or were you too busy with your main squeeze. Tell me we've got a plan this time."

Dan looked over, smiled, and shook his head. "If I did, you'd be disappointed...or argue about it with me."

"Enough you guys. We need to get along," Uri said.

"It's okay, Uri," Roland said. "Just a running joke between the three of us. But you must know that from your two missions with Dan. He makes it up as he goes along."

"Now that you mention it, things did seem a bit confused at times."

"Seriously," Dan said, "this guy seems to try to present last minute confusion and change. It worked for the bombings and could work here. So, we have to be quick on our feet, and flexible."

The men lapsed into silence as they reached the outskirts of Baghdad, and the traffic thinned. Soon, they were going through irrigated farm fields along Rt. 10, which went past Abu Ghraib and Fallujah on its way to Ramadi.

"Any of this bring back memories?" Marcus asked Dan.

"Yep. For you as well?"

"A bit. My longer experience was in Afghanistan. This was pretty nasty though. Both Roland and I felt it."

"Both were confusing places," Roland said. "You were a fool if you trusted the Afghanis too much. Some were selfless in their support, others were vipers you couldn't turn your back on."

"Hard times," Uri said. "We know who our enemy is. But undercover work is always tense. I prefer direct fighting, but I speak Arabic too well. My bosses always wanted to send me in undercover."

He shrugged his shoulders.

"Now I get to fight. I prefer it."

"Roger that," Roland said.

Chapter 69

The four men drove into Fallujah, a town with a population of around 280,000, late that afternoon. They navigated the side streets, working with their maps, until they found the one with the shop on it.

"Let's drive past. We need to check it out," Dan said.

Roland took out his phone and held it up just over the sill of the backseat side window. "I'll take some pictures. We can check them out later."

The shop sold a mishmash of packaged goods, along with snacks and some fruit.

"Looks like he sells about everything," Uri said. "Typical of some small merchants. Kitchen utensils, snack food, dates, tea, anything you might run out of and want to just go down the street to get."

"The Iraqi convenience store," Marcus said. "I've seen versions of it in the States."

Dan sat silent, watching, shifting his eyes from the narrow street to the rooftops. He looked for ambush points. Places where his adversary could monitor the shop and learn who came to see his contact.

The street was narrow, and few cars drove down it. People stared at the four occupants, three of whom looked like foreigners.

"We can only make one pass," Uri said. "We stand out too much."

"Roger that," Roland said. "We're getting the look."

"Drive around the block, let's see if there's an alley behind the store, another way out."

There was an alley, only wide enough for pedestrians. Each block had buildings backing up with a walking space between them and the opposite building fronting the next street.

"Pretty straightforward grid here. Easy to navigate, but hard to hide," Uri said.

After a thorough check of the area, the men drove to a small, local hotel that Eitan had reserved. He used the cover story. A visit by three Westerners would raise enough local interest, but the story might help explain their presence. They would be stopping there briefly before going on to their primary work in Ramadi.

Ramadi was rebuilding, and the cover story was that this team of archeologists was going to check construction sites to try to identify and collect artifacts from antiquity before excavation began in order to help preserve them for the Iraqi government. The permission letters gave them easy access to sites around both cities.

That night, the men sat around in the hotel room, talking quietly. They had eaten in a local restaurant, with Uri explaining their presence to the curious owners and customers. He indicated they would be moving on to Ramadi, where most of their work would be done.

"What do you think?" Marcus asked Dan. "You texted this Muntaqim that Jetmir was on his way and would see his contact either tomorrow or the next day. So it's fish or cut bait time. We can't sit on this too much longer."

"I'm worried—"

"We're all worried," Marcus said.

"I'm worried that if this Muntaqim is as cagey as he seems to be, he might have surveillance set up around the shop. He'll see westerners going in. That could cause him to bolt."

Marcus lifted his hands as if to say, what can we do about that.

"Yeah. Not much we can do," Dan said. "Still, we can't blow things at this point. We're getting close."

"Does Uri look anything like Jetmir?" Roland asked. He was relaxing on one of the beds. The others were sitting in uncomfortable chairs.

Dan looked over at the Israeli. "He's stocky like Jetmir. But his hair isn't as black."

"You mean too gray?" Roland asked. "As in getting old?"

"Fuck you. Always the jokester," Uri said.

"Someone's gotta be."

"Still, it's an idea," Marcus said.

"I need to be there. I'm sorry, but this one has to be me," Dan said.

"Maybe we dress you up a bit to blend in. You could act like the fixer bodyguard to Uri being Jetmir. He might come with someone like that? It doesn't sound like he was a familiar figure in the Middle East," Marcus said. "Plus, he'd be spooked and want some protection if he had almost been killed by the assassin.

"Worth a try, don't you think? It may be enough to fool any security cameras. At least give Muntaqim pause. He probably doesn't want to bolt without talking to Jetmir. Find out more about his encounter with you," Roland said.

Dan thought about the idea. "Could work. Wouldn't hurt anyway. I can't pass as Jetmir. I go in and then there's a phone call, or whatever signal they've agreed to. This Revenger doesn't see anyone resembling Jetmir if he's got videos. He'll be immediately suspicious." He thought for a moment. "If he sees Uri and Uri looks a bit like Jetmir, then the call might seem to be legitimate."

"You willing to try it?" Marcus asked, looking at Uri.

"What do we have to lose? Sure, I'll try it. Having two of us in the shop is also safer."

"Good!" Roland got out of the bed and started pacing around. "We get some shoe polish, darken Uri's hair—"

"He'll need a pair of sunglasses," Dan said. "Jetmir always wore them. And new shoes."

"Fine. Sunglasses and shoes it is. We'll need to darken your skin as well. Make you look a bit less white."

"Looks like we go shopping tomorrow," Roland said.

The men talked late into the night, refining the costumes each would wear and what role Marcus and Roland would play.

Chapter 70

The following morning, Dan and Uri set out. Marcus and Roland, both well over six feet tall and weighing in at 230 and 250 pounds, respectively, would stand out too much. They remained in the room. The decision frustrated both of them, but they understood it. No hint of suspicious activity could come to the shopkeeper's attention before Dan and Uri visited him.

The two returned later that day with what they needed for disguises that they hoped would work. All four men had been letting their beards grow for some time, and now they were sufficiently filled out to help them blend in. They had purchased a face cream, which they mixed with a dab of brown shoe polish. Dan applied this to his face and hands. Uri mixed some black shoe polish with the cream and massaged it into his hair. It took two applications before his critics proclaimed the result dark enough. They added a pair of sunglasses along with some dressy shoes to his costume.

"These damn shoes are too tight," Uri said. "They're killing my feet. If this guy decides to run, I won't be any good."

"Don't worry. It's just for today and if he runs, I'll chase him down."

With the costumes set, they decided on the final steps.

"Roland and Marcus, you guys watch each end of the street. Take a magazine and sit in a café. Sip coffee and keep watch. If anyone tries to seal off the street, let us know," Dan said.

All the men except Uri wore a wire. Dan figured the interest would be on Uri standing in for Jetmir. He was going to be just a bit player.

They all carried their 9mm side arms. The SUV was parked nearby. In the rear compartment, under a cover, were the M4s fully loaded with 30-round magazines. Along with the carbines were tactical vests for all four men with spare clips for both the M4s and their pistols.

"If the shit hits the fan," Marcus said, "we can punch our way out of town, but we'll be screwed in the end. The army or police will come running and we'll be off trying to hide in the desert."

"Better to have a chance, than to be trapped here," Dan said.

"Just saying. It's pretty long odds. And we don't get Muntaqim."

"I hear you."

"Forget that talk," Roland said. "You two just get in there, get this fellow to tell you where Muntaqim is and get the hell out. Then we're off to the next step in our plan. If the boss *has* a plan." He looked directly at Dan.

"Speaking of a plan," Uri said. "What do we do with the shopkeeper, this Waahid Mustafa? We leave him there, and he calls Muntaqim. Then this Revenger is gone."

"I've been thinking about that. He may just be a bit player, not part of the bombing. Muntaqim might just use him because he knows little and can only tell us what Muntaqim wants us to know."

"Us meaning Jetmir?" Uri asked.

Dan nodded. "He may not deserve to be killed. And if I do, it might alert Muntaqim. Someone could find him. We don't have time or the capacity to sneak a body out of town and dispose of it."

"Take him with us. At least for a while," Marcus said.

"That's what I was thinking," Dan replied. "We'll see when we get to talk to him."

"The old play-it-by-ear routine again." Roland smiled and sighed. "But you're the boss. We just get to save your butt."

"And don't you forget it either," Dan said.

Once everyone had dressed for their roles, they exited the room. Marcus and Roland went down to the street separately and walked to the SUV; Dan and Uri followed. The four men got into the vehicle, and Marcus drove them the five blocks to the street where Waahid Mustafa had his shop. They dropped Roland off at one end of the block. Marcus drove past the shop and stopped to let Uri and Dan out. Then he continued to the other end of the street and found a place to pull over and park.

Roland and Marcus, trying to fit into the role of being part of Jetmir's security, would also try to remain as inconspicuous as possible. Dan would act as the personal security for the arms dealer.

The two entered the shop. It was a small space crowded with tall shelves loaded with a variety of goods. One shelf near the rear of the store, next to a cooler, was filled with local produce. One other patron, a woman dressed in a long, black gown with a hijab over her head, was in the shop. Dan and Uri pretended to look at the merchandise while waiting for the woman to finish her purchases.

When she left, Uri approached the counter.

"Are you Waahid Mustafa?" he asked in purposefully broken Arabic.

The man looked at him suspiciously. Uri obviously was not a local.

"I am Jetmir. I'm here to see Muntaqim. He said to see you for directions."

"Ah, the foreigner. He told me you would be coming here."

"You are to tell me where to meet with him."

"That is correct. But first I must call him."

Uri shook his head. "No more calls, no more chasing around. I have been patient and now I must see Muntaqim." He filled his voice with a mixture of anger and fear.

"I...I...can't do that. Muntaqim told me to have you call."

"He doesn't want calls. He is not stupid. My phone could be tracked. Who knows what abilities the ones who are after me have? They are also after Muntaqim. It is safer to just meet. If my phone is tracked, it could lead to Muntaqim."

"But—"

"No! They could be tracking you by now. Better that I just meet with him and he helps me hide. I cannot go back and I cannot wait longer. My life is in danger."

Dan admired Uri's acting, his desperation. His forcefulness seemed like it would be typical of Jetmir, entirely in character.

"I can tell you what I know, but he will not like it."

"Do not worry about that. I will explain that I forced you to tell me. I will make it my problem."

Waahid looked doubtful. Uri nodded to him.

"Go ahead. Tell me where I should meet him."

Waahid paused for a moment and then shook his head.

"No, I must call. It will only take a moment. Then you can be on your way. He's in the Ramadi area. Not far from here."

He reached for the cell phone on the counter beside his cash box. Dan reached out his hand to stop him and, at the same time, pulled his 9mm out of his pocket.

"You will not call him," Uri said. His voice now was openly threatening. "You will not call him and you will come with us."

"I can't leave my shop. Why are you doing this? Muntaqim told me he was going to help you."

"You can leave your shop, or I can shoot and kill you here. The choice is yours."

"Please. I don't want to be a part of this. I just do what Muntaqim says. I'm just someone to make the last connection for you."

While he was talking, Dan went around behind the counter and took Waahib by the arm.

"If you want to live, walk with us. You close your shop for a few hours. We take a ride and you deliver me to Muntaqim. I will arrange a ride back for you and a substantial amount of money for your trouble," Uri said.

"I can't close my shop."

"You can. And I will pay you more than you will make today for the trouble. Do you want to earn a lot of money? Or should my guard kill you here?"

The man was shaking now. Uri went over to the door and flipped the latch to lock it.

"If you kill me, you won't find Muntaqim. Just let me call him."

"If we don't find Muntaqim, you will die, but it will be slow and painful. Something you can't imagine."

He walked up to the shopkeeper and poked his finger into the man's chest.

"Money or slow death?"

"What about Muntaqim? He will do worse to me."

"I will make it right with him. But I will not be led around anymore, by him or you."

Dan spoke into his mic. "Bring the car around to the shop. We're leaving."

The shopkeeper's head jerked towards Dan as he heard words spoken in English.

"Who are you?" He asked, looking back at Uri.

"Jetmir. You find it odd I have an American keeping me safe? They are very well trained for this."

He pushed Waahid to the door.

"No more talk. We go now."

They went outside, and Waahid locked the door behind him. The SUV pulled up, and the three men piled into the back seat. Roland came striding up and joined Marcus in front. They drove off in silence and got onto Route 10, which went to Ramadi.

"Now tell me exactly where I will meet with Muntaqim," Uri said.

He took out a map of Iraq and pointed to it.

Waahid pointed to a junkyard on the southwest side of Ramadi. It was the same junkyard where Uri and Dan had captured Jamal.

"He is here?" Uri asked.

Waahid nodded. "That is where he said to send you."

Chapter 71

U ri glanced over at Dan. Being in the same place where they had gone after Jamal would make it easier. They already knew the route and how to approach the building.

"You know where this place is?" Marcus asked. "In that case, what do we do with Ali Babba?"

Waahid could not understand but watched fearfully, stuck in the back seat between Dan and Uri.

"Secure the current package," Dan said, "before we get the next one."

"Understand," Marcus said.

They drove on in silence.

† † †

Muntaqim hadn't heard from Waahid all the previous day. He expected this would be the day Jetmir showed up so he would get the confirming call. He didn't like spending too much time in Ramadi, especially at the recycling yard. The men who kidnapped Jamal had struck here. It was known to others, but Muntaqim, in line with his strategy to always be creatively disordered in his activities, felt no one would expect him to visit here. It was a satisfactory choice for meeting with Jetmir. He would not let the man know about any of the more secret, discrete locations he used.

That idea, though, only went so far. He felt the more time spent waiting here, the more he risked exposure. If Jetmir did not show up today, he would leave, and the man might not get to meet with him. After pacing around most of the morning, Muntaqim called the shopkeeper.

† † †

The phone rang in the car. Dan grabbed Waahid's arm as he reflexively reached for it.

"It might be Muntaqim," Waahid said. "I should answer."

Uri replied again in Arabic, making himself sound limited in the language. "Don't answer." He pointed to the sky. "Drones. The phone could alert them, and they could send a missile. Kill us all."

The shopkeeper's eyes grew wide with fright.

As they continued, Uri and Dan briefed the other two men about the layout of the recycle yard office. In English, they discussed how they would go in. Roland and, to some extent, Marcus favored a rapid frontal assault. Go in quick, overwhelm any opposition, kill everyone in sight. Then confirm Muntaqim with their shopkeeper and get out of town quickly. Dan and Uri favored a more stealthy approach so they could learn how many were in the office and whether or not Muntaqim had stationed any additional men outside. They would eliminate the outside guards silently if they could and then be able to assault the office without worry of others joining the fight. While the conversation was going on, the shopkeeper sat silently, seeming to try to understand what was being said.

† † †

Muntaqim looked at his phone after the call didn't go through. It hadn't rung out the entire length, which made him suspect someone had declined the call. The shopkeeper would not do that. He had been told not to identify the number in his directory, but Muntaqim had made sure he knew it was him calling and that he was always to answer. *Why would he not respond?*

His men were lounging around the office. Muntaqim had assembled them to be present when Jetmir came. Muntaqim knew Jetmir would not come alone but would bring some bodyguards with him. He wanted there to be no doubt in the arms dealer's mind that he could not exert force in their meeting. He was on Muntaqim's ground and would not dictate terms to the terrorist.

But something was wrong. If Jetmir had not shown up, something else would have caused the shopkeeper to not respond. If Jetmir had shown up, was he up to something? Something Muntaqim would not like?

The instincts Muntaqim had developed over the past years to be unpredictable rose up in him. The dropped phone call was odd. He didn't like odd. Odd often indicated danger from an unseen source. Often seen too late. He survived by staying ahead of or side-stepping odd things. If they turned out benign, the interruption his actions caused was a small price to pay for the added security of his unusual responses.

If the dropped call was a sign of some threat to him, he didn't have much time. Muntaqim knew it would take less than an hour to get from Fallujah to Ramadi. He could shut down this meeting with Jetmir and disappear. Or, he could set up a trap. If this was the enemy, it might be the one or ones who had killed his men. They were efficient and would probably pursue him. Maybe it was better to ambush them now and end the threat. They would think they were ambushing him, but he could turn the tables.

He needed to prepare. There were no explosives at hand, but he could make do with the munitions he had.

"Go get some grenades from the storeroom," Muntaqim told one of his guards. Without a word, the man went out to the building behind the office. He came back a few minutes later with four grenades in his hand.

"Is this enough, *zaeim?*"

Muntaqim nodded. He stood around the large office. *Four grenades should kill everything in the room.* A plan formed in his mind. It was complicated but could be done. He smiled. It was not one of warmth but one of cold satisfaction. He just needed to place them in the right position. Muntaqim told the same man to get some rope and duct tape.

The men watched without a word as Muntaqim paced around the room, examining the space with an unusual intensity. But one did not ask questions of their leader. He did unusual things. They had become accustomed to this behavior and understood it to mean he kept them secure. His seemingly erratic style certainly had worked in the bombings that some of them had participated in. Now, they stood around as Muntaqim walked the office space in a calculating manner.

† † †

As they approached Ramadi, Dan hooked Uri up to their communications with an earpiece and throat mic.

"We're going to reconnoiter the area before we assault," Dan said. "I don't disagree with a strong attack, but I don't want to go in blind."

"We risk getting spotted and blowing our surprise," Marcus said. "If this guy is expecting to meet Jetmir in the office, that's where he'll be. We just have to go in and take him out."

"I'm with the big guy on this one," Roland said. "Sorry, boss."

"Do I get a say in this?" Uri asked. "Since you all seem to be doing this in a very democratic manner."

"It only seems that way," Marcus responded. "When the shit hits the fan, Dan is in charge. It's his mission."

"My mission as well, this time," Uri said. "I'm not just the cover guy for all of you."

"What do you think?" Dan asked.

"We check the place out from a distance. Minimize our chance of being detected. The biggest danger is from any backup he has that jump into the fight after we begin. We need to know where his men are located, in and out of the office. You can be sure he's not there alone. We roughly know the office layout. Dan and I were there. No decisions needed on that part, we just kill everyone in sight. But we need to know if there are other hostiles who can enter the fight."

"I can live with that," Marcus said.

"That's settled then. We won't try to see who's in the office. We don't get too close. But we'll check out the surroundings."

"We'll draw up a diagram of the area when we get off the road," Dan said.

Chapter 72

The next part was more complicated. After Muntaqim decided where to place the grenades, he had them taped to the backs of chairs. Now, he had to find a way to trigger them without killing himself or his men. The rope was a little large, but it would have to do. There was certainly no danger of it breaking. He tied the rope to a pin. One man held the pin to keep it from being pulled out while Muntaqim led the line through the office, through a hole in the bottom of the back door that he had punched out, and across the dirt to the outbuilding. From there, he pulled hard while the man held the pin clenched in his hand as if his life depended on it, which it did.

There was a sizeable amount of slack to take up, but the man reported a strong pull on the line. It could pull the pin, activating the grenade. Muntaqim repeated the process for the other three grenades. When the slack was taken up just far enough, Muntaqim tied the various-length lines together so they would pull simultaneously with one great yank of the ropes.

Muntaqim stood in the storeroom with his men, who kept watching him closely. They vaguely understood what was going on. The arrangement of the grenades was enough to make them uneasy. The office was now booby-trapped with the ropes tied to the pins and running from there to the back door, coming together to go through a

368 David Nees

hole in the bottom of the door. Then the line ran across the ground to the building at the rear and through another hole in the bottom of that door to wind up on the floor. If anyone but Jetmir showed up, they would get a lethal surprise. If Jetmir came, Muntaqim would dismantle the trap and put it away. He would not be sorry for the additional work it had required.

To complete his surprise, Muntaqim needed a decoy. But he had to figure out how to do it without making the man a martyr. He looked over his men. Some of them had been with him for years, some for less than one. His principal lieutenant was a man around his age and could easily stand in for him. He paced the room, careful to not trip over the four ropes gathered on the floor.

"Ebin," Muntaqim called out. His lieutenant stepped forward. "You have been with me for a long time."

"Yes, *zaeim*."

"I have a hard task. You do not have to do it, if you feel it is too dangerous."

Ebin looked steadily at Muntaqim, his face inscrutable and calm.

"Someone is coming to see me. I have told you all that earlier. That is why you are here. But it may be a trap. I have some signs. So, as you can see, I've prepared a counter trap. If whoever is coming is not who it should be, they will be destroyed."

He put his hand on Ebin's shoulder.

"I need a decoy. Someone to sit in the office. To stand in for me. If someone other than who is supposed to come arrives, they will not know it is not me. They will come in and be killed. But if you do this,

I need you to escape the office alive."

Ebin looked confused.

"This has to be timed very carefully. If whoever comes in is not who it should be, you have to get out of the back door and I have to pull the cords." He looked at his lieutenant with a stern face. "You must get out of the office, just before I blow it up. It is dangerous. If you are a second too late, you will die."

"How will I know it is not the right person?"

"I will monitor the office from here in the back building." He handed Ebin a radio. "If it is not the right person, I will click the call button. You will hear it and you dive out of the back door. When you exit, I will pull the cords."

"I will do this," Ebin said.

† † †

When they got close to the recycle yard, the men pulled off the road to review the map Uri was drawing.

"Do we do a drive-by?" Roland asked.

"Too risky," Uri said. "Not enough traffic on the road. We stop a block away and two of us go forward on foot. Check out the scene with binoculars."

"Can't get a whole lot of information that way," Marcus said. "They could have men hiding that we can't see."

"Maybe can't see them from a drive-by either," Uri said. "Only a close-up survey could let us know everything. And that's too risky."

"It's sketchy," Marcus said.

"It always is," Roland replied.

"Let's just get on with it," Dan said.

He got out of the SUV along with Uri. "Uri and I are going to enter the office. Marcus, you and Roland position yourselves at the fencing on either side of the office. You can let us know about their backup and can intervene and slow them down."

They walked two blocks to the corner of the road that fronted the recycle yard's grounds and office. The road they walked along led out of town, parallel to Rt. 10. It had more traffic than the dirt side roads or the one passing in front of the recycle yard. The two men carefully peered around the corner and studied the office and parking area in the front. Behind the office were two buildings. They could see men coming out of one and walking around the yard or going into the front office.

"Looks kind of normal," Marcus said.

"Except some of those guys are carrying rifles. Not the usual equipment for dismantling cars."

"Yeah. They're here for the meeting with Jetmir. He wouldn't even meet with his arms dealer without backup. Probably doesn't go anywhere without them."

"You might be right. We need to get a look at the office from the other direction. I want to see through one of the windows."

Dan put his binoculars down and stood back from the corner.

"Let's walk back a block and go up the road. We can approach from the other side."

"We don't want to take too long. We know they're here, but we don't know how long it will be before Muntaqim gets suspicious. Remember that shopkeeper isn't answering his phone anymore."

The men walked quickly back to the side road, which was also dirt, and hurried down it to another approach road. They turned and headed back towards the recycling yard. Again, they stopped at the corner to peer around a building shielding them from view. Both men studied the office with their field glasses.

"Looks like someone inside, sitting at a desk at the back," Dan said. "Can't see too clearly."

"Roger that," Marcus said. "A few moving around. Someone just left to go out the back door." He put his glasses down. "Could be our guy?"

"Yep. If he's here. And he's supposed to meet Jetmir today, that would be him."

"Got a plan?"

"Just the basics. You know me." Dan smiled.

"Yeah. But I thought I'd ask anyway."

David Nees

Chapter 73

Roland looked at Dan. He waited.

"You'll like this," Dan said. "Uri and I go in while you and Marcus position yourselves along the fence line on either side of the office. You should be able to have eyes on the rear so you can intercept anyone coming from the back building or the yard."

"Intercept as in take them out." Roland said.

Dan nodded. "We'll give you a shout out when we've cleared the office and we'll all beat it out of here."

"Have to move fast after our attack," Uri said. "I don't want another running gun battle like before."

"Right," Dan said. "We race out of here and when we've gotten separation, we leave the way we came in. Just ourselves and our failed archeology mission, in case anyone asks."

"Mark this down," Roland said. "It's a first. A complete plan including the exit, even if it's a bit on the light side regarding details."

"You and Roland get into position before Uri and I drive up. You'll need to get across the road and closer than from where we reconnoitered."

"Roger that," Marcus said. "On this end, one of us can walk across the road like we're hiking out of town. On the other side, I'll have to cross the street, which puts me up against the yard fence. I checked it out, and I'll be out of sight from the office. I can move forward and try to get eyes on the back area. I'll find a spot.

"Sounds like you've picked your side," Roland said.

Marcus nodded.

"Okay, gear up," Dan said. "Use our communications. You alert if there's a threat from the back. We'll let you know when to bug out."

"If we're engaged and can't break away—"

"Let Uri and me know. We'll help from the office after clearing it."

The men donned their tactical vests and checked their magazines. Five 30-round mags for their M4s plus two more for their 9mms."

"If we have to use all of this, we're in deep shit," Roland said.

"Better have extra than to run out. But I don't disagree," Dan said. "We take too long, they'll have reinforcements coming. Let us know when you're both in position."

With that grim thought, Roland and Marcus stepped out of the Toyota and headed for their positions. When they left, Uri went to the rear of the vehicle and brought back a length of rope. He used it to tie the shopkeeper down in the back seat. Uri made sure the man could not sit up and attract any attention.

"When we are gone, you will sit quietly. Do this well, and we will release you when we return. Make a problem for us and we'll kill you. *Tafahm?*" Understand? The man nodded with his eyes wide in fear.

† † †

When all the preparations were done, Muntaqim returned to the rear storeroom building with the rest of his men. He stationed two out at the rear. If anyone was checking out the building beforehand, they would expect to see armed guards somewhere. However, he didn't want any additional men in the office. They would only get in each other's way in their rush to get out of the back door. No, in this situation, Ebin had to be alone, standing in for the target in order to annihilate those who showed up if it was someone other than Jetmir.

With a kiss on both cheeks, Muntaqim bade Ebin well and sent him off. "You do a brave thing today. You are a warrior and we will sing your praises tonight as we celebrate the destruction of those who come to kill us."

After sending Ebin to the office, Muntaqim called the shopkeeper. Again, the phone rang, with no one picking up. He nodded, thinking to himself. Something was definitely wrong, and he was doing the right thing to be suspicious. But the hunter would become the hunted. The one who would ensnare him, kill him, would be killed. He would prevail. A cold smile appeared on his face.

† † †

Roland casually crossed the side road on which the recycle yard faced. He had his head down, a scarf around his neck and head, and a jacket over his tactical vest. It was hot, but he needed to cover his obvious military equipment, including the M4 slid under his coat and following his leg to stay out of view. Two cars passed, one heading into Ramadi, the other out of the city. Neither seemed to hold combatants, but that was one of the problems in Iraq. One could never tell who was a combatant and who was not. If their raid didn't go well and a call went out for help, either one of those vehicles could show up with armed men inside.

At the wall, he inched forward towards the office. There were no windows on this side, so Roland felt comfortable getting closer. He could not be seen from the front windows, and when close enough, he could straighten up and peer over the irregular top to watch the rear.

Marcus paused at the corner to study the office. His crossing the street would be more obvious. Seeing no one looking in his direction, he quickly walked to the board fence. When he reached it, he began to move forward. Nearing the dirt parking area, the board fence gave way to chain link. He crouched down behind some metal drums to conceal himself from anyone in the office. Seeing no one at the window, he stood to peek over the fence to make sure he had a good view of the rear.

"In place," Marcus said into his mic.

"Copy that," Dan replied.

"In place and ready," Roland said.

"Copy that," Dan replied. "We're on our way. We'll let you know when we exit the vehicle and are heading inside."

"Guns blazing," Roland said.

Chapter 74

Muntaqim was standing in the outbuilding, his hand on the ropes. Ebin sat at the desk pretending to look at a computer. He was nervous. The men coming, if they weren't the ones Muntaqim was expecting, if they were the enemy, might come in ready to shoot. There would be no reason to wait if they didn't want to capture Muntaqim alive. He wondered what chance he had to get out of the back door, not before being blown up, but before being shot.

Whatever Allah wills. The thought came to his mind. Still, he'd try his best to put the odds in his favor. He shuffled his chair around so he'd have a more direct path to the door without taking time to turn around.

Dan and Uri got out of the car. There was not going to be any possibility of subterfuge. Muntaqim would recognize that Uri was not Jetmir. They would have to kill him right away when they entered.

As they approached the front door, Roland came on the radio. "Something looks odd, boss."

"What is it? We're almost ready to go in."

"There's a bundle of lines running from the back building to the rear of the office. And I only see two guards in the yard. They're standing around and not heading inside. Marcus you got eyes on the office?"

"Affirmative. Only one person inside. And I can see just the guard out back, closer to me."

"Something's up," Roland said. "I can sense it. You'd think Muntaqim would have his guards inside, as a show of force, if nothing else."

"Can't go back now. We'll crash in, shoot the occupant, and get out. Be in the office less than thirty seconds."

They were at the door. "Going in now," Dan said.

Marcus trained his field glasses on the window to see what would happen. As he scanned across the office, he saw it. A grenade taped to the back of a heavy wooden chair.

"It's a trap!" He shouted over the radio as Dan burst open the door.

At the sound of the door beginning to break, Ebin jumped up and ran for the back door. He dove through the opening as Dan and Uri broke through from the front. Muntaqim saw Ebin and yanked all the cords with a mighty pull.

"Grenades!" Marcus shouted, trying to be heard over the gunfire that erupted inside the office as Dan and Uri shot at the disappearing Ebin.

"Get out, get out!" Marcus shouted.

When the two shooters paused momentarily as their target had disappeared, they heard the warning. Both men turned to the front. Uri dove through the doorway, followed by Dan. He had almost cleared the door when the blasts occurred. The shock wave and the shrapnel flung Dan down the steps, slamming him into Uri, who was just ahead of him. Shrapnel ripped through the office; nothing inside could have remained alive. The windows shattered outward. Multiple pieces of metal, glass, and other debris hit Dan as he dove after Uri.

The two guards in the rear had dropped to the ground. Roland opened fire and quickly downed one of them as he got up to run to the back building. The door opened, and a man peered around the frame. Roland shot him center mass, and he fell back inside. Marcus shot the other guard as he got up to run.

"Dan's hit!" Uri shouted. "One of you help me get him into the car."

"I'm coming," Marcus said, and he ran to help drag Dan to the SUV.

"They got men in the back building," Roland said. "I can keep them bottled up. Get loaded and drive to me. I'll jump in."

Shots were now coming his way from the windows as well as the doorway. No one tried to stick their head out; the shooting was not well aimed. Roland put some rounds through the windows to suppress fire. Then, shots came from the back corner of the building.

"They got a back door," Roland said between shots. He spoke as he continued to fire with deadly precision, making each round count. "They'll spread out in the yard. Plenty of cover for them. They'll be coming from multiple directions. We should get the hell out."

"Coming to you," Uri said. He threw the bound shopkeeper out onto the front lot, and he and Marcus helped get Dan into the back seat. Then Uri jumped in and drove down to where Roland was firing. Roland loosed one more long burst and ran to the SUV. He jumped in front with Marcus in the back. Uri raced off with the tires spitting dirt out the back. Shots chased them down the street until they turned.

Uri flung the older SUV around the corner, heading into Ramadi. The machine leaned dangerously to one side, with the tires slewing across the dirt, grabbing for traction. He sawed away at the steering wheel, trying to correct the slide. They crashed through potholes with violent jolts as Uri kept the throttle pinned.

"Careful!" Roland shouted. "Don't tip us over. He craned his neck around to see if anyone was coming. "No pursuit so far."

"It'll come," Uri said. His voice sounded grim.

Marcus was busy in the rear seat, checking Dan, who was recovering his senses from being knocked out by the blast.

"What the hell happened?" he asked. His voice sounded strained, and his breath came in short gasps.

"Booby trap," Marcus said. "They rigged the office with multiple grenades. You two would have been mincemeat if it had caught you inside. Luckily, I spotted it. The lag between pulling the pin and explosion helped you escape."

"Feels like I didn't get all the way out," Dan said.

"I'm checking. Looks like multiple wounds. I want to find any bad bleeders. Can you roll over on your stomach?"

He helped Dan take off his tactical vest. It was torn by the shrapnel in the back.

"Looks like your vest helped protected you."

Dan grunted. "Somewhat. My back, legs, and butt, are burning like I've been flayed by a whip."

"Looks like it. You're pretty torn up all over. But it could have been worse."

"I could be dead."

The Toyota bounced over the road at speed. The motion continually shoved the team back and forth. Marcus found himself slipping off the seat to the floor. He had to support Dan to keep him from falling off the bench seat as he labored to roll over.

"We can't go back into town," Roland said over the din of the roaring engine. "You race through the city and you'll draw all the cops and military to us. We don't need that. Who knows who sides with who? At the least, they'll arrest us and then we're screwed."

"If we can get through and on the north side, we can head for the border."

"Fuck that. We won't cross with Dan in this condition. They'll stop us there. We need to get out of town and find someplace to hide out," Roland said. "Turn around and get into the desert."

"I'm with Roland," Marcus said. "I need to do some triage on Dan and can't rocking around in this shit box."

Uri glanced in the rearview mirror. Dan wasn't answering.

"Hang on," he said, and he flung the SUV around in a 180-degree turn and headed back down the road.

Before they got to the recycling yard, Uri turned right and found a different road heading west, out of town.

"We'll skirt the yard. Maybe they didn't see the vehicle so don't know what to look for. We can be sure they'll be out looking."

"So slow down," Marcus said. "Don't draw attention to us. I need to cut off some of Dan's clothes and check him out."

He reached into the back area for the emergency aid kit. It contained wrap bandages along with disinfectant and clotting powder.

"I'll try to find an abandoned building we can hide out in until dark," Uri said.

He slowed his pace, and Marcus went to work on Dan. Roland kept his head swiveling around, searching for any indication of hostiles approaching.

The reputable-looking houses gave out, and they passed a tractor-trailer yard. Uri slowed. To the west of the yard was empty ground sprinkled with a few empty-looking houses and some larger buildings. Some showed bomb damage, others just looked abandoned. Uri turned off and headed towards one of the buildings that had an intact wall partly surrounding it.

"We can pull in here, hide the truck."

"He steered the SUV off the road and through an opening in the wall where a gate used to be.

He pulled the machine up against the wall, facing the opening. Anyone driving by would not be able to see it.

"Let's get Dan inside," Marcus said.

Chapter 75

Dan staggered into the building with Marcus' help. He didn't seem fully aware of everything around him.

"I think you got a concussion from the blast," Marcus said. "Are you with us?"

"Feel spaced out. My ears are ringing like mad and I can't quite remember what happened."

His shirt and pants were bloody from the shrapnel that had hit him from behind.

Once inside, the men helped Dan onto a table. Marcus helped him out of his vest and shirt and pulled down his pants. Then he rolled onto his stomach. After pouring some alcohol on his hands, Marcus went to work. Dan had multiple cuts and gouges all over his back and legs. There was a large gash on the back of his head, which was probably the source of his dizziness.

"Jesus," Roland said, looking over Marcus' shoulder. "Your backside is mincemeat."

"Don't sugar coat it, tell me how I really am," Dan said.

"Sorry boss. But you're going to have a sore butt for a while. Sitting may hurt."

"At least there are no major bleeders," Marcus said. "Lots of blood, but no arteries hit."

"Thank God for small favors," Uri said.

"You came out pretty well," Roland said, looking at Uri.

"All thanks to Dan. He gave me cover when we dove out of the door."

"You're welcome," came a weak voice from the table.

"We got a couple of problems here," Marcus said.

The others came over to look.

"Pieces of shrapnel still stuck in him. When I pull them out, they could cause the bleeding to increase."

"Can't leave them in," Roland said.

"Yeah. Damned if I do, damned if I don't."

"Not your call," Dan said. His voice strained to be heard as his face was down against the wooden table.

"Yours?" Roland asked.

"Damn right. Pull those fuckers out, pour on some antiseptic, and put some clotting bandages on the worst of them."

"You a doctor now?" Roland asked.

"No, but I don't want any metal shifting around inside me. I'll seep blood, but I shouldn't bleed out."

"Okay boss. I'm on it," Marcus said.

The others watched as he began to pull the metal shards out. Dan grunted as new waves of pain swept over him.

"Fuckers are cutting you some more," Marcus said.

"Can't be helped. Get 'em out."

After a minute more of pulling, with Dan grunting and breathing heavily, Marcus lifted his head. "Done!" he said.

Numerous gashes along Dan's back and legs were now bleeding more profusely. Roland helped Marcus press the clotting bandages on Dan's multiple wounds.

"Son of a bitch!" Dan shouted with a strained voice.

"Sorry boss. They're bleeding pretty badly."

"We should disinfect the wounds," Roland said. He dug through the contents of the first aid kit and pulled out a plastic bottle of alcohol, handing it to Marcus. "Pour this on to start."

Then he pulled out some povidone iodine. Marcus poured some alcohol on the pad he held over the wounds, causing Dan to shout out a round of curse words. Next, Marcus painted the iodine on the cuts, pouring some inside.

"Some of these really need sewing up," Marcus said.

"Not now," Dan said through clenched teeth. "Just tape them closed."

"We got a couple on your back and one on your leg that probably won't stay closed. At least let me sew those."

"You just want to play doctor at my expense you son-of-a-bitch."

"Call me whatever you like, boss, but that's my professional opinion as a temporary doctor."

"How many?"

"Two on your back and one on your left leg."

"All right. But be quick. There's still some numbness. Take advantage of it."

Marcus took out the needle and suture thread and began stitching through the torn flesh to pull the worst of the gashes closed. Dan grunted and growled as Marcus went to work. The work took ten minutes before Marcus stepped back.

"Best I can do," he announced. He finished by placing another clotting bandage over the sutured cuts and then put some gauze bandage over them, anchored by generous adhesive strips.

"Now for the rest of the wounds," Marcus said. "I'll just tape a gauze pad on them. None hit dangerous areas."

During this time, Uri returned to the door to watch the road. When Marcus was done, he helped Dan turn on his side. Roland gave him some water to drink.

"I've got one hell of a whack on my head," Dan said after a few minutes. "Going to have a massive headache."

"Yeah. You got knocked silly."

"How's Uri?" Dan asked.

"A few cuts and bruises. Some from when you knocked me down. You must have literally flown through the air."

"I don't remember it," Dan said in a weak voice. He paused for a moment. "I'm thinking more clearly now, though. What's our situation?"

"We got to a hideout of some sorts. On the outskirts of Ramadi," Marcus said.

"No sign of pursuit so far," Uri called out from the doorway.

"So far," Roland said. "That won't last."

"We need to go north," Dan said. "Uri knows the way."

"Not north this time," Uri replied. "I think we go west towards Jordan. Our cover story may work there. We can say we came under attack from some leftover ISIS gang. Barely escaped with our lives."

"We play the freaked-out researchers," Roland said.

"Won't Muntaqim expect us to go west?" Dan asked.

"Probably," Uri said. "But there are two roads going that way, so we have a fifty-fifty chance of not running into them."

"Unless they have enough men to cover both roads," Marcus said. "Way out in the desert, away from the government, they could set up a checkpoint and stop all west-bound traffic."

"But getting across into Syria is just as dangerous. Especially with our wounded man," Uri said. "There'll be lots of questions."

"Tough choices," Marcus replied.

Just then, they heard the sound of a truck. All three men rushed to the windows or doorway. A pickup loaded with men carrying what looked like AK47s was driving slowly down the dirt road.

Chapter 76

Muntaqim's lieutenant, Ebin, escaped the carnage of the four grenades with only a few cuts and ringing eardrums. After the blasts, he jumped up and ran to the outbuilding, diving through the door. One of the men stepped into the doorway after Ebin rolled inside and was immediately shot. Whoever had tried to ambush Muntaqim had brought backup. His men immediately went to the few windows and, with more care, to the doorway to return fire. The shooting came from only one source, but it was deadly accurate. Muntaqim sent men out of the back door.

"Go, spread out. Use the cover of the vehicles and close in on the shooter from different positions."

Five men nodded and slipped out of the door into the recycle yard. From inside, Muntaqim heard the truck start, stop, and then roar away. There was no more shooting coming from the fenced area. One of his men shouted back that the SUV had driven off, heading into Ramadi.

Muntaqim walked to the office, hoping to find the remains of the ones coming to assassinate him. He looked around the shattered space, desks overturned, file cabinets and walls riddled with shrapnel, the windows blown out. But no bodies. He heard someone calling from the front yard. The men with him went to the blown-out front door and found the shopkeeper tied up and lying in the dirt. Muntaqim went over to him and gestured for someone to untie him.

"You brought these men to me, to kill me?"

The shopkeeper shook his head violently. "No, no. They made me come. He said that you didn't want him to call you, but to have me guide them to you. He threatened me if I didn't tell him where you were going to meet with them. I didn't know they meant you harm until they had the information."

"Why did they bring you?"

"So I could not warn you. They seemed to already know the way."

Muntaqim digested this bit of information. If they knew where the recycling yard was, they were probably the ones who took Jamal. The pursuit was getting too close. Jetmir had only helped make the situation worse, and now he was probably dead after helping to set up this ambush. Infidels could not be trusted.

Muntaqim was angry. His improvised ambush did not kill anyone. There were shouts from the ambushers; maybe one or more were injured, but it was clear the grenades had not claimed any victims.

"We must pursue them," Muntaqim said. He looked at the shopkeeper. "What vehicle did they have? You rode in it."

"It was an old SUV. Nothing special. Black paint. I don't know the brand. I am not smart about cars."

He hung his head, knowing his answer would not please the man who stood before him.

Muntaqim turned to one of his fighters. "Did you see the vehicle? Do you know what it was?"

The man who reported the departure responded. "I only saw that it was an SUV, not a pickup. It was old but I don't know what brand."

"Headed into the city?"

"That's the way they turned." The man looked frightened, unsure of Muntaqim's reaction.

Muntaqim turned to Ebin. "Call the others. We have to find them. Alert the police. Give them a description of the vehicle but not too much information. Let's assume they are westerners. That will give the police something to look for."

His lieutenant took out his cell phone and began to make calls. After laying out the bodies of those shot, Muntaqim ordered his men to split up into two groups. They gathered their weapons and jumped into the backs of two pickup trucks. One headed towards Ramadi, the other headed west on the main road towards the Jordanian border hours away.

† † †

"What do you think?" Marcus asked Uri as they watched the pickup go slowly through the group of empty buildings.

"Looking for us, for sure," Dan said.

"You think they'll come back?" Marcus asked Uri.

"Who knows? If they see the Toyota, they'll know we're here."

"And we'll be trapped. The truck's out by the wall."

"Yeah. That's why they didn't see it," Dan said. "But it's too dangerous to move with them nearby. They might hear it."

Marcus shook his head. "I don't like it."

"Watch for an opportunity," Uri called out. "We need to bring the truck closer. We need an escape route. This way we're trapped and it's a fight to the death."

"Let's see if they leave or come back," Marcus said.

"They come back, it'll be too late," Uri replied. "If we're gonna do something, we got to do it now."

"I'll get it," Roland said. "Watch them. If they go behind a building, I'll retrieve the truck."

"Get ready," Uri said.

Roland went to the door and waited while Uri watched from another window. The pickup was making the rounds of the scattered shells of abandoned buildings, some in better repair than others. When the truck disappeared behind a building, Uri said, "Go!"

Roland ran to their Toyota. He jumped in and started the engine. Keeping it near idle, he slowly drove to the side of the building. There was a door opening, partially shielded from the direction of the pickup.

"Mission accomplished."

"So far," Uri said. "If they come back on the street, they might see it."

"If they retrace their steps, they won't see the vehicle and we have a way to escape."

"I hope you're right," Uri said, almost to himself.

Chapter 77

The truck slowly trolled through the area and finally turned towards the highway.

"Looks like they're leaving," Marcus said. "We lucked out."

The men started to relax when Uri called out to them. "It's coming back."

Marcus and Roland jumped back to the windows to look.

"Damn. Did they see something?" Roland asked.

"Maybe they were told to check again," Marcus said.

"Doesn't matter. Let's get ready," Dan said

They watched the pickup advance. There were two men in the cab and four in the bed. All armed with AK-47s.

"If they turn in, we take out as many as we can before they find cover. Then disable the truck so they can't get away," Dan said.

Roger that," Roland settled into a position to shoot from a window.

Dan was up and putting his torn clothes back on. He grabbed his M4 and went to another window.

The pickup turned into the opening in the wall where the four men had driven earlier. As soon as they cleared the wall, they could see the Toyota on the side of the building. The truck stopped abruptly, and the ones in the bed jumped out. They scrambled for cover behind the pickup as gunfire erupted from the building, killing the two men in the cab. The other four quickly returned fire, pinning down Uri and the others, suppressing their return fire.

"They'll try to spread out and surround the house," Dan said. "Come at us from all sides."

"We can't wait too long," Uri said. "One of them will have called their boss and he'll be sending backup, if not the police or military. None of that is good."

"Got it," Marcus said. "We'll have to take out the ones trying to flank us before we can get out."

During a momentary lull in the shooting, two of the remaining four men slipped behind the walls and headed to separate sides of the building. One of the two who remained hidden behind the truck called Muntaqim. He reported that they had found the attackers and the location of where they had them pinned down. He was told that help was on the way.

Muntaqim put down his phone, and a smile cracked his face. He would capture them yet, capture and kill. With the threat eliminated, he would not have to look over his shoulder quite so much, although he knew his routine of purposeful disorganization was working. Whatever source of information the enemy had, high-tech or spiritual, he was countering it. A few calls sent two more trucks racing towards the Ramadi suburb.

The men at the truck opened fire again on the building. Dan lay on the ground at the door. Most shots were aimed higher. He stayed in place, ignoring the wounds on his back, which had begun to bleed again. He watched where the shots came from. One shooter was near the front. *The engine will protect him.* Dan looked for the second shooter. After the man fired a few rounds, he saw that the shooter was lying behind the right rear wheel. He opened up on automatic, spraying the ground around both wheels. The tire burst with a bang and a spray of dirt. Dan watched. Looking from his prone position, he could see underneath the pickup. The shooter was backing away on his knees. Dan fired another burst on automatic, aiming under the truck. There was a scream of pain and a tangle of movement barely visible to Dan. *Got him.*

Roland was watching the wall along the side of the building where the Toyota was parked. He saw a lock of hair near a broken part of the top of the wall. Roland brought his carbine to bear on the spot and waited. He wouldn't need much. Through the earpiece, he could hear Uri talking about the shooters who remained at the truck. *Three down, three to go.* Marcus didn't report any sightings from his vantage point.

The lock of hair grew to a larger crop. Roland stayed patient. In the next moment, a forehead began to emerge. The man was slowly exposing his head, wanting to get a look at the SUV and what was happening on this side of the building, but also knowing how dangerous it was to expose himself.

Roland settled his iron sights on the strip of skin. *Give me just a bit more.* The head rose. Now, the eyebrows were exposed. He squeezed off a round. The head flung back and out of sight.

"I got the shooter covering our exit," he shouted into his mic. "Bug out time! Let's go!"

Without another word, the men came running out of the side door with their gear and piled into the SUV. Uri jumped into the driver's seat, with Dan gingerly setting himself on the passenger side. Marcus and Roland dove into the back, piling onto one another.

"All in!" shouted Marcus.

They bounded over the rough terrain, aiming for the road that crossed behind the building.

"Where are we going?" Dan shouted over the engine noise. He was trying to brace himself against the bouncing.

Uri didn't answer. His hands flew back and forth, fighting the steering wheel to keep the truck on course. Shots came from behind them, and everyone shrank down in their seats. When they reached the crossing road, still dirt but at least graded smoother than the raw desert between buildings, Uri turned left and accelerated.

"Going to the highway and then west. As fast as we can go," he said.

"They probably have reinforcements coming," Dan shouted.

"Yeah," Uri replied. "This group just wanted to hold us there until they arrived. They'll probably pursue as well."

"What about the border?" Marcus asked.

"We'll figure that out when we get there. First thing is to put distance between us and the bad guys. We'll be even more outnumbered next time."

Chapter 78

The four men raced through the growing darkness. They could see no sign of pursuit, but everyone knew it was coming.

"Think they could call ahead?" Roland asked. "Maybe set up a roadblock?"

"Don't know," Uri replied. "There's not much out here between Ramadi and the border."

The men lapsed into silence as Uri hammered down Route 1, staying off the more-traveled Highway 10, which paralleled it. The night quickly grew dark, and the temperature cooled as the desert heat escaped into the atmosphere.

"How you doing, boss?" Marcus asked Dan

"Uncomfortable. Sore butt, like Roland predicted. And still bleeding, but I'll be okay."

"Lean forward. Let me take a look."

Dan hunched forward, and Marcus looked at his wet vest. "You're right. Still bleeding. You want to take that off and let me see what's going on?"

"Not much you can do about it."

"Maybe reset your bandages if they've slipped."

Without a word, Dan began to shrug out of his vest and then unbuttoned his shirt.

"Fuck," Marcus said.

"What's up?" Dan asked.

"The bandages came off. You're bleeding more than I like. Let me get the first aid kit from the back."

He twisted around and rummaged through the packs.

"Don't use up everything in it," Dan said.

"What are we saving it for?" Marcus asked. "That gash that I stitched up is bleeding a lot."

"But it's not arterial, so don't worry."

"Still creates a problem. What about your leg?"

Dan felt around the back of his left leg. His pants were damp. "Got some bleeding there as well. Look, throw a patch on the worst if you feel you should and that's all. I'll deal with it."

"You're the boss," Marcus said and proceeded to re-bandage Dan's wounds.

"Where's the satellite phone?" Dan asked.

Roland reached into the back area and grabbed the bag with the phone, handing it up to Dan.

When it had synched with some satellites, Dan punched Jane's number. After a few rings, she answered.

"Jane here."

"It's Dan."

"This is not the most secure line on my end," Jane said.

"Doesn't matter. We have a situation."

"Go ahead."

"We're on our way to Jordan. Mission aborted. Need some assets to meet us. We've got some injuries and probably won't get across the border. Too suspicious."

"How bad?"

"Mostly inconvenient."

"You're crossing at Highway 1, the Trebil Border Crossing?"

"Aiming for that. But like I said. We may get detained."

"How long out?"

"How long to the border, Uri?"

"Four hours, maybe less."

Dan relayed the information to Jane.

"All right. What's Uri say about the border situation?"

"He suggests a story about either an accident in the field or an attack by some leftover ISIS gang. The Iraqis don't think highly of them."

"Listen to Uri on that. He'll have a good idea. I'll have help coming your way. Contact me when you reach the border, then hide the phone. It'll only create more suspicion. You just need to get out. The Jordanians will be more friendly since you're on American passports and coming back from a research mission."

"Roger that. Talk to you in a few hours." Dan shut down the phone.

Chapter 79

When Muntaqim's men reached the abandoned
building on the outskirts of Ramadi, They
found their quarry gone. The three attackers,
one badly injured with his legs shot up, and the other two,
uninjured, reported that the men drove off and headed
west towards Jordan.

Muntaqim digested the news when he was told. He had
remained at the recycle yard. He ground his teeth in
frustration. His men had failed to deal with these
intruders who came to disrupt and destroy what he had
established. Their seeming incompetence only spoke to the
skill of the ones sent against him. Worthy adversaries.
Worthy, but ones he had to eliminate, or his security
would become more fragile.

He told the men gathered on the outskirts of the city to
set out in pursuit. They were to split up, one truck going
down the main Highway 1, the other on the older, more
local Route 10. The two roads crossed not too far west of
Ramadi, but Muntaqim thought his quarry would get past
that point. He had to have his men outrace them as they
headed towards Jordan.

Somewhere, farther west, he would set up a roadblock
and capture them. He didn't fear the local authorities.
There were none to speak of in this empty part of Iraq. He
could operate a blockade for some hours before any

military or police came to stop him. Not far west of Rutba, a small village along Rt. 10, the local road came close to Highway 1. He would set his teams up there. They could manage two blockades, and when they stopped the vehicle he was after, the other team could quickly come to help eliminate them. He would destroy them yet, no matter how skilled they were.

† † †

"We need to be ready for a blockade, or checkpoint, or ambush," Uri said. "There's an interchange ahead where this road comes close to Route 1. They may try to set up there."

"We can't stop. They'll just riddle us with bullets," Roland said.

"May do that if we don't stop," Marcus replied.

"We're better moving and shooting than standing still," Dan said.

Silence descended again on the group. Each man wondered how this would all turn out.

"You thinking what I'm thinking?" Roland asked Marcus.

"I'm never sure what you're thinking, but go ahead and enlighten me."

"This could be our most dangerous moment."

Marcus thought about that statement for a moment.

"Could be. When we go on these crazy adventures with Dan, we get a lot of these moments."

"I know. But if they've got something like an M240, or worse, we're in deep shit."

"We'll improvise, like we always do," Marcus said. "But we shouldn't stop and we need to lay down a lot of fire. Keep those bastards' heads down."

"I hear you," Roland said.

They roared on through the dark, uncertain of what lay ahead.

"We'll get through, guys," Dan said. "There's always opportunities and these fuckers so far haven't been all that great."

The Toyota raced on towards Jordan and relative safety.

Chapter 80

One of the two pursuing teams sped down Highway 1, the newer, better-paved road. They reached the ambush point and quickly set up. The highway was divided with two lanes in each direction. They were narrow, and the traffic, never very thick, drove as if each side were one lane. The men arranged two pickup trucks sideways to block the full width of the pavement. The trucks faced one another. It would be hard to punch through the middle, with both engines adding weight and strength to the blocking effect.

Once in place, the men settled down to wait. The night was dark; the moon hadn't yet risen. On one side, they lit a small fire to ward off the chill and sat around it with their rifles nearby. They engaged in small talk centered on this group of men that had proven so deadly and elusive. The men knew the group had been after their leader and had failed only due to Muntaqim's anticipation of their attack. They considered the approaching men to be a formidable enemy to deal with.

Along Route 10, the going was slower. Muntaqim's men drove as fast as they could. Both teams were told to get to the blockage point as quickly as possible. Both groups understood that one of them could catch up with the fleeing fighters before the checkpoint. They had to be ready for that. Few vehicles were traveling at night, especially along the more local Route 10. The ones they came upon caused much tension as they approached and tried to determine if it was the fleeing enemy or a local out late. Most were going slow, and once they decided it wasn't the ones they were pursuing, they quickly passed them and accelerated down the road.

† † †

Dan broke the silence in the SUV. "Let's talk about what we do before we get to the interchange."

"You have a plan?" Uri asked.

"Only that we don't stop. We can't let them get close or get us pinned down."

"Check the map," Uri said. "See if you can determine what the geography is around the area. Does it give us any options?"

"Probably pretty clear ground if there's an intersection for the two roads," Dan said. "We've got three shooters so we should be able to lay down a lot of rounds. The M4 has a better range than the AK, so we're in luck there."

"As long as they don't have a machine gun. The last time they did," Uri said.

"We left that pickup dead in the desert. Let's hope they didn't revive it yet," Dan replied.

The men went silent. They were a wounded group. Their leader, Dan, had a torn-up back that was still bleeding. He would not get stronger if he kept losing blood; they could not afford a drawn-out fight. Marcus, like Roland, watched to the rear. His thoughts were dark. Marcus realized that Dan was the glue that held them together. He had the vision. He was the one the Watchers had chosen. Without him, their war against the terrorists, this war of different ideologies, which seemed to have no end, would falter and lose its way. Dan was the focal point, the tip of the spear. He, Roland, and even Uri made up part of that spear, but it was a blunt, ineffectual weapon without this man trying to ignore his bloodied back and concussion.

"We may be getting company." Roland's voice was partly torn by the wind as he looked out of the rear side window.

"What is it?" Marcus asked, yanked out of his reverie.

"Some headlights. Pretty far behind, but going our direction." Roland yanked his head back inside the window. "How many vehicles have we seen on this road?" There was no answer. "Right. Not a whole fucking lot. Now there's one coming our way. And it must be going faster since I'm seeing it now. I didn't see it a few minutes ago."

"Can you go faster?" Marcus asked.

"Do my best." Uri was bent over the steering wheel, concentrating on the dark road. He pressed the accelerator, and the old Toyota began to sway and shudder more as Uri struggled to make it go beyond what the road and the machine could manage.

Roland and Marcus watched in silence while Uri kept wrestling the steering wheel. The bouncing and swaying increased. The cab of the SUV was buffeted by the cold night wind coming from the open windows as they raced down the road.

"Definitely getting closer," Roland announced after five minutes.

"We can't just start shooting when they get within range. Could be non-combatants," Dan said.

"That's a problem. Let them get close enough to identify, they shoot the hell out of us. If they hit our tires, we're shit out of luck." Roland yelled to be heard over the roar of the engine. His voice expressed his disgust and anger at having to deal with subtleties. He seemed to want a clear-cut fight.

A few more minutes passed.

"I can see another set of headlights," Marcus said. "There's two vehicles and they're definitely getting closer."

"That tells me enough," Roland said. "Dan, when they're within range we're going to start shooting. We're a whole lot better shooters than this pile of rag heads. Those fuckers are out to kill us and I'm not going to let them."

"Your call," Uri said, risking a quick glance over at Dan.

"You keep driving like a bat out of hell. And don't crash," Dan said. "The three of us will try to take out the lead vehicle. That should stop the second one. Then we cruise on to the border and decide on our story."

"They may have sent others along Highway 1. It runs parallel to this one," Uri said.

"Let's worry about the immediate threat," Dan replied. "Marcus, you and Roland man the side windows. I'll squeeze through the sun roof opening."

"Works for me," Roland said.

"When they get within range," Dan said, "let us know if you get to a straight section. It doesn't have to be long. Steady up the truck and we can take better aim. With some luck, we can take them out."

They watched as the vehicles grew closer. They came in and out of focus through the dust raised by the Toyota.

Chapter 81

The Toyota came to a small village. Not much more than a collection of rundown, mud-brick houses and a few shops along the local Route 10. Uri didn't slow down. One late-night pedestrian had to dive out of the way as he blasted past.

The pursuing pickups sped through behind them. They were closing in.

"Definitely the bad guys. It's going to be a fight," Roland said. His voice was calm. The warrior taking over the jokester. "They're almost in range. Can you steady it up?"

"Straight section ahead," Uri said as the SUV slewed around a curve.

"Steady then."

All three men had their heads out of the vehicle with their carbines pulled tight to their shoulders. They waited.

"I think we're good," Marcus said.

"Let's give them a welcome," Dan replied.

They opened fire, aiming just above the headlights, hoping to send rounds into the cab. No one fired on auto. They fired one shot at a time when they could steady their aim for a split second on the target. The rifles wavered all over the place with the wind buffeting them, the SUV lurching even with Uri's best efforts, and the target moving around. Still, each shooter had moments, fractions of a second, when their sights were on target. They anticipated the swings of the barrel and, with almost instantaneous reactions, pulled their triggers.

The men in the pursuing pickup trucks looked eagerly ahead at the taillights. They could see they were closing in. There was little doubt the vehicle they were pursuing held the men who tried to ambush Muntaqim. It was going way too fast to be part of the local traffic. As they roared through the small village, the driver and passenger in the lead truck smiled at each other. The men in the back held on for dear life, with only one man braving the motion to stand and look over the cab.

Then, the rounds started coming.

"Call the other team," shouted the driver. "Tell them we have them on the local road. They should switch the road block."

He pulled out his cell phone and made the call.

The man standing in the back of the pickup fell back into the bed after the first rounds were fired. He landed on some of the other men with a mixture of brain and blood covering him. The men in the back jumped up, and three of them crowded over the cab and started firing back. After delivering his call, the passenger leaned out of the window and began to fire on full auto.

"Incoming," Marcus said as he kept up a steady stream of rounds aimed at the pickup.

The rounds coming from the pursuing pickup were all over the place. Their volume was intense, with some shots hitting the SUV. The men could hear them shriek as they spun off of the bumper. A dull thump accompanied the rounds, slamming into the truck's body.

"Got to stop them," Uri said. "If they hit the gas tank we're done. We won't make the border."

None of the shooters replied but kept up a steady stream of rounds aimed at the pursuing truck. A headlight disappeared. Then, the pickup wavered back and forth, indicating something wrong.

"We hit the engine, or the driver," Roland said. "They're slowing and having trouble steering."

In the pursuing pickup, a couple of rounds whistled through the cab, almost hitting one of the men in the back bed. The windshield erupted into a spider web of cracks as the high-velocity 5.56mm round went through it. Two more rounds slammed into the front, one taking out a headlight, the other landing somewhere in the engine.

"Keep shooting!" the driver shouted. "There are more of us."

The pursuer's rounds were now hitting the SUV with more frequency.

The pickup's windshield was hit again. Part of it blew out this time, spraying glass fragments through the cab. The driver slammed back in the seat and then slumped over the wheel. The man next to him reached over to try to stabilize the steering. He held the wheel with one hand and, with the other, pulled out his phone and called the other team behind them.

"We're hit. Can't drive. I'll try to pull over and you go ahead."

He tried to stabilize the swerving truck, which was not slowing down. The dead driver still had his foot on the accelerator. After two swerves back and forth, the pickup tucked in the front end, and the inside wheels lifted into the air. The passenger vainly tried to twist the steering wheel from his side to correct the slide, but the truckvan dug into the dirt and flipped up and over. A violent series of rolls ensued that spit out the men in the back and flung the passenger through the shattered front window. The

following pickup jammed on its brakes to avoid the
tumbling truck.

"One down, one to go," Roland said as he watched the
lead vehicle swerve and then start a series of barrel rolls.
When it stopped, the second truck accelerated past and
began to close again. The men resumed their shooting.

"I'm down to two mags," Roland declared.

"I've got three including what's in the rifle," Marcus
shouted back into the cab.

"Same," Dan said. "Check the back. There may be more
there."

"Check my pack," Uri said.

Marcus pulled in from the window and draped himself
over the back seat to rummage through the packs as they
continued to race down the highway.

"Got 'em," he said. He pulled the pack up and dragged
it forward. An incoming round shattered the rear hatch
glass and slammed into his left shoulder. He spun sideways
and fell against the driver's seat.

"Fuck! I'm hit," Roland shouted. He pulled in from the
window.

"Where?" Marcus shouted.

"Shoulder."

Marcus pulled in from the window. "How bad is it?"

"Don't," Roland shouted. "Keep shooting. I'll take care
of myself."

He dug out the first aid kit with his good right arm.
Then, he began to take off his tactical vest and shirt.

They had increased the distance between themselves
and the pursuing trucks, but the second truck was now
gaining on them.

Marcus went back to the window and started firing
again, along with Dan.

"Save some ammo for getting through the blockade," Uri shouted.

"You sure they'll have one?" Dan asked.

Uri didn't answer. Dan and Marcus kept up a steady, careful volley of shots at the pursuing pickup. Bullets whistled past him, to the sides and over his head. *They get any closer, they'll ventilate this truck with shots. It'll be a death zone.*

David Nees

Chapter 82

U ri, we have to stop this pickup," Dan said.
"What? I thought the idea was to not stop."
There was a pause in the shooting as the road got
curvy as it turned north. When they went around the
corners, the pursuing truck had no target to shoot at.

"These guys will just keep peppering us until the truck's
disabled. We're gonna stop it now. When you get around
one of these corners, stop. We can smother them with
gunfire when they come around and end this threat."

"Risky, but I like it," Marcus said.

"I'm in," Roland replied. "We get a rifle in Uri's hands as
well and we'll have the four of us laying down fire."

"We don't take them out, we're done," Uri said.

"They hit a tire and disable the truck, we'll be done
anyway."

Short bursts of gunfire from the pursuing truck every
time they came into view interrupted their conversation.

"We're going to have to move fast," Uri said. "Get my
rifle up here and make sure there's a mag in it. Your
shoulder okay?"

"Enough to kill some terrorists," Roland said.

Marcus busied himself, setting up Roland and Uri's
carbines. Uri pushed his pace even more to create
additional space between the two vehicles.

"Here we go," he shouted as he sped around a sharp turn. The road bent around a steep hill, which blocked the view looking forward. As soon as they were out of sight, Uri jammed on the brakes and yanked the SUV over to the side. He and Roland pushed their rifles out of the left windows while Dan and Marcus jumped out of the truck to aim over the roof.

At that moment, the pickup came sliding around the corner, and the four opened fire. The men in the cab were riddled instantly; then, the shooters directed their fire to the men in the bed. Before they could react, they were hit. The pickup slewed violently left and right and then jammed itself into the ditch.

"Wait here," Marcus shouted. "Uri and I will go check."

"Grab a couple of their AKs and ammunition," Dan said.

A minute later, two shots rang out from the pickup, and shortly after, Uri and Marcus returned with four AK47s and loaded magazines. A fire began under the pickup as Uri drove off north. He looked back in the mirror as the fire grew larger.

"Good riddance bastards," he said.

"Roger that," Marcus said.

Roland went back to work on his shoulder with Marcus' help. The round had gone through, but there was a great deal of tissue damage. The clotting bandage worked, and Marcus finished binding the joint tight.

"That should hold you 'till we get out of here."

"It's going to stiffen. I'll be shooting one-handed for a while," Roland said.

"You always did like to show off," Marcus replied.

"I can think of better ways."

"The blockade," Dan said. "Let's talk about it."

The wind noise from the shot-out rear window competed with their voices.

"They'll probably have two pickups, like this group that followed us," Dan said.

Like the others, he spoke loudly to be heard above the buffeting wind.

"Agreed," Uri said.

"Anyway around? Through the truck depot?" Marcus asked.

"Hell if I know," Uri said. "Probably only one way in and out. It's basically a large, fenced-off parking lot for the trailers."

"Going off-road will be too slow and make us an easy target," Marcus said.

"We hit them at full speed, guns blazing," Roland said.

"You are dramatic, aren't you?" Marcus replied.

"I'm just saying. It may be our best option. The more time spent near them is time in the kill zone."

"I don't know what they'll expect," Uri said, "but it won't be for us to stop like law-abiding citizens."

"You got that right," Roland said. "But we just have to do what they expect at a faster, more lethal level. That might be enough to throw them off."

"We need just a few seconds of surprise, whether it's where we head as we approach, or how fast we approach. Just get them to pause to recalibrate. Then we stand a chance," Dan said.

"So fast and furious it is?" Uri asked.

"Just like the movie," Roland replied.

There were a few minutes of silence as Uri drove through the now more winding road as it got closer to the newer Highway 10. Dan studied the map for clues about the terrain around the intersection.

"We're losing gas at a high rate," Uri said. "The tank must have taken a hit."

"We got enough to get past the blockade?" Dan asked.

"Probably. But I wouldn't bet on getting to the border."

"As we blast our way through, we should try to dismantle the trucks so they can't follow. I know it's a stretch, but we should try," Dan said.

"Stretch indeed," Marcus said. He was rooting around in one of the backpacks. The rear seat was a mess with packs and spent magazines littering the area, along with Roland trying to not aggravate his shoulder wound. Suddenly, Marcus lifted his hand up high.

"Christmas came early," he shouted. "Oops, sorry, Uri."

"Forget it. What do you mean?"

"I'm holding two grenades."

"All right!" Roland said. "That'll change the equation."

"Question is," Uri said, "how do we deliver them before getting shot to hell?"

"Same question as to how we get through the blockade in the first place," Dan replied. "Roland, you're the strongest one here, how far can you throw a grenade? And can you do it with your injured shoulder?"

"Yes. And fifty yards."

"Okay. Let's work around that. Can you do it from the SUV?"

"I can stand up through the roof vent and throw."

"You'll be exposed."

"Not much more than anyone in the truck. I throw it and then get back down inside."

"If they feel they've got a secure blockage, they may hold off shooting in an attempt to capture us," Uri said.

"You think?" Roland asked.

"Maybe this Muntaqim wants to know more about us. We didn't get him, but we did a lot of damage to his fighters."

"Let's rethink this," Dan said, looking up from the map. "We might want to go off-road. Keep some distance between us and the blockade. The map shows a possibility.

If we can head away from them, why should we just drive into it? Why not just divert?"

"I'd rather have the bastards shooting at us from a distance than up close," Roland said.

"The M4 gives us a greater range," Marcus said. "Maybe try that and save the grenades for later."

"We better decide," Uri said. "We'll be there soon."

"Roland," Dan said, "you get up through the roof vent. We'll plan on a wide detour. If it's not there, we charge and you throw the grenades, Marcus and I will start shooting and we hope we get through this alive. If we can detour, Uri, don't baby the truck. Flog it for all its worth."

"It's not going to get us to the border in any case," Uri replied.

"Right," Dan said. "And that brings up another problem."

"We deal with that later," Roland said.

"No. we need to deal with it right now. If we get through, where do we go with the gas remaining?" Dan addressed his question to Uri.

"There's a road going north. We take it and then head west through the desert. There's a small collection of houses where there used to be a military installation. I studied it on the map. People may still live there We go there and try to get transportation to the border."

"It's as good a plan as any," Dan said. "At least we'll be in the desert and able to fight in the open."

Chapter 83

M untaqim's men rushed over to the local route and reset their roadblock. They set up just before the road split, with a lane turning right towards the Highway 1 interchange and truck plaza and the main lane continuing west as Route 10. Near the interchange, the road was paved. On the southwest side, there was a deep ditch that would prevent any vehicle from leaving the roadbed to drive around their blockade. The other side had no such impediment. The desert was flat, with only a shallow depression at the edge of the pavement. In addition, there was an abandoned oil derrick a hundred yards from the road.

Roland stood up and maneuvered his body through the roof vent, careful to not pull at his injured shoulder. Meanwhile, Dan and Marcus manned the left and right windows. Everyone scanned the surrounding terrain as the intersection came into sight. They could see the two pickups parked nose to nose in the center of the road. Men were visible behind the trucks, their rifles aimed at the oncoming SUV.

"We got room to the right!" yelled Roland. He could see the terrain best from his higher perch. They were about 500 yards out, beyond the range of the AK carbines. "Go right!" he yelled again.

Uri swerved off the road without slowing down. The SUV lurched and bucked over the uneven ground. Roland grunted as his body jerked back and forth in the sunroof opening.

"Head to the east, around the oil derrick," Roland yelled. The wind was buffeting him and trying to drown out his voice.

Shots came from the blockade, but no rounds came near them.

"We're out of range," Marcus said.

Marcus had no shot from the right side of the truck, but Dan and Roland sent some rounds downrange.

"They're ducking," Roland said. "That means we're reaching them."

"Try to get rounds into the truck cabs. Maybe disable them," Marcus shouted.

The two men steadily fired at the trucks, trying to hold their sights on the cabs as the SUV bounced over the ground. Uri wrestled with the steering wheel. He wanted to avoid the bushes, which could damage the undercarriage or launch the truck off the ground. It was a continuous battle. The headlights bounced with the vehicle, offering him erratic lighting of the desert floor ahead. He hit a bush and sent the SUV lurching both into the air and to one side, throwing all the occupants around. Dan tried to jam himself against the door and seatback to keep his aim on the terrorists' pickups. Roland was tightly wedged into the vent but grunted as the lurching truck shoved his rib cage hard against the side of the opening.

On the far side of the derrick, a two-track emerged, coming from the derrick and running parallel to the road for a quarter of a mile. Uri aimed for the track and then increased his speed.

"This is faster," he said. His voice was panting, indicating his effort to keep the SUV from crashing. There was a deeper ditch along this section, but it shallowed up ahead. "I think I can jump back onto the road from here."

He looked for a spot with a minimal depression and swerved to the left. The SUV bounced up onto the road, now paved as it was part of the Highway 1 interchange. Uri planted his foot to the floor, and the tired SUV responded, its engine roaring more loudly now.

"Sounds like a muffler got torn," Marcus said.

"Doesn't matter," Uri replied. "I doubt we'll be sneaking up on anyone from here on out."

Roland twisted himself around to look back. Dan pulled himself back inside. His back and butt felt like they were on fire.

"They got one truck coming after us," Roland shouted to the others. "We must have hit the other one."

"Some lucky shooting," Marcus said.

"I'll take it," Roland replied. "Hopefully, some will remain to try to get the truck running. We'll have less to deal with. But we're going to have to deal with them."

Uri drove north through the interchange.

✝ ✝ ✝

Muntaqim received the news that the attackers had avoided the roadblocks and were headed north with only one of his trucks pursuing. He could feel his anger rise. This small group of men, he didn't know the exact count, but it couldn't have been more than five or six, more likely only four, had slipped through his men twice, delivering many casualties.

"They will not go north for long. Syria is that way. They'll turn west to Jordan. Do not let them get away. Do not try to capture them. Just kill them...or else answer to me."

He slammed the phone down and paced the office. It was time to go back to his ranch hideout. He would be safer there and could just as easily receive news. If he had to disappear, that was the place from which to do it. He called his bodyguards, and they got into their vehicles.

† † †

"How will you know where to turn?" Dan asked.

Uri remained hunched over the steering wheel. He was not wrestling it as before, but he seemed to have a death grip on the wheel as the SUV strained to reach top speed. The road was smoother and had few curves, but there was still much bouncing as the bulky machine tried to maintain a straight line.

"Should be easy to see, dirt tracks going off to the left. Even if the houses were abandoned, there must have been lots of traffic at one time."

Suddenly, Uri braked hard. Everyone lurched forward.

"What the hell?" Roland said.

Not replying, Uri cranked the steering to the left, and the SUV careened off the road, leaning dangerously on its side. He barely slowed as he pushed the truck down the two-track path into the desert. It was well used, or had been in the past, and still well defined. The potholes jolted the truck and caused painful grunting from Dan and Roland, the two wounded men.

Marcus turned to watch the road they had just left. There was no cover in the open, flat desert, and he was sure anyone following could easily see their headlights.

"They'll see us and turn off. We're not going to shake them," Marcus said.

"That's okay," Uri said. "We'll stop at one of the house compounds and set up for them. Roland's got a good surprise for them when they show up."

"The plan is to eliminate them and then head to the border? Across the desert?" Roland asked.

"You got a better one?" Uri replied.

Roland paused for a moment. "Can't say I have."

It was the time of a gibbous moon, one that was waning. It rose after midnight and was now climbing higher in the sky in the hours before dawn. Although less than full, it created a good amount of light in the clear desert air. Uri turned off the headlights and slowed to navigate by its pale light.

Ahead, they could see the dark shadows of a building or collection of buildings but could make out no details.

"Let's get in there and wait to counter attack," Uri said.

"I'm for that," Roland replied. "I'd like to go on the offense. We've been playing defense too long."

"Roger that," Marcus said.

"I'm good with it." Dan completed the vote.

Uri pulled closer and then slowed. Marcus looked back at the highway. He could see the headlights. The pursuing truck was going along the road, and some men had powerful flashlights. They were shining them along the road's edge and out into the desert.

"They're coming," he said. "Looking for where we might have turned off."

As they approached the dark building, they saw it was part of a group scattered around a small area. Some were larger, like one-story apartments or dormitories; others were single houses.

"Looks like the remains of a barracks setup," Marcus said.

Uri drove up to the first one. It had a partial wall, and behind it was a long, low concrete block and mortar building. There were multiple doorways indicating individual apartments. He pulled up to the last door at the end.

"Not much time," Uri said.

"We need to get inside and then spread out to ambush our pursuers," Dan said.

Without a word, the men climbed out of the truck and headed to the door with their gear. Inside was a table, some chairs, and two beds in a corner. Opposite the beds were the remains of a kitchen: a sink, counter, and cabinets. The stove and refrigerator had long since been removed. Two windows were facing the front, along with a side window.

Roland stood in the doorway looking out. He could see flashes of headlights above the wall as the pursuing truck bounded through the potholes. He turned back to the others.

"They'll be here in a few minutes. I'm going outside. There's a pile of rubble just inside the wall. I can hide behind it and lob the grenades at the pickup. I'll take out some of them. You guys open fire from here and we'll finish them off."

"Just don't get yourself killed," Marcus said.

"You either.

"Mics on everyone," Dan said. "We need to be able to communicate."

Roland grabbed an AK-47 along with two extra magazines and ran out to the wall.

Uri and Dan manned the windows. All of them had switched to the AK carbines, having more ammunition for them than what remained for the M4s.

Marcus opened the side window. He'd shoot from there, or if the pickup wasn't in sight, he'd go out of the window and shoot from the corner of the building.

The men waited. They could now hear the engine of the approaching truck.

"They'll be cautious entering the area," Dan said.

"Once bitten, twice shy," Marcus said.

"They might even park outside and approach on foot," Uri said. "Will Roland pick up on that?"

"He's experienced. He'll get it and adjust," Dan said. "Battle plans always need adjusting."

This was shaping up to be a life-or-death moment. Either they died, or the pursuers died. There would be no middle ground.

Chapter 84

The approaching terrorists could see the recent disturbance in the two-track indicating the passage of the SUV they were pursuing. There were no other vehicles in the area. When they saw the tracks turning into the barracks just past the wall, they stopped before following through the gap. They knew the ones they pursued were accomplished fighters and might have an ambush planned. To drive around the end of the wall and approach the building might be to put themselves into a killing zone.

After some muttered consultation among themselves, they split up with one group of four, heading in the opposite direction from the end of the wall, and the other group of six unloading from the pickup. They decided to enter the compound using the truck as a shield. One man lay down in the driver's seat to idle the pickup forward, with the others following behind and to the far side, using the truck for cover. The truck would draw the fire, and the second group could enter undetected and complete the attack.

Some men harbored thoughts that they might be heading to their deaths but didn't voice them. One should be ready and willing to die for the faith.

"They've stopped outside the wall," Marcus said into his mic.

"Probably going to split up," Roland said. "I may have them at my six. Don't let anyone come over the wall behind me."

"We got your back. If it's two groups, use the grenades first. You'll do the most damage."

"Roger that."

The men waited patiently. There was nothing to do until the enemy showed themselves. Roland moved around the pile of blocks until he was between them and the wall, giving him partial cover from either direction. *Better partial than fully exposed.*

The group that headed away from the opening had to go around a corner before coming to a break in the wall. This put them along the side of the building and quite a distance from where Dan and the others were hiding. One of them placed a call to the group near the opening where they parked, letting them know they were in position. On the leader's signal, they rushed around the corner.

Roland heard the truck engine start. He readied himself. He was the wild card, the surprise. Not only his position outside the building but having two grenades to throw. The M57 grenade was shaped like a baseball for easier throwing, with a lethal zone of five meters and an injury zone out to fifteen meters.

The truck appeared, going forward slowly with seemingly no driver. Roland took in the situation in an instant. It was being used as a shield. The attackers were behind and to the far side of it. He pulled the pin and lobbed the grenade. It fell just on the near side of the truck. Roland ducked. He heard one man shout out something in Arabic. The weapon exploded, scattering metal shards that tore into the pickup. Shrapnel flew underneath and hit some of the men. There were shouts of pain. The truck stopped

Roland then stood up and turned to see the second group, further away, running towards the side of the building. He lobbed the second grenade in their direction. They were farther away, and it landed short, exploding in the dirt as they disappeared around the corner of the building. He could only hope some of them were within the injury zone. While he wasn't looking, one of the attackers crawled back outside and around the wall.

Gunfire erupted from the building. The three were shooting at the attackers pinned down behind the pickup.

"Status on the other group?" Dan asked between rounds.

"They got to the far side of the building. I lobbed the grenade at them and might have injured some, but I've got no eyes on them."

"I can go out the side window and around back," Marcus said. "We don't want them coming at us from behind."

"That works. Uri and I will lay down cover fire for you. Find a place around back to intercept them."

"Unless they run off into the desert," Roland said.

"We should be so lucky," Dan replied. "One from the truck crawled back out. Did you see him?"

"Negative. I'll deal with him later," Roland said.

"You need a backup?" Uri asked Marcus.

"Negative. Just keep them suppressed so I can get around back."

He raised the sash window. As Uri and Dan laid down a heavy volley of fire, Marcus jumped out of the window and ran for the back of the building.

He peeked around the corner. There was no one in sight. He scanned the ground, looking for a spot to set up. There was a small shed about twenty yards from the barracks. He stood up and ran for it. Shots flew past him with their deadly whistle just as he reached the cover. He dove for the ground. Multiple rounds slammed into the wall of the shed. Luckily, it was made of the same concrete and block material as the barracks. It would stop the rounds the attackers were using.

Switching to the left hand, he lay in the dirt and edged his carbine around the corner. He could just make out two men partially exposed at the corner of the barracks, one kneeling, one standing. Marcus fired, and the man standing flew backward and out of sight. The other ducked back around the corner.

"One down, not sure how many more to go."

"Keep 'em at bay," Dan said. "We're working on the main group out front. It'll take a few minutes."

Uri and Dan kept sniping away at the men behind the pickup, keeping their heads down and suppressing any serious return fire. Occasionally, one man would raise his carbine over the truck without aiming and fire away on automatic, hoping to hit something.

Roland watched this and noted the shooter's location. The bed would offer little protection against the 7.62 round from the Kalashnikov. When the shooter stuck his carbine up again, Roland fired a burst through the truck bed. The rifle dropped from the man's hands as Roland's shots hit him.

"Got one," he announced over his comms. "Going to try to flush them out. They'll either run back to the wall or forward. Be ready," Roland said.

He started firing repeatedly through the pickup bed and cab. Soon, the only safe place was to hide tight against the front, protected by the engine.

Suddenly, two men bust forward from the cover of the pickup, heading to the side of the barracks and out of the direct line of fire. Dan swung his carbine over and shot the first one. He hit him in the side, and the man went twisting to the ground. The other one reached the side of the building as Uri's shot missed.

At the same time, two others ran for the protection of the wall to the rear. Roland dropped one of them, but the other dove out of sight behind the wall.

"Get to the side window," Dan said to Uri. "He can shoot in from there."

Uri turned to the window Marcus had used just as a barrel poked through the opening. The man opened fire on automatic. Dan dove to the ground as rounds flew through the air. Uri ducked and returned fire, but there was no one to hit. Dan rolled over and trained his rifle on the window. Uri ran forward to the wall and then crawled under the window to the rear of it. He crouched near the floor just past the opening with his rifle trained on it.

A head appeared, and both men opened fire. The head fell away from the opening. Uri peeked out and gave Dan the okay signal.

"Got him."

"Sitrep," called Marcus. He had heard the gunfire coming from the front.

"Pickup neutralized. One man escaped behind the wall. There's another out there," Dan said.

"Copy that," Marcus said. "I've only taken one down. The others aren't showing themselves and I don't know how many there are."

"If they try to come forward at the front of the building, I've got them," Roland said.

"What about the one's behind the wall?" Marcus asked.

"I'll take them," Uri said. "I'm uninjured and used to close-quarters shooting."

"You go around the corner, they'll be waiting for you," Roland said.

"I'll figure it out. You guys flush out the other ones. They're still a threat."

Chapter 85

The two men behind the wall looked at one another. They were stunned by the reversal of their situation. They had gone from confidant pursuers to being pursued with most of their fellow jihadists killed.

"We must go," the man who had just come around the wall said in a whisper.

"I can't. I'm injured in the leg. I could never make it."

"They will kill you if you stay."

"If it is Allah's will, so be it."

"I will not stay. There is little chance to kill any of these infidels. They are too good. I will try to get help so we can fight another battle."

The injured man gave him a dark look but didn't comment. The other man patted him on the shoulder and took off, running back towards the road.

The injured man slumped against the wall and awaited his fate. His leg was bleeding, and he could only crawl. In his hurry to escape, he had dropped his rifle and now had no weapon.

Uri switched to left-hand shooting and swung his rifle around the wall from the prone position. He paused. There was only one fighter lying up against the wall with no weapon. He scanned the area and saw a figure running in the distance.

Uri got up and walked to the man. He was wounded in the leg. A jagged opening from the grenade. The man looked up at Uri with a mixture of fear and anger in his eyes. Uri spoke in Arabic.

"Is that your friend running away?"

"Balaa," yeah, the man answered.

"He left you."

The man nodded. Uri took out his knife and began to cut away the man's pant leg. He cut a strip of material out of it and fashioned a tourniquet, which he tied tightly to the man's thigh to stop the bleeding.

"Hold this tight and loosen it when your leg gets numb," Uri told him.

The man looked at him for a long moment and then nodded.

"How many went around to the back?" Uri pointed in the direction away from the opening of the wall.

"Arbe," four, the man said.

Uri relayed the information to the others. Then he turned to the injured fighter.

"I will be back and clean your wound."

He ran towards the far end of the wall.

"I'm going to follow to the end of the wall. Hopefully, I can get eyes on them," Uri said over the radio.

"Let us know when you're in position," Dan said. "I'm going around back to help Marcus."

"When you get to the corner, we'll open fire. We'll have them in a crossfire with no cover."

"That works for me."

"I just sit out the fun?" Roland asked.

"You take out anyone who might bolt and head your way."

"I'm in position," Uri said. His voice was low. "There's three of them. They seem to be discussing their next move.

I'm guessing they know the others are done for. They may want to run."

"They haven't yet," Dan said. "Marcus and I are coming forward. I'll click the mic when we're in position. We'll wait for your shots."

Marcus dashed across the open ground and pressed himself to the back of the building. Dan joined him, coming up along the back wall. From there, they moved as quietly as possible forward to the corner. Both men had rifles trained on the edge of the wall where any shooter might appear, one high and one low. They would have only one chance to get off the first shots. If they missed or were too slow, both could get shot. When they reached the corner, Dan whispered into his mic. The enemy was just around the edge of the wall. They kept their breathing quiet. When Uri opened fire, they would swing into action.

Uri lay on the ground and trained his sights on a fighter on the right side of the group. Once he had taken the shot, the others would try to scatter like a herd of deer. Dan and Marcus would take care of any going their direction. That most likely left only one to take down on the run.

He steadied his aim and gently squeezed the trigger. The AK barked, and the man collapsed to the ground. The other two immediately bolted towards the desert. He heard Dan and Marcus shoot. The fleeing terrorist dropped to the ground and thrashed around in pain.

All three men ran forward to check the downed fighters.

"All clear," Dan said over the coms. "Three killed and the fourth is not going to make it much longer. Sucking chest wound. Let's get back to the room and decide what we do next."

Without a word, Uri returned to the man he left at the wall. He pulled him up and told him he was going to take him inside to clean his wound.

"Limadha a?" Why? The man asked.

Uri didn't answer but pulled the man's arm over his shoulder and started forward.

Chapter 86

The four gathered in the room. Uri had half dragged, half carried the fighter inside with him.

"What's up with that?" Dan asked.

"I want to take care of his wound and then interrogate him."

"I doubt he'll give you much," Roland said from the side of the room. He was leaning against the wall in an attempt to rest his wounded shoulder.

"Give it a try, but let's not stay long," Dan said. "There'll be more. Some of them escaped."

"Speaking of leaving," Marcus said. "Do we just hike from here?"

"Let me take care of this guy, then we'll see what options we have," Uri said.

He pulled the man over to the side and had him sit on the ground. He tore open his pant leg and began to disinfect the wound. When he was done, he wrapped it in a clotting bandage, and they re-tied the torn pant leg over the area.

"This will keep the wound from being infected. It will also stop the bleeding." He spoke in Arabic. "I want to know where this Muntaqim lives. He's your leader, isn't he?"

The man looked long at Uri. "You bandage me up, save my life. Now you ask for information that will get me killed if I tell you. Me and my family."

"No one will know you told me. We are not going after him today. That is for another day. A day in the future that no one will connect to this day or what you tell me."

"I may be a dead man just for you bandaging me. The others will know the enemy gave me medical help. They will wonder why."

Uri smiled. "You can take the bandage off after a couple of hours. Use your pant leg strips to bind the wound. I will leave you a knife."

"Why should I tell you? You have already taken care of my wound, what more do I gain?"

A crafty smile spread over the man's face.

"A good question. The answer is that I know how to create much pain and then leave you here to die slowly. You can choose to live with a good story of how you survived, or you get to experience much pain and then die."

Uri smiled back at the man.

"I will start with fingers and toes. I will cauterize the wounds so you won't bleed out. Then nose and ears. You will not make a pretty corpse. I will also pour pig's blood on you so you can't get to paradise."

"Pig's blood?" the man's eyes went wide.

Uri nodded. "I keep a container for just this situation."

The man sighed and began to speak rapidly in Arabic. The others watched the scene. Uri kept nodding, staring intently at the captive as he told his story. When he was done, Uri turned to the others.

"You get something interesting?" Marcus asked.

Uri nodded. "Let's not talk about it now, let's get going."

"Where?" Roland asked.

"I suggest we hike to the next collection of buildings. Someone may be living there. these compounds offer a valuable asset in shelter. They have wells, so there is water. Squatters may have established themselves nearby."

"And they didn't run off after the gunfire started?" Marcus asked.

Uri shrugged. "Who knows. It's towards the border in any case. Let's go find out."

They got up and reorganized their gear, and headed out. They moved as quickly as the two injured men could maintain. The night was giving way to daylight, which would bring with it the intense heat. They needed to find transportation and water soon.

Two miles farther into the desert, they came upon another small group of houses. Individual ones this time instead of a barracks. Outside one house, in the fenced yard, were some animals, donkeys, and goats.

"This is the ticket," Uri said. They didn't spend much time examining the dwelling but charged up to the door and began to knock. Uri called out in Arabic that they were lost and needed help.

Finally, a sleepy-eyed man cracked open the door, only to be met with a 9mm pistol in his face. He stepped back, now much more awake, as the four barged inside.

"What is going on?" the man asked. "Who are you? We have nothing. We are poor herders. There is nothing for you to steal."

Uri concentrated on the man while the others scanned the room for any threats. A woman's voice called out from a back room. The man told her to stay there. He turned to Uri.

"We need your help. We need water and food. Help us and there is much money in it for you. Give us trouble and we will kill you and your family. *Hal tafahm?*" Do you understand?

The man nodded.

"Good. Hurry. We must be quick."

After the husband explained the situation to his frightened wife, the woman went to the well and drew some water in a bag. She brought it back to the house, and the men filled their empty water bottles. She then went to make some tea and put out some bread. They thanked her, looking more awkward than dangerous, and ate with urgency and gusto, taking long swigs of water. They politely took time to sip the tea she had made while Uri gave the man five hundred U.S. dollars. His eyes were wide with wonder at such a fortune.

After checking Dan's and Roland's wounds, they set out on their way to the west in the growing dawn. They had replenished their water at the herder's house. They walked through the heat of the day, the sun burning down on them relentlessly. When they came to the occasional abandoned building or a rock outcropping, the four stopped in the meager shade it provided to rest and drink.

By evening, they had reached the fencing that indicated the border between Iraq and Jordan. Spaced along the fence line were the scattered remains of gun emplacements and defensive fortifications, all now abandoned.

"We just cut the wire and walk right through?" Roland asked.

Uri nodded. "In some places there is no fence, just a stone pillar or marker, or geography, a canyon or set of hills, to indicate the border."

"Then what are we waiting for?" Roland asked.

The four men crossed from Iraq into Jordan and began to walk away from the border.

"That was anticlimactic," Roland said after a few minutes of walking.

"Agreed," Marcus replied. "An odd way to end a tumultuous week."

"Always with the big words," Roland said.

They walked on in silence, weary and nursing various wounds, some large, some small.

Once a couple of miles into Jordan, they found a sheltered place to stop. Dan called Jane on the satellite phone and gave her their coordinates. She promised a support team would arrive within eight hours.

Chapter 87

Once back in Tel Aviv, the men suffered through another debrief session with Eitan. Marcus and Dan had their wounds attended to at a private clinic. There would be no official report of any medical action taken by a hospital. With the briefing over, Dan skipped Uri's invitation to celebrate their mission and left with Jane on one of the agency's private jets. Jane had insisted that it was not a danger to Dan's cover to fly into Venice since it was the CIA's plane and her flight manifest.

All through the flight, Dan sat quietly. He answered Jane's questions in a perfunctory manner using few words. When she finally gave up on engaging him in conversation, he sat silent for the rest of the flight. After landing, they took a cab to the Maghera district outside of Venice. They stopped to purchase some fresh groceries and then walked the last mile to Dan's restored Italianate-style mansion. Dan evidenced a great amount of fatigue but had insisted on the walk, not wanting any random cab driver to know the whereabouts of his home. After reaching the large house, they put their bags in the bedroom, and Dan lay down on the bed.

"Do you want something to eat or drink?" Jane asked.

Dan shook his head. "No. I just want to rest. I'm exhausted."

"You lost a lot of blood in spite of no arteries being hit. And you're coming off three weeks of intense, almost non-stop action. It's no wonder you're tired."

"Seems like more than that."

The words came out slurred as Dan sank into unconsciousness. Jane stared at him for a long time, watching his breathing grow soft and steady. She felt a sadness creep over her. This man, the man she loved, the man whose boss she was, seemed so fragile at this moment. How did he change so quickly?

She shook her head as if to clear it and headed back downstairs to the kitchen. She poured herself a glass of wine and sat at the table. It was an elegant house, large and impressive, without being overly ostentatious, something difficult to pull off. She smiled as she remembered her efforts to help Dan decorate it. He had simplistic ideas, some of which were correct, but many of which were at odds with what the house demanded. It had been a wonderfully busy, irritating, and enjoyable time together. The effort gave her a sense of belonging that she would never have felt without participating in bringing the building to life as a home.

Now her man, her warrior, lay exhausted, somehow more affected by this latest battle than the others. If his will was faltering, she sensed what she had to do. It would be up to her to ensure Dan recovered his energy, his enthusiasm, and confidence...his old self. Not just so she could have her warrior back but so she could have her man back as well. She picked up her phone and called her boss, Henry.

Dan slept through the rest of the day and night. When he woke the next morning, he had a ravenous appetite. He made his way down to the kitchen to find Jane putting out fresh-squeezed orange juice along with plates and silverware.

"I'm going to make breakfast, are you hungry?"

Dan nodded. "Quite."

"Sit down, have some juice and coffee while I make your signature 'eggs with stuff in them'."

Jane repeated the phrase Dan had used describing his combination of scrambled eggs mixed with different vegetables and some chopped ham or sausage. It was a joke between them that the concoction would never be successful, however good it tasted with such a name.

Dan sat at the island counter with a black coffee and a glass of juice. He watched Jane move around the kitchen like it was her domain. She had never shown herself to be much of a cook, but this simple breakfast was definitely part of her repertoire.

They ate in silence. Dan consumed a large serving of the unfortunately named dish along with three slices of local bread, toasted with butter and jam. When they were done, Jane refilled their coffee cups and led Dan onto the screened-in porch to sit in the cool morning.

"How do you feel?" she asked.

Dan shrugged. "Okay...I guess."

Jane shook her head. "Not okay from my perspective. Something's off. You seem down since you got back. You hardly spoke on the plane, slept the clock around, and now seem morose. Usually, you're recapping your mission with a detailed after-action report for me. Something you give with enthusiasm and clear analysis." She raised her arms in a helpless gesture, "Now, nothing."

"There doesn't seem to be much to say. We failed to get the head of the bombings, this Muntaqim. That's a new one for me...failure."

"It's not failure. You killed both of the ones who headed each bombing along with some of their men. You took care of the arms dealer and learned more about this Muntaqim, who he is and where he lives. He'll have to go underground now. Eitan said that a drone is going to level the compound. His home base. He'll be on the run now."

"Sounds good when you say it like that." He gave her a slight smile. "But it doesn't feel like a win. We walked into a trap and it was just luck that Marcus saw it. If he hadn't seen the grenade through the window, I'd be mincemeat."

Jane was quiet for a moment. It was not like Dan to dwell on what-ifs. He knew all the missions were dangerous, a matter of life and death. This one was not any different, except that the ultimate target had slipped away. Some easy words of encouragement were not going to fix this. It seemed to be more profound.

Jane suggested they go into Venice and walk around. It was a clear, early fall day, and she hoped getting out would improve Dan's mood. He agreed, although without much enthusiasm. They took the *vaporetto* or water bus into the city and disembarked along the Grand Canal. Dan led them through a labyrinth of narrow back streets with small bridges crossing equally narrow canals. Their circuitous route was taking them to Piazza San Marco, although Jane would not have ever guessed the destination from the confusing path. Dan seemed to enjoy the walk, showing off his intimate knowledge of the back "streets" of the city that no tourists ever visited. The few people they met along the way looked at them in surprise but greeted them warmly when Dan spoke in his excellent Italian.

"Can you talk about what's bothering you?" Jane asked. "I'm concerned on a personal level, as your partner."

They walked in silence while Jane waited for Dan to speak.

"This mission made me feel suddenly vulnerable." He paused. "It's not a good feeling and not one that is helpful in the field." There was another long pause. "I almost got blown up...twice. Once from a drone and the second time was the trap Muntaqim set. I've been going over it in my mind...over and over. Trying to think of how I could have anticipated or avoided those incidences." He looked at her. "I haven't come up with anything."

"And that's what bothers you?"

Dan nodded. "I don't know how to protect against something like that in the future. It seems like my fate is not in my hands."

He stopped and turned to her.

"Do you know how that feels? Not being in control in extremely dangerous situations? I'm beginning to feel like I'm just rolling the dice with each mission. My number is going to come up, sooner or later. *And*, I'll have no control over that."

Jane was silent. Part of her wanted to protest. His skills, his training, all kept him ahead of the curve in dealing with the terrorists. He was better than they were. But just protesting would not dissolve Dan's feelings. Was this a form of PTSD? Did Dan want to get out of the fight? That is what he constantly railed on about. He needed to be out there, taking the fight to the enemies of the U.S. Taking down the ones who wanted to destroy us. Making them live in fear. She was concerned about the answer, but she needed to ask it, whatever it might do to their relationship.

"Do you want to get out of the fight? Or maybe take a long time off?"

Dan turned and started to walk again.

"I don't know. I don't know. I need to figure this out."

They continued in silence towards the piazza. Jane slipped her hand into Dan's. He grasped it firmly. When they reached the piazza, they slowed to take in the scene. Vendors were setting up on the fringes. Tourists were beginning to mill about, having arrived at the plaza by *vaporetto*. Then Dan's eyes locked onto a vendor, the small, intense gypsy woman who had talked to him and Jane before. She was a Watcher. She beckoned him to come over to her. Dan nudged Jane, nodded in the old woman's direction, and they started towards her.

When they reached the Watcher, she immediately turned to her daughter and told her in the Roma tongue to watch the stall. She gestured to Dan and Jane to follow her and immediately set out for a side street off the open piazza. They walked down it until they came to a house that Dan recognized. It was where she had first talked to him.

After entering, they went into the kitchen and sat down. The old woman stared at Dan intently, seeming to read his mind.

"You have begun to doubt your mission, your calling," she said.

"You can read my mind?"

She shook her head. "Your moods, the energy you project. I can sense much of the truth from that."

She paused before continuing.

"You have done much injury to the enemy. You must not dismiss the value of what you accomplished."

"That's what I told him," Jane said.

The old woman gave her a quick glance but didn't answer.

"This Revenger, Muntaqim, is now like a fox on the run with no place to hide, no den to rest in. His life is now changed for the worse." She raised her finger at him. "But he suspects us. He is a formidable foe because of that."

"He knows about the Watchers?" Dan asked.

"He remembers old tales from his grandmothers. He does not discount them as just stories. He does not know exactly what is going on or how it works, but he has taken steps to defend against it. He uses confusion, chaos, and changes his plans without warning. It makes it hard for those he commands, but also makes it hard for us to see what is happening. That is why we did not know of the bombings until too late. That is why he understood you were setting a trap for him. You must take that into account as you fight against him."

"That is my problem. I'm not sure I'm up to the fight."

The old woman uttered a dismissive sound. "You had a difficult mission. One in which you were often not in control and so you want to quit? Tell me, what will you do if you quit the field of battle?"

She waited for Dan to answer. He didn't provide one.

"You will sit back and watch the terrorists continue to attack? And you will not feel you have betrayed the ones who needed you to defend them? The Shaman gave you a gift. He awakened it in you and taught you what it was. It has grown in you and become part of your weaponry. You would now abandon it? Your insight grows but this Revenger still works in the dark, only on suspicion. He will never have this special sight.

"This is your destiny. Maybe a quiet life sometime in the future. We do not read the future like fortune tellers. But now you are the warrior, the tip of the spear that this battle needs."

Dan shook his head in doubt.

"You must not deny your destiny. If you abandon the fight, you will sicken, both in mind and body, because you deny your role...what you are here for."

She rose from the table.

"Go rest. Take time to strengthen your relationship with this woman. She understands you best. She is your helpmate in this fight. Take comfort in each other. Take refuge in each other. But you must go back. The dark does not rest. You know that. It continues to grow; in the far east, in the Middle-East, and in the West on your southern border."

Dan and Jane stood. The old woman reached up to touch Dan's cheek.

"And do not trust those who seem to be on your side. There are forces within your organization that do not want you to uncover certain truths. They are willing to sacrifice you and those around you," she nodded to Jane, "to keep their agenda alive."

"What's their agenda?" Jane asked.

"Power. Power and the money that comes with it."

She led them out to the street and quickly strode away, radiating energy from her small frame.

Dan and Jane slowly walked back to the piazza. Dan's head swirled with the words she had delivered. *Was* this his destiny? He knew deep down inside what she said was true. He always sensed it and had no answer for what he would do if he left the fight. If he was honest, it was such an alien idea that he could form no picture of his life outside this battle against the dark forces of terror and tyranny. So be it.

Dan sighed. Jane looked over at him and clasped her hand in his.

He would find a way to gather the strength to fight again and to prevail against a more sophisticated opponent. And at some point in the future, he would take the fight to Rashid. The illusive man who seemed to be pulling all the strings.

The End

Afterword

The Revenger is the eighth book in the Dan Stone series.

If you enjoyed this tale, please consider writing a review on Amazon. Reviews do not have to be lengthy and are extremely helpful for two reasons: first, they provide "social proof" of a book's value to a reader unfamiliar with the author, and second, they help readers filter through thousands of books in the same category to find choices worthy of their investment in reading time.

You provide an essential service to other Amazon readers with a solid review. I very much value your support.

You can get access to behind-the-scenes activities and special features by joining my Reader Group. Go to my website, davidnees.com and click the button "Get My Free eBook". You'll receive a free copy of my novella which fills in the timeline between *Payback* and *The Shaman* and be registered in the group. No spam; I never sell my list and you can opt out at any time. You can also follow me on Facebook at facebook.com/neesauthor.

Other novels published by David Nees:

Jason's Tale	book 1 in the After the Fall series
Uprising	book 2 in the After the Fall series
Rescue	book 3 in the After the Fall series
Undercover	book 4 in the After the Fall series
Escape	book 5 in the After the Fall series
Payback	book 1 in the Dan Stone series
The Shaman	book 2 in the Dan Stone series
The Captive Girl	book 3 in the Dan Stone series
The Assassin and the Pianist	book 4 in the Dan Stone Series
Death in the Congo	book 5 in the Dan Stone Series
The Scorpion	book 6 in the Dan Stone Series

Rogue Mission   book 7 in the Dan Stone Series

Thank you for reading this book. If you enjoyed the story, please leave a review on Amazon. Reviews provide "social proof" of a book's worth and help readers unfamiliar with my writing to give the story a try.

As always, your reading pleasure is why I write my stories.

Made in the USA
Columbia, SC
25 September 2024

42998030R00274